The Bastard's Pearl

CONNIE BAILEY

DSP PUBLICATIONS

Published by
DSP PUBLICATIONS

5032 Capital Circle SW, Suite 2, PMB# 279, Tallahassee, FL 32305-7886 USA
http://www.dsppublications.com/

ISBN: 978-1-63216-878-8
Digital ISBN: 978-1-63216-879-5
Library of Congress Control Number: 2014953889
First Edition April 2015

Printed in the United States of America
∞
This paper meets the requirements of
ANSI/NISO Z39.48-1992 (Permanence of Paper).

For Danielle

Author's Note

This story is an homage to the wonderful pulp sword and sorcery paperbacks I read as a teenager.

A glossary of world terms is available on page 309.

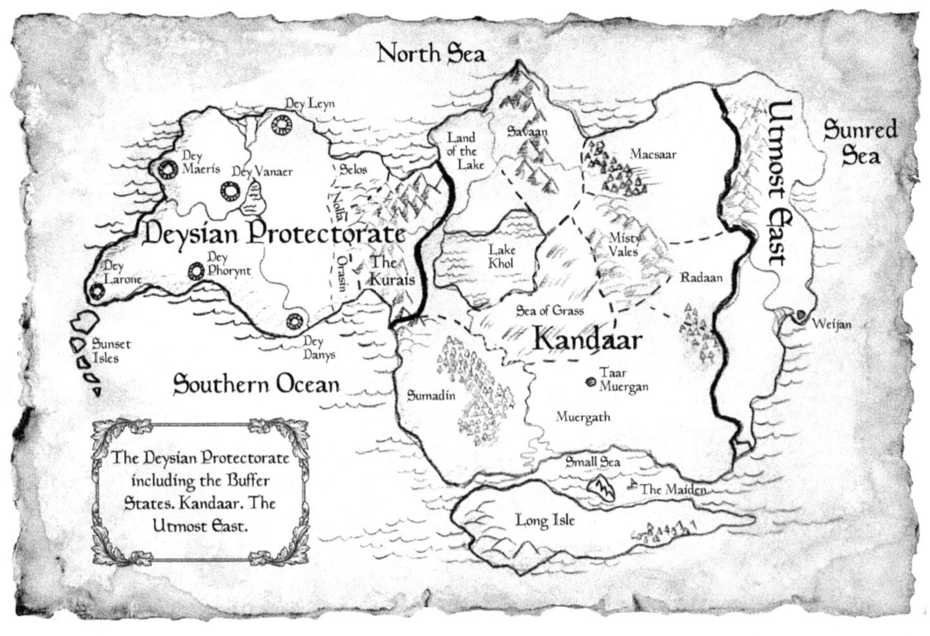

North Sea
Sunred Sea
Utmost East
Dey Leyn
Savaan
Macsaar
Land of the Lake
Dey Maeris
Dey Vanaer
Selos
Nolla
Dey Phorynt
Deysian Protectorate
Orasin
The Kurais
Lake Khol
Misty Vales
Radaan
Dey Larone
Weijan
Sea of Grass
Kandaar
Sunset Isles
Dey Danys
Southern Ocean
Sumadin
Taar Muergan
Muergath
Small Sea
The Maiden
Long Isle
The Deysian Protectorate including the Buffer States. Kandaar. The Utmost East.

Chapter

1

THE HIGH, vaulted ceiling echoed with the sounds of labored breathing, the slithering scrape of boot soles on the wooden floor, and the whistle and clash of metal striking metal. There were no drapes on the windows of the fencing gallery, and the afternoon sun streamed over the two men who sparred with slim sabers. The older man had the compact body of an acrobat, nut-brown skin, and short, graying black hair that gleamed with oil. His opponent stood a head taller, though he looked at least two decades younger. The lad was as long-limbed as a thoroughbred colt with none of a colt's awkwardness. His pale braids caught the light like ivory as he dipped, bending his knees and spinning on his heel. He rose smoothly from his crouch, sword poised to strike, only to find his opponent waiting for him.

"And now, you're dead." The fencing master touched his student's throat with the point of his saber.

"That hurts."

"It's your fault for growing angry and reckless and trying a technique beyond your skill. I should give you a scar to remind you to stay in control of your emotions when fighting."

"You wouldn't dare!"

"No, I wouldn't… not quite." The Eastron sighed and stepped back, lowering his sword. "My days of glory are over. Now Master Tezwar rests on his reputation and teaches fencing to spoiled aristocrats."

"Are you referring to me?"

Tezwar bowed briefly. "Would I be so imprudent?"

Rosheyn Lir Merisolle, fifth of that name, called Sheyn, looked down his nose at the fencing master. "I trust not. I may have only eighteen years, but I'm counted a man. And even if I weren't, I was born a prince of the House of Merisolle, and my bloodline goes back to the Great Division. You're not even a citizen."

"Your words are true. Where I am from, a man who excels at a craft, such as swordsmanship, is also given honor."

A slight frown dragged at Sheyn's sharply cut, delicate features. He couldn't quite take exception to Master Tezwar's words, but he wanted to. The swordmaster had always been mocking in his manner, and though Sheyn believed all souls were equal, it was a fact that a society had layers. He drew breath to explain the concept but then realized it was beneath him to argue with a hired man. "You needn't bother attending me next week," he said instead.

"May I know why you'll be missing a lesson?"

"I'm going on a journey that will take a year at the least."

"Where are you going?"

"I want to see the temples and libraries of Weijan."

"That shouldn't take a year. I'd reckon six months at the most, even if you see every book in the Utmost East. Ships these days take less than a month to make the trip. When I was a boy, you'd be lucky to do it in three."

"I'll be going by caravan."

Tezwar's eyes widened in a rare display of surprise. "Overland? Young lord, surely you know how dangerous—"

"I'm not ignorant. I'm at the top of my class at the university. I know the dangers, and I'll make provisions for them."

Tezwar thought a moment before he answered. "This is all I will say before I say farewell. As a student you show good form, and you have a true talent for swordsmanship. When you spar, the blade becomes a part of your hand, and you have the will to wield it. However…." He paused before he went on. "You're headstrong, and until you learn to master yourself, you'll never master the sword. I wish you a safe journey, though I don't think you'll have one."

Sheyn sniffed. "I suppose I should thank you."

"Only if your thanks are sincere."

"Well, then…." Sheyn lingered a moment more and then turned on his heel.

Tezwar shook his head as he watched the tall young man sweep out of his practice room. He didn't expect to see Rosheyn Merisolle again in this life, and despite the boy's prickly personality, he thought it was a shame to lose him. With the right mentor, Sheyn would blossom into a formidable man, but given the way he was coddled, he'd most likely live and die as a useless ornament of the Laronese royal court. But only if he stayed in the elegant, cultured, and so very civilized city-state of Dey Larone. If Sheyn traveled to the Utmost East by caravan, he'd most likely die in the dust beside the road with a bandit's arrow in his chest.

Swordmaster Tezwar was from Orasei, a small country below the Kurais—which Deysians called the Greiwoll—a towering range that marked the border between West and East. The only people who lived in the mountain wilderness were bandits who came down from their forts to pillage and rob travelers. And beyond that barrier was Kandaar, about which little was now known.

Tezwar had grown up hearing farfetched tales of the wild lands on the other side of the vast range of forbidding peaks. Everything he knew about Kandaar he'd learned from his uncles' stories. Kandaar was divided into ten savage tribes at constant war with one another. Kandaari boys were given their first sword at birth and killed their first man before they were six. Kandaari men preferred the company of their horses to that of women. In Kandaar, gods and goddesses still took a personal interest in human affairs and often appeared to meddle in the lives of those who caught their interest. In Kandaar, there were eagles the size of horses, fish that could fly, and tiny dragons that were kept as pets.

Tezwar didn't know if the stories were true or if they were tales invented by his ale-loving uncles. However, he suspected the parts about the warring tribes were true. The fact that no merchant from the trade-loving coastal nation called the Utmost East had ever traveled west into Kandaar spoke volumes about the danger. It was known that no one went to Kandaar voluntarily.

Under his breath, Tezwar spoke a charm he hadn't thought of since he was nine. Having wished his pupil luck, he'd done all he could for him. He was too old for bodyguard work, and young Lord Merisolle was not family. After placing his saber on its wooden cradle, he donned his jacket and went to seek the company of friends.

SHEYN PAUSED outside the fencing school and unfastened the braid he wore when practicing. Shaking free his pale, waist-length locks, he crossed the university grounds, strolling over green expanses of lawn, past carefully tended trees and shrubs and the graceful buildings of creamy marble. When he returned, he would resume his studies here, but only after his journey to the mysterious lands that had fascinated him from childhood. He was going to travel to the Utmost East, to the ancient city of Weijan, and no matter what anyone said, he wasn't going by sea. Sheyn had no wish to spend a month on a boat, and he was just as curious about Kandaar as Weijan. So he was going overland, over the Greiwoll that separated Deysia from the forgotten world beyond the Kurais wasteland.

His parents disagreed strongly with his plan. It was Lady Merisolle's fear that he would be killed in any number of ways. His father agreed, presumably. He'd have to take his mother's word for that, as he hadn't spoken with his father in weeks. His mother had rallied the family against him, and even his suitor thought he was mad to consider such a route.

The thought of Aeriq Toureyn slowed Sheyn's steps as he reached the edge of the orderly collection of colleges and academies that made up the Classical District. Instead of continuing over the bridge to Crescent Isle and the grounds of Merisolle House, he turned right at Grand Canal and entered the Garden District. Aeriq's mansion was here, part of an enclave of young, wealthy merchants who specialized in importing exotic goods. It would be much more pleasant to have dinner with Aeriq than to eat with only the servants for diversion. A short walk brought Sheyn to the gated courtyard in front of Aeriq's home, and he caught Aeriq returning.

"Sheyn!" Aeriq called out, his handsome face brightening as he smiled. "I'm so happy to see you. What a wonderful surprise."

"Could we have dinner together? Both my parents are at court this month."

"I'd like that very much. Please come in." Aeriq pushed the gate open, and he and Sheyn crossed the courtyard to the double doors of the large house.

Sheyn hung his velvet cloak and his saber on hooks in the wood-paneled front hall and followed Aeriq to a sitting room that faced west. The setting sun struck rainbow sequins from the corners of the beveled glass windows and gilded the contours of the polished wood and rich fabrics. It was nowhere near as grand as the homes Sheyn had grown up in, but it was luxurious enough to make him feel comfortable.

"Have you been fencing?" Aeriq asked as Sheyn sat down.

"Why do you ask? And yes, I'd like something to drink."

"I saw you had your sword with you." Aeriq crossed the room to a table that held various bottles and glasses. He poured an inch of honey-colored liquid into a blown-glass goblet and added chilled water.

"What if I said I'd been fighting a duel?" Sheyn inquired archly.

"Duels are illegal within the city."

Sheyn sighed as he accepted the drink from Aeriq. "Do you have one iota of romance in your soul?"

"Swordfights are romantic?"

"Don't treat me like a child."

"Believe me, that is not my intention at all." Aeriq leaned close to brush his lips against the part in Sheyn's hair.

Sheyn moved aside. "Why must you always be touching me?"

"Because I'm courting you, of course."

"There's more to courting than indulging in love play."

"I know." Aeriq held out a slim, black-lacquered box.

Sheyn's gaze was caught by the three pearls set in a triangle, the sigil of Moon Trine, master jewelers to the ruling house. "Is that for me?"

"A token." Aeriq shrugged. "In promise of what I'd give you were you mine."

A pleased smile curved Sheyn's lips as he reached for the box. When he opened the lid, the light kindled in the precious stones inside. He picked up the ring and held it before his eyes. Lustrous darqsilver had been shaped into an interlacing pattern of vines hung with dewdrops of polished reynstones. As much sculpture as jewelry, the delicate ring gleamed softly in the failing light.

"It's beautiful," Sheyn said.

"May I see it on you?"

Sheyn put the piece of jewelry on his finger. "It really is an exquisite piece."

Aeriq looked over Sheyn's shoulder at their reflection. "It suits you," he said. "It's almost as beautiful as you are."

Sheyn smiled. "*Now* you're being courtly."

Aeriq took hold of Sheyn's arm and turned him around. Looking into Sheyn's dark eyes, he leaned in and kissed him. When Sheyn responded to the kiss instead of rebuffing him, Aeriq's pent-up desires slipped their leash. He let his hand drift down Sheyn's back to his round butt and squeezed as he deepened the kiss. He gently worked his fingers between the globes of Sheyn's ass as he pressed his hardness to Sheyn's groin.

Sheyn shuddered and closed his eyes as the past took him. He was twelve the year it happened but had the height, vocabulary, and manners of someone years older and was allowed to attend his mother's parties. It made him feel grown-up to mingle with the dignitaries, philosophers, and artists who attended Lady Merisolle's gatherings. He could taste the syrupy sweetness of the drink the Weijan envoy had given him. He had been so flattered that the worldly emissary from the Utmost East spoke to him as though they were equals. He was in his own home and had thought nothing of going with the man to another room. He was surprised when the Eastron pulled him behind a tapestry, but not alarmed. It wasn't until the man pushed his face into the wall and yanked his leggings down that he realized he was in trouble. Sheyn's nose was full of the cloying perfume of the oil in the man's hair and the earthy musk of his sweat as he was crushed against the stone wall by the emissary's weight. Sheyn opened his mouth to call out for help, and the man clamped a hand over the lower half of his face. Something hot and hard poked at his bunghole; he wasn't supposed to use that word, but it fit somehow. The Eastron cursed and then spat, and the hot hardness prodded at Sheyn again. And then the worst pain he'd ever felt split him in half. It was so big that it pushed out everything else. He couldn't move, couldn't scream, couldn't think. All he could do was endure in a numb limbo until it ended. The man let go of him, and he slid down to his knees.

"Tell no one of this," the envoy said. "They'd never believe you."

Sheyn didn't answer. He didn't stir or make a sound until the man was gone. Trembling violently, he got to his feet, pulled up his leggings, and slipped away to his room. Still numb, he wiped himself clean with a cloth soaked in cool water. As he stared at the red stains on the white fabric, he broke into weeping. When the storm of tears ended, he dried his face and fetched a fresh pair of leggings from his wardrobe. The stained pair was stuffed down the midden hole in his water closet, and he stuffed the incident down there with them.

Sheyn never told anyone what had happened to him behind the tapestry. At first, he wasn't really sure what had happened, and later, he was too ashamed of his gullibility and weakness to tell anyone. He'd managed to forget about it, but it surfaced when he was under a particular kind of stress. And when it did, he relived it in vivid detail.

"Sheyn?" Aeriq said. "Are you all right?"

Sheyn pushed Aeriq away with a convulsive movement.

"Sheyn!" Aeriq recoiled from the panicked look on Sheyn's face. "What's wrong?"

Sheyn caught his breath. "Why must you always be pawing at me?"

"Why do I have to keep answering that question?" Aeriq sighed. "I've been courting you for six months, and a bit of affection is not out of the bounds of propriety."

"I'm well aware that you've been on my heels since I came of age."

"Must you put it like that? I've wanted you as my partner since I first saw you. While I waited for you to come of age, I built up my personal fortune so I could woo you properly. As soon as it was fitting, I requested an audience with your parents and declared my intention. I—"

"Do you imagine for a moment that my parents would allow me to become bonded to a jumped-up smuggler's get?" Sheyn continued, ignoring the stunned look on Aeriq's face. "My mother has found your donations to her causes very useful, but you'll never be anything to her but a source of funds. As for my father, on the rare occasions he mentions you, he refers to you as 'that trader.' I myself find you a very useful diversion."

"Your words are painful, as you intended, but—" Aeriq swallowed. "I know you don't mean them. Why don't you tell me who you're really angry with?"

"I'm angry with everyone who thinks they know what's best for me."

"Did you fight with your parents?"

"If you must know, they've forbidden me to travel by caravan."

"Good," Aeriq said, and then paused. "I know I don't usually agree with them, but I think they're right in this case."

"Yes, I know you do."

"Honestly, why do you insist on taking this route? You can have the use of any of my ships."

"I get seasick. You know that."

"You can design a personal cabin, and I'll have the ship outfitted any way you like."

"I'm not spending my trip puking, no matter how nice the cabin is."

"At least wait until I can go with you."

"I want to go alone." Sheyn reached into his cloak pocket. "And don't worry," he said, holding up a voucher for a berth on a passenger ship. "Despite my protests, I've given in."

"When do you leave?" Aeriq asked, greatly relieved.

"In three days' time. I couldn't make arrangements any faster."

"We should have a party to send you off with good wishes."

"That sounds very nice. Shall I leave it to you?"

"It would please me if you'd let me host the party for you."

"Just don't invite my parents. I'll have dinner with them before I leave."

"I doubt they'd attend a party at my house."

"True." Sheyn took off the ring. "I should go now."

"You can stay the night if you like."

"I don't like." Sheyn put the piece of jewelry carefully back in its box and slipped the box into an inner pocket. "But I'll see you tomorrow evening, and we can talk about the party." He offered his cheek for a kiss.

Aeriq kissed Sheyn's cheek and stood aside to let him walk out the door. He smiled fondly as he indulged in watching his beloved, who had no equal for beauty in his eyes. He loved the shining cape of pale hair that fell to Sheyn's waist, his willowy frame, and the haughty carriage that proclaimed his royal blood faster than he could. As though he owned each patch of ground he stepped on, Sheyn strode out of sight, and Aeriq called to the servants to lock up for the night.

Sheyn went directly to the Eastern Coach Station, where he dropped his voucher in a rubbish bin. He approached an agent and purchased a seat on the next passenger carriage leaving Dey Larone. After shopping for a weatherproof oilskin bag and a few essentials to go in it, it was time to leave. He boarded the coach and rode out of Dey Larone, alone and unencumbered as he had planned. He supposed that

Aeriq and his family would be upset he'd tricked them, but he didn't spare much sympathy for them. They'd simply have to accept that he was an adult and that he made his own decisions about his life. Meanwhile, he had a three days' journey ahead. He would travel through marshes, green meadows, and tame forests. The road would take him past Dey Larone's sister city-states of Dey Danys and Dey Phorynt, across the countries of rolling hills, orchards, and planted fields that fed the people of the Protectorate, and thence to the rocky rising lands and desert plains of the buffer states. Sitting back against the well-padded seat, he daydreamed about the adventures that awaited him beyond the Deysian Protectorate.

Chapter

2

SHEYN GOT down from the carriage and waited for the Eastern Coach porter to fetch his bag. After pressing a small coin into the man's hand, Sheyn put the pouch's strap over his shoulder, patted the little bag of gems under the neck of his tunic, and looked around. This was the last stop on the longest coach route in the Protectorate, and when his boot had touched the ground, he was on foreign soil. He let the feeling sink in before calling out to the driver.

"Where will I find someone to give me directions?" he asked.

"You'll find an Eastern Coach agent in the building behind you." The driver touched the brim of his hat in an abbreviated gesture of deference. "He'll be able to help you, sir."

Sheyn parted with another coin, tossing it up to the driver as he turned to go into the building. The agent inside was polite and happy to help but also puzzled.

"Lord Merisolle, may I ask why you need this information?" the agent asked.

"I journey eastward, and I need to hire a guide."

"I don't understand. Why would you do such a thing?"

"You don't understand why I'd travel east?"

"Exactly, my lord."

"I'm curious."

"Curious?"

"Don't you wonder what's beyond the Greiwoll?"

"No. Never. Forgive me for saying it, but only someone very foolish or very brave—"

"I've heard this speech before," Sheyn said as he stood. "All I need from you are directions."

Stiffly, the agent told Sheyn where he might find what he was looking for. "But won't you consider a safer—?" His words were cut off by the closing door as Sheyn left.

SHEYN RETURNED to the dusty square and looked about. He recognized the building on the corner from the agent's description and walked toward it. At the cross street, he turned right and soon found what he was searching for.

The market was a hive of activity that sprawled across the apron of beaten earth outside the city's western gate. Sheyn had seen bigger markets, but none so busy. The air was thick with the buzz of myriad languages being spoken, shouted, and sung. Pulling his hood up to block out some of the noise, he picked his way through the maze of stalls, tents, and wagons laden with all manner of goods. Cloaked in the confidence born of a sense of superiority, he haughtily ignored the calls of the vendors as he headed for the northeast corner.

Sheyn stopped when he reached the open area where caravans formed to take the Trade Road east across the buffer states or west to the shores of the Sunset Sea. A line of packhorses and oxen was moving out to take advantage of the cool early-morning air, and Sheyn watched them for a moment before turning his gaze on the small groups of men standing idle. According to his information, these were bravos looking for hire as guards, and they certainly looked the part, if one could judge from the number of weapons on display. Choosing one who looked a bit less disreputable than the others, Sheyn approached him and broke into his conversation.

"A moment of your time, mercenary."

The dark-haired man turned from his red-bearded companion and gave Sheyn a measuring look. "What do you want, boy?" he asked.

"As I said, a moment of your time."

"What's your business here?"

"I want to hire you."

The mercenary glanced at his friend and both men smirked. "Now what could I possibly do for *you*?" he asked.

"You could show a bit more respect for someone who's offering to pay for your services."

"Where are you from, pretty boy?" Redbeard asked.

"I'll wager he's a Laronese aristocrat," said the other man.

"I *am* from Dey Larone," Sheyn said. "If you'd care to step away from your colleague for a moment, I'd like to discuss business." He jingled the bag of coins in his hand. "It will be worth your while."

The chiming sound awakened a gleam in the dark man's eyes. "Please forgive me, my lord. I'm Captain Merlan, at your service." Merlan flapped a hand at his friend as a signal to clear off.

Sheyn cleared his throat. "I wish to travel as far east as you're willing to go. I don't want to haggle with any caravan chiefs, and I want to feel safe against bandits. The less contact I have with other travelers, the better." He lifted his chin. "I can pay well."

"My road ends where the Kurais begins," Merlan said, giving Greiwoll its Eastron name.

"Then arrange to take me there."

"The fee would be steep. Not as steep as the mountains at the end of the world, but steep enough."

"I'm sure I have enough gold to satisfy you."

"You probably shouldn't tell a stranger something like that. Fortunately for you, I'm not a bandit. If you ask around, you'll find I have a good reputation."

"How much will it cost to hire you as guide and bodyguard?"

"What coin are you paying in?"

"Laenir."

Merlan's eyes gleamed. Laronese was the most desired currency in the Protectorate and the Buffers. The small, thick oval coins were made of highly refined gold and never lost their value. "Twenty and we have a bargain."

"Twenty! I could buy horses and a carriage and servants to drive it for twenty laenir."

"Then perhaps you should do that." Merlan smiled. "It's not an unfair price, and I'll pay any caravan fees out of my pocket."

Sheyn bit his lip in thought. Twenty laenirs represented nearly a quarter of his coinage, but he still had the bag of gems. "Very well," he said. "We have a bargain."

Merlan noted the gesture when Sheyn reflexively patted the front of his tunic. "When did you wish to travel?" he asked.

"As soon as you can arrange it."

"And where shall I call for you?"

"That won't be necessary. I'm not leaving your side until we reach the end of the Trade Road. And don't think of robbing me." Sheyn pulled his dagger with a speed that made Merlan blink. "I'm not as helpless as you might suppose."

"So I see." Merlan smiled. "You've got more pride than a hundred kings, but you've got heart as well. Come. It's time for midday meal, and I know a place that makes a stew to put hair on you."

"That sounds repellent, but I *am* hungry."

"This way, my lord, and try to keep up, will you?"

"You won't lose me."

"I won't try. Let's go." Merlan glanced at Sheyn's hair. "And pull your hood back up. No one here has hair like that, and you don't want to be singled out."

Sheyn uncharacteristically did as he was told and followed Merlan. This was to set the pattern for the next few weeks as Sheyn chafed at what he saw as Merlan's high-handed manner. The self-described captain seemed to delight in giving Sheyn orders and watching Sheyn get annoyed. Somehow, Merlan always had a good reason and a reasonable explanation for his orders, but Sheyn found him disrespectful. On the other hand, Merlan did as he'd promised, dealing with the caravan leader and the local merchants in the towns they passed through. It was hardly ideal, but Sheyn reminded himself of his goal and let the foreign landscapes distract him until they reached the end of the route in the lively town of Orasei, largest city in the buffer state of Orasin.

Chapter

3

MERLAN LED Sheyn a short distance away from the caravan. "This is it," he said as he tapped his staff against a pillar of stacked rocks. "This marks the easternmost boundary. On this side, Deysia, on that side, the Kurais, or Greiwoll as it's known to civilized folk."

"A maze of barren peaks, and beyond it, Kandaar the unknown."

"You've been here before?" Merlan's voice was sharp with surprise.

"Of course not. But I've read every book I could find that mentions the lost tribes of Kandaar. Did you know that the continent of Ondey was once one nation? But two thousand years ago, the Great Division—"

"Yes, yes," Merlan said quickly. "Every schoolchild knows that story. A goddess grew angry and gave birth to the Kurais, forever dividing East and West. Religious rubbish."

"Of course it is. The Great Division was a natural occurrence, but wouldn't you like to take that road and see what lies on the other side of those mountains?"

The captain made a sign of warding off evil. "No. Even if you survived the Kurais, beyond that are tribes of barbarians who eat human flesh. No thank you. If I want to trade goods with the Utmost East, I will sail around the bottom of the world like everyone else."

Sheyn smirked at the man's ignorance. "I think it would be fascinating."

"I think you're moon-touched. If you've seen enough, I'd like to get into Orasei before the sun sets. This is smuggler country."

"What is there to smuggle and where would it be smuggled to?"

"I can't tell you."

Sheyn slipped a small gem from the pouch under his tunic. He held it out. "Tell me about the smugglers," he said.

Merlan took the jewel. "Not very many people know this, but there are those who travel to Kandaar."

"And?"

"That's all I know."

"If there are people who know a route through the Greiwoll, I want to hire them."

"No, you don't. These are the kind of people who stop at nothing to gain a bit of coin."

"I pay well, as you know."

"These people would kill you and take your money and save themselves the trouble of taking you to Kandaar."

"I think I can find someone at least as honest as you, Captain."

Merlan snorted and walked faster.

MERLAN BROUGHT Sheyn to the caravan wayhouse in Orasei. They arrived as the evening meal was being served and were pointed toward empty spaces on one of the long benches. Clay bowls of stew and wooden spoons were set in front of them, and they began to eat the gray-brown, gravy-coated lumps.

Sheyn spit his mouthful of food back into the spoon and dropped the spoon into the bowl with a clatter. "This is slop!"

"You don't care for the food?" Merlan asked mildly.

"I just told you it was slop. Pigs eat slop. Are you saying I'm a pig?"

The captain ground his teeth and reminded himself of the gold he'd been paid and the gold he'd been promised. Into his thoughts crept a reminder that his employer carried something of value around his neck. Perhaps it was time to satisfy his curiosity. Once he knew for certain what was in the pouch, he could decide what to do with his employer. "Of course I'm not calling you a pig. Come with me, and I'll take you to a tavern."

Sheyn followed Merlan out of the wayhouse, blinking in the torchlight after the gloom inside. At least the hanging reek wasn't any stronger, just different. Inside, the air was an amalgam of old sweat, cooking grease, and stale smoke. Out here, a miasma of piss, manure, and sour vomit rose from the gutters to hang over the narrow streets. Sheyn pulled a fold of his cloak over his nose and mouth, and Merlan turned to look at him.

"Pull up your hood," Merlan reminded Sheyn. "That hair draws too much attention."

Sheyn drew the hood up over his head, putting his face in shadow. Feeling quite daring, he trailed the captain deeper into the warren of noisome alleys. The walled city was no different from a dozen the caravan had stopped at, but its status as a border town gave it an alluring aura of lawlessness. It was likely that the colorful characters they passed were engaged in nothing more sinister than seeking a glass of whatever passed for wine here, but in Sheyn's eyes they took on the aspect of smugglers and brigands. Behind each dilapidated door, he pictured a stolen chest of exotic gems or cache of rare spices.

"In here," Merlan said, gesturing to a small structure built of fieldstone and salvaged boards. He passed between the two torches that marked the entrance, and Sheyn followed him inside.

The only light in the tavern came from gaps in the walls and an open hearth between the main room and the kitchen. The air was thick with smoke and the guttural sounds of the local dialect. Sheyn could feel a layer of grease forming on his skin as soon as he stepped inside. A man in a leather apron pointed Merlan to a table. Sheyn and the captain sat down on unpadded benches at a rough plank table with several other patrons.

"Keep your voice down and your hood up," Merlan told Sheyn. "Food will be here soon."

The man in the apron returned with a large platter of sliced bread, roasted meat, and two bowls of something that looked like chowder. Sheyn started to ask what it was, but instead, he picked up the wooden spoon and tasted it. The thick liquid was blandly sweet but left a lingering burn on the back of his tongue. The chunks were some sort of pale meat, but whether fish or fowl, he could not discern. The bits that had the texture of vegetables were likewise pale and boiled to a consistency that did nothing to satisfy the tooth. However, it was hot and filled his belly, and he was soon swallowing with the same gusto as the peasants around him. His bowl commanded the greater part of his attention, and he simply nodded when Merlan expressed his need for the privy. It wasn't until the food was gone and he looked around for a servant that he realized the captain had been missing for quite a while.

"What a bother!" Sheyn said under his breath as he rose and went to find the man in the apron. He knew a few words of the local tongue, enough to find food or a place to relieve himself, but certainly not enough to convey the complicated ideas that his guide was missing, he was lost, and needed directions to the wayhouse. As he'd feared, the man either had no idea where Merlan had gone or had no idea what Sheyn was saying. Sheyn gave up and decided to check the privy himself.

He went to the door, where he was accosted by the owner with his hand out in the universal sign for payment. Sheyn reached for his purse, but it was missing from his belt. He assumed Merlan had robbed him, and his desire to find the guide doubled, particularly since Aeriq's ring was in the pouch. Shoving a hand in his pocket, he found a few coins and tossed them at the man before walking quickly away. Certain he'd entered the tavern from the left, he turned down the first cross lane he came to. Behind Sheyn, Merlan came out of the alley with another man at his side. The gray-clad man accepted a small ruby from the pouch Merlan held, nodded his understanding of Merlan's instructions, and set out after Sheyn. Merlan went back the wayhouse and retrieved Sheyn's bag. He took the pouch of gold laenir and a very valuable-looking ring, which he later sold to buy his way out of imprisonment. The rest of Sheyn's belongings were tossed on an offal heap, and the last traces that Sheyn had been in Orasei left town with Merlan.

SHEYN SEARCHED his robes as he walked and confirmed that his purse was gone as well as the bag of small jewels he'd worn around his neck. When he found the local authorities, he would report the theft, but right now, it was of paramount importance that he find the caravan as quickly as possible. He had more currency in his oilskin pack, but it did him no good until it was in his hands. He only hoped the caravan guards would hand over his bag without Merlan there to act as go-between.

Sheyn emerged from a winding street into a square lit by tall torches. A crowd had gathered to drink and dance to the music of a group of men sitting on the steps of a fountain. Jostled and assailed by the fumes of some noxious local drink, he made his way around the eastern edge. As he entered the alley on the opposite side, a man spoke from the shadows.

"Are you lost?" the stranger asked in the tongue Sheyn knew as Ondey.

Sheyn had studied the rustic version of Deyrien, the Protectorate's official language, and the lessons came back to him as he concentrated. "I don't converse with strangers," he said slowly. "Show yourself and give me your name."

"Where are you from?" A man dressed all in gray stepped into Sheyn's path. "I don't know that accent at all."

"I won't speak with you until you give me your name."

"The slavemaster named me Thursday, but my mother called me Taranz."

"Clear out of my way, Taranz."

"Where are you going?"

"That's not your business."

"It could be." Taranz smiled, his teeth very white in his tanned face. "If you were in need of a guide."

"If you can take me to the wayhouse by the eastern gate, I can pay you when we get there."

"We have a deal." Taranz bowed. "Now, tell me where you're from. It will pass the time as we walk."

"Why are you so curious?"

"You speak Deyn, which is very odd. Even odder is that I knew it was your language as soon as I saw you."

"It's not my language. No one with any culture speaks Ondey."

"No? What a pity." Taranz gestured down the alley. "This way, my beauty."

"Don't address me as though we're equals. Simply show me to the wayhouse, and you'll receive your fee."

"I think I'll take my reward now." The man who called himself Taranz crowded Sheyn against the wall and put a hand over Sheyn's nose and mouth. He held Sheyn tightly until the drug that permeated the leather of his glove put the young man to sleep. After hefting the dead weight to his shoulder, he walked the short distance to a tavern owned by a friend. He paid a boy to carry a message for him and waited for the visitor he was sure would arrive as quickly as possible. Windfalls like this happened once, perhaps twice, in a lifetime.

TARANZ ANSWERED the door on the first knock. "Come in, Harkot," he said as he stood aside to let the rotund man into the room.

Harkot the slave merchant sniffed audibly. "Why do you insist on conducting business in a whorehouse?"

"Strictly sentimental reasons. If you're in a hurry to leave, let's get down to business."

"There's no excuse to flout my dignity. I supply pleasure slaves to the nobility, even to kings."

"Everyone knows this. You brag enough." Taranz grinned. "Forget custom for a moment and look at what I've brought you."

"You said he was special, or I'd have sent my overseer."

"I don't think you'll want very many people knowing what you've come into possession of." Taranz removed the cloak that covered Sheyn and stepped aside. He had the very distinct pleasure of seeing Harkot's pudding face go slack with surprise. "Did I lie?" he asked.

Harkot shook his head slowly, rubbing a hand over his close-cropped ginger hair without taking his gaze from the unconscious young man.

"Have you ever seen anyone who looks like this?" Taranz loosened the ribbon that held Sheyn's hair back. "It's pale as fresh milk and feels like silk floss."

"He's entirely unique," Harkot said.

"And quite valuable, I imagine."

"Priceless," the slave merchant said before he caught himself. Harkot glanced at Taranz, trying to gauge whether the thief knew just how special his prize was. The merchant regained his equilibrium and got ready to bargain.

"What will you give me for him?" Taranz asked.

"Come to my door in a few hours, and you shall have a ring of gold for each finger, gold bands for your wrists and ankles, and a collar of gold that reaches to your waist."

"I'd rather have something else."

"Any dealer in precious metal will give you enough coin for you to retire on four times over."

"And how would I carry it around? I'd have to hire servants and guards. Too much work. I want something else."

"Name your price."

"I want land."

"A thief like you imagines he can become a landowner?"

"You have land. Give me some of it."

"No one trades land for a pleasure slave."

"Ah, but he's not an ordinary pleasure slave, is he?" Taranz paused. "His coloring alone makes him priceless."

Harkot relaxed a bit more. Taranz knew his catch was exceptional, but he didn't know just how special the foreigner was. Not that it made a difference. Harkot could pretend to deliberate on the price, but he knew he would pay it. The pale-haired stranger was exactly what he'd been looking for. If Harkot bargained shrewdly, he could trade this foreigner for enough wealth to buy a minor title. His children would be born noble and might marry into noble families. He could sell his less than respectable business and retire to a place where no one knew his reputation.

"Very well," Harkot said. "Bring him to my smaller warehouse at midnight. I'll have the deed to a piece of land for you."

"I knew you'd come around."

"Be on time," Harkot said.

Taranz grinned. "I'll come to the door on the west side," he said. "Look for the rag cart. That'll be me with your delivery."

TARANZ PUSHED the two-wheeled cart into the empty warehouse and let the long handles rest on the ground. The bed tilted, but the cargo didn't shift, and the thief began tossing aside the rags that covered Sheyn.

"What did you use to keep him quiet?" Harkot asked as he looked into Sheyn's slack face.

"That will cost you extra. Where's my payment?"

Harkot took a rolled piece of parchment from his sleeve and handed it to the thief.

Taranz unrolled the sheet and doffed his hood to read it. The buttery light of the oil lamps smoldered in his close-cropped, ruddy hair as he bent his head over the document. "It looks real enough to me," he said.

"And it's the farthest from my other holdings, so I suppose we're both content."

"My, how lordly you've grown. Have you forgotten we were born in the same sty?"

"I choose to put that history behind me. I hope this will be the last time we do business."

"What if I find another like him?" Taranz jerked his chin at Sheyn.

Harkot chuckled. "Then I'll make an exception," he said. "But until then, I hope you'll take this land and start another life."

"Is it truly your wish to never see me again?"

"It is."

"So be it." Taranz gave Harkot a small bottle. "A gift to keep your new pet sweet. Good-bye, brother." He went out the door and closed it behind him.

Chapter
4

AFTER TARANZ had gone, Harkot spoke. "You may come out now."

A man stepped from the concealment of an empty row of shelves and came to the cart. He stared down at Sheyn, seeming to fall into a trance.

"Well?" the slave merchant said loudly. "Will he do?"

The green-robed man jumped. "Help me put him on the table," he said in a dull voice.

"Do it yourself, priest. I'm paying you, not the other way 'round."

"Don't call me that. I'm not a priest."

"So you say, but you took vows. I don't reckon you can just quit something like that."

"You can become unworthy."

Harkot snorted. "As long as you can still perform the ritual, I don't care if you're worthy or not."

"I can perform the ritual, but as I've told you before, there are no guarantees."

"Look here, Yozif. You'll do what I've paid you to do, or I'll tell everyone who you really are. What do you think will happen if people around here find out you're not just a harmless drunkard, but a dark wizard of Kandaar hiding from justice?"

"No one would believe that."

"Why not? It's true."

"It wasn't my fault," Yozif cried out, as he'd cried out many times since the tragedy. He'd lost control of the magic for just a moment and a life had been lost. That wasn't his fault. It was the magic that had killed, not him. Yet... it *was* his fault, and he knew it. He should've been sober.

"Are you drunk right now?" Harkot asked.

"I'm never completely sober anymore." Yozif set his bag down on the plank table and came back to the cart. He bent down and lifted Sheyn in his arms. With slow, staggering steps, he made it to the table and dropped Sheyn onto it.

"Well?" Harkot said again.

"He's heavier than he looks." Yozif put his palm against Sheyn's forehead and felt the unmistakable energy signature. In this young outlander's veins flowed a drop of the blessed blood of Anaali, the Goddess Yozif served. And he was of a type that had not been seen in the world since the first *daaksim* were created. The most numerous incarnations were the redheads who burned with Her Fire. Second in number were the sun-haired beauties who embodied Her Earth. Third were Sea children with ivory skin and hair dark as ink. In all of known Kandaari history, there had been only two Ice daaksim, unique with their white hair and diamond black eyes. Yozif didn't have to see the foreigner's eyes to know they were dark and depthless as the sky at midnight.

Harkot observed the priest's change of expression and smiled in satisfaction. "I was right, wasn't I?"

"Yes." Yozif sighed.

"I can't explain how I knew, but he felt... different."

"You have a gift," Yozif said as he turned away to rummage in his bag. It was a travesty that this trader in flesh should have such a gift, but as Yozif knew, the Gods were rarely fair or logical when bestowing their favors. This merchant, who knew nothing about daaksim, had twice now sniffed out a candidate, and this was the second time he'd coerced Yozif into performing the ritual. When Yozif had braved the Kurais to escape Kandaar and his Goddess, he'd thought he'd find a haven of forgetfulness in the west, but such was not his luck. A few indiscreet words over a skin of wine had put Yozif in thrall to Harkot and Harkot's greed.

After the slave merchant had learned of the existence of daaksim from Yozif, he became wildly obsessed with finding and selling one, believing it would bring him enough wealth to retire. To Yozif's shock and dismay, Harkot found a candidate among the attractive young men and women he sold as pleasure slaves. Yozif was summoned to one of Harkot's properties and shown into a room where a young man was bound to a table. Yozif scoffed at Harkot's claim that this lad was "different." How could anyone not born in Kandaar harbor the spark of Anaali's Favor? However, the ebony-haired bandit's son did indeed prove to have the potential, and Yozif had performed the ritual that transformed him into a daaksi.

Harkot had no idea what sort of miracle a daaksi was and planned to sell the lad to highest bidder. Yozif had protested passionately, insisting that daaksim could only be owned by kings, Kandaari kings. Harkot listened and recognized a unique opportunity. He sent the new daaksi to Kandaar by a route Yozif mapped for him. His emissary found his way to the court of a local king, and the daaksi was offered as a gift. Since then, Harkot had enjoyed sporadic but profitable trade with King Yevdjen of Sumadin and was constantly scheming to expand that trade.

Everything Yozif had done since fleeing Djenaes had gone awry, and he had reached the point where he no longer cared what happened. What difference did it make if he performed the ritual for faith or for money? He had no power over his fate, so why not do as Harkot wanted and enjoy the comforts Harkot's gold bought? A jug of good wine could drown a lot of guilt.

One by one, the disgraced priest set out the items he needed, his movements taking on a measured cadence. He lit the sacred candle and sprinkled the dried flower petals, and a faint, sweet scent filled the air. Breathing deeply of the smoke, he murmured the words of the Invocation and let calmness possess him. Yozif picked up a small, curved knife, and the edge of the blade glowed as though heated in a forge. He bent over Sheyn and touched the point of the knife to the outside corner of Sheyn's right eye. With a sudden, decisive gesture, he made a curving, downward cut following the contour of the high cheekbone. As blood welled up and trickled down like a red teardrop, Yozif repeated the action on the other eye. Setting the knife on a folded square of red silk, he took up a small metal container with a pierced lid. He shook powder from the filigreed tube onto the small wounds, and the blood clotted instantly.

Yozif's gaze was caught by a glint of light between Sheyn's eyelids, and he was abruptly seized by something he'd thought he'd never feel again. The Goddess took hold of him and lifted him up, infusing him with Her light, love, and joy. The container of powdered herbs fell from his hand and struck the table with a sound like a great golden gong. Sheyn's skin began to glow with a faint luminescence like the inside of a shell, and Yozif heard the merchant gasp. The moment stretched out as the air itself seemed to take on weight, and then the ringing ceased and the light sank back into Sheyn's flesh.

For several moments there was silence in the chamber. Yozif leaned heavily against the table as the glorious feeling of exaltation faded away. Harkot stood frozen, his mouth open, as he stared transfixed at what had been wrought. The new daaksi's skin had a slight pearlescent glow like the inside of a shell, and his pale hair glimmered like moonlight on water. His lips and cheeks were touched with the faintest stain of rose, and his eyebrows and eyelashes had darkened to sable. There was nothing about him that wasn't pleasing to the eye. And he had something beyond sheer beauty that drew the heart. Harkot took a step toward the table, and Yozif stirred. Slowly, the priest reached out and touched Sheyn's cheek. When Yozif brushed away the reddish crust at the corners of Sheyn's eyes, the small cuts had healed, leaving two crescent-shaped scars.

"It's done," the priest said.

"Excellent," Harkot said. "The first one bought me exclusive trading rights with the Sumadinim. This one will buy me—"

Yozif interrupted. "You cannot sell him to any but a king."

"Yes, no need to make pronouncements. You've explained it many times. Don't worry. Who but a king could afford him?" Harkot smiled. "The Sumadi ruler is eager to acquire another daaksi. He likes making gifts of them."

Yozif nodded. "Where else would you sell him but Sumadin?"

"It's true Sumadin is the only trade ally I have in Kandaar, but that will change. I'm the only merchant who trades on the other side of the Greiwoll, and someday everyone will have to come to me to sell their goods in Kandaar."

"Do you really believe that? If so, you're as foolish as you are greedy."

"And you're an outcast whose opinion doesn't have any more weight than a beggar's fart."

"True. Why am I so weak?"

"Because you drink liquor and burn *kataash* all day and night."

"Also true." Yozif's expression hardened. "Our bargain stands. You won't tell anyone about me."

"You have my word." Harkot patted the priest's cheek. "I won't tell anyone a single thing about you. Why do you worry so much?"

"It's forbidden to awaken a daaksi outside of Her Temple."

"Yes, so you've said."

"I don't deserve Her Grace."

"I don't disagree." Harkot glanced at the door, eager to be gone with his prize. Yozif had become invaluable to him, but Harkot found the man's religious ramblings unbearably boring.

"And yet…." To Harkot's annoyance, Yozif continued. "Anaali has graced me twice since I turned my back on Her." He held out his hands to Harkot. "What does it mean?"

"I'm no sage." Harkot unfastened a clinking pouch from his belt and tossed it to Yozif. "Here, go buy yourself some comfort. Maybe you'll find some answers in a wineskin."

Yozif took a last look at his handiwork, packed his bag, and left the warehouse. The moon on the snow turned the wall of mountains into a silver carving, and the ashes of his soul yearned toward them. He'd thought he would never go back over those mountains or see his homeland again, but why shouldn't he? If Anaali hadn't blasted him for his sacrilege by now, he doubted She ever would. So why was he still cringing in this hateful foreign land? If he could make daaksim for Harkot, why not go back to Kandaar and make daaksim for kings? If he had the protection of the rulers, he needn't fear the Shrine's wrath. Instead of searching out liquid solace, he went to his squalid room, packed his few belongings, and began walking homeward.

IN THE city of Taar Muergan, capital of Muergath in the heart of Kandaar, in the Red Temple of Taankh, God of the Shadoworld, High Priest Chanesh sat up in his bed. Clutching the ragged edges of his dream, he reached for parchment and ink. With several strokes of the quill, he recorded what he could remember. When the vision had faded, he lay back and rang for an acolyte.

"Reverend Lord?" A young man entered Chanesh's sleeping chamber. "How can I serve you?"

"Come here, boy." Chanesh gestured with a hand like a vulture's claw. He was little more than a collection of bones held together by wrinkled, papery skin, no more substantial than a cobweb. This frail elder was the most powerful man in Muergath, the third largest nation of Kandaar.

The acolyte stopped beside the high priest's bed and stood with his head bowed.

"Which one are you?" Chanesh asked.

"Moksha, Reverend Lord."

"Fetch the pitcher on the ledge there and pour a cup for me."

"At once." Moksha hurried across the room and back. He poured some liquid from the pitcher into the cup beside Chanesh's bed.

Chanesh sat up gingerly and took the cup of restorative herbal wine. "Take up the quill and make notes," he said.

It was not the first time Moksha had acted as night scribe to Chanesh, and he knew where to find writing materials. He seated himself at Chanesh's worktable and lit the oil lamp. "I'm ready, Reverend Lord," he said.

"I had a vision tonight," Chanesh said. "The Way is opening. It has begun."

Moksha hid his start of surprise.

"After centuries of banishment, our lord Taankh shall walk in the Waking World again." Chanesh took another long drink of his potion. "The one who will open the Way is here."

"The Gate?" Moksha blurted out.

"Yes, the Gate," Chanesh said impatiently and paused to catch his breath. "I saw a vision of the Threshold of Worlds. I saw Him reach across the barrier, and I saw the one who will be the channel. He is just as the Ophidian Prophecies describe."

"I haven't read them, Reverend Lord."

"Of course you haven't. You're an acolyte."

"What does he look like, Reverend Lord, so that I may record it?" Moksha asked with quill poised.

"He is young, his skin as pale as a statue carved from ivory, and his hair is white." Chanesh paused. "And he is a daaksi, of course."

Moksha bit his lip. He was curious but afraid of the high priest. Reminding himself he needed all the facts to make a faithful record, he worked up his nerve. "Reverend Lord?"

"Yes?" Chanesh looked over at the acolyte and noted the anxious look in the lad's eyes. "If you need the privy, go use it. If you have something to say, out with it."

"Why does the Temple need daaksim?"

Tongue loosened by the herbs in the wine, Chanesh answered candidly. "Because the sacrifice of an ordinary person wouldn't be enough to call a demon."

Once again, Moksha hid his shock. He'd heard rumors that Taankh's Children were being summoned again after two hundred years under ban, but he hadn't believed them. "I don't understand," he said.

"To call up a minion of Taankh, what must you do first?"

"I'm an acolyte, Reverend Lord. I haven't read the—"

"First you need a strong body to act as your Gate. The gate will need stamina to stay alive for the entire ritual. If the Gate dies before the ritual ends, the demon cannot cross over the Threshold. There must be a certain amount of suffering to attract such a creature and lure it to the Threshold. The longer the sacrifice suffers, the more powerful the demon that responds. A daaksi's connection with the Lost Goddess, curse Her name, gives them the power to heal quickly. A daaksi can be tortured almost forever."

Moksha shuddered. "Would you like more to drink?" he asked.

"Yes, pour me another cup. And put that parchment in the drawer. No need for anyone to see that until I decide how to present the news."

"Will it help our cause, Reverend Lord?" the boy asked as he filled the high priest's cup.

"When Taankh crosses the Threshold, there will be none who can stand against him. The world will be His… and ours. Does that answer your question?"

"Aye, Reverend Lord. That will make High King Kezlath happy."

"I daresay it will. Those who shunned our king as a pretender and put the crown of high king on the head of Djulyan of the Misty Vales will soon bow to Kezlath of Muergath." Chanesh lay back on his pillow. "Go, boy, I need to think."

After the acolyte left, Chanesh let his mind drift as he pondered the implications of his dream. In the vision, he had looked down from above as a green-robed man turned his back on a new-made daaksi. He could feel the tendrils of fate that uncoiled around the pale figure of the Gate. And he could sense the boiling cauldron of rage that simmered under the daaksi's icy exterior.

His vision told him many things, but the knowledge that struck him hardest was that someone knew how to create a daaksi outside the Shrine at Djenaes. Even in the Shrine, it was almost unheard of for the ritual to be performed these days. Chanesh suspected that the priests couldn't produce daaksim any longer and concentrated on the healing arts. It was certain that they'd turned down every extravagant offer from the Servants of Taankh. Perhaps Taankh's old adversary Anaali had turned Her back on this world completely.

Chanesh grew ever more drowsy until he couldn't keep his eyes open any longer. As he fell asleep, his last thought was that the Temple could make good use of a man who could create daaksim.

A DRAFT slave carried Sheyn to Harkot's compound and left him in the hands of Harkot's slavemaster. Slavemaster Raun tied the unconscious young man's wrists and ankles to rings on the corner posts of a cot designed for such a purpose. The cords he used were woven silk, strong but less abrasive to valuable skin than chains or leather. He was making a visual inspection of his new charge's physical attributes when Harkot arrived.

"He still sleeps," Harkot said, his voice sharp with disappointment.

"Give me a moment, master." Raun unstoppered a small bottle and held it under Sheyn's nose. "This herb never fails no matter what they've been dosed with."

Harkot smiled as Sheyn stirred. Anticipation fluttered in Harkot's belly as Sheyn opened his eyes. Never had Harkot beheld anything so exquisite that he considered keeping it for himself, but this boy tempted him. Harkot shook his head; this foreigner was worth too much to keep as a personal indulgence, and Harkot preferred women anyway. Why had he even entertained the notion? Harkot turned away from the daaksi.

"Treat him carefully, Raun," Harkot said. "He's not like the others. He's special."

"As you command." Raun bowed, puzzled that Harkot wasn't staying for the first training session. The master's policy was to take each slave once, and Raun had never questioned the practice. The slaves belonged to Harkot to do with as he wished. Raun would have found it odd if Harkot *hadn't* taken advantage of the endless supply of young flesh.

Raun's thoughts were disturbed when Sheyn lifted his head. "Easy there, beauty," Raun said.

Sheyn tried to sit up and found he was bound to a bed. "Where am I?" he asked and was horrified by the croaking sound of his voice.

"You are in the slave quarters of Master Harkot."

"Slave quarters? Let me go at once!"

"Slaves don't give orders," Raun said. "That's your first lesson."

"Obviously, you've no idea who I am. My parents are very powerful and wealthy. If you let me go now, you'll be rewarded. If you don't—"

Sheyn's words were cut off when Raun's hand covered his mouth.

"Listen to me, Your Highness. You're a slave now. No one knows where you are, and your Mam and Pap can't help you. I'm Raun and I'm here to break you in. If you're wise, you'll do as you're told and avoid a lot of pain."

Sheyn glared at the slavemaster.

"All right, then," Raun said as he reached for a leather strap. "We'll do it your way."

HARKOT VISITED the slave quarters the next day right after his morning meal. The bright-haired daaksi was bound as he'd expected, but he was surprised to see the young man muzzled. "Is the gag necessary?" Harkot asked.

Raun held up a bandaged finger. "He nearly bit it off," he said. "And he won't be silent."

"What sorts of things does he say?"

"Threats mostly. He says he's from an important family that will pay to have him back. I tell him he's worth more as a pleasure slave, but he won't listen. Stubborn as stone."

"He's strong-willed, eh?"

Raun nodded. "Granite between the ears. Fights every step of the way. I pity his new master."

Harkot met Sheyn's gaze. "Look how he glares," he said. "His eyes are so dark, so… deep." Harkot's voice slowed as a smile spread over his face. "Dawnglories!" He took a deep breath through his nose. "They smell so sweet."

"Master?"

Harkot turned toward the sound of Raun's voice. He blinked and focused on the slavemaster. "What a strange feeling," he said, glancing at Sheyn. "It was as though I was sixteen again and waiting under the dawnglory vines to meet my darling Tareza. I felt young and eager to see what the next moment would bring." Harkot stopped speaking and cleared his throat.

"May I speak freely, master?" Raun asked.

Harkot nodded.

"Forget about training this slave. I could break him, but he'd be too broken for use. Send him off to Sumadin and collect your payment. That Eastron king is going to pass him off on someone else, so no harm done."

"Are you getting lazy?" Harkot teased.

"I'm getting old, and I tell you that slave is not worth the trouble. He's a disaster in the making."

"Very well, then. Prepare him for travel and I'll send a message to the Sumadi court. I'll be going now."

"Will you be visiting the slave quarters later?"

"What?" Harkot turned from the door.

"Forgive my boldness, but I thought you might enjoy a bit of time alone with this one before he leaves. I'll make sure he's drugged and tied down good and tight."

Harkot shook his head. "No. I think you're right about this one, and besides, that scowl of his would wilt my sprout."

"I'll say good-bye, then, master."

"One moment. Which handler are you sending with the daaksi?"

"I'll be doing that duty. I'd like to see a bit more of the world before I get too old."

"A good journey to you, then." Hartok took a pouch from his belt. "Draw funds from my quartermaster and take this gold for yourself."

"Thank you, master." Raun bowed. "Until my return," he said as he left.

Chapter
5

SHEYN WOKE and peered into the gloom. He sat up and banged his head. After a moment, he realized he was in an enclosed sedan chair and that it was moving. A knocking against the side made him jump.

"Are you all right in there?" Raun called out from the back.

"Let me out!" Sheyn shouted.

"No. But if you stay quiet, I'll open the panels."

After several moments of silence, Raun bade the draft slaves halt. While the burly slaves balanced the sedan chair on their shoulders, he unhooked the wooden panels and removed them from the screened openings. After placing the panels in a rack under the conveyance, Raun gave the order to walk on. Once they were over the mountains, Harkot's emissary knew an inn where they could hire a wagon, but for now, walking was the only way to follow this narrow, rocky path.

"It's cold," Sheyn said.

"Yes. We're high in the mountains."

"I'm freezing."

"You have furs in there. Use them."

Sheyn picked up a cape made of supple pelts and put it around his shoulders. "Where are you taking me?"

"To the court of the King of Sumadin."

"Why?"

"Because he bought you from my master."

"A king you say?" This sounded promising. Surely, one prince would recognize another and Sheyn would be set free.

"That's what I said. Sumadin is the westernmost nation of Kandaar."

"Yes, I know. And the easternmost is Weijan. The ones in the middle are debated, but the one along the—"

"Quiet! Unless you want another dose."

Sheyn sat back and brooded. The limited view showed him nothing but snow, rocks, and more snow. He huddled in the fur blankets and tried to stay warm until Raun called a halt to give the slaves a rest. Sheyn was allowed out of the box to relieve himself and promptly ran. After he was caught, Raun drugged him again.

SUMADIN'S KING was not in his palace when Raun delivered Sheyn, but instructions had been left with the master of the royal slave quarters. Harkot's emissary left messages for the king and received messages for Harkot in return. The small caravan returned to Harkot laden with gifts, and Sheyn was carried to King Yevdjen's hunting lodge in the lowland forest. The only bright spot for Sheyn was the warmer temperature.

Yevdjen was enjoying one of his jaunts pretending he was a warrior on a hunting trip with his best-loved comrade. Aside from Lord Ognyan, Yevdjen's chief general and royal champion, the only other occupants of the lodge were a few servants and Yevdjen's daaksi, Luks. They did a bit of hunting early in the mornings but spent the greater part of their days lounging on the breezy porch while cat-footed servants kept their plates and cups filled.

Ognyan watched over the rim of his carved, amber goblet as the lithe daaksi leaned against the king and offered his ripe, red mouth for a kiss. Rank envy rose in the general, threatening to choke him. Luks, whose name meant *velvet*, was physical perfection. His limbs were long and graceful with well-formed muscles covered in smooth skin that glowed like a sun-warmed peach. He had eyes like a deer, large and soft, and his dark, silky curls had a warm touch of red. He also had a sweet and compliant nature that drew Ognyan like a staked lamb draws the hungry wolf. But of course, the daaksi belonged to Ognyan's king and closest friend, and by law, Ognyan would have to be a king to claim such a treasure.

Yevdjen noticed his warlord's envious glance and chuckled. "You look like a bear with a bee-stung snout who didn't get any honey."

"The honey is all reserved for you."

Yevdjen grinned. "What shall we do about this grumpy man?" he asked Luks.

Luks didn't look at Ognyan. The burly warlord felt like a thundercloud that could wreak devastation at any given moment. It made Luks as nervous as a one-eyed cat to be in the same room with the massively muscled, bushy-bearded mountain of a man. Nor did the daaksi answer the king's question; he knew it was rhetorical. His master was not the sort to share his playthings, so Luks had no fears on that score, though it sometimes made him shiver to imagine being forced to serve Ognyan.

Yevdjen chuckled again. "While you were tramping about frightening the game this morning, I received a delivery. Would you like to see my gift?"

"A distraction is always welcome. Where is it?"

"I can have it brought here."

"Then I'm guessing it's not a horse."

Yevdjen rose from the divan and pulled Luks to his feet. "Come," he said to Ognyan. "Come and see this jewel in a proper setting."

Curious, Ognyan followed his liege from the open-air sitting room into the rambling stone-and-timber lodge. One of the four honor guards on staff bowed as Yevdjen stopped in front of a door in the west wing. The guard opened the door, and the king and the warlord walked through into the royal sleeping quarters. Ognyan stopped in his tracks and stared over Yevdjen's shoulder.

Luks hid his shock when he saw the occupant of the royal bed. How had Yevdjen managed this without his knowing anything about it? Why hadn't Yevdjen asked for his daaksi's help in this matter? And why did Yevdjen need another daaksi?

"Well? What do you think?" Yevdjen said.

Ognyan cleared his throat. The young man tethered to the bed with chains of gilded silver was unlike anyone the warlord had ever seen. To someone else, this pale beauty would be a prize beyond price, but Ognyan didn't like things that were different. To him, the slave was colorless, except for his eyes, which were a cold, fathomless, unwelcoming black. The pleasure slave looked as warm as snow, and that beak of a nose was—

"My gift doesn't please you?" the king prompted.

"I don't know what to say. It's too great a gift."

Yevdjen slapped Ognyan on the back. "Not too great a gift for the man who saved my son's life."

"It was battle. I'd have done the same for any Sumadi soldier."

"But somehow, you always manage to stay at Djenosh's side."

"I don't tell you how to rule your kingdom, so don't tell me how to fight a battle."

"You have a bargain." Yevdjen gestured toward the bed. "And you have your own daaksi. I've seen the way you look at Velvet, and I see no reason you should not have what you so greatly desire. I've been searching for over a year, but finally, I can present you with a proper reward."

Ognyan bowed to his king. "It's too much, but I thank you."

"Would you like to be alone with him?"

Ognyan shrugged. "As you wish. I've topped both lads and wenches in your presence."

"Sometimes side by side." Yevdjen shook his head. "Remember when we were the prince's age? Battle today is not the same as it was then."

"That's the sad truth. When we were pups, we took what we wanted and held it by the strength of our arms. These days, there's more apt to be a battle of words than swords between two clans."

"I thank Father Suma and all the other Gods that I was born Sumadi."

Ognyan knocked his fist against Yevdjen's before he walked across the room. He looked down at Sheyn, running his eyes over the contours of smooth flesh draped in a red robe as light as a whisper. "He's not soft," he said approvingly. "Why is he gagged?"

"He bites."

"Does he now?" Ognyan showed Sheyn his teeth in a carnivorous grin. "That's a bad habit we'll have to break him of."

"I'll leave you to it then." Yevdjen clapped Ognyan on the shoulder. Putting an arm around Luks's lithe waist, the king left the room.

Sheyn stared apprehensively at Ognyan. This man could not possibly be the king the slavemaster had spoken of. This man was clearly a brute, probably a brigand who robbed travelers. From what Sheyn had heard when he'd woken in this bed, he had been given to this barbarian as a reward. How could this be happening to a scion of the House of Merisolle?

"Do I see fear in those black eyes?" Ognyan said as he leaned over the bed.

Sheyn composed his face into the expressionless mask favored by his fencing instructor. His features gave away no clue as to what he was thinking and gave no advantage to his enemy. And this brute *was* his enemy, of that Sheyn had no doubt. This barbarian meant him nothing but harm. There was barely repressed violence in every line of the man's body and in the pitch of his voice. He awaited the slightest spark to flare into a storm of destruction.

For a moment, Sheyn was back behind the tapestry, crushed against the wall, frozen in terror and pain, and then abruptly, he snapped out of the trance. His mind had seized on a few remarkable facts. It had struck him that these savages weren't speaking his language as he'd supposed. Somehow, he understood theirs. And not only could he understand and speak their tongue, he knew what they were feeling. It was a disorienting sensation, and Sheyn's curiosity at that moment outweighed his fear.

Sheyn was reminded that this wasn't a classroom exercise when Ognyan grabbed a fistful of his robe.

"Look at me when I speak to you," Ognyan growled.

Sheyn met the warlord's gaze without a trace of fear in his eyes. He was frightened of what might happen to him, but he wasn't going to let this barbarian see him cringe.

"That is not how a slave looks at his master." Ognyan ripped Sheyn's robe from neck to crotch. "But I wager your expression will change when I take you for the first time."

Chapter

6

YEVDJEN RETURNED to the sitting room and pulled Luks down onto his lap. "What is that pout for?" the king asked indulgently. "Is there some food you're craving that you don't see here?"

"No, my lord," Luks said.

"Something is keeping the smile from your lips."

Luks smiled fetchingly at his master.

Yevdjen shook his head. "Tell me what has displeased you." He watched Luks pour wine before he spoke again. "You're not jealous of the new slave, are you?" As Luks handed him his cup, Yevdjen stroked the young man's cheek. "He's a gift for Ognyan, not for me. Now, be merry."

"Where is the new slave from?"

"His strangeness has made you curious too?"

"Yes, my lord. And I'm curious about something else."

"Speak freely."

"Though he bears the scars of a daaksi, I see nothing of the Shrine's training in him."

"He didn't come from the Shrine in Djenaes."

A fine line appeared between Luks's brows. "How is this possible?"

"What difference does that make? Ognyan wanted a daaksi and I procured one for him. What more is there to know?"

"Daaksim are for kings. They are not vulgar trophies for—" Luks stopped speaking and stared at his master in utter shock as he brought a hand up to his burning cheek. Not once in over a decade had the king laid a hand on him in anger, and surprise robbed him of speech.

"Nonsense," Yevdjen said dismissively. "It's true you're a rare beauty and you have an uncanny talent for pleasing a man, but there's no magic in that."

Luks bowed his head, letting the auburn waves of his hair slide forward to hide his face.

"Have I hurt you?" Yevdjen asked.

"Not you, my lord. I am only sad that my kind has fallen so low in the regard of this world and the one above."

"They filled your head with nonsense at that Shrine." Yevdjen put his fingers under Luks's chin. "I indulge you because you please me, but when all is said and done, you're a pleasure slave. You should remember your place."

"Yes, my lord."

Yevdjen set down his goblet. "This wine is sour."

"I'll fetch another jar."

"Go into the cellar at the right of the ladder and take a jar from the farthest corner. I'm in the mood for something special."

"Aye, my lord."

"And I wish you to join me, so bring another cup."

Luks bowed his head and left the room.

"Enjoy it," someone said as Yevdjen lifted his cup to his lips. "It will be your last drink."

Yevdjen reached for his sword, but a boot came down on it. The king looked up. "Bastard!"

"Yes," said the tall man. "It is the Bastard of Savaan." He put the point of his long sword against Yevdjen's neck.

Yevdjen swallowed. "Prince Kashyan," he said. "Welcome to my court."

"Not surprised? Well, I suppose you knew this day would come."

"I knew you'd try to kill me if you had the chance."

"Perhaps you shouldn't have abducted my mother and held her for ransom."

"That was twenty-five years ago. I was a boy of fourteen."

"There is no time limit on my mother's honor."

"She's dead."

"I'm aware of that."

A drop of blood trickled down the king's neck. "How did you get so close to me with your life?"

"I've had scouts watching you since I got my first command. It took patience, but at last, I have you where I want you. I've killed your guards, and my lieutenant is taking care of your warlord right now. Prepare yourself for death."

"You'd kill an unarmed man?"

"You want a fair fight? Did you give my mother a weapon?"

"She was just a woman!"

"She was my mother. You took her, and you defiled her, and you sold her back to a husband who was ashamed of her. She died alone and heartbroken, believing herself worthless because of you. You deserve no mercy from me."

"Ognyan!" Yevdjen bellowed.

"Shout all you like," Kashyan said. "No help is coming to you."

"Let me stand up, at least."

"Did you let my mother stand up?"

"Do you want to hear about it? Or would you rather stay with whatever story she told you?" Another trickle of blood flowed down Yevdjen's neck.

Kashyan cursed under his breath and took a step back, afraid he'd kill Yevdjen too quickly. "On your feet," he said. "And pick up your sword."

"Why give me this chance?"

"Because simply killing you wouldn't be satisfying enough. It would be over far too quickly."

"Oh, Bastard." Yevdjen grinned. "I do like your spirit." He drew his sword and faced Kashyan. "You're wearing riding leathers, and I'm in my robe, but I'll not complain. Fight for your life, boy, because I intend to."

"I fight for your life and the privilege of ending it."

Yevdjen grinned wolfishly. "My blood is stirring as it hasn't done in years. If I die today, at least it will be by the sword and not in my bed of old age."

SHEYN FROZE, every muscle rigid as iron, as Ognyan seated his rod. He felt pressure at his entrance, and his breath congealed in his throat until he felt as though he was suffocating. There was no distraction from the reality that he was helpless to stop what was happening to him. He could feel Ognyan's excitement, and it fed his horror.

Ognyan grinned as he leaned forward, trying to force his thick length into Sheyn without the aid of lubricant. The petrified look on Sheyn's face was sweeter than honey to Ognyan, and he reined himself in to savor the moment. His greatest pleasure had come from mounting prisoners in the aftermath of a battle when his blood was up and he felt like the God of war himself. However, that custom had been outlawed by the high king. To Ognyan's surprise, forcing this foreign daaksi gave him the same thrill. The pale lad wasn't as attractive as Luks, but Ognyan was beginning to see his charms. If only the daaksi would make a little noise, Ognyan was sure he could find release.

"Feel that?" Ognyan said as he pushed again. "You'll soon know what it's like to be topped by a man. When you feel my thrust, you'll make plenty of noise."

Ognyan grinned, and then he went still, straining to hear a faint noise. Climbing off Sheyn, he slid from the bed. As his feet touched the floor, he pulled down his kilt and grabbed his sword belt. Buckling the belt around him as he ran, Ognyan followed the unmistakable sound of metal striking metal. He saw Luks coming up from the cellar and ordered the daaksi to hide until the king came for him. Luks set down the jug he was carrying and hurried away.

Sheyn was stunned and relieved by Ognyan's abrupt departure. As he shivered in reaction to the assault, he wished with all his heart for someone to come and take him away from this misery and make everything all right again. He wished for the power to take revenge on those who hurt him. He pulled at his chains as he tried to curl up around the awful pain at his core, and he wished he could go back to moment before he left Aeriq for the last time. He didn't understand what had happened to him, but he knew it was worse than anything his mother could have imagined. And when that bloody-minded brute Ognyan came back, he was sure it would happen all over again.

KASHYAN LUNGED, Yevdjen skipped back out of reach, and the duel continued. Both men were tall, broad shouldered, and deep chested, with strong muscles forged in hours of practice with heavy weapons.

Neither had an advantage in height or reach, but Kashyan was fifteen years younger than Yevdjen. On the other hand, Yevdjen had fifteen years more experience and a familiarity with his surroundings. The fight was even, intense, and shockingly brief.

The deciding factor was the difference in the weapons in their hands. Kashyan carried a long fullered blade that had been passed down for generations. The ingot used to make the sword came from the Utmost East hundreds of years ago, and the metal was difficult to work. It took two gifted smiths three days to forge the blade, and they needed a team of six men to keep the bellows going day and night to ensure a hot enough fire. Grinding the edge took another month. In the fist of a strong, fearless man like the Bastard of Savaan, the sword had no equal.

Though Yevdjen was a powerful and wily swordsman, the first time he solidly blocked a blow, his weapon was shorn in half. Kashyan's stroke was not deflected at all; it barely lost any momentum as it slashed through Yevdjen's robe and the flesh beneath. Yevdjen fell back, raising the broken sword as a makeshift shield, as Kashyan hammered at him. The hilt flew from Yevdjen's hand, and he ducked away from the blow aimed at his neck. He kicked a large cushion under Kashyan's feet, but the Bastard leapt nimbly over it. Yevdjen looked swiftly around, but he knew there was nothing within reach that could be used as a weapon. Sumadin's king accepted the inevitable and spread his arms, inviting the killing stroke. Kashyan didn't hesitate to stab his enemy through the royal boar of Sumadin embroidered over Yevdjen's heart.

As Yevdjen fell, a flicker in the dying man's eyes alerted Kashyan. The Bastard spun around in time to block Ognyan's sword. Ognyan pressed the attack, driving Kashyan back with his greater weight. Kashyan recovered from his surprise and went on the offensive. He was beginning to gain ground when another man appeared in the arched doorway. Ognyan glanced over, saw that the warrior was no friend of his, and abruptly broke off the fight.

"Coward!" Kashyan barked as Ognyan turned and ran. "Don't let him get away, Djenya!"

Ognyan avoided the doorway, smashing directly through a plaster wall into the room next door. He dove out the window, tucked into a ball, and rolled to his feet. A few running steps brought him to the stable, and he jumped onto his horse's back. Without bridle or saddle, he clung to his mount with hands and knees as the animal bolted. He grunted when an arrow pierced his back, but he held on and urged the horse to run faster.

"Raas damn your eyes!" Kashyan cursed as he caught up with his lieutenant. "I told you to catch him, not let him get away."

Djenya Fairhair leaned on his bow and shook back the dark gold locks that were his namesake. "It would probably have been a good idea for us to have tethered our horses a bit closer."

"Rascal!" Kashyan gave his best friend and second-in-command a dark look. "You don't have to remind me. But it was too great a risk."

"It was your revenge and your decision." Djenya smiled. "I'm just trying to avoid blame for letting Yevdjen's best general escape."

"Yes. Let's talk about that," Kashyan said as he walked back to the lodge. "Weren't you supposed to kill him?"

"That was my intention, but I was foiled by sorcery."

Kashyan gave his friend a sidewise glance, his glacial eyes glinting with something like humor. "Magic, eh? I see. Well, I suppose I have no right to scold you for failing to follow orders."

"No, not really. How could I be expected to fight magic?"

"Exactly what sort of sorcery was it that prevented you from killing Ognyan?" Kashyan asked as they entered the royal sitting room.

Djenya glanced at the dead king. "It would be easier to show you than try to explain."

"Lead on." Kashyan paused. "Just a moment." He bent down and looked into Yevdjen's face, but whatever he was seeking, he didn't find it there. Yevdjen was just another corpse. It had occurred to him at an early age that Yevdjen might well be his father—they had the same distinctive pale green eyes—but that had no bearing on his vengeance. And his father could have been any one of the young Sumadi nobles who'd taken part in the raid. He only knew one thing for certain about his father: he was most definitely not King Nakhol of Savaan. Nakhol had told him so on many occasions.

Nakhol had branded Kashyan a bastard, and Kashyan had taken up the name like a badge of honor. He refused to be put aside; he was the son of a queen of Savaan, if not Savaan's king. He never forgave Nakhol for abandoning his mother, and he'd taken grim pleasure in the king's failure to produce another heir with any of his increasingly younger brides. These days, Kashyan stayed far away from the royal palace, serving as a captain of cavalry in his brother's mercenary army, the Horde of the Hawk. The Horde was in Muergath at the behest of Muergath's king, and Kashyan had taken the opportunity to settle a matter of honor in nearby Sumadin.

Kashyan looked around as he followed Djenya down a broad corridor. He rightly guessed they were in the lodge's sleeping quarters and tapped Djenya on the shoulder.

"Where are we going? If it hadn't occurred to you, Lord Ognyan will certainly return as soon as he finds reinforcements."

Djenya grimaced. "Are you sure? He ran away quickly enough."

"Yes, that surprised me. His reputation is of a man who fights likes a bear."

"In here," Djenya said, as he opened an elaborately carved door.

Luks backed across the room when Djenya entered.

"Don't be afraid," Djenya called softly. "We're not here to hurt you."

Kashyan pushed the door wide open and stared at Luks. "Great Raas! Djenya, are you mad?"

"I'm bewitched. Didn't I mention it?"

Kashyan groaned. "That would be Yevdjen's daaksi?"

"I was as surprised as you when I saw him. Why would Yevdjen bring a pleasure slave on a hunting trip?"

"I heard daaksim used to go into battle with their masters."

"And you have the hide to say I'm addled?"

"You *are* addled." Kashyan paused. "You let your short spear think for you."

"At least I employ it for something."

"Let's go," Kashyan said.

"Are you joking? We can't leave him here."

"Why not?"

"It would be cruel."

Kashyan sighed. "All right. If you want him, then bring him, but he's your responsibility."

"Of course." Djenya started across the room with his empty hands held in front of him. "Come with me, pretty one. I'll take care of you."

Luks shook his head. "I belong to the king. If you touch me, he'll kill you."

"Yevdjen is dead," Kashyan said. "I just killed him."

Luks paled. "Dead?" He heard the truth in the big man's voice, but he didn't want to believe it. With his protector gone, he was at the mercy of chance until he found another master.

"It was a matter of honor," Djenya said. "Now come with us. We won't let anything happen to you."

"You," Kashyan said. "*You* won't let anything happen to him. I don't care what becomes of him."

"How can you be so cold? Just look at him," Djenya said. "He's… perfect."

"He's beautiful," Kashyan said. "What of it?"

"Do you even have *naaks*?"

"Yes, and they're shriveling right now as I imagine Ognyan riding back with the Sumadi war band."

"Come along," Djenya said to Luks. "I don't want to hurt you, but I can't leave you here."

Luks considered the outcome if Ognyan did return with an army. Ognyan would no doubt claim the kingship and everything that went with it, including Yevdjen's daaksi. Between the prospects of belonging to Ognyan or being taken by a raider, Luks chose the evil he didn't know. Once the decision was made, Luks acted upon it immediately. With ingrained grace, he walked across the room and put his hand in Djenya's.

Djenya smiled. "You won't regret this," he said as he led Luks away.

"Wait," Luks said when they passed the royal bedchamber.

"Wait for what?" Kashyan turned and glared.

"There is a prisoner in that room."

Djenya shrugged at Kashyan. "Any enemy of Sumadin is a friend of ours, yes?"

Chapter
7

WITH A put-upon look, Kashyan kicked the door in. Sheyn stopped yanking at his chains and stared at Kashyan through the curtain of his disheveled hair. Luks sensed the invisible bolt that pierced Kashyan's soul, and a great foreboding filled him.

"Can you believe our luck?" Djenya said. "Two of them."

"*Ayeesh*! The Gods hate me," Kashyan said.

"Yes, they do, or why would they have made you so weak and ugly?" Djenya grinned. "Come on. Let's free this one and get back to camp."

"You do remember that we have several leagues of forest between us and the horses?"

"These lads look fit enough."

"What if one of them changes his mind and raises an alarm? The pale one looks angry enough to eat my liver raw."

"You would say something like that when I'm starving. Hurry and free him and let's be gone."

Sheyn scowled at Kashyan as he pulled away to the limit of his chains. He was determined to keep a brave face, but when the bright sword flashed down, he flinched. The blade cut through the gilded silver as though it were butter, leaving Sheyn with two awkward bracelets. In another moment, his legs were free, and he scrambled off the other side of the bed.

"Stop," Luks said. "I know you understand my words, foreigner, so listen to me. If you run, these men will kill you. Surrender, and they'll care for you."

"I'd rather be dead."

"No, you wouldn't."

Sheyn bit his bottom lip in indecision. He didn't want to go with these brutes, but he had no idea where he was, and he had nothing but the torn robe that barely covered him. It would be wiser to bide his time and trust the ruddy-haired lad. Yes, he should trust him. This one wouldn't harm him. He should go with him. Everything would be all right if—Sheyn shook his head. For a moment, he'd felt dizzy and drowsy at the same time, but his wits returned quickly.

"Who are you?" Sheyn asked.

"I am Velvet, who had the honor to be daaksi to the King of Sumadin. You should come away with me. Lord Ognyan will surely return, and I think you would rather not see him again."

"That animal you left me alone with?"

Luks nodded. "Come on," he said, holding out his hand.

"I can't go outside in this." Sheyn glanced down at the ruined bed gown.

"Enough!" Kashyan said loudly. "We're leaving *now*."

"Where are they taking us?" Sheyn asked Luks as they walked out of the hunting lodge.

"Keep your voice down," Luks said softly as Kashyan glanced back.

Sheyn was blinded by the rays of the setting sun, and he missed Kashyan's scowl. "Why are we going with these barbarians if you fear them so much?"

"Are you completely ignorant?"

"Look here, you little savage, I won't stand for—" Sheyn's words were cut off when Kashyan spun and took hold of his jaw with bruising force.

"You! Lapwarmer," Kashyan said to Luks. "Make this one understand that I don't like a lot of chatter."

"Yes, lord," Luks said softly as he gave Kashyan an appealing look.

"It's useless making eyes at him," Djenya said. "You should try them on me."

Luks turned to Djenya. "Pearl was only asking where we're going."

"His name's Pearl, is it?"

Luks nodded. It was as good a name as any, and prettier than most. "Please, lord, who are you and what is to be our fate?"

"We have no time for these fancies," Kashyan said as he let go of Sheyn. "Keep up or you're on your own." He strode away toward the trees.

Djenya winked at Luks. "My friend's bark is worse than his bite," he said. "Follow me and you'll be taken care of, my word as a Savaani soldier."

"Are you not a noble?" Luks asked.

Djenya chuckled. "Come, hurry. Kasha won't wait for us." He trotted off, and after a moment, Luks followed.

"Wait." Sheyn stopped rubbing his jaw and caught up with Luks. "Where are we going?"

"If you insist that I guess, I'd say we're going to Savaan."

"What is that and where might it be?"

"Savaan is a kingdom in the Shieldwall Mountains. They breed brave warhorses and fierce warriors, not as fierce as the Sumadinim, but good fighters."

"And why, again, are we going with these…?"

"Raiders," Luks said.

"Why are we going with these raiders?"

"We need their protection. Now be quiet. I need my breath for running."

Sheyn pursed his lips in thought as he kept pace with Luks, his long legs giving him an advantage. He saw no reason to stay with these violent savages. He needed to find the nearest agent of the Protectorate and arrange his passage home. After he recovered from this experience, he might consider traveling again, but right now, he wanted a hot bath, some fresh clothing, and someone to tell him the nightmare was over.

Sheyn stopped in his tracks, turned around, and started back to the lodge, but after a few steps, his feet began to drag until he stopped. Though he willed his legs to move, he remained frozen in place, and the compulsion to follow the bandits was growing stronger by the second. He struggled against it, but inexorably, he was drawn to reverse his course.

"Thank the Goddess, you came to your senses," Luks said when Sheyn trotted up beside him.

"I don't want to be here, but it seems I have no choice."

Luks glanced at Sheyn and sighed. "I hoped I was wrong."

"About what?" Sheyn craned his neck to see Luks's face. "About what, you irritating savage? And try being a bit less cryptic."

"Do you feel as though you must follow our protectors?"

"Yes. It's the poxiest thing, but I can't seem to do anything else."

"Then keep moving." Luks ran faster to catch up with the two Savaanim.

"Curse it," Sheyn said under his breath as he hurried after him.

Luks was beginning to flag when they reached a clearing among some willows by a stream. Two massive horses in leather tack studded with bronze stood under one of the ancient trees. The chargers' reins trailed on the ground as they moved toward the men. Kashyan and Djenya patted their horses' glossy necks and murmured to them.

"There you see the bond between a warrior and his steed," Luks said.

"There are only two steeds," Sheyn pointed out.

"We ride with our masters."

"You're joking."

"Do you really think I'd joke at this moment?"

Sheyn turned his back on Luks and watched as Kashyan swung up into the saddle of the blue roan charger. The tall, heavily muscled animal looked capable of carrying double, but Sheyn had no wish to share a mount with a barbarian raider. When he looked back, he saw Luks already on the chestnut behind the fair-haired man.

"Come," Kashyan said sternly as he held out his hand.

When Sheyn didn't move, Kashyan came closer. Sheyn wanted to run, but he was rooted to the spot. The barbarian took hold of his arm and hoisted him up to lie belly-down over a saddle that was little more than a piece of leather over felt padding. Limp as a sack of rice, he bounced helplessly as Kashyan urged the horse to a faster pace.

"WE'RE ACROSS the border," Djenya called out. "And dusk will be on us soon. Why don't we stop for the night?"

"We have an hour or more of daylight left," Kashyan called back.

"Are you so eager to return to camp and face your brother's wrath?"

"Where should we spend the night, then?"

"If we ride on, we'll be in the open, but if we stop now, we'll be under the cover of the forest."

"Choose a spot, then."

"We passed a trapper's cabin on the way in. Can you find it again?" Djenya grinned as Kashyan took up the challenge.

As the sun sank below the tops of the trees, Kashyan led them to a stone-and-timber cabin in a corner of a small meadow.

"I'll take care of the horses if you can manage dinner," Kashyan said as he dismounted.

"You have a bargain." Djenya dismounted and helped Luks down.

Kashyan put Sheyn over his shoulder and carried him into the cabin. After dropping Sheyn on a cot, he left him there and went to feed the horses.

Luks entered the cabin behind Djenya and came to where Sheyn was sitting. "Are you all right?" he asked.

"Of course not. I've been kidnapped, sold into slavery, assaulted, and abducted. And I was made to ride in a most undignified manner." Sheyn swiveled his neck. "My entire body is sore."

"You'd have an easier time of it if you'd just—"

"What?" Sheyn said loudly. "If you're going to advise me to surrender to these barbarians, you can save your breath."

Luks glanced nervously at Djenya. "Lower your voice. Did they teach you nothing?"

"Who?"

Luks's frown grew deeper. "You've no idea what I'm talking about, do you?"

"No, I don't."

"By the Goddess's law, only She and Her priests can create a daaksi in Her Shrine at Djenaes. You've never been in Djenaes, have you?"

"I was on my way to Weijan when I was kidnapped. That's near Djenaes, isn't it?"

Luks frowned. "This is very bad," he said, ignoring Sheyn's question.

"Yes, I agree." Sheyn paused. "What's a daaksi?"

"How can you not know what you are?"

"I know I'm a prince of the House of Merisolle, but who do *you* think I am?"

"You're a daaksi like me." Luks saw the look of irritation on Sheyn's fine features and hurried on. "In the Dawn of the World, the Gods and Goddesses walked this realm and created nations and people, each to His or Her own design."

"Yes, that's a fairly common creation myth, but go on."

"Only Anaali stood apart and created no tribe. Many years went by, and the different clans of men warred with one another, with their patron Gods joining in, until the numbers of man dwindled. The Gods met and agreed to retreat beyond the Threshold, all save Taankh, God of the Shadoworld, and Anaali of the Moon. Taankh and Anaali submitted to the judgment of their brother and sister deities and each gave their reasons for staying. After deliberation, the council favored Anaali, and Taankh was forced to leave and His children were banished as well."

"That's fascinating," Sheyn said sincerely. "Tell me more about this Anaali."

"Anaali is the Goddess of the Moon, the Lady of the Sword. She alone of the Gods remained to wander this world spreading Her Blessings. Under Her hand, the plants, the beasts, and man prospered and grew numerous again. Kings arose and looked covetously upon the kingdoms of others. When Anaali beheld the return of strife, She was disappointed and heartsore, but after a time, She grew determined to stop the violence."

"It seems She failed," Sheyn said. "But tell me what She did."

"She created Her tribe at last. Djeyd Flamehair, Araan Fairbairn, Yozi Brighteyes, Khandi Heartsease, Pharaan the Golden, Taafi Honeytongue, Oseah Swanneck, Gaazi Silkenlocks, Fasha the Wise, and Treijan Moonborn. There were only ten, ten daaksim, one of each nation, one for each king, and they were the most perfect creatures ever formed."

"How so?"

"At great sacrifice, She imbued each daaksi with a measure of Her divine life force. None of the other Gods did this, and so their children were doomed to age and suffer damage. Anaali's daaksim didn't grow old and they healed instantly. They were faster, stronger, and cleverer than other mortals. And they were beautiful, a perfect blend of the best traits of man and woman with an irresistible allure."

"If they live forever, where are they now?"

"She took them back into the Unseen Realm."

"Why?"

"Why don't you just let me tell the story?"

"Please continue," Sheyn said stiffly.

"Anaali sent a daaksi to each of the rulers of the ten tribes, to bring comfort, beauty, and joy to their lives. For a time, there was peace as the daaksim influenced the rulers to build up their nations rather than destroy others. But men are men and ever covetous, and war returned as they fought over ownership of the daaksim."

"How ironic."

Luks glanced at Sheyn before he began speaking again. "Anaali called all the rulers to council and gave them a choice. They could keep the daaksim and rule over peaceful, prosperous kingdoms, or She could bestow on Her priests the ability to turn an ordinary young man into a diminished version of a daaksi, thus allowing any with royal blood who had enough power and wealth to possess one. Do I have to tell you what choice they made?" He sighed. "Anaali was so disheartened that She took Her daaksim and disappeared. And that is why She's called the Lost Goddess. Her only remaining temple is the Shrine in Djenaes."

"Have you finished?"

Luks nodded.

"May I ask questions now?"

Luks nodded again.

"How could this happen to me?"

"I don't know," Luks said. "But I don't like it."

"Well, I'm not happy about it either."

Luks chewed his lower lip a moment and then spoke again. "It shouldn't be possible, but you exist, so I must accept that the rules have somehow changed. I wish I could speak with someone at the Shrine."

Impatient, Sheyn sought more information. "Why couldn't I run away?"

"Because a sacred, unbreakable bond exists between you and—" Luks fell silent as Kashyan entered the cabin.

Kashyan glanced distrustfully at the daaksim as he crossed to the hearth. "That smells better than expected," he said to Djenya.

"Last of the rabbit jerky with a few roots. The stew will be thin, but it'll warm our bellies." Djenya pointed a toe at a large wooden box. "Crockery in there," he said. "I don't know who the trapper is, but he's well-provisioned."

"I'm just glad it's not trapping season."

"Truly. I'll leave a few coins for our use of his belongings."

"What kind of raider pays for what he steals?" Kashyan joked.

Djenya grinned. "Speaking of loot," he said, tossing a look at Luks and Sheyn.

"What about them?"

"Are you made of wood? Look at them. Don't you want to—?"

"No! I don't. I'd as soon chop off my right hand as put my *jaavi* in one of those witches."

"You're missing out on a rare opportunity."

"I'm not interested."

"You can't let one bad experience put you off for life."

"Yes, I can. If you've a mind to top one or both, have at them, but stop trying to persuade me. I'm not one to trade a few moments of pleasure for a lifetime of regret."

"But it's a few moments of *divine* pleasure."

Kashyan noisily took pottery bowls and wooden spoons from the cache box, and Djenya fell silent until the stew was ready. Djenya ladled stew into the bowls Kashyan held, and Kashyan set two down near the cot. Luks picked them up and handed one to Sheyn.

"Thank you, my lord," Luks said.

"I'm not your lord, and I don't want your thanks, lapwarmer," Kashyan said.

"There's no need for rudeness," Sheyn snapped without thinking.

Luks gasped. "Pearl, no!"

"Speak to me in that tone again and you'll earn yourself a slap," Kashyan said.

"From you?" Sheyn sneered.

Luks took hold of Sheyn's arm and turned him until they were facing. "Please, stop."

Sheyn's pride would not let him stop. "You think I'm afraid of these savages?"

"You would be if you were smarter," Luks answered.

"Be quiet and eat your stew," Kashyan said. "The sound of your voices annoys me."

It was Sheyn's opinion that most things probably annoyed Kashyan, to judge from the constant scowl, but he held his tongue. He wasn't afraid of a slap, but he didn't want one, either. Resentfully, he ate the watery stew. When Luks and Sheyn were finished eating, Luks carried the bowls to where Kashyan and Djenya were sitting.

"Forgive me for interrupting," Luks said. "What will I do with these?"

Before Kashyan could speak, Djenya answered. "Leave them on the hearth."

"Lord?"

"I'm not a lord," Djenya said. "But ask your question."

"May I know your names?"

"I'm called Djenya Fairhair. My noble companion is Kashyan of Savaan."

Luks took a step back.

"You've heard of me?" Kashyan asked wryly.

"Everyone knows of the Bastard of Savaan."

"You show a proper respect, at least," Kashyan said. "Why don't you explain to your friend why he should fear me?"

Luks bowed and hurried back to Sheyn.

"What did they say to you?" Sheyn asked.

"We've been taken captive by Prince Kashyan, the Bastard of Savaan."

"That means nothing to me."

"He has a fearsome reputation. They say he's ruthless in battle and has the strength of three men. I have also heard that he killed a daaksi with his bare hands."

"I could well believe it of such a brute." Sheyn glanced at Kashyan. "What makes him so angry all the time?"

"He's a bastard."

"Literally?"

"What?"

"Are you saying his mother and father weren't wed?"

"His mother was queen, but the king refused to claim him."

"I see." Sheyn watched Djenya rise and walk toward him. "What does *he* want?"

Luks looked over his shoulder, gauged the look in Djenya's eyes, and then stood.

Djenya stopped in front of Luks and ran a hand over Luks's auburn curls. "You're very pretty," Djenya said.

"What do you want?" Sheyn asked as he got to his feet.

"Stay out of it," Luks told him.

"Tell me this beast doesn't intend to—"

"I intend to enjoy this pretty boy," Djenya said to Sheyn. "Do as he says, and stay out of it."

Djenya dismissed Sheyn from his attention as he took hold of the hem of Luks's tunic and pulled it up. Sheyn stepped forward, shoved Djenya hard, and swung a fist at him. Knuckles met nose with a distinct popping sound, and Djenya reeled back, holding his hands over his face.

"What are you playing at over there?" Kashyan asked.

Djenya turned, and Kashyan saw the blood pouring from between Djenya's fingers. Kashyan's eyes went to the daaksim, and he saw Sheyn standing in front of Luks with his fist cocked.

"Did Snowhair do that?" Kashyan asked his friend.

Djenya nodded. "Hurts like fire."

"Let me see."

Kashyan walked over and Djenya let his hands drop to his sides. After looking at the damage for a moment, Kashyan grabbed Djenya's nose and twisted it.

"That hurt even worse," Djenya complained.

"But when it heals, you'll be as handsome as ever. Wash off the blood before it crusts."

Grumbling, Djenya went to the bucket, saw it was empty, and went out to the well.

"I should beat you for striking my friend," Kashyan told Sheyn.

"Then beat me, but for Leynys's sake, don't bore me talking about it. Your voice annoys me."

Luks hissed at Sheyn. "What is wrong with you?"

"What's wrong with *you*?" Sheyn countered. "Why do you cower before these swine?"

"The next time you disrespect me, I'll give you a new scar, you venomous piece," Kashyan said.

"Charming," Sheyn said under his breath.

Kashyan looked away from Sheyn as Djenya came back in. "How does your nose feel?"

"Broken."

"It's swelling fast. Looks more like a snout than a nose."

"Thank you for telling me that."

"No trouble." Kashyan stretched out on the floor. "Have you lost interest in sex for now?"

"Oddly, yes."

"Then take first watch." Kashyan closed his eyes and was asleep between one breath and the next.

"We might as well get some rest too," Luks said to Sheyn. "Take the cot if you want."

Sheyn didn't think he could sleep, but once he was horizontal, he felt abruptly exhausted. The last thing he heard as he drifted off was the sound of Djenya and Luks talking.

Chapter

8

"WAKE UP," Luks said as he shook Sheyn's shoulder. "We'll be leaving soon."

Sheyn focused on Luks's face, and he groaned. "I dreamed I was home."

"No time to feel sorry for yourself."

"Why are you so cruel to me?"

Luks looked surprised. "Cruel?"

"Don't you long to go back to your home?"

"I was told I was given to the Shrine when I was born, and I grew up there. When I was old enough, a priest performed the ritual, and I became a daaksi."

"So this is the only life you've ever known?"

Before Luks could answer, Kashyan strode into the cabin. "The horses are saddled," he said. "Let's go!"

Luks and Sheyn followed the Bastard outside. To Kashyan's astonishment, Sheyn trotted to his horse, put a foot in the stirrup, and swung into the saddle. Even more surprising, the battle-trained horse didn't object to the stranger on his back. The charger stood in docile stillness as Sheyn scratched between his ears.

"My eyes see it, but I don't believe it," Djenya said. "How is it that the daaksi still has all his fingers?"

"How is it that Karkaran hasn't thrown him?" Kashyan stalked over and took the reins from Sheyn's hands. He didn't think the big horse would obey the daaksi's commands, but he wasn't taking the chance they'd gallop off and leave him looking a fool. He mounted behind Sheyn and slackened the reins.

"Do you have something I can use to tie back my hair?" Sheyn asked.

"What?"

"I need something to tie back my hair."

"Do I look as though I carry hair ornaments with me?"

Sheyn shrugged. "It's all the same to me if you want to chew on my hair until this ride is over, but I'd sooner have it out of the way."

Kashyan ground his teeth as he drew his knife. "Why don't I remove the problem for you?"

"Stop! Take this." Djenya held out his neck scarf. "Be a shame to chop off hair like that."

Sheyn pulled his hair into a tail, doubled it, and used the length of cloth to bind it. "I'm ready now," he said arrogantly.

The muscles bulged along Kashyan's jaw. Abruptly, he dug his heels into Karkaran's flanks, and the horse bounded forward in a serious of great leaps until he settled into a gallop.

"This promises to be entertaining," Djenya said as he followed Kashyan.

Luks put his arms around Djenya's waist and held on.

A RIDE of a day and a half took them into the lowlands of Muergath. On the plain before the city of Taar Muergan were several cultivated parkland areas reserved for royal hunting parties. A small army was camped in one of them with tents set up under the trees of a miniature forest. The sentries recognized Kashyan and Djenya, and they rode to the center of the camp to the command tent. They dismounted, and Djenya turned to offer Luks his hand. Sheyn was on the ground a second behind Kashyan. The two guards at the tent's entrance were too well trained to react, but they couldn't take their eyes off Luks and Sheyn.

"Is my brother inside?" Kashyan asked the group of officers who were leaving the tent.

"Aye, Bastard," the older officer replied. "Go right in."

Kashyan nodded his thanks and strode into the tent, dragging Sheyn by the wrist, and Djenya followed with Luks. A man of Kashyan's build with the same hawkish features looked up from his plate as the four entered.

"Where have you been, little brother?" he asked.

"I had some leisure time and I wanted to see a bit of the countryside."

"I ordered you to stay away from Sumadin."

"Yes, you did."

"And you'd never disobey my orders."

"I'd be a fool to disobey your orders, Kholya."

"Yes, you would." Kholya let his gaze rest on Luks and Sheyn. "And who are these two?"

As Kashyan struggled to find words, Sheyn spoke up.

"I'm Rosheyn Lir of the House of Merisolle of Dey Larone, and this is…. Velvet. He's a… daaksi."

"Yes, I know a daaksi when I see one," Kholya said in a droll voice. "Who is Velvet's master?"

"The King of Sumadin was my master," Luks said.

"Was he indeed?" Kholya looked at Kashyan. "Anything to add?"

"I might have run in to Yevdjen while I was riding about. His death is most likely my fault."

"You realize you've just started a war with Sumadin, when Muergath has just hired us to fight a war for them."

"With Sumadin?" Djenya asked hopefully.

"Your wit isn't appreciated at the moment," Kholya said. "Kashyan?"

Kashyan cleared his throat. "I didn't know when I'd be this close to Sumadin again, so I had to go."

"I understand why you did it, but you've just undone all my work here."

"You reached an agreement with King Kezlath?"

Kholya nodded. "He was not shy about his intention to declare himself high king, and as soon as he does that, we'll have all the fight we can handle. When High King Djulyan hears of it, he'll send as many troops as he can muster to crush Kezlath."

"I don't think I like this job," Kashyan said.

"Have you ever known me to make foolish decisions?"

"There was the time you defied Father and took my side. Look what that gained you. You were the heir to Savaan's throne, and now you're a commander of mercenaries."

"I command the best army-for-hire in the world," Kholya corrected. "So have a bit of faith in me. Kezlath isn't ready to make his announcement yet. He's waiting on his priests for some sign or other. And when he does make his bid for the Crown of Kand, it will take some time for Djulyan to gather his armies and march to Muergath. A lot can happen between now and then."

"What's your plan?" Kashyan asked.

"Who did I swear fealty to?"

"High King Djulyan."

Kholya glanced around before he spoke again, but he knew he could trust Djenya, and the daaksim didn't register as people to him, so he felt safe in speaking freely. "Once I knew Kezlath was set on treason, I sent a message to the high king."

Kashyan shook his head. "I can't believe I ever doubted you."

"You doubted me?" Kholya stood, pretending outrage.

"No need to hang me, but I did wonder why you'd take a contract with lowlanders. Their treachery is legendary."

"What would you have done if I'd truly allied us with Kezlath?"

"I'd have followed your orders."

"Even if I ordered you to fight the true high king?"

"I love you, Kholya. You never once denied I was your brother. You broke with Father over the way he treated me. I can never repay you, but I can fight for you."

Kholya put a hand around the back of Kashyan's neck and drew him forward until their foreheads smacked together. "Now," he said as he leaned against his worktable. "Let's talk about the loot from your raid."

Chapter

9

HIGH PRIEST Chanesh faltered in his recitation of the Chant of Abasement, and the acolyte at his elbow looked up at him in concern. They were alone in the ancient First Temple, but there were guards at the outer door, and Moksha was prepared to run and fetch one. The High Priest had been pushing himself hard since he'd had the vision of the Gate. Chanesh was not young by any means; in fact, he was the oldest man the acolyte knew of, and that was worrisome. Without the High Priest to oversee the Temple, it would fall into confusion and fail. Moksha did not doubt the truth of that. And if the Red Temple fell, the nation of Muergath would fall with it.

The acolyte didn't quite dare interrupt Chanesh's morning prayers, but he edged closer, ready to catch the old man if he collapsed. Moksha was very relieved when the High Priest resumed the chant, though he didn't care for the breathiness of the reedy voice. He was even more relieved when Chanesh cut the prayers short. After an interval of silence, Chanesh spoke.

"*He* is here."

Moksha looked around the gloomy space. "Reverend Lord?"

"Not here with us but very near." Chanesh smiled wearily. "The one who will bring the doom of this world and the birth of a new one."

Moksha's mouth went dry. "Would you like a cup of your tonic, Reverend Lord?"

"What? Yes. Yes, that would be good. Come." Chanesh rose and they left the small temple within the temple. "I'm going to my chambers. Find Brother Mardjan and send him to me."

Moksha hesitated just long enough to earn an annoyed glance from the High Priest.

"Are you still here, boy? I gave you an order."

The acolyte hurried away, though he had no wish to visit the barracks of the Temple's militia. It was understood that all Servants of Taankh were soldiers in His army, but the Red Monks were battle-trained and went about with swords at their sides. An air of imminent violence hung about them, and their eyes were never still, always searching for a reason to use their sharp weapons.

Moksha slowed down when he saw a novice younger than he was. He sent the boy to the barracks with Chanesh's message and went to Chanesh's chamber by way of the kitchens. He consumed a meat pie in several large bites, and licked his fingers clean as he approached the High Priest's door. Once inside, he busied himself setting out Chanesh's evening prayer robes while he waited for Brother Mardjan.

It wasn't long before the antechamber door opened and a towering man in a dark red tunic entered. Moksha bowed to the captain of the Red Monks. "Please come with me," Moksha said.

Mardjan followed the acolyte into Chanesh's sitting room and bowed to the High Priest. "How may I serve you?" he asked as Chanesh gestured to Moksha to leave the room.

"Sit," Chanesh said. "I can't speak to you while you're looming over me like that."

Mardjan sat and waited for the High Priest to speak again.

"I need someone found," Chanesh said.

"Give me a description and I'll start a search, Reverend Lord."

"It isn't quite that simple."

"Explain, please."

"I can give you a description, but the search must be discreet. I don't want anyone to know we're looking for him until he's in our hands."

"That isn't complicated."

"He's a daaksi."

Mardjan ran a hand over his shaven head as he sat back. "You're right, it isn't simple."

"WHAT WERE you thinking?" Kholya asked his brother as he ran his eyes over Sheyn and Luks.

"I honestly don't know," Kashyan answered. "Maybe I thought that you'd be so angry about the raid that you wouldn't even blink at a pair of daaksim."

Kholya gave his brother an incredulous look.

"It was my idea," Djenya said. "I thought it would be cruel to leave them on their own."

"Is that what you thought?" Kholya said. "You had no other motive?"

"Well… perhaps one." Djenya made a comically lustful face.

"As I thought," Kholya said. "I expect you to follow the wishes of your jaavi." He looked to Kashyan again. "But you… I'm baffled that you'd have anything to do with daaksim. Your contempt for them is legendary."

"What else could I feel for such creatures?"

"Pity?" Sheyn suggested. When everyone turned to look at him, he shrugged. "I'm not saying that *I* want your pity, but you could have a little sympathy for poor Velvet. By all accounts, he was enjoying some sort of honored position with his king, when these two ruined his life." Sheyn looked surprised and then insulted by the laughter his speech provoked. "I fail to see anything amusing about this situation."

"The daaksi's honored position is on all fours with the king on top," Kholya said.

"Royal concubine is a position of some honor," Sheyn stated.

Kholya looked at Kashyan and Djenya. "Is this daaksi debating me?"

"It's only one of his annoying habits," Kashyan said.

"It's oddly fascinating," Kholya said. "As if my horse decided to speak up and disagree with me about a point of strategy."

"How dare you refer to me as an animal?" Sheyn said.

"Pearl is a foreigner, lords," Luks said quickly. "He knows nothing of Kandaar or its ways."

"You're joking," Kholya said drily. "Tell me, where do they grow boys with hair like that?"

"I'm from the city-state of Dey Larone in the Deysian Protectorate," Sheyn said. "And I'd be grateful if you'd return me there. My parents will pay—"

"You're a daaksi," Kholya interrupted. "You can't go home."

"That's ridiculous. Of course I can go home. I just need some gold and an escort to the coast."

"You'll not leave Kandaar while Prince Kashyan lives," Luks said softly. "You're bonded to him and cannot leave his side."

Sheyn was silent for several moments as he realized he could actually feel the truth of Luks's words. He remembered his odd paralysis when he'd tried to run away in the woods. "No!" he said loudly. "I don't accept this. How is it even possible? I demand that you help—"

"Enough," Kholya said. "Kashyan, control your daaksi."

"He's not mine. I only gave him a ride."

"Forgive me, but Pearl *is* yours, lord," Luks said.

"No," Kashyan said. "The Gods wouldn't be this cruel."

"The truth," Kholya said, putting a hand on Kashyan's shoulder. "Do you feel a bond?"

"I feel something," Kashyan said grudgingly. "I feel I want to strangle the white-haired witch."

"You do enjoy making threats, don't you?" Sheyn said as Kashyan's gaze met his.

Kashyan had never seen eyes so dark, so deep that you could fall into them forever. He could feel the wind of passage on his face, as though he rode across a plain of sweet grass, his horse's hooves raising a subtle scent. The perfume of frostflowers filled his nostrils, and he could hear the chuckling of the brook they grew beside in the meadow where he'd played as a child.

"Kasha," Kholya said. "What are you thinking about? You have such an odd look on your face."

Kashyan sighed. "If honor says I must claim this daaksi, I will, but if there is a way to escape this fate, I hope someone will tell me."

"Claim me?" Sheyn said. "I want nothing to do with you, brute." He looked at Kholya. "Couldn't I stay here with you until we find a way home for me?"

Kholya laughed. "I've never seen, or heard, a daaksi like this one," he said and then glanced at Luks. "And what shall we do with you? There are only two men in this camp with royal blood, and I doubt my brother wants a pair of you."

"Kholya, please," Kashyan said. "Take him into your tent."

"I won't say it isn't an attractive proposition, in some respects," Kholya said.

"Please, lord, give me your protection," Luks said, going abruptly to his knees.

Kholya smiled. "Now, how can I refuse such a sweet request? I'm afraid you'll be bored, though. I'm hardly ever in my tent."

"Then perhaps you wouldn't mind if I spent that time with Pearl," Luks said.

"If that pleases you, I have no objections. Kashyan?"

"I don't care."

"Then it's settled," Kholya said. "The daaksim can stay together in my tent for now."

"I need clothing," Sheyn said.

Kholya chuckled again. "It's the haughty tone that makes it so amusing," he said to Kashyan and Djenya.

"I'm glad you think it's funny," Kashyan said. "I want to slap him."

"Maybe you could try being amused instead of annoyed." Kholya picked up his helmet from the table. "I'm going to review the archers at their request. Care to come along?"

As Kashyan and Djenya followed the commander out of the tent, Sheyn turned on Luks. "What just happened?"

"Lord Kashyan claimed you," Luks said as he got to his feet. "You're lucky. You have a master now."

"What does that mean exactly? Am I a slave?"

"Only to your bond with your lord. You'll find it hard, sometimes impossible, to leave him."

"He just left."

Luks paused as he thought about that. "Do you feel as though you want to run after him?"

"No."

"But when we were taken by the Savaani, you felt as though you had to follow."

"Yes, I remember. It was most vexing."

"I don't understand," Luks said softly.

"This isn't fair!" Sheyn burst out. "I only wanted to see Weijan."

"I don't know how you became a daaksi, but whatever your life was like before the ritual, you should forget it. You can't go backward."

"I don't believe you. I'll find a way to undo whatever was done to me."

"No, you won't."

Sheyn stared at Luks for a long moment before he looked away. He couldn't read Luks's thoughts, but he could feel Luks's emotions, and

Luks utterly believed what he was saying. It was the oddest thing to feel the emotions and motivations of those around him. It frightened him, though it was terribly useful. Who knew what other changes this "ritual" had wrought in him? Sheyn shook off the temptation to despair and concentrated on the situation at hand as his mother had taught him. "What do we do now?"

"First, you need something else to wear." Luks picked at the tatters of Sheyn's diaphanous bed gown. "This might be fine for a royal bedchamber, but you can't walk around among warriors dressed like this. You'd be had five times before you went ten steps."

"Don't be vulgar."

Luks smiled for the first time since Sheyn had clapped eyes on him. "Come with me," he said.

At the entrance to the command tent, Luks spoke to one of the sentries. "Does the commander have a body servant?"

"No, he doesn't, nor a cook neither. Commander Kholya doesn't keep a household. He lives like one of his warriors."

"He has a household now," Luks said. "He's taken us under his protection. Where is his tent?"

"The tent he sleeps in is just behind this one. I'll escort you."

Luks gave the sentry a willowy bow of gratitude. Taking Sheyn's hand, he followed the guard. The soldier waited until Luks and Sheyn were inside the commander's tent and then went back to his post.

Luks looked around, noting the practical wooden furnishings that were designed to collapse flat for transport in a wagon. "It's not so bad," he said. "For a military man's home."

"You're joking. It's a *tent*."

"But the ground is covered with woven mats and there are soft cushions for sitting." Luks walked to a low table and inspected the objects sitting on it. "Would you like something to drink?"

"I'd murder a stranger for something cool and wet."

"Here." Luks poured water from a pitcher into a wooden cup. "Now, let me see what I can find to cover that long body of yours."

Sheyn gulped down the water. "Is there something wrong with being tall in your land?"

"Most men prefer a daaksi whose height is less than theirs."

"That doesn't surprise me. I have a feeling that men in your land prefer forcing their will on others."

"It's different in your land?" Luks asked as he opened a chest.

"Won't you get into trouble snooping around like that?"

"The commander took me into his tent. I live here now."

That answer didn't satisfy Sheyn, but he let it drop and answered Luks's question. "Yes, it's different in my land. Violence is illegal in Dey Larone. There hasn't been a war in the Deysian Protectorate in over a hundred years. Those who prey on those weaker than themselves are held in the greatest contempt, and the punishment for a crime of violence is so severe that there hasn't been a murder in my lifetime."

"No wars?" Luks said.

"Differences between rulers are settled by ambassadors instead of generals."

"You have no warriors, no soldiers?"

Sheyn shook his head. "I remember a speech my mother made before the League of States Council on the Day of Memoriam. She spoke of how happy she was, how happy every mother was, that no sons would ever die in battle again. Most moving."

"Your mother?"

"Yes?"

"Is a woman."

"Of course."

"She spoke in public… in front of men?"

"She's Dey Larone's chief ambassador."

His head spinning, Luks turned to Sheyn and held up a tunic of dull red. "This might do for now," he said, changing the subject.

"It will cover me at least," Sheyn said. "Can you find some leggings?"

"Daaksim don't wear—"

"No!" Sheyn barked. "I don't want to hear the words *daaksim* and *don't* used together ever again."

"I'm only trying to save you a few slaps."

"I have nothing but pity for anyone stupid enough to strike me."

Luks handed Sheyn the tunic. "The world you came from is very different. I can't even imagine a woman appearing in public, much less giving a speech. And if you continue to behave as you do, you'll suffer more than slaps. Prince Kashyan has been very merciful, but—"

"You may consider me warned, so don't feel as though you have to mention it again." Sheyn finished stripping off the remains of the bed gown and pulled the tunic on over his head. "Maybe I will get slapped or worse, but what I won't do is live in fear."

Luks bit his lip as he swallowed the words that came to his mind. Coming closer, he tugged the tunic into place across Sheyn's shoulders and wrapped a length of silky yellow cloth around Sheyn's waist. He tied the sash in a complicated knot that resembled a flower bud and let the ends dangle to flow fetchingly when Sheyn moved. After tweaking a few folds of fabric, Luks stepped back to inspect his handiwork.

The tunic was too large, but cinched by the belt, it draped Sheyn's narrow frame in flattering billows. It was nothing finer than medium-weight linen, and it was dyed or faded to the color of drying blood, but it was a vast improvement over the filmy rags Sheyn had been wearing.

"I suppose it's too much to hope that there's a mirror in this tent," Sheyn said.

"The commander may have a small one for shaving. His signal corps might have some large enough for you to see most of yourself."

"You're awfully knowledgeable about military matters."

"My master was a general as well as a king. I went on many campaigns and raids with him."

Sheyn cocked his head. "I don't mean to be callous, but do you miss him?"

"I'm… not sure how I feel." Luks poured himself a cup of water and took a sip. "At first, I was shocked, and then terrified, but now… I don't know. I'm just trying to stay alive."

"I understand."

"We've both seen great changes in our lives recently, haven't we?"

Sheyn's lips twitched in an imminent smile. "We have that much in common, at least."

"Then… shall we be friends?"

"Allies, at the least."

Sheyn was taken aback when Luks embraced him, but he controlled the urge to recoil. Gingerly, he put his arms around Luks and held him for a few moments. To Sheyn's surprise, he didn't feel awkward or uncomfortable; he felt the soothing evidence that he was not alone, and it comforted him.

"Now," Luks said as he stepped back. "Let's see what can be arranged for the evening meal."

Chapter
10

"WELL, ISN'T this pleasant?" Kholya said as he and Kashyan entered his tent.

The sun was down, and the oil lamps had been lit, lending a gilt-edged glow to every surface. The low table held a number of dishes, and a delicious smell pervaded the air. Luks and Sheyn sat on cushions playing with a set of dice.

"If you say so." Kashyan sat down on the floor and helped himself to a plate.

"How was this accomplished, Velvet?" Kholya asked as he sat down.

"One of your sentries sent a message to your quartermaster for me, and he sent someone to see to your needs, my lord," Luks said. "They took my word that I spoke in your name, so I think news must travel quickly in your army."

"You did well," Kholya said. "I'm very pleased. All my favorite foods are here." He looked over at Kashyan. "It's not so bad having someone see to my needs."

"I manage well enough on my own."

Kholya looked over at Kashyan, who was devouring half a roasted rockhen. "If you say so." He took a drink from his cup and spoke to Luks again. "Have you eaten?"

"We have, my lord, but if you wish for us to wait and eat with you next time, we will."

"Eat when you're hungry," Kholya said. "I'm impressed with how quickly you've settled in."

"I behave according to my training, lord," Luks said. "But if I displease you, you must let me know."

"How pleasant," Kholya said. "Kasha, how can you frown at this beauty?"

"He's a daaksi with all a daaksi's well-known habits of treachery, deceit, and betrayal."

"Look at this lad," Kholya said, nodding at Luks. "There isn't an ounce of deceit in him."

"It's that innocent look that makes them so good at deception."

"You've got a habit too, you know—the habit of bitterness. You let it influence everything you say and do."

"You sound like an educated man, commander," Sheyn said.

Kashyan and Kholya turned to stare at Sheyn in surprise.

"You shouldn't interrupt," Luks whispered.

"I'm giving the man a compliment," Sheyn said.

Kholya shook his head at the foreign daaksi's audacity, but he answered. "You're right. I had the best tutors my father could afford, and he could afford the very best."

"The best your country had to offer, you mean." Sheyn pursed his lips. "At least you got a decent vocabulary out of it."

Kholya chuckled. "Kasha, honestly, how is it you aren't amused?"

"He's not trying to be funny. He's insulting you."

"Yes, I know that. That's why it's amusing. Imagine… a fierce daaksi. That's like saying—"

"A trustworthy Sumadi?" Kashyan suggested.

"Bitter to the bone." Kholya shook his head again. "I miss the Kashyan who laughed the loudest of all at a good joke. I wish you weren't so devoted to getting yourself killed."

"You're exaggerating. I don't want to die."

"Then why do you put yourself in such dangerous circumstances?"

"Are you going to scold me again about taking revenge on our mother's defiler?"

"No, though I should. If you'll take my advice, you'll enjoy this good food and drink and then take that astonishing creature to your tent and enjoy him."

"I was hoping he might stay here."

"If that's what you want, I don't mind," Kholya said.

"Good." Kashyan got to his feet. "Do you want me with you when the delegation arrives?"

"If you like, but I won't need you."

"I'd rather remind my troops that life is hard when I'm around."

"Why don't you lead your Black Hawks past the command tent while the delegation is there? I'd like the Muergathim to see what well-trained cavalry looks like."

"That will be my pleasure," Kashyan said. "Good night."

Kashyan had been gone for several minutes when Sheyn noticed the beginning of discomfort. He felt vaguely queasy, and his pulse was pounding in his temples. He could tell he'd soon be nauseous and his head would ache horribly.

"Are you feeling unwell?" Luks asked.

Sheyn nodded. "I feel terrible."

"You should go with your master. While the bond is fresh, you'll feel worse the farther you are from him."

"I was fine when he left earlier. Explain that."

"It's the Goddess's will."

"I hate your Goddess."

"You really shouldn't say such things. Why don't you go to your lord's tent so you'll feel better?"

"I'd rather die in excruciating pain."

Before Luks could answer, Kashyan strode back into the tent.

"Did you forget something?" Kholya asked.

"My head feels like Raas's thunder. Damn this daaksim nonsense." Kashyan scowled at Sheyn. "Come with me."

"Go," Luks urged Sheyn. "I'll come find you in the morning." He smiled. "Don't worry. You'll be all right."

"How do you know that?"

"If you calm down long enough to read your master's feelings, you'll know it too. Go now."

Sheyn wanted to ask more questions, but he was compelled to follow when Kashyan left the tent for the second time that night. Kashyan didn't speak as he led Sheyn to the edge of the camp and a group of tents set apart from the others. Under a line of awnings stood twenty-five horses. Sheyn recognized the blue roan charger beside the first tent.

"In there," Kashyan said. "Try and keep your mouth shut so I can sleep."

"Just show me where I'll be sleeping and you won't hear a sound out of me."

"Here's a blanket." Kashyan grabbed the covering off his cot and tossed it to Sheyn. "Sleep anywhere you like as long as it's as far from me as possible."

"That would be my preference." Sheyn looked around. "Do you really expect me to sleep on the ground?"

"I don't expect anything. Sleep standing up if that suits you."

Sheyn spread the blanket on the opposite side of the tent from Kashyan's cot. He found two cushions stacked beside a small fire pit and placed them on the blanket. After several minutes of pillow punching and rolling from side to side, he lay still. Just as Kashyan was drifting off to sleep, Sheyn spoke.

"Do you really mean to keep me like a slave?"

"Do you think I have any more choice than you do?" Kashyan snapped. "Go to sleep, or I'll bind your wrists and ankles and put a gag in your mouth."

Sheyn turned his face to the wall of the tent and distracted himself by imagining the revenge he'd take on this barbarian and the others responsible for putting him here. There had to be a way back to his life as a scholar and privileged son of nobility. He didn't see the way yet, but he was intelligent, and he'd solve this problem. It was plain to him that he was the only one who cared about his plight. Even Luks, who was sympathetic, wanted him to accept his fate. Sheyn clenched his fists and willed his tears not to fall. He was smarter than these savages, and he'd find a way home.

Sheyn didn't notice the moment he went from brooding to sleeping, but he noticed Kashyan banging around early the next morning. "Great Leynys," he grumbled. "Did someone let an ox in here?"

"Shut up," Kashyan said automatically.

"Why are you making that racket?"

"I'm looking for my shield."

Sheyn glanced around the tent. "It's there." He pointed. "Behind that rack thing."

Kashyan snatched up his shield and clipped it to the back of his weapon harness. "Don't cause trouble," he said as he went to the opening of the tent.

"Wait! I want to go to the commander's tent."

"No. He's meeting with the Muergathim this morning, and I'm showing off our cavalry. When I return, you can go."

Sheyn told himself it was childish to pout. "I suppose I'll go back to sleep then. There's precious little else to do around here. You don't have a single book, do you?"

"Shut up." Kashyan glared at Sheyn before he left the tent. The nausea roiling in his stomach and the pounding in his head worsened with each step he took away from the daaksi. Kashyan set his jaw and kept moving.

Sheyn sat up again and went to the entrance. He lifted the flap and watched Kashyan mount his horse and ride away. "You can't order me around like a servant," he muttered.

He felt the onset of the sickness that had come over him last night, but he was determined not to let it affect him. After finger combing his hair and straightening his tunic, he went outside. The area around the tents was empty of people, and he had no difficulty retracing the path to the command tent.

Chapter

11

MUERGATH'S ROYAL herald arrived with an entourage of twenty soldiers and an honor guard to hold his banner of rank. Beneath the square of silk with the Muergathi bull and the feather symbol of diplomacy, the herald bowed deeply to Kholya. "I greet you in the name of King Kezlath," he said. "I am Lord Beshar, and I hold sufficient rank to treat with a prince."

"Thank you for coming outside the city to meet with me," Kholya said. He gestured to the large open-sided tent that had been set up in the open square in front of the command tent. "Please come out of the sun and sit."

"First, let me make my companions known to you, great lord," Beshar said. "I'm escorted today by a troop of the finest warriors in Muergath. You see here twenty of the legendary Red Monks, sworn to serve the Shadow of Death."

The twenty scarred, bald men in red tunics lifted their swords as one and shouted, "For the greater glory of Taankh!"

"They seem very dedicated," Kholya said.

"Indeed. Their leader is Brother Mardjan. He's never lost a fight."

"Very impressive." Kholya took a closer look at the Red Monks' leader. Could the stories about these warriors possibly be true? Legend said they took no wives because they were wed to Death. Kholya suppressed a shudder and returned to business. He feared nothing he met in the light of day with a sword in his hand, and he gave little credence to the supernatural. "What did you want to discuss?"

"King Kezlath has heard rumors concerning your brother, the Bastard."

"Already?" Kholya grimaced. "What are these rumors?"

"A messenger came in the night from the court of Sumadin. King Yevdjen was slain in a raid on his hunting lodge. General Ognyan names Kashyan, Bastard of Savaan, as the killer."

"If that is Ognyan's claim, he should make it to Kashyan's face."

"Is that your only answer?"

"What other answer could I make? He's my brother, and I've seen no proof of this accusation."

Beshar nodded as he leaned toward Kholya. "Of course, I understand. For your ears alone, the loss of Sumadin's king is no loss to Muergath." He straightened up and raised his voice. "If Sumadin seeks justice of your brother, Muergath cannot provide refuge."

"I understand. I hope these rumors won't affect our contract."

"No, my lord."

At the sound of hooves, the Red Monks assumed battle stance. Kashyan rode up at the head of a troop of twenty-four, drawing everyone's eyes. Taking advantage of the opportunity, Sheyn made his way unseen to the entrance of Kholya's personal tent.

"How did you get here?" Luks asked.

"I walked."

"Alone?"

"Calm down. I'm fine. And I have a question. Why did I feel ill last night, but this morning, when the barbarian left, I felt fine?"

"You had no reaction?"

"Not exactly. I could feel it coming on, and I knew what to expect, so I was able to control it."

Luks muttered under his breath about some people's luck and then raised his voice, changing the subject. "Have you eaten?"

"Not a thing."

"Sit, and I'll pour *khai* for you. There's a loaf already sliced on the table."

"I like you more and more," Sheyn said as he sat and smeared honey on a thick piece of bread.

"Then will you listen when I give you advice?"

"If it's good advice, but I have to say, you're not all that well-informed."

"About what?"

"When I ask about this magical bond you claim exists, you don't have satisfactory answers."

"That's not my fault. You're just so… different. You're not like any daaksi I've known or heard of. It's as though the rules don't apply to you."

"Well, that's not very helpful, is it?"

Luks ground his teeth and made an effort to answer pleasantly. "Will you at least listen? For safety's sake, you shouldn't walk around alone."

"I can defend myself."

"As you are? Against an armed man?"

"You'd be surprised."

"You have too much pride," Luks said as he handed Sheyn a cup. "Be careful, the khai is hot."

Sheyn sipped the steaming liquid. "It's bitter," he said and took another sip. "I like it."

Luks sat down and picked up his half-finished cup. "Why are you so determined to break the rules?"

"I don't even know them."

"When I try to explain them to you, you get angry."

"Then tell me whatever you wish. I'm content to sit here and break my fast."

"You mustn't go around without an escort."

"Explain that further, if you will. Am I supposed to believe that my allure is so great that no man can resist it? I know I'm fairer than most, but I'm hardly irresistible."

"The spark of the Goddess's fire that burns in you attracts all manner of men, but especially fighting men and other men of power. The danger of assault or abduction is very real. Some men cannot be deterred, not even by the severe punishment for such an offense. Some men would have to have you though it costs their lives."

"Are we so valuable?"

"Beyond price."

"Is a mere physical function such as sex rated so highly here?"

"It's more than that. We're not simply concubines. We bring luck to the man we bond with. Luck in battle. Luck in wealth. The man who possesses a daaksi has the Goddess's favor."

"Luck," Sheyn scoffed.

"Do you believe in nothing beyond yourself and your five senses?"

"Permission to enter," a man said from outside.

Luks and Sheyn looked up as a trooper drew back the tent flap.

"The commander wants you," the soldier said to Luks.

"In what manner?" Luks asked.

"He didn't say, but I believe he wishes to impress the Muergathi dignitary with your beauty." The soldier paused as if gauging how improper it would be to keep talking. "The talk between the nobles turned to daaksim, and the commander could see that the Muergathi was curious. The King of Muergath doesn't have one, you see."

"I understand. Give me just a moment," Luks said as he got to his feet.

"What about me?" Sheyn asked.

"The commander said nothing about you," the soldier said, doing his best not to stare at the pale daaksi.

"I'm going with you," Sheyn told Luks as Luks wiped his face with a wet cloth.

Luks ran his fingers through his mop of burnished curls. "You weren't called for."

"I wasn't forbidden to go, either."

Luks looked at the trooper. The trooper shrugged. "I suppose I can't stop you," Luks said. "But for the love of the Goddess, comb your hair."

"With what comb?"

Luks sighed. "No time for it now, but when we return, I'll comb and braid your hair for you."

Sheyn gathered the tangled strands at his nape and let them fall to the middle of his back. "I'm ready," he said.

"You're hopeless," Luks said as he tugged at Sheyn's tunic, settling the folds into place. He sighed again. "In the past, you'd have been draped in silk and satin and cherished as a jewel beyond price, but look at you. You're like a fine colt with burrs in his mane."

"Are you saying I chose a bad time to become a daaksi?"

Luks smiled despite himself. "Yes, you did, foolish foreigner." He turned to the soldier. "We're ready."

The trooper held the tent flap open and gestured for Luks and Sheyn to precede him. Outside the tent stood another soldier. Accompanied by the two guards, Luks and Sheyn walked to the shade awning set up in front of the command tent.

Kholya smiled when he caught sight of his messenger returning. "Ah, here we are," he said. "Perhaps this will satisfy your curiosity."

"Thank you. As I said, King Kezlath doesn't keep a daaksi, and I've never seen one in person." Lord Beshar looked suitably impressed, and even the stone-faced leader of the Red Monks took notice from his position at Beshar's back. Luks bowed gracefully and greeted the emissary with formal words that deepened Beshar's appreciation of his beauty and demeanor. "I see the appeal," Beshar said to Kholya. "I'm not a lover of boys, but he stirs me."

"Velvet is perfection, isn't he?" Kholya said in a tone of slight boredom.

"Are the legends true?"

Kholya chuckled. "I can tell you he's as sweet as honey and paradise lies between his thighs, but thus far, I've seen no evidence that he can predict the future, read minds, or shoot lightning from his eyes."

Beshar laughed. "What of the other one?"

"Ah, that one." Kholya looked at Sheyn. "That one *can* shoot lightning from his eyes."

"I don't doubt it. I've never seen anyone who looks like that. What nation is he from?"

"He claims to be from Far West. I don't know if I believe him, but it's certain he's not from Kandaar."

"Does he speak Andaar?"

"He rarely stops."

Beshar smiled. "I wonder if I might speak with—" Kholya cleared his throat, and Beshar realized he'd overstepped bounds. "I wonder if Kandaar will always be separate. There are many, many Kandaarim who have no idea there's a world beyond our borders. What's your thinking on this, Commander?"

"I think we've probably been isolated long enough, but it's not up to me to open a road to the West. It would take more than one man to do that."

"I think it would depend on the man." Beshar smiled again. "And now I must go and report to my king." He rose to his feet. "Allow me to say it was a true pleasure to meet with you, Kholya of Savaan. You are a most unusual mercenary commander."

"Have you dealt with many?"

"Sitting in the middle of the plains, Taar Muergan is an easy target for an army. I've negotiated with dozens of mercenary leaders as foes and as allies. You're nothing like them." Beshar paused. "But of course, you were a prince before you became a sword for hire."

"I'm still a prince. King Nakhol hasn't renounced me."

Beshar bowed. "I didn't mean to give offense."

"You meant to poke me a little and see if I'd jump." Kholya took Luks by the wrist, pulling him into Beshar's line of sight. "I'd do the same if I were in your boots. Go and give Kezlath your assurance that all is well."

Luks raised his head and met Beshar's eyes.

Beshar gazed into Luks's melting eyes as he replied to Kholya. "Yes, I can see you're a man to be trusted. I'll tell His Majesty that he can go ahead with his plans."

Kholya ran his hand over Luks's hair, drawing Beshar's eyes. Beshar blinked and looked up at Kholya.

"It was a pleasure to meet you also," Kholya said as he rested his hands on Luks's shoulders.

Beshar bowed again. "The king will be very pleased with my report. He glanced at Luks and back up at Kholya. "Kezlath of Muergath is the true high king, and we will put the Crown of Kand on his head."

Kholya nodded and remained on his feet as Beshar left with his entourage. "Well done," he said as he let go of Luks. "The Muergathi couldn't take his eyes off the pair of you. I swear I could see his mind being swayed."

Luks bowed. "I'm glad we were of service."

"I'm seeing more and more advantages to having a daaksi around." Kholya gestured to the honor guards. "These men will take you to my tent. I'll try to think of a suitable reward for your assistance." Kholya gave Luks and Sheyn a brief nod and went to the command tent.

As SOON as the Muergathim returned to Taar Muergan, the Red Monks split from Beshar's party and marched directly to the temple. Mardjan left his men in the barracks and went to report to Chanesh. When he was admitted to the high priest's chamber, he blurted out his news. "Reverend Lord, I've found him."

"Why didn't you bring him to me?"

"I couldn't."

"Why not?"

"He belongs to the Bastard of Savaan."

Chanesh banged his withered fist against the table. "What jest is this?" He was quiet for a moment as he sucked his knuckles. "Why would Taankh show me the Gate and then make it so difficult to acquire?"

"Our God tests us," Mardjan said. "And I will not fail Him. Give me a few hours."

Chanesh nodded. "I'll ready the Ritual of Summoning. Bring the daaksi to the Gate Chamber as soon as you have it in your possession."

Mardjan bowed and left the high priest's office. Chanesh reached for a bellpull and called for one of his personal servants.

"How may I serve?" Moksha asked as he came into the room.

"Which one are you?" Chanesh asked brusquely as he rose from his chair.

"Moksha, Reverend Lord."

"Moksha, I need the red-and-gold robe. Bring it to the antechamber of the Gateway."

Moksha bowed and hurried away, unhappy with his errand. Fetching a heavy, gem-crusted ceremonial robe was routine, but a visit to the Gateway area of the Temple was not. The acolyte was content with his clerical position. The Temple paid well and regularly, and as the oldest son in his family, it was his responsibility to help support his younger brothers and sisters. He had no wish to go any deeper into the mystical elements.

Moksha entered the high priest's chambers and went to the tall wardrobe. Carefully, he lifted out the Summoning regalia and laid it out on a table before calling for two novices. He supervised the younger boys as they took up the robe, sash, cape, and cap. He carried the ceremonial jewelry as he led them from the residential area of the Temple compound.

"What are you whispering about?" Moksha said, turning to the give the boys a disapproving look.

"Sorry," the taller novice said. "Adjal is nervous and I was trying to calm him down."

"What's the matter?" Moksha asked, bending to look Adjal in the eyes. "You can tell me."

Adjal glanced at his friend. "I don't want to get in trouble, Ruernan," he said.

"I won't tell anyone else," Moksha assured him.

"I don't like going into First Temple. I'm afraid of it," Adjal admitted.

Moksha straightened up. "Of course you are," he said calmly. "We're all afraid of it, but it's part of the Temple and it's right in the center, so you'll have to get used to walking through it once in a while."

"Yes, sir," the boys said at the same time.

"I know my words aren't any comfort," Moksha said. "But don't feel as though you're weak or cowardly for being scared. First Temple is a scary place."

"Why do we need it?" the taller boy asked, encouraged by Moksha's kindness.

"It holds the Gateway, the sacred door to the Shadoworld."

"Yes, we know. The priests taught us that," Ruernan said as they began walking again. "But why do they want to bring Taankh's Children from the Shadoworld into ours?"

"It's a sacrament." Moksha's tone said the conversation was over.

Ruernan glanced at Adjal, and Adjal shrugged. He hadn't really expected to get any answers from an acolyte. Only the most important priests knew anything. The rest of Taankh's Servants did as they were told.

Moksha walked faster and kept his mouth shut, though he was as uneasy as the pair of novices. He didn't understand any more than they did why the priests were so set on bringing Taankh's Children over the Threshold. He'd never seen a demon, but he'd seen depictions of them in some of Chanesh's books, and he never wanted to see one in the flesh. Why would a God create beings so hideous to the eye? He shook his head as he broke into a trot. What business did he have questioning a God or His priests? His business was to do the High Priest's bidding as quickly as possible.

Chapter

12

AFTER DISPLAYING their skill for the Muergathi emissary, the Black Hawk cavalry troop unsaddled their mounts and tended to them. Djenya led his horse over as Kashyan finished brushing Karkaran and gave the charger some feed.

"I think we impressed the Muergathim," Djenya said, leaning against his horse's warm side as the animal ate. "Your brother isn't called the Savaani Fox for no reason. He dazzled the envoy's eyes and addled his brain. Why don't you look happier about it?"

"My daaksi…. Great Raas, I can't believe I'm saying those words." Kashyan took a deep breath and blew it out again. "I despise him, and yet, I yearn to be with him. My stomach is in knots, and I can barely keep from retching."

"You could call him Pearl like the Sumadi lad does," Djenya suggested. "And the sickness will go away in time, or so I've been told."

"Pearl left my tent after I told him to stay."

"You aren't surprised, are you?"

"A little. A daaksi is supposed to obey his master's orders. Where does he get the naaks to behave like that?" Kashyan shook his head. "And I'm not happy with Kholya, either. Parading daaksim around like that. Does he really think that's wise?"

Djenya shrugged. "I think he was using them the way they were intended to be used."

"That's all well and good for him. He's not bonded to one of them, is he?"

Djenya put a hand on Kashyan's shoulder and felt the tension in the hard muscles. "I'm sure that never occurred to him. He's not used to thinking of you with a daaksi, and to be fair, you haven't given Kholya any reason to believe you're fond of Pearl."

Kashyan's expression lightened, as Djenya hoped it would. "That's true," Kashyan said. "And now, I have the unappealing task of disciplining my daaksi."

"I know you're capable of handling your own problems, but if I can be of any help to you, all you have to do is ask. I could hold him over my knees while you—"

Kashyan cuffed the side of Djenya's head. "Lecher."

"Monk," Djenya retorted. "Hey, where are you going?"

"I told you."

"I'll go with you."

"No. I'm not giving you fodder for future jokes at my expense. Find something useful to do."

"If you won't entertain me, I'm going to find a dice game." Djenya gave Kashyan a comic salute as he walked away.

"I wish I could forget my troubles as easily as you, my friend," Kashyan said as he left for Kholya's tent.

"WHY AREN'T you where I left you?" Kashyan asked as he walked into the tent.

"I didn't want to be there," Sheyn answered.

"I'm no happier about our situation than you are. But at least I have enough honor to fulfill my role."

Sheyn stood up. "Honor? Are you implying that a creature like a daaksi has such a thing as honor?"

"Don't use my words against me."

"Choose them more carefully, then."

Luks set his cup down with a loud rattling sound. "I'm sure I'm needed elsewhere."

"Wait," Kashyan said. "You're a sensible sort. Can you tell me how it's possible for a daaksi to defy his master?"

"I don't understand it, lord," Luks said. "Once there is a bond, a daaksi is subject to his master's will. That has always been the way of it. I can't explain Pearl's willfulness."

"That's not my name," Sheyn said peevishly.

"It is now, and it's such a pretty name." Kashyan smirked. "*Pearl.*"

Sheyn gave the warrior a dark look.

"He doesn't understand our ways, lord," Luks said apologetically.

"So you've said. All right, then, you have one more chance to teach him. If *Pearl* can't learn his place, I'll turn both of you over to the Sumadinim when they come looking for vengeance."

"You can't go five sentences without making a threat, can you?" Sheyn said.

"If Pearl speaks again before I leave, I'll punish *you*," Kashyan told Luks.

Sheyn clenched his jaw to hold in his response.

"Are you hungry, lord?" Luks asked.

"I'm eating with my men, but that was an excellent daaksi ploy to distract me from my anger at your friend."

"Do you wish Pearl to stay here until you return?"

"Yes, I wish that, but I've never had much luck with wishes." Kashyan gazed at Luks's bowed head for a moment. "Did you want to say something else?"

"Yes, lord. I'd like to speak about clothing."

Kashyan glanced at Sheyn. "His tunic's too big."

"Yes. He needs proper clothing."

Kashyan paused before he spoke again. "I'm not taking proper care of him, is that it? Don't cringe. I'm not angry. I'm… I shouldn't have to have my duty pointed out to me by the likes of you. I'll be back to fetch Pearl after the evening mess."

"He's the most infuriating person I've ever known," Sheyn said as soon as Kashyan was gone.

"Listen to you." Luks sighed. "You don't realize what just happened, do you?"

"My *master* stormed in and barked at me and threatened you before storming out again."

Luks rapped his knuckles against Sheyn's skull.

"Ouch!" Sheyn drew back with a deeply affronted look.

"You disobeyed your master, but he didn't punish you. Both these things should be impossible."

"Nonsense. You keep prattling about some mystical bond, but I see no evidence of it. It's true that I felt ill last night, and you convinced me it was because of this bond, but I've thought about it and decided it was the result of eating strange food."

"*You're* the most infuriating person *I've* ever known."

"Finally." Sheyn smiled. "I knew you were hiding a temper somewhere."

"Why do you enjoy making people angry?"

"I don't enjoy it, but it does seem to happen quite a lot."

"You'll find life easier if you listen to me."

"Why do you care if my life is easier?" Sheyn asked.

Luks looked puzzled. "Why would I want you to suffer?"

"I don't know." Sheyn paused. "Why do I assume people mean me harm?" He sighed. "Very well, you can teach me Kandaari manners, but I still intend to leave this barbaric land as soon as I can."

"Until then, try to remember to speak softly. Wait for your master to acknowledge you before you speak. Never raise your voice or disagree with him."

Sheyn shook his head. "And this seems right to you?"

"It's tradition."

"I thought you said daaksim once served as advisors to kings."

"That was a long time ago, before Anaali turned Her back on Kandaar."

"So daaksim were intended as companions and became pets."

"Why do you have to make everything sound so awful?"

"I'm only pointing out the truth. If I have to live by your rules until I return home, I can manage it. But I won't pretend I think it's right or that there's any honor in it."

"It's an honor to be the comfort a warrior seeks after he has battled to defend his people."

"I can see how that would seem noble to you."

"Why do you always speak as though your ways are better?"

"Because they are. I was born a prince in a civilized country. Kandaarim aren't quite the pelt-wearing nomadic savages I imagined, but you are inferiors."

Luks's shoulders drooped. "I don't know what will become of you."

"Don't be sad. It isn't your responsibility."

"Yes, it is. Your master has made it my responsibility."

Sheyn gave Luks an exaggerated wide-eyed look. "Do you think he was serious?"

Luks stared at Sheyn for a moment before he broke into a grin. "You have an odd sense of humor," he said. "Let's continue your lessons later. I want to take a nap so I'll look fresh when the commander returns."

"What will I do while you sleep?"

"Practice speaking in a tone that's not so sharp."

Sheyn watched Luks curl up in a pile of pillows. Luks's tunic rode up far enough for Sheyn to notice several large freckles on the otherwise flawless skin of Luks's hip. He hadn't noticed the dark splotches before and assumed Luks took care to keep them hidden. After prowling about for a bit, Sheyn found some scrolls, but he couldn't read the writing. He listened to Luks snore softly for a few minutes before he went to the entrance. The soldier outside glanced at Sheyn and then resumed walking his post. Sheyn watched the man's shadow circle the tent, and when he returned to the front, Sheyn went under the wall at the back. Earlier, he'd seen peddlers hawking wares in the camp. Surely, he could find someone to take a message for him in return for the promise of payment. At the least, he might find clothes that fit him, though what he'd use for money, he had no idea.

Sheyn walked quickly behind the cloth stall of the commander's private latrine and paused there until he heard the sentry make another round. He darted off, but after a few minutes, he was sure he was being followed. Though he couldn't see anyone, he could feel the interest of a presence nearby. A shiver ran the length of his body, and he decided he'd rather be in plain sight than endure another second of this dread. As he stepped from the shadow of a tent, someone yanked him back out of sight. A cloth was held over his nose and mouth, and he went limp.

A few minutes later, a sentry stopped a man carrying a roll of carpet from the Savaani camp. The Muergathi laborer produced the name of a merchant he worked for and was allowed to go on his way. It wasn't until later that the sentry realized why the porter looked familiar. By then, Sheyn's disappearance had been discovered.

Chapter
13

"I'M SORRY, lord," Luks said when Kashyan returned for Sheyn. "I should have stayed awake, but I thought the guard on duty would be enough to discourage Pearl from leaving."

"It's not your fault," Kashyan said. He could barely restrain himself from stalking out of the tent, mounting his horse, and galloping off on a wild search.

"Well, no one in camp has come forward to say they saw—" Kholya broke off as the door guard called out. "What is it?"

"A sentry with some information for you, sir."

"Send him in."

"I came as soon as I heard," the sentry said. "A man carrying a rug went through my checkpoint this evening. I didn't think anything of it at the time, but now I'm sure I've seen him before. He was the leader of the Muergathi soldiers that were here this morning."

"The Red Monks?" Kholya said.

"Yes, sir. The leader. He was wearing a wig, but I'm sure it was him."

"Kashyan!" Kholya shouted. "Stop!"

Kashyan paused in the entryway. "Kholya, you know I have to go." He grimaced at the stomach-clenching wave of nausea that flooded his body. The pain that radiated from his core threatened to put him on his knees, and only his will kept him upright.

"Yes, but not alone." Kholya stood and took his sword belt off the back of his chair. "We'll go to Taar Muergan with your Black Hawks, and I'll demand to see Lord Beshar. I'll tell him what happened and demand he take us to the Red Temple to confront this monk."

Djenya cleared his throat. "Suppose King Kezlath heard Beshar's description of Velvet and Pearl and coveted them?"

"He'd send his war band, or he'd simply demand one or both daaksim and wait to see what we'd do. He wouldn't send Temple soldiers," Kholya said.

"How do you know?"

"Have you forgotten that he and I learned battlecraft together?"

"He might have changed."

"Not judging by his side of our correspondence." Kholya squeezed Kashyan's shoulder. "We'll get your daaksi back."

"It's maddening," Kashyan said. "I can't bear Pearl's presence, but I ache for him."

"Wait just a moment and we'll ride." Kholya thanked the sentry and called for his horse.

Kashyan whistled piercingly as they left the tent, and in a few moments, Karkaran trotted up to him. Kholya's charger was brought, and they left camp at the head of Kashyan's cavalry troop. When they reached the gate of Taar Muergan, Kholya set a messenger running to court to find Lord Beshar and deliver Kholya's scroll. It was now almost dark, and Kashyan was out of patience when a different messenger ran up at top speed.

"Lord Beshar will meet you in the square in front of Taankh's Temple," the gate guard said. "I'll send a guide with you, but your men must wait here."

"We allowed your soldiers into our camp," Kholya said. "At least let me have a decent honor guard."

"Six men, then." The head guard stood aside as he gestured to another Muergathi soldier. "Lead Lord Beshar's guest to the Temple," he ordered. "And don't dawdle."

"You see?" Kholya said to Kashyan as they followed their guide. "Diplomacy has its uses."

Kashyan looked over his shoulder at Djenya, and Djenya winked. Kashyan faced front again and rested his free hand on the hilt of his sword as they entered the Temple square. True to his word, Beshar was waiting with an entourage of three.

"Commander," Beshar said as Kholya and his men dismounted. "Your message was brief, but obviously deserving of my attention. May I ask some questions before we enter the Temple?"

"We don't have time for—" Kashyan began but subsided at a look from Kholya.

"The captain is a bit anxious," Kholya told Beshar. "But it's to be expected of a man of royal blood when his daaksi is stolen."

Beshar cleared his throat. "As you know, this is a very serious crime. Are you certain your daaksi was taken by Taankh's Servants?"

"A witness saw a Red Monk."

Beshar looked queasy when he replied. "I've spoken to King Kezlath about this matter, and he's given me the authority to settle it. Come with me, and we'll speak to High Priest Chanesh. We'll have to go through him before we search the Temple."

Kashyan didn't look satisfied, but he kept his mouth shut and followed Kholya and the Muergathi nobleman into the Red Temple. It was gloomy and cool in the large space that held the bull-headed statue of the God of the Shadoworld. Six times the height of a man, the seated depiction of Taankh was forged of bronze. The midsection was hollow for use as a furnace and had a barred hatch at the front so worshipers could see into it.

"Why would you need a window there?" Kashyan whispered to Djenya.

"You really don't know?"

"I don't know anything about Taankh, except a few nursery stories. I might end up in His realm after I die, but until then, the less I know about Him, the happier I am."

"I understand." Djenya walked closer to Kashyan and lowered his voice. "I know quite a bit about Taankh and His Servants. My aunt lived in Muergath after she married. Twelve years later, she came home with her children. I wasn't born yet when she left Savaan, so I'd never seen her before, but I could tell my mother was shocked at the change in her."

"I just want to know about the window in that ugly statue."

"Right. My aunt told me many stories about her life in Taar Muergan, and being a typical bloodthirsty boy, I begged her to tell me about the worst of it. That window in the ugly statue is there so Taankh's faithful can watch people being roasted alive."

Kashyan shot Djenya a look, saw his friend wasn't joking, and shook his head. "That's…."

"Yes, it is. And it's not even the worst thing they do here."

"But why?"

"It's how they praise their God. Taankh thrives on suffering and misery. Cries of pain are His incense and tears are His sacramental wine, according to my aunt."

"Why would anyone worship a monster who enjoys their pain?"

"Taankh is known to reward those He favors. For a powerful or wealthy man who doesn't care who he kills, worshiping Taankh makes perfect sense. You sacrifice a slave a day to the Lord of Shadows, and he brings bad luck to your enemies."

"It makes no sense to me," Kashyan said as they came to a halt in front of a set of doors. "I don't rely on anything as unpredictable as luck or the favor of Gods."

"You don't rely on anything except that big sword." Djenya fell silent when Beshar spoke up.

Lord Beshar had talked to the guards and wasn't happy with their answers. "The high priest isn't here," he told Kholya. "He's performing an evening ritual. Just a moment!" Beshar raised his voice. "You there, acolyte!"

Moksha stopped a few feet from the high priest's chambers. "Yes, my lord?"

"Do you serve High Priest Chanesh?"

"Yes, my lord."

"Where is he? I have a message from the king."

Moksha swallowed. "My lord, I—"

"If you know where the high priest is, take us to him, boy!" Kashyan said.

"Yes, my lord!" Moksha turned and started back the way he'd come.

"There was no need to terrify the lad," Kholya said as they followed the acolyte.

"This is taking too long," Kashyan growled.

They left the residential section and crossed through the main temple again. On the other side, they entered the complex of rooms where much of the real work of the priesthood was done. Kashyan's discomfort abated as they moved farther into the temple. When Moksha stopped before a door faced with rough stone in contrast to the dressed blocks of the rest of the building, Kashyan knew Pearl was near.

"I've never been this far into the Temple," Beshar said. "Where are we, acolyte?"

"This is the Gate Chamber, my lord," Moksha said.

"Open the door."

"I'm sorry, my lord. I cannot." Moksha bowed his head. He'd been overjoyed when Chanesh dismissed him an hour ago, but now he was back in the last place he wanted to be. His luck God was asleep today.

"How dare you refuse to obey me! I'm a minister of the court and a personal friend of King Kezlath. If you don't open that door, you'll wish you'd never been born."

Kashyan tensed like a hound hearing a strange noise. "Out of my way," he said as he drew his sword.

"Kashyan!" Kholya shouted, but Kashyan had already swung the great blade.

Moksha and Beshar jumped aside as the sword cleaved wood and metal. Kashyan yanked the blade free and raised it again.

"Wait!" Moksha shouted.

"No more talk. Pearl is in there," Kashyan said through clenched teeth. He brought the sword down again and sheared off part of the lock.

"You'll all die if you go in there!" Moksha cried out.

Kholya looked at Beshar.

"I have no idea what's going on in there," Beshar said. "I'm not a particularly religious man. But you have official permission to break the door down if you believe the daaksi is in there."

Djenya looked at the other five men of the Savaani honor guard. "What are you waiting for?" he asked.

The double doors burst open under the impact of eight men. With Kashyan in the lead, the soldiers spilled into the room and stopped in their tracks, eyes wide with shock. Though they were veterans of many battles and had witnessed butchery and madness, the scene was a form of horror beyond any they'd beheld.

Sheyn was chained to an altar of rough stone. His pale skin was crisscrossed with the red lines of countless fresh and healing cuts. An ancient man in ornate robes chanted as he circled the altar, darting out his hand to inflict another wound at the end of each drawn-out word. The air above the altar roiled with dark, oily smoke. A shape formed in the smoke and grew more distinct by the second. Sheyn screamed as a dark claw emerged and raked his shoulder, opening deep gashes.

Kashyan's paralysis broke. The Bastard focused on the knife the old man held as he sprang to the gory altar. Sheyn opened his eyes as

Kashyan's sword struck the manacle on his left wrist, and the high priest shouted in fury. Sheyn's gaze fastened on something over Kashyan's shoulder, and Kashyan's blood went cold at the look in those dark eyes. Throwing himself to the side, Kashyan cut through the chain on Sheyn's right wrist as he slid to the floor. He dodged around to the foot of the altar, focusing on his goal of freeing Sheyn. In two rapid strikes, he severed the remaining chains. Yanking Sheyn off the altar, Kashyan covered the daaksi's body with his own. Only then did he look up.

"Great Raas," Kashyan breathed. "What is that thing?"

"I can't say for certain," Djenya said as he stepped in front of Kashyan. "But I'd guess it's a demon, or at least part of one."

Kashyan stared at the great limb—as thick as a man's waist and gnarled as oak bark—that appeared out of the smoke. The claw at the end of the arm was mottled white and yellow and had six talons, each as long as a dagger. He thought the hide was glittering until he realized he was looking at countless tiny creatures moving about like fleas on a dog. Everything about it repulsed him at his core. Leaving Sheyn on the floor, Kashyan jumped atop the stone table and slashed at the hideous limb. A great bellow shook the walls, and dust sifted down from the ceiling. Kashyan struck again as Djenya leaped up beside him.

"Stop!" Chanesh screamed. "What are you doing?"

"Stay out of the way, priest," Kholya said as the rest of the Savaani troopers entered the fray.

A massive shoulder pushed through the smoke, giving the arm a longer reach. The warriors hacked at the arm as it slashed blindly at them.

"Stop!" Chanesh shouted again, but no one paid him any attention. Shaking with fury, he went to the hall to call for the Red Monks.

"Where are you off to, Reverend Lord?" Beshar asked.

"Step aside, fool."

"I'd like to, but I'm here at His Majesty's behest. He'd like an audience with you."

"Hinder me any longer and I'll not be responsible for the consequences."

"I'll make a note of it." Beshar glanced through the doorway. "I look forward to hearing you explain this to the high king."

"He isn't the high king yet."

Beshar hid his reaction to the treasonous remark. "He was born high king."

"But he needs me to put him on the throne, me and my God, and you're standing in the way."

"It looks like you were summoning a demon." Beshar tilted his head to one side. "That's against the law."

"Laws change." Chanesh cringed at the sound of another pain-filled bellow. "Get out of my way so I can call for help."

"I don't believe I will. I believe I'll follow King Kezlath's orders. As soon as the Savaanim are finished in there, we're going to the king."

"You idiot. You think the king doesn't know about this?"

Beshar looked into the chamber again as the claw withdrew into the boiling, black cloud. The dark green blood that splashed every surface evaporated into wisps of steam. The Savaani warriors watched the ceiling warily for several moments, but nothing else appeared. Kashyan and Djenya jumped down from the altar, and Kashyan went to Sheyn. Lifting the unconscious daaksi, Kashyan put him over his shoulder.

"We're leaving," Kashyan said to his men. "Right now. Before anything else comes out of that smoke."

"Go," Kholya said and waited until everyone was out of the chamber before he left.

Kashyan moved away with Sheyn over his shoulder. Djenya was right behind him with the other five soldiers on his heels.

"King Kezlath gave me orders to bring you all to the throne room if you found your daaksi here," Lord Beshar said when Kholya appeared.

"Why are we standing here?" Kashyan asked. "Let's leave this cursed place."

"The king wants to see us," Kholya said.

"He'll not be in a good mood when he hears what you Savaani scum have done," Chanesh said.

"Shut up, worm," Kashyan said. "Kholya, I'm leaving." He stalked away.

"Are you going to let him go?" Djenya asked Kholya.

"I'm going with him. We left our horses in the same place, after all." Kholya turned to Chanesh. "Let's go, priest." He gave Chanesh a shove to get him going.

Chanesh gave Beshar a smug smile. "It will be a pleasure to see your faces when you realize that the Temple holds the true power in Muergath."

"I cannot believe the king would condone such a practice as I saw today," Beshar said, gesturing to his three guards to keep an eye on Chanesh.

"Then you don't understand how badly he wishes to be high king."

"Quiet," Kholya said.

Sheyn regained consciousness as the group walked down the Temple steps to the square. "Put me down," he said.

Kashyan was so startled that he almost dropped Sheyn. He set Sheyn down and was astonished to see that all the daaksi's wounds had healed to thin pink lines. "Are you all right?" he asked.

"I can walk," Sheyn said. "But I'd like to borrow your cloak."

Kashyan unfastened his cloak pin and gave Sheyn the garment.

"Were you planning on carrying me all the way back to camp naked?" Sheyn asked as he put the cloak around him.

"I hadn't thought about it. I was busy fighting a demon."

"And after that?"

"Get on the horse."

"I really must insist that you come with me to the palace," Beshar said.

"Please tell the king that we'll attend him tomorrow," Kholya told Beshar. "Surely, your report will be enough for now, and I need to make sure my brother doesn't start a war with Muergath over this."

"I'll explain to His Majesty," Beshar said. "Accept the apologies of the Crown and know that the thieves will be justly dealt with."

Kholya saluted Beshar and left at the head of the small troop. A few minutes later, several royal guards marched into the square.

"Our escort is here," Beshar said.

Chanesh smiled. "Captain," he called out to the leader of the guards. "Savaani raiders are headed for the west gate. Send men after them while I call out the Red Monks."

To Beshar's dismay, the captain did as the high priest bade him.

"Yes, I like that look on your face," Chanesh said before he walked back into the Temple.

Chapter 14

DJENYA RODE up from the rear to report. "We're being followed, and they don't look friendly."

Kholya looked to the rear, saw the royal guards, and gave orders. "Ride for camp and prepare for battle!"

The small company of Savaani warriors used their horses to shoulder a way through the more crowded streets. When they sighted the gate, they urged their mounts to a faster pace and rode through at a gallop. Once outside the walls, they were joined by the rest of the troop and increased their speed in a race to the camp. The sentries looked surprised but immediately took a battle stance when their commander shouted at them to be ready for an attack.

Kholya rode straight to the command tent and dismounted. "Get your daaksi safely stowed and join me with all the Hawks," he ordered Kashyan.

"I'll go find Velvet," Sheyn said as Kashyan took him by the arm. "That hurts, by the way."

Kashyan let go of Sheyn as though he'd touched fire. "Velvet's likely in my brother's tent."

"Where else would he be?" Sheyn moved away from him.

"I'll walk with you." Kashyan glanced aside at the willowy foreigner. "Are you all right?"

"What a particularly stupid question. I was abducted, chained to an altar, and tortured for hours… and that was *before* the demon arrived."

"I should have kept a better watch on you."

Sheyn was startled into silence by his apologetic tone.

"Whether I want a daaksi or not, I have one," Kashyan said. "I'll make sure you're better protected from now on."

"So I'll be under constant guard? That sounds terribly pleasant." Sheyn grimaced.

"Would it be more pleasant to be back in the Temple?" Kashyan asked as they reached Kholya's tent.

Sheyn shot him a dark look as he entered, and then Luks was on top of him.

"Thank the Goddess!" Luks exclaimed as he simultaneously hugged Sheyn and checked him for injuries. "I was so worried about you." He looked to Kashyan.

"He was taken to Taankh's Temple and—" Kashyan swallowed. "They did horrible things."

"I can tell the story," Sheyn said. "Don't you have orders?"

"I still can't believe it," Kashyan said. "You were covered in cuts when we found you, but now your skin looks as smooth as…." His voice trailed off as he ran his eyes over Sheyn's body.

"Would you like your cloak back?" Sheyn asked pointedly.

Kashyan looked up. "I'll collect it later," he said as he turned on his heel and left.

"What an odd man," Sheyn said as he sat.

"Wait just a moment and I'll bring you a cup of khai," Luks said. "Take off the cloak so I can have a look at you."

Sheyn held out his arms, turning them over as he examined his skin. "Not a mark," he said softly.

"It's a bit breathtaking when you experience a miracle for the first time," Luks said as he handed Sheyn a cup. "Now tell me what happened to you."

Sheyn shuddered and took a drink of the hot khai before he answered. "I went out looking for the peddlers. I was trying to stay out of sight, and someone grabbed me. I didn't see him, but I'd recognize that smell again. He put a cloth over my nose and mouth and I went to sleep. When I woke, I was chained to a stone altar." He shivered again. "I was naked, and the stone was cold and rough, but that was hardly the worst of it." He paused. "I don't think I can describe it, but the room made me feel very small, and I felt as though something large and hungry was watching me every second. I could feel eyes on my skin like ants." Sheyn took another drink of khai. "I knew the thing watching me wanted to tear me to shreds and devour the pieces. And I knew I'd be alive while it happened, and that the thing would devour my suffering as well."

"A demon," Luks said.

As Sheyn met Luks's eyes, he suppressed a shudder. "I didn't know they really existed. I've read tales with demons in them, but they're just made-up stories, not history books."

"They're real."

"Why? Why should such a terrible thing exist?"

"All things have an opposite," Luks said. "Pure good exists, so pure evil must also exist."

"You're certain about the pure good?"

"There is one perfect creature created by all the Gods together, an avatar who embodies the best traits of every race of men." Luks saw he had Sheyn's full attention and continued. "This being has no name, unless it's the sound of laughter, and no one who ever saw the avatar could agree on what it looked like. However, all agreed that it was the most beautiful thing ever created, and it inspired joy in all who came near."

"That does sound like the opposite of a demon." Sheyn jumped at the distraction. If he didn't stop thinking about what he'd endured, he would start screaming. "What happened to this avatar?"

"No one knows. My faith teaches me that the avatar still wanders this world."

"If that's so, I don't think it's visited Kandaar in some time."

Luks was quiet for a moment. "Are you really all right?"

"I'm... I've been shaken up a bit by recent events, but physically, I'm well." Sheyn smiled. "When you told me that daaksim heal quickly, I had no idea you meant that quickly."

"I didn't. I've never seen a daaksi heal so fast."

"What about knowing what other people are feeling?"

"What?"

"I can feel other people's emotions, even the intentions behind their words sometimes."

"Of course you can. It's another of the Goddess's gifts. It's much easier to deal with people if you know their mood."

"My mother says the same thing."

"I wish I could meet such a woman. What a marvel that would be." Luks stood and walked to the other side of the tent. "I almost forgot," he said as he picked something up and returned to where Sheyn sat. "Here."

Sheyn took the length of bright red material and held it up. It was a thigh-length tunic decorated at the neck and hem with gold-embroidered birds. "It's not horrible," he said. "Where did you acquire it?"

"Prince Kashyan bought it for you, but when he came here to give it to you, you were gone."

Sheyn slipped the tunic over his head, enjoying the feel of the fine cloth sliding down his body. "This is the silkiest wool I've ever felt. I wonder what the sheep look like."

"It's made from the hair of a goat that lives high in the mountains. They're not easy to find or catch, so the cloth is very expensive."

"How interesting." Sheyn yawned. "I'm suddenly exhausted."

"Healing takes a lot of energy. Put your head on this pillow," Luks said.

When Sheyn was comfortable, Luks took out a wooden comb and began working on the tangles in Sheyn's long hair. It was rough going with all the dried blood, but Luks did what he could until there was an opportunity for a bath. After a while, Sheyn spoke in a drowsy voice.

"Such an awful old man."

"Who?" Luks asked.

"The one who cut me. He was almost as frightening as the demon. That feels very nice," he said as Luks divided his hair into strands for braiding. Sheyn smiled sleepily. "He wouldn't speak to me, no matter what I said to him. He used the knife on me as though I was a piece of wood he was whittling. He just kept chanting, and the look in his eyes...." His features tightened at the memory of his torture and then smoothed out again as he fell into exhausted sleep.

"Pearl?" Luks looked down and saw that Sheyn's eyes were closed. "Good," he whispered. "Sleep and don't have bad dreams." He kissed the top of Sheyn's head and busied himself in another part of the big tent.

A short time later, the soldier on guard duty came into the tent and passed a message to Luks. Luks's eyes widened as he read it, but he suppressed the urge to panic. He needed a cool head just now, and he needed help.

"Pearl, wake up," he said, kneeling beside Sheyn.

"What is it?" Sheyn blinked groggily.

"We have to pack. The army is moving."

"When?"

"Now. Get up and help me, please."

Sheyn sighed. "I haven't rested well since I came to Kandaar," he said as he got to his feet. "Tell me what to do, and I'll do it."

By the time Kholya sent a detachment to strike the tent, Luks and Sheyn had the commander's belongings ready to be loaded on a wagon.

"Are we going to be loaded like the rest of the baggage?" Sheyn said.

"The things you say!" Luks made a comically scandalized face.

"You have definite potential," Sheyn said. "It's only a matter of time before you're talking back to your master."

Instead of the smile Sheyn was hoping for, Luks looked troubled. "I don't have a master," he said. "Prince Kholya has not claimed me."

"Why not?" Sheyn was genuinely surprised.

"I don't know, but when I find the fault in me, I will correct it. Prince Kholya would be a very good master."

"What if the fault lies in him? Maybe he prefers women."

"That has nothing to do with it."

"How can the commander's preference have nothing to do with it?"

"He's a man of power and will, a prince and a warrior. He's exactly the sort of man Anaali created the daaksim for. A man like him can no more resist me than I can resist—" Luks stopped speaking when Kholya's quartermaster approached and addressed him.

"Very neat job," the quartermaster said, looking everywhere but at Luks and Sheyn. "I'm to tell you that an escort will arrive shortly to take you to a wagon."

"Thank you," Luks said, bowing slightly as the man moved away. "Yes, the commander would be a good master," he said to Sheyn. "With all that he has on his mind right now, he still spared a thought for us, even though neither of us belong to him."

"He does seem to be a decent sort," Sheyn said. "His brother, on the other hand…."

"Prince Kholya is several years older. He has more experience. Give Prince Kashyan time, and he'll become a man like his brother."

"How much older?" Sheyn seized on the most interesting item in Luks's speech.

"At least ten years. The gossip in the royal courts said that Savaan's queen was barren, and then she gave birth to a second son, nine months after her abduction by Sumadi raiders."

"Thus proving Savaan's king impotent," Sheyn said. "He should've claimed the child and saved his pride."

"Ah, but the baby's eyes were the same color as Prince Yevdjen's."

"You speak as though you were there."

"I was presented to Prince Yevdjen by his father on the prince's thirteenth nameday."

"That's not possible. You can't be any older than me. In fact, you look younger than me."

"I was born forty-two years ago."

Sheyn looked into Luks's eyes. "You're not lying," he said. "But you look like a lad of sixteen."

"I was sixteen when the ritual was performed." Luks smiled. "Did I forget to mention that we age very slowly?"

"I would remember a detail like that. Is there anything else you'd like to mention?"

"I did tell you."

"You said the original ten didn't age."

"We age but very, very slowly."

"Tell me more."

Luks and Sheyn talked and watched the quartermaster direct the loading of the cart until their escort arrived. Four Black Hawk troopers stopped in front of Sheyn and Luks, and their leader spoke.

"I'm Sergeant Leksi. Captain Kashyan has given me and my comrades the honor of escorting you to your wagon."

"I know you," Sheyn said. "You were there… in the Temple. You fought that thing."

The trooper bowed, straightened up, and tossed the light brown bangs out of his eyes. "I had the honor to fight beside the Bastard," he said. "I'm happy you're all right."

"Accept my gratitude," Sheyn said. "You fought well."

Leksi maintained his bearing, but it was obvious that he was pleased by Sheyn's praise. "I'm a Savaani horseman. So I have a reputation to uphold."

Luks cleared his throat delicately.

Leksi took the hint. "We shouldn't delay any longer." He and another trooper preceded Sheyn and Luks, while the other pair walked behind the daaksim. They went to the edge of the camp where the draft animals were usually pastured. All the beasts were now harnessed to laden wagons and carts surrounded by men carrying burdens.

"Why are we leaving?" Sheyn asked.

"It's common knowledge around camp, so I don't think the captain will mind if I tell you." Leksi glanced back at Sheyn and Luks. "We're leaving because King Kezlath sent soldiers to take you—" He glanced at Sheyn again "—back to the Temple. The commander refused to give you up, and now there are Muergathi troops lined up on the town side of the camp. Also, General Ognyan has claimed the Sumadi crown, married the queen, and formally adopted the dead king's son. He sent a message demanding the Bas—Captain Kashyan's head. The commander refused him too."

"What makes you think the Muergathim will let you go?" Sheyn asked.

"They're Muergathi. We're Savaani. If they stand in our way, we'll march over them."

"After watching you and your comrades fight that demon, I'm inclined to believe you."

"I'm glad you have a good opinion of our fighting skill," Leksi said. "We'll do our best to protect you... both of you."

"Thank you," Luks said.

"Here's your cart," Leksi said. "You'll be riding with the bedding, so you'll have a soft journey."

"Where are we going?" Sheyn asked.

"You'll have to ask the commander," Leksi said. "There'll be a detail of soldiers around your wagon at all times. Make yourselves comfortable. It shouldn't be much longer before we move out." He bowed and walked away, leaving behind two men as guards.

"You shouldn't do that," Luks said as he and Sheyn climbed into the back of the covered oxcart.

Sheyn settled himself on a stack of down-filled pallets. "What did I do this time?"

"You shouldn't flirt with them. It's a sure way to bring trouble on yourself."

"I wasn't flirting," Sheyn said indignantly. "And make up your mind. Do you want me to be nice to them or not?"

"You have a master. You should spend your time pleasing him." Luks paused. "I can see that you're used to everyone trying to please you, but things are different now."

"I don't like your way of doing things," Sheyn said as he relaxed against the piled bedding.

"You don't even care that your master may have to fight today, do you?"

"I think he enjoys it."

"Your heart is made of stone."

"You're not the first to tell me that." Sheyn covered a yawn with his hand. "Now, do you mind if we speak later? I'd like to sleep for a while."

Luks almost said something critical but reflected that Pearl had been through a lot that day. He made himself comfortable and let the other daaksi sleep until they started moving. Sheyn woke and crawled to the back of the wagon. He opened the curtains and leaned out to look at the train of wagons, horses, and marching men. The trooper riding off the corner of the cart nodded briefly to Sheyn before Luks pulled Sheyn back in and yanked the curtains closed.

"Have you no modesty?" Luks asked.

"Not when compared to you, though I was considered very well-mannered by my friends."

"You were about to speak to that warrior, weren't you?"

"I like talking and finding out new things. I'd very much like to know the name of the region we're heading toward." Sheyn put his eye to the crack between the curtains. "And the name of that tree we just passed."

Luks knelt beside Sheyn and peered. "Which tree?"

"It's gone now. Wait! There's another like it, though not as tall."

"That's djunir. The leaves stay green all year. The Muergathim make a fermented syrup from the sap. It's very costly and can have a man seeing wood nymphs after a few drinks of it."

"You have wood nymphs here?"

Luks frowned. "Of course not. They're just creatures in legends. Do you have wood nymphs where you're from?"

"Dey Larone," Sheyn said. "And no, we don't. No wood nymphs, nor water nymphs, nor dragons, nor demons, either. Nothing magical at all."

"No magic? What about your Gods and Goddesses?"

"We worship Leynys. He's our only God, and he was a man before he became divine."

"You're trying to make a fool of me."

"I'm telling you the truth."

"I can't imagine your homeland."

"I wish I could take you there, right now."

"Well, you can't. Why don't you try to fall asleep again? I'll finish braiding your hair if you like."

"I'd like that," Sheyn said, and Luks moved closer. "You know, it's very good of you to look after me, but I wish you didn't worry so much."

"Be quiet and try to sleep," Luks said. He unraveled the hair he'd braided a few hours ago and combed out the shining, rippled locks.

Despite the swaying of the cart, or because of it, Sheyn fell into a deep sleep as Luks sang softly. After a few minutes, Luks became drowsy and leaned back against a stack of bundled cushions. As he was dropping off, someone pulled the curtains open, and Luks was instantly wide-awake.

"Softly," Kashyan said. "Don't wake Pearl."

"I won't, lord," Luks whispered.

"I just wanted to see that you were all right." Kashyan leaped down from the back of the cart and caught up with Karkaran running alongside. He swung up into the saddle and rode to the front of the column.

Chapter
15

IT TOOK a day to cross the plain and another to navigate the foothills. Apart from regular stops to rest the beasts, the Horde of the Hawk traveled by moonlight as well as by sun. By the second night, Sheyn was heartily sick of sleeping in the wagon. When he woke feeling sore, it was noticeably colder. He pulled a blanket around his shoulders and peeked out of the curtains. It was dark, but he could see more djunir trees, and the ground was rocky. From the way the wagon bed was tilted, he assumed they were entering highlands.

"Do you know what mountains these are?" he asked.

"We're probably over the border by now. This land is a vast hunting preserve that belongs to the high king. We're probably on Mount Eyrie."

"How long did I sleep?"

"Half the night. Prince Kashyan came by again to check on you."

"Why would I care?" Sheyn shivered. "Is it going to get colder?"

"Probably. Let's put the blanket over both of us. And here's another."

Sheyn flinched when Luks put an arm around him, but the warmth was welcome and he soon relaxed. Though he'd slept for hours, he drifted off again with Luks's even breathing in his ear. When he woke again, it was dark, and he could tell by the motion that the cart was not on a road any longer. Luks woke, and they looked outside.

"We're making camp," said one of the guards.

The wagons were lined up in rows in the large meadow, and the draft beasts were unhitched to graze. Horses were unsaddled and bedrolls laid out beside them. Everyone ate a cold dinner and went to sleep, except for the sentries and scouts.

Sheyn and Luks weren't the least bit sleepy. After they ate the bread and cheese brought by one of the quartermaster's errand runners, they fell into conversation.

"You seem different since the Red Temple abducted you," Luks said.

"Seeing my first demon did have an effect on me."

"No, I'm not talking about the shock. I expected that. This is something else. I can't quite get my mind to focus on it, but there's something different about you."

"Well, I found out that I heal instantly and that I'm going to live for a very long time without getting old. Both of those things are difficult to accept."

Luks shook his head. "You're not like any daaksi I've ever known. Maybe it's only that you're the first foreign daaksi I've ever known." He frowned. "And how can someone not of Kandaar become one of the Goddess's chosen?"

"You're worrying again. That will give you wrinkles."

"Why don't you feel the bond?" Luks said. "Except for one time, you haven't felt the separation sickness, have you?"

"I hope you're not looking to me for answers. I'm a scholar, but this is out of my realm."

"What happened the first time Prince Kashyan bedded you?"

"You must be joking with me. I'd never allow that swine to touch me."

"You haven't—?"

"No!"

"Unbelievable," Luks whispered.

"What?"

"I'm just amazed at Prince Kashyan's restraint."

"Restraint? He has none."

"He hasn't thrown you down and topped you, though he must burn for you."

"He wouldn't dare force me, and I'll not consent to it."

"You feel no desire for him?"

"Of course not," Sheyn lied. In fact, he felt uncomfortably aroused when he was near Kashyan, but nothing would make him admit it.

"I was wrong. You haven't changed. You're as hard-headed and willful as ever." Luks softened his voice. "If you don't complete the bond—"

"And why would I want to do that?"

"It's your destiny."

Sheyn made a rude noise.

"If the bond doesn't exist, why don't you run away?" Luks asked.

Sheyn was quiet for a long time before he spoke again. "I can't deny that something holds me here. But I won't mate with that savage. When I choose a partner, he'll come from one of the finest families in the Deysian Protectorate. He'll be an educated man and quite wealthy. I wouldn't be surprised if he wielded a fair amount of political power."

"How can you still be lying to yourself?"

"Why do you want me to give up hope?"

"Your life has changed in a way that cannot be changed back. One day, you'll believe that."

"I don't want to. And I will never rut with that savage."

"It's no use talking to you," Luks said.

"ANYTHING?" KHOLYA asked as Kashyan rode up to him. The commander's well-trained stallion showed his teeth but tolerated the nearness of Kashyan's charger.

"Nothing. We rode the perimeter twice. The sentries haven't seen anything out of the ordinary."

"The scouts report the same." Kholya dismounted and stretched. "Great Raas, it feels good to be out of the saddle."

Kashyan dismounted and gave Djenya a hand signal. The lieutenant led the Black Hawks away, taking Kashyan's horse with him.

"Eat with me," Kholya said.

"No. I'm going to look in on the daaksim."

"Then let's find a loaf and a skin of something, and I'll go with you."

Kholya and Kashyan acquired a round loaf and a jug of beer as they walked toward the line of wagons. They devoured the bread in chunks and washed it down with the flat beer.

"I've given some thought to claiming the Sumadi boy," Kholya said.

"I think he suits you, if you want to court that kind of trouble."

"He takes care of me, and he's easy to be with."

"Have you taken him?"

"Of course."

"Liar."

"There hasn't been time."

"Crawl into the wagon with him when we get there. I'll take the other one out of the way."

"Do you like him any better yet?" Kholya grinned. "Has his strange beauty bewitched you?"

"Of course," Kashyan said in the same tone Kholya had used.

"Have you taken him?"

"There hasn't been time." Kashyan paused. "I do want him, though."

"I'd be very surprised if you didn't. You're a hard man, brother, but you're human."

Kashyan clenched his fists. "This has to be some joke of the Gods. I despise daaksim."

"Take him and ease your pain. Truthfully, it will be a relief for both of you."

Kashyan threw a chunk of bread that bounced off Kholya's ear. "I'd have to gag him so I wouldn't lose my desire."

"Then gag him. He's your daaksi."

"Would you?"

"No, probably not. I prefer my bed partners willing."

"And there you have my answer as well."

Kholya patted Kashyan's shoulder as they reached the far end of the line of wagons. "You're a pitiful excuse for a man, but I love you."

"LET'S TALK about something else," Sheyn said. "It's boring just sitting here."

"All right. Tell me again, is it really true that women are the equals of men in your land?"

"Yes, it's true," Sheyn said. "Women in my country own property. There are female merchants and artists and every other occupation you can imagine."

"Next you'll tell me there are women warriors."

"Well… there are women in the Imperial Honor Guard. They don't fight, but they look very fine in their armor."

"You're making all this up. It's not—"

Sheyn held up a hand and Luks stopped talking. Both listened intently for a few seconds.

"I thought I heard someone outside," Sheyn said.

"It was the guards walking around."

"No. I'm used to the sound of their footsteps."

As Sheyn finished speaking, something struck the cart, jostling it. Sheyn looked at Luks and then crept to the back of the wagon. He looked out through the crack and saw a Savaani soldier fall to the ground with a knife in his throat.

"We're being attacked," Sheyn said. "Can we get out the front of the wagon?"

Luks nodded. "We can squeeze between the covering and the wood."

"Come on, then."

Without questions or argument, Luks followed Sheyn. When they were both on the ground in front of the cart, they saw the body of the other guard. They heard the sound of curtains being yanked open and a muffled curse. Sheyn flattened himself in the snow-patched grass and started crawling away from the wagon. Luks hesitated and then threw himself under the cart as a man dashed from behind it.

The dark-clad stranger whistled, and three more men in identical tunics and head wraps surrounded Sheyn. Luks darted in the opposite direction in search of help and ran into Kashyan and Kholya. Kashyan took Luks by the arm to steady him.

"Where are you going?" Kashyan asked.

"Pearl!" Luks gasped. "Raiders!" He pointed at the cart.

Kashyan and Kholya drew their swords as they broke into a run. Four men walked from the cover of the wagon with Sheyn in the middle. Sheyn's wrists were bound behind him, and he was gagged, but his feet were free. The kidnappers saw Kashyan and Kholya and drew their weapons. Three stood their ground while one fled with Sheyn.

"Take one of them down and go after the daaksi," Kholya said. "I can handle the other two."

There was no more time for speech. The five men met in a flurry of flying metal. The intruders fought well and without a care for their lives. They were ready to sacrifice themselves so their leader could escape with the Temple's prize. The sounds of fighting attracted attention, and soon more Savaani warriors arrived.

"Go!" Kholya shouted at his brother. "I have more than enough help."

Kashyan didn't hesitate long enough to reply. He dodged around the man he was fighting and ran after Sheyn.

SHEYN RECOGNIZED the scent of the man who was gripping his upper arm. It was the same man who'd kidnapped him before and taken him to the Temple. Sheyn fought the fear that wanted to paralyze him and worked at the ropes around his wrists. His bonds had been hastily tied, and he managed to loosen them enough to slip them off. Letting the cords fall to the ground, he reached up and removed his gag. After taking a deep breath, he shouted for help.

Mardjan flinched, then whirled around to give Sheyn a backhanded slap. Sheyn bent backward from the waist and easily avoided the blow. Mardjan grabbed for Sheyn, and Sheyn danced away almost too fast for the eye to follow.

A Savaani sentry ran up with his sword drawn and shouted a challenge. As Mardjan turned to face the soldier, he drew and released his dagger. The knife pierced the sentry's throat, silencing him. The soldier reached up to grab the hilt and a second dagger entered his eye socket. As the soldier crumpled, Mardjan spun about to chase Sheyn, but to his surprise the daaksi wasn't running away. Sheyn was running toward the fallen man. Mardjan thanked Taankh for his luck as he launched himself at Sheyn. He was surprised again when the daaksi turned and faced him. In Sheyn's hand was the sentry's sword.

Kashyan ran up as the gleaming point of a sword appeared between Mardjan's shoulder blades. At the other end of the sword, Sheyn was frozen in a lunge that would have made his fencing master proud. He'd driven the tip of the blade up under the Red Monk's ribcage exactly as Tezwar had taught him, keeping his wrist straight as he followed through. Mardjan had died when the sword pierced his heart, and it was the only thing holding him up.

Kashyan went to Sheyn as more soldiers arrived. Sheyn looked up as Kashyan stopped beside him.

"You can drop the sword now," Kashyan said. "He's dead."

Sheyn didn't react.

"Let go of the sword," Kashyan ordered. He saw how the young man's arm muscles quivered with strain, and he reached out to take the sword from him.

Sheyn wrenched the blade free and put the point under Kashyan's chin. Though he'd had years of extensive training with a fencing saber, he'd never been in a real fight until tonight. His nerves were singing like a plucked bowstring, and his racing blood made him reckless. He'd killed once. What difference would another death make?

"Easy there," Kashyan said. "I can see you're on edge, but you don't want to kill me."

"I don't?"

"All right. Maybe you do want to kill me, but it would be a bad idea. If you kill me, these men will kill you. And they might not do it quickly."

"Oh very well. Can I keep this sword?" Sheyn said as he lowered the blade.

"Can you keep—?" Kashyan blinked. "You want a *sword*?"

"Let him keep it," someone called out from the crowd. "He earned it."

Kholya arrived, and despite circumstances, had a difficult time keeping a grin from his face. "Do you need any help?" he asked Kashyan.

"I'd disarm him, but I don't want to hurt him," Kashyan said.

"Don't speak of me as if I'm not here," Sheyn said.

"May I have the sword?" Kholya asked. "It should go to the man's family. He might have a son."

Sheyn handed the sword to Kholya. "I feel odd," he said. "I've never killed anyone."

"Do you feel like you're going to lose your dinner?" Kholya asked.

"It's a bit like that."

"Let Kashyan take you back to the wagon. Luks will make you feel better, I'm sure."

"He wants you to claim him," Sheyn said distantly as he listed to one side.

Kashyan put a hand under Sheyn's elbow and kept him upright. When Sheyn sagged, Kashyan put an arm around his back.

"Take him to bed," Kholya said and looked surprised at the sound of cheers. "Why are you all standing around gawking?" he said to the crowd. "Go back to your posts, rascals."

Sheyn was asleep on his feet when Kashyan got him back to the wagon. Kashyan lifted him inside, and Luks put a pillow under Sheyn's head.

"What happened, lord?" Luks asked.

"He killed the man who tried to kidnap him."

Luks gasped. "Surely he didn't."

"He did, though. Ran the villain through as neat as you please."

"I don't know what to say."

"Don't say anything. Let him sleep. I'll be back at first light."

IN THE Temple, the high priest received word of Mardjan's failure and ordered the messenger out of the chamber. He rose from his chair, paced, and raged against the outcast Savaani princes. When his fury was spent, he turned to the acolyte standing silently by the door.

"Which one are you?" Chanesh asked.

"Moksha, Reverend Lord."

"How old are you?"

"Sixteen."

"Good. Are you yet innocent?"

"I don't understand, Reverend Lord."

"Don't pretend to me," Chanesh snapped. "I've lived more than a hundred years and had charge of hundreds of boys like you. Your minds always return to the same thoughts unless they're channeled by someone wiser."

Terrified he'd say the wrong thing, Moksha remained silent.

"Admit it," Chanesh said. "Rutting is all you think about when you have idle moments."

Moksha had a vivid flash of yanking his jaavi before getting out of bed this morning. He swiftly banished the thought, afraid the High Priest was reading his mind.

"Answer me," Chanesh said. "Have you rutted with man, woman, or beast?"

Moksha shook his head.

"Good. Now go and fetch my visitor."

Moksha bowed and left the High Priest's quarters. When he reached the central hall, he sent a novice to find Chanesh's guest. A short time later, a green-robed man with a scanty beard approached Moksha.

"I was told High Priest Chanesh wished to see me."

"Come with me," Moksha said and led the man to Chanesh's chambers.

"It is time, Yozif," Chanesh said by way of greeting.

"I thought that might be why you summoned me." Yozif held up a leather bag. "I brought what I need for the ritual." He turned to look at Moksha. "I assume this is the candidate?"

Moksha spoke out of turn for the first time in his life. "Candidate?" He fixed his gaze on Chanesh's fissured face. "What ritual, my lord?"

"Be silent," Chanesh said. "Or scream if you like. It makes no difference." He called to the door guards, and they made short work of subduing Moksha and binding his wrists. After tying the acolyte to the top of a large chest, the guards went back to their posts. "You may begin," Chanesh told Yozif. "And don't disappoint me."

Yozif lit the Goddess candles and took up the small knife.

Moksha wanted to beg for mercy when Yozif leaned over him with the gleaming blade, but his tongue was frozen to the roof of his mouth. He lay rigid with fear as Yozif chanted, but after a while, the scent of the candles and the rhythmic words lulled him into a stupor. He didn't feel the bite of the silvery metal as he drifted into unconsciousness, and when he woke, nothing was the same.

LATE IN the afternoon, the Horde of the Hawk came to the end of their stony road. The wagons had been sent by another way to sheltered fields on the border of Savaan, but the main force of fighting men had climbed to the top of Mount Eyrie. Perched on the peak, as though it had grown from the rock of the mountain, was a large fortress. Kashyan reined in to look at the view as the troops marched through the gate.

"What do you call this grim place?" Sheyn asked from behind Kashyan.

"This is Karkaran Castle, once the most formidable fortress in Kandaar," Kashyan said. "It's been abandoned since the high king four high kings back turned this into hunting land."

"Karkaran? That's your horse's name, isn't it?" Sheyn furrowed his brow in thought. "It means something like Falling Hawk."

Kashyan grinned. "It means *Diving* Hawk."

Sheyn was about to ask another question when Djenya stopped beside them.

"There's our new hero," Djenya said. "When are you going to get him his own armor, Kasha?"

"Do you need a beating?" Kashyan responded. "I'm in the mood to give one to somebody."

"Spare me." Djenya pretended to cower.

"Are you making fun of me?" Sheyn asked.

"Not me," Djenya said. "I fear you too much."

Kashyan gritted his teeth as the men of his troop laughed. "I don't want to hear any more about that ridiculous incident," he growled.

"What a shame," Djenya said. "At least allow us to praise him just once, this battling daaksi of yours. Such a spirit deserves recognition."

Djenya led the Black Hawks in a cheer, each man raising his sword in salute to Sheyn. Kashyan clenched his jaw until it ached, but he wouldn't deprive his troops of their sport.

"Have you humiliated me enough?" Kashyan asked his lieutenant.

"For today." Djenya clapped Kashyan on the shoulder. "I'll see to getting the men settled."

Kashyan nodded his thanks. "I'll find you as soon as I put this one in a safe place… if such a place exists."

Kashyan and Sheyn dismounted, and Djenya took Karkaran's reins. After a brief search, Kashyan found the quartermaster and rooms were allocated to the daaksim. Taking Sheyn by the arm, Kashyan pulled him down a drafty corridor.

Sheyn shivered with cold, and abruptly it was all too much. Everything that had happened in the last four days crashed down on him at once, and he began to shake in reaction. He'd been tortured. He'd been attacked by a demon. He'd been forced to kill a man. By the time Kashyan escorted Sheyn into his quarters, Sheyn was a mass of nerves.

KASHYAN SHOVED Sheyn into the chamber set aside for the daaksim. "Stay put," he ordered.

This was the last straw. Sheyn would not tolerate being treated like unwanted baggage. "Or you'll do what?" He raised his chin as he stared Kashyan in the eye. "Nothing. That's what you'll do."

Kashyan wanted to leave, but the daaksi's tone got under his skin. "I wouldn't wager all I had on that, if I were you," he retorted.

"I would, because I know your weakness."

"And what is my weakness?"

Sheyn knew he should stop talking now, but the words kept coming, racing as fast as his heart. "You're brave and strong and you have no trouble killing in battle, but for all you're a brute—and you *are* a brute—you can't bear to cause pain."

Kashyan laughed.

Sheyn smiled at him. "I believe I could provoke you to such anger that you'd strike me, or put me in chains, but you'd relent. You'd relent, and you'd feel shame and remorse. After a time…." His voice trailed off.

"What? Speak!"

"You're not a stupid man, though you wish others to think you are. In time, you'd change your behavior to avoid the pain of guilt." Sheyn paused. "Or you'd rid yourself of me entirely." He tilted his head to the side. "But you can't do that, can you? Not without suffering even greater pain and loss of honor. You're stuck."

"Shut your pretty mouth."

"Another threat? Must I repeat myself? We both know now that you won't hurt me."

Kashyan grabbed for Sheyn's wrist, but his hand closed on air. "I've never seen anyone move that fast," he said in amazement.

"You've never met my fencing master."

Kashyan calmed himself before he spoke again. "I'm tired of your insolence. You'll do as I tell you, or—"

"Stop blustering for a minute. I'm thinking."

Shocked into silence, Kashyan stared at Sheyn. Sheyn concentrated and blocked out all distracting thoughts, as he used to do in the crowded library of the university. He put his excellent brain to work as he'd not done since he'd been kidnapped. Swiftly, he reviewed all that had happened since he came to Kandaar and formulated the best plan possible for leaving here someday.

"My lord," Sheyn said. "Let's have an understanding."

"I'm listening."

"I'll play the part of daaksi when others are watching, so you needn't worry about your honor." He met Kashyan's eyes. "It's now as precious to me as my own."

"What are you babbling about?"

"My standing here depends on yours, isn't that right?"

"Your standing? Ayeesh!" Kashyan exclaimed. "When is it going to penetrate your skull that you're a slave?"

Sheyn narrowed his eyes at Kashyan. "Understand this, barbarian. I am not now, nor ever will be, a slave."

"You're making more sense now, but you're still soft in the head."

"Yes, you've told me that more than once. Don't you get tired of repeating yourself?"

"If you ever speak to me this way when we're not alone—"

"I won't."

"And stop interrupting me."

"Why? Does it irritate you?"

"It's disrespectful."

"We're alone," Sheyn pointed out.

Kashyan pursed his lips. "So we are," he said and leered broadly at Sheyn.

Sheyn swallowed hard as he took a half step back. His hands clenched into fists in the folds of his tunic as he struggled for control. By an effort of will, he suppressed the sudden wave of panic, and his voice was steady as he replied. "I am not in mood for bedplay, and we both know you won't force me," he said, praying it was true.

"You didn't think I was serious? We both know I don't find you attractive at all."

Sheyn took a deep breath. "For which I am everlastingly grateful. Do we have a bargain?"

Kashyan snorted. "You're in no position to bargain, and I need to return to my duties."

"Wait!"

"What is it now?"

"It's cold in here."

Kashyan sighed, but the sight of the pale daaksi shivering with his arms wrapped around himself stopped the harsh words that sprang to his tongue. "I'll see what I can do about that," he said as he left.

SHEYN STOPPED pacing when he heard a key in the lock. He would've welcomed any distraction but was pleased to see Luks and a line of men carrying furnishings. After a few minutes work under Luks's direction, the chamber was habitable. Luks thanked the soldiers and they left.

"You're a genius," Sheyn said as he reclined on a mattress.

"And you're… I don't have a word for what you are," Luks said as he sat on a cushion. "As soon as the ovens are fired, someone will bring us food," he added.

"Good. I'm starving. In fact, I'm always hungry. I haven't been able to get enough to eat since…."

"Since you became a daaksi," Luks finished for him. "We give a lot of our energy to our masters, so—"

"That's nonsense," Sheyn said.

"No, it isn't. I'm weary of you making fun of my faith."

"I'm sorry," Sheyn said quickly. "You're right. It's ill-mannered of me."

Luks watched Sheyn for a moment. "You've changed again."

"Have I? Then I suppose I should stop consorting with demons and killing kidnappers. It seems to have an effect on me."

"You're hopeless. You turn everything into a jest."

"Would you rather I wept?"

"No, but…." Luks sighed. "You should hear the soldiers talking about you."

Sheyn sat up. "What do they say? I'm sure it's crude and ignorant, but simply out of curiosity, I'd like know."

"They say that you're as brave as you are beautiful, and more things of that sort. I believe half of them are in love with you."

"Such nonsense," Sheyn said, but the corners of his mouth turned up in a pleased little smile. "They don't think I'm beautiful. They think I'm too tall, too thin, and too pale."

"It's true you're not a typical Kandaari beauty, but anyone with eyes can see how fine you are. You don't look like you belong to this world. When I think of the avatar now, I see your face."

"I think I'd rather look like you." Sheyn tilted his head as he gazed at Luks's face. "You look as luscious as a ripe peach. Your skin even has that glow." He paused. "I've wanted to ask you about that. Sometimes your skin actually glows."

Luks's eyes widened. "Have you looked in a mirror since you became a daaksi?" When Sheyn shook his head, Luks went to the door and talked to the guard outside. He smiled as he returned to his seat. "You've no idea what you look like now," he said. "But soon you will."

"While we wait, do you have any more gossip?"

"Did you really kill a man?"

"I had no choice. He was taking me back to the Temple. I didn't think about it at all. I simply picked up the sword and used it."

"I heard you killed him with a single perfect thrust. That's what the soldiers are saying. Anaali must have guided your hand."

Sheyn snorted. "It wasn't magic. It was hours of practice with a pitiless perfectionist."

"Nothing makes sense to me anymore," Luks said.

Sheyn looked at Luks's bowed head and rethought his flippant reply. "It's been hard for you, hasn't it?" he said instead. Tentatively, he touched the back of Luks's hand.

"I don't know what horrible thing will happen next," Luks said in a choked voice.

Sheyn looked down as a teardrop splashed his hand. Something broke inside him, and he crumpled, pulling Luks with him into a clutching hug. For several moments, they clung together, awkwardly balanced halfway between the couch and cushion, but neither wanted to let go. When the knock came at the door, they moved apart, but the warmth of the embrace stayed with them.

One of the quartermaster's men came in carrying a long, flat bundle. He unwrapped a tall rectangle of polished metal and set it against the wall. Without exchanging more than a dozen words, he was gone.

"Look," Luks said, giving Sheyn a little shove toward the mirror.

Sheyn conquered a few irrational fears and went to the mirror. It was tall enough to reflect his full length, and his first thought was that the Kandaari were right. He was too long for his weight with hardly more breadth than a youth of sixteen. His shoulders were broad, but they tapered to a waist as willowy as that of an untried maiden.

In the midst of cataloging his faults, Sheyn noticed that his skin looked extraordinarily smooth, almost like porcelain. Then he realized that his skin was as softly radiant as the inside of a shell. He looked up into Luks's reflected gaze. "Am I glowing?" he asked.

"Anaali's spark shines in you," Luks said. "You can hardly see it in the daylight, but it makes our skin as lustrous as pearls."

"I have scars." Sheyn traced the lines from the corners of his eyes to his cheekbones. "Just like yours. I thought they were some sort of tribal symbols that marked you as a pleasure slave." He paused. "And I suppose I was right."

He looked into the eyes of his reflection. Had his gaze always been so deep? His eyes so large? So heavily fringed with lashes? He was certain his eyebrows were different. Before, they were barely visible, and now they looked like the delicate charcoal strokes of a talented artist. His lips had bloomed from pale pink to rose. His flaxen hair had always been silky and shiny, but now it was so fine that it flowed with his slightest movement and gleamed like moonbeams breaking through clouds.

"Now do you see?" Luks asked.

"Yes, I see, but how is this possible?"

"I told you. During the ceremony, if you're chosen by the Goddess, you receive a measure of Her divine essence. It changes you."

"I'm a freak."

"You're a miracle. You'll never convince me otherwise."

"I don't want to be either of those things."

"You have no choice."

"Exactly." Sheyn turned from the mirror. "I didn't choose this. Did you?"

"I was raised for this purpose. The Goddess chose me, and I've done my best to follow my training and my faith."

"What about your family?"

"I know nothing of my life before the Sanctuary at the Mother Shrine. I was told I was left there as infant, only a few months old."

"I understand that you were trained from birth, but why are you so content with your lot?"

"This is the life I was given, and I'm trying to live it as well as I can."

"But surely you must long to be free."

"I wouldn't know what to do."

"You'd do just as you pleased."

Luks sighed. "I can't understand why Anaali would choose someone like you, but I must follow my beliefs and trust that She has a purpose."

"While you're doing that, I'm going to find a way out of this cage."

Luks shivered with the same unease he'd felt the first time he'd seen Pearl. In spite of everything, Luks liked the prickly foreigner, but the shadow of foreboding never completely went away. "You should seal your bond with your master," he said. "Until you do, you'll be out of balance."

Someone knocked, and Sheyn was grateful for the interruption. He called out permission to enter, expecting a tray of food and khai, but it was a pair of Black Hawks. Each carried an armload of furs they could barely see over. Sheyn recognized one of them.

"Hello, Leksi. What's all this?"

"From the captain," said Leksi. "Two fur cloaks and bed covers." His lips twitched as he suppressed a smirk. "He said he wanted to make sure your hot blood didn't cool down."

"Should you be repeating such things?" Luks interrupted.

"Don't be cross," Sheyn said as he picked up one of the cloaks and put it around his shoulders. "This is a beautiful pelt."

"It's crag bear," Leksi said. "They go all mottled white and gray like that in the winter. The worst-tempered creatures ever born."

"Not according to your captain," Sheyn said. "He thinks *I'm* the worst-tempered creature ever born."

"I think you're very brave," Leksi said, leaning toward Sheyn.

"I hope we aren't keeping you from your duty," Luks said.

Leksi glanced at Luks and resumed his military posture. "We should get back to our posts," he said. "May I take a message to the captain?"

"Take a message to the Black Hawks for me," Sheyn said. "Give them my thanks for protecting me, and tell them I wish them luck on their raids."

"I will." Leksi bowed and left with his comrade.

"You wish them luck on their raids?" Luks said as soon as the door was closed.

"Was that the wrong terminology?"

"You can't start planting ideas in their heads."

"What ideas? I extended my thanks and good wishes. What could be wrong with that?"

"You can't be this simple." Luks chewed his lip for a moment before he continued. "You said you wished them luck on their raids. Do you know if raids have been authorized?"

"If they aren't authorized, then what's the harm?"

"Because Pearl the Perfect just hinted that he admires raiders. You've given them incentive to disobey orders... if there are orders against raids."

"I think you're making too much of this."

"Why won't you accept that I know more about this than you?"

"You worry too much. Nothing is—" Sheyn broke off as someone knocked at the door.

Luks went to the door and returned with a tray. He set it down on the floor between the bed and the cushion and poured two cups of khai.

"You left in the middle of my sentence," Sheyn said.

"I didn't need to hear any more. Drink your khai while it's hot." Luks broke a loaf in half, spread soft, baked cheese on both pieces, and handed one to Sheyn.

"Why aren't there any female daaksim?" Sheyn asked before he took a bite.

"I'm going to let you think about your question for a moment before I answer." Luks chewed a piece of dried apple and watched Sheyn's face.

"Of course," Sheyn said. "What a foolish question. Your culture would never allow a woman near a battlefield or a camp full of strange men."

"Or any number of other places." Luks looked around as someone knocked. "Whoever could that be?" he wondered aloud.

"I'll answer it this time," Sheyn said as he got to his feet.

When Sheyn opened the door, there was no one there but the guard. "Did someone just knock?" Sheyn asked.

"I'm not saying anyone did," the soldier said. "But if someone did, they left this for you." He handed Sheyn a stone jar.

"Thank you." Sheyn took the jar inside and gave it to Luks. "A gift," he said.

Luks opened the lid. "It's honey!" he said. "The Goddess's blessings on whoever brought this, but… I'm not sure we should accept it."

"You're joking. It's just a jar of honey. Pour some on your bread and give it back."

"You're right. It's a harmless gift." Luks passed the jar to Sheyn and bit into his honeyed bread. "It's surprising how much you can come to crave something sweet," he said after he swallowed.

"Very true." Sheyn thought about Luks's words as he ate his bread and honey.

CANDLES AND incense burned once again in the Gate Chamber. Again, High Priest Chanesh sought to call one of Taankh's Children into the Waking World. On the rough altar, a daaksi struggled against his chains and begged for mercy.

"Reverend Lord," Moksha said. "Please don't do this. I beg you not to hurt me."

Chanesh took no notice of Moksha's words. Though the acolyte had served him well for two years, the young man might have been a stone in the wall for all the attention the high priest paid to him. Chanesh was concentrating on the words of the chant. At the end of the third line of each stanza, his hand snaked out, and the ceremonial blade cut into Moksha's flesh. Soon the sound of screams filled the air that was already heavy with musky incense. A puff of murky mist appeared above the altar and began to expand.

Moksha saw the demon taking form above him, and his terror doubled. The waves of fear emitted by the sacrifice opened the door between the realms. Guided by the high priest's chant, one of Taankh's Children squeezed through the crack and manifested as a winged creature the size of a boar with a bat's face and the yellow, knobby hide of a toad. Held captive in the altar's aura, the creature writhed and gibbered, gnashing its four-inch tusks at the young man chained to the stone just out of reach.

"A goblin," Chanesh said in disgust. He glanced at Moksha, who'd bloodied his wrists trying to pull free of his manacles. It was clear this daaksi wasn't powerful enough to attract anything larger. Chanesh needed the Gate, the moon-haired daaksi who'd escaped him. But the Gate was guarded by the Bastard of Savaan and the army of the Bastard's traitorous brother. To defeat them, Chanesh needed more demons. To get more demons, he needed more daaksim. He spared another glance at Moksha. And if they were all as weak as this one, he was going to need a great number of them.

Chanesh spoke the words of command to the goblin and sent it on its way. He had no confidence that it would succeed in its mission, but it would have an affect on the morale of the rogue Savaanim. Leaving Moksha on the altar, Chanesh went to his office and sent for Yozif. They had plans to make.

At last the long day was over, and the Horde of the Hawk was settled in and around the fortress. The men and horses had been fed and were bedding down. The commander took a few minutes to breathe and walk the parapet with his best warrior.

"Now we wait," Kholya said and Kashyan nodded. "I don't think Kezlath will pursue this. He knows his fellow kings would take my side as soon as they hear his high priest stole a daaksi."

"Some might say the daaksi was already stolen goods that I had no right to."

Kholya shook his head. "The Council of Kings would recognize the bond and honor it."

"I hope you're right. Those Red Monks worry me. They need Pearl for one of their filthy rituals, so I don't think they'll give up so easily."

"If it comes to a siege, we can hold them off. We have a well, a large store of grain, and a tunnel to the hunting grounds. And we know our noncombatants will be safely in Savaan soon."

"What if the king decides not to give them sanctuary?"

"He has no authority over my lands, and since you're not anywhere near his kingdom, he'll pretend not to notice."

"I've always wondered, why did he keep me around?"

"To torment you," Kholya said bluntly. "He couldn't bear the sight of you, and yet, he wanted his eye on you. You remember how he looked for the slightest fault and pounced on it. But even when you were small, and one of his slaps would send you flying, you never cried."

"I shed plenty of tears."

"Never in front of him."

"Let's speak of something else."

"As you wish," Kholya said. "Your daaksi is a proper hellion."

"Something else."

Kholya chuckled. "I must be tired. I can't think of a single thing to talk about."

"Then take some rest."

"A wise suggestion. You should come with me."

"I want to think for a while."

"All right. I think it's good that you're taking up a new pastime."

Kashyan aimed a punch at Kholya's shoulder. Kholya dodged and continued on to the ladder. His grin was the last thing Kashyan saw as he climbed down out of sight. Kashyan took a moment to thank Raas for giving him such a fine brother, and then his thoughts turned to Sheyn.

"I CAN'T breathe," Sheyn said.

"I know. You've told me at least a dozen times." Luks opened his eyes. "I can't make a window."

"Go to sleep, then. You're of no use to me."

Luks curled back up and fell asleep. Sheyn went to the door and opened it.

"Do you need something?" the guard asked.

"Do you know where Prince Kashyan is?"

"Not at this moment. But I could send a message for you."

"I'll take that message," Djenya said as he approached. "Good evening, blossom," he said to Sheyn. "Kasha sent me to see if you have everything you need. Why don't we go into the chamber?"

"Luks is asleep."

"You should get some sleep too."

"I can't. I feel trapped in all this stone. I need to feel the wind."

"I could walk with you as far as the nearest window," Djenya said.

"Thank you!" Sheyn pulled the fur cloak around his shoulders and shut the door behind him.

"This way," Djenya said, giving the guard a salute before he led Sheyn down the hall.

"Couldn't we go outside?" Sheyn asked.

"You're *really* feeling caged, aren't you?" Djenya chuckled. "I understand that feeling all too well. I'm not happy unless I'm on horseback under the sky." He paused. "Come on. I'll take you to the donjon tower."

After climbing a set of winding steps, Djenya opened a hatch and he and Sheyn emerged on the platform of a large, squat tower. There were no pennants for the wind to play with, so it made do with Sheyn's hair, turning it into a banner of white silk. Djenya lounged against a merlon and watched the daaksi's long hair dance on the air currents as Sheyn leaned out of the crenellated wall to look into the courtyard. The sun had set, and the light was grainy, but Sheyn could see men still moving about, preparing for a siege.

"Do you think the Temple will try again?" Sheyn asked as he turned to look at Djenya.

Djenya didn't answer. He was staring at something above Sheyn's head. As Sheyn spun to look, he heard Djenya's sword leave its sheath. When he spotted the thing that had made Djenya gape in horror, he froze.

"Get down," Djenya yelled as he shoved Sheyn aside.

Sheyn hit the planks of the platform with bruising impact, and his paralysis broke. He scrambled to the hatch and lifted it and then looked back for Djenya.

Djenya leaped away from a swiping blow of the demon's talons. The demon flapped its leathery wings and rose a few feet before swooping down again. Djenya raised his sword and cut at the monster as it slashed at him. He fended off the daggerlike claws and cut at the beast as it flashed by. The goblin's head seemed to split in half as it opened its fanged maw and bellowed in pain. Down in the courtyard, men looked up as the demon flew a circuit around the tower. Its warty, yellow hide glistened like sulfur in the torchlight as it dove on Djenya again.

"No," Sheyn whispered as he realized the demon intended to smash into Djenya like a living battering ram. The hatch banged down as he threw himself at Djenya, grabbing him around the waist. Sheyn and Djenya tumbled to a stop against the notched wall as the demon passed over them. Sheyn coughed in the stench the monster left in its wake.

"What are you doing?" Djenya shouted. "Get out of here!" He pushed Sheyn toward the hatch as the demon swooped again.

As Sheyn rose to his hands and knees, he was yanked violently backward.

"Get down," Kashyan barked as he shoved Sheyn toward the open hatchway. Without waiting to see if Sheyn obeyed, he ran to help Djenya.

As Sheyn watched in horror, the demon caught Djenya's blade in one of four claws and clutched his head with another. Djenya grasped the giant talons that squeezed his skull and tried to pry them loose. The demon used its other pair of claws to tear at Djenya's arms as it beat its wings rapidly to hover in place. It was so intent on its prey that it didn't see Kashyan until Kashyan's sword clove through one of its limbs. As the arm fell to the ground, the monster clenched its talons and crushed Djenya's skull. It dropped Djenya's body as it flew up, keening in agony. Kashyan shook off his horror and raised his sword above his head. He would have to grieve later.

The demon dropped below the level of the platform and flew halfway around it. With three powerful surges of its ribbed wings, it rose up and spotted the target. Tucking its wings close, the monster swooped, grabbed Sheyn around the waist, and rocketed upward again.

Kashyan threw himself across the platform and caught hold of Sheyn's ankle. He pulled backward and succeeded in keeping the goblin from flying away, but he was afraid Sheyn's hip would be dislocated if he continued. Raising his sword to the limit of his reach, he slashed at the demon, trying to cut a tendon that would make it release its grip.

Though it squealed like a teakettle on the boil, the monster would not let go. It twisted in midair and lashed out with two of the three remaining sets of talons. Kashyan parried the strikes, shearing through another claw but suffering two long slashes down his arm. As Kashyan swung his sword and kept his grip on Sheyn, the goblin raked his chest, opening deep wounds.

"Let go," Sheyn shouted.

Kashyan tightened his grip on Sheyn's ankle and raised his sword again. He was growing weaker with each drop of blood that fled his body, but he would fight until his strength was gone. He would not let the demon have Sheyn.

Sheyn looked down into Kashyan's face, and something turned over in his heart like the tumbler of a lock. "No," he said. Abruptly, he couldn't bear it if this brave man died, and he wished for the power to save him, to slay the demon, and punish those who sent it. His fear became a white-hot rage so large he couldn't contain it. It seeped out of him, and where it touched the demon, it burned like molten metal.

Kashyan was surprised when the demon let go of Sheyn, but he didn't hesitate to take advantage. As Sheyn fell the short distance to the platform, Kashyan gripped his sword with both hands and leaped. At the top of his arc, he brought the sword down, severing one of the wings from the monster's body. Kashyan landed badly, stumbled, and went to one knee beside Sheyn. For a moment, their eyes met, and then the thrashing demon raked a claw across Kashyan's back. Kashyan reversed his grip on the hilt and thrust backward into the creature's guts. As several Savaani soldiers emerged from the hatch, Kashyan shielded Sheyn with his body and let them finish the thing off.

Kholya arrived as a soldier wearing a Black Hawk badge hacked through the demon's neck. The monster flopped a few times and went still. An oily dew formed on the lumpy hide, and in moments, the carcass melted into a viscous puddle that evaporated like spit on hot iron. When Kholya could tear his gaze from the bizarre sight, he saw Kashyan.

"I need men to carry him to a surgeon," Kholya shouted as he knelt beside Kashyan. He glanced at Sheyn. "Are you hurt?"

"Not as bad as he is," Sheyn said. "Will he live?"

"I don't know," Kholya said as he and three other men lifted Kashyan. "We need to get him to the surgeons."

"And Djenya," Sheyn said.

Kholya shot a look at Djenya's headless body. "I'll take care of him," he said. "Come with me."

Sheyn followed Kholya through the fortress, accompanying the men who carried Kashyan.

"Are you all right?" Kholya asked.

"I'm a little shaky, but my wounds are almost healed."

"Do you need anything?"

"Could you send for Velvet?"

Kholya nodded and dispatched a man. When they reached the surgery, the physicians barred everyone but Kholya from entering. Sheyn was left to wait outside the door and was relieved when Luks arrived with his escort.

"What happened?" Luks asked, staring at the rents in Sheyn's blood-soaked tunic. "I heard people shouting about a demon."

"It would have taken me if Djenya hadn't fought it off and—" Sheyn's voice choked off for a moment. "He's dead."

Before Luks could answer, Kholya came into the hall. "Why are you still here?" he asked. "You'd be more comfortable in your quarters."

"I want to see him," Sheyn said.

"It's not a pretty sight," Kholya said.

Sheyn met Kholya's gaze. "Please."

Kholya was startled by the raw emotion in Sheyn's voice and eyes. Without a word, he held the door open so Luks and Sheyn could enter. In the quiet room, Kashyan lay unmoving on a narrow bed.

Sheyn stared at the horrible wounds on Kashyan's body, shocked that anyone could endure such damage and still breathe. "I did this," he whispered.

"What?" Luks leaned closer.

"This is my fault. It happened because of me."

"You're bonded. Of course he defended you."

"It isn't fair. Those awful priests in that disgusting Temple are the ones who should suffer and die." Sheyn clenched his hands into fists as a great bubble of rage rose in him. On fire with righteous anger, he trembled and his voice shook. "This man shouldn't die." Sheyn bowed his head. "I want him to live." His fists thumped down on Kashyan's chest and shoulder. "Bastard," he said. "It's not fair for you to leave just when you became interesting."

Luks stared in awe as Kashyan's visible wounds began to close. He put a hand on Kholya's arm when Kholya started forward and urged him to stay where he was. Silently, he took one of Sheyn's hands and placed it over Kashyan's heart.

Sheyn felt the faint heartbeat and willed it to be stronger with every fiber of his being. He closed his eyes and let whatever was happening continue to happen.

"What's he doing?" Kholya whispered to Luks.

"Healing Prince Kashyan."

"He can do that?"

"Once all daaksim had this power, but it faded away. It seems it has returned in Pearl."

"If Kashyan lives, I'll give him his weight in pearls."

Luks looked over at Sheyn. He was joyful that the lost gift of healing had returned, but part of him wondered at the Goddess's choice. Why had She given Her Blessing to a foreigner who had no appreciation for what it meant to be a daaksi?

When Sheyn collapsed from the energy drain, Kholya caught him. The commander put Sheyn on a bench while he fetched a surgeon. When he returned, he lifted Sheyn in his arms.

"Lead me to your chamber," Kholya said to Luks.

"Yes, my lord."

Kholya carried Sheyn to the bed Luks pointed out and set him carefully down. "Sleep as long as you like," he murmured. "You've earned a rest."

"I'll see that he isn't disturbed," Luks said softly.

"And I'll put guards at each corner of the hallway as well as at the door." Kholya smiled fondly at Sheyn. "My brother will live and so will this flower. Any who wish him harm will find an enemy in me."

Luks's throat grew tight, squeezing his words small. "You're a noble man, Your Highness."

"Then I should probably claim you, shouldn't I?"

"You look happy."

Luks smiled. "I wish the same happiness for you."

"I just need a good bout of bedplay, is that your opinion?"

"That's not what I meant. You wouldn't be so troubled if you would accept your destiny."

"You keep saying that."

"But you don't believe it." Luks took Sheyn's hand.

"I don't want to." Sheyn pouted. "And I don't want to feel this way."

"What way?"

"I want to see the barbarian."

"Prince Kashyan?"

"Yes, *Prince* Kashyan, if he really is one."

"He may be a bastard, but his mother was a queen of Savaan and a princess of Macsaar before that. His blood is royal enough, especially if King Yevdjen was his father, as the rumors have it."

"It's maddening, but I actually *crave* his presence at this moment."

"I'd like to sympathize with you, but I think this is a good thing."

"He saved me." Sheyn went on as though Luks hadn't spoken. "He never hesitated even after he saw what he'd be fighting. Neither did Djenya. What kind of men do they breed in Savaan?"

"They follow the old ways in Savaan. Duty and honor are sacred. By the time their boys are five, they've been sent away to the home of a nobleman to be taught a warrior's skills. They return home at twelve and the rest of their training is up to their sires. It's not very different in Sumadin, except that Sumadinim send their sons to camps run by the military."

"So Kashyan has spent his entire life either fighting or training to fight."

"Like all Kandaari men."

"Except you," Sheyn pointed out.

"Daaksim aren't considered men."

"What?"

"We're not considered women either," Luks said hastily.

"Then what are we?"

"We're just ourselves."

Sheyn was about to retort when the guard knocked. Luks called out, and the door opened. The guard came in a few steps and held out his hand.

"Some Black Hawks brought this for Pearl," he said.

Sheyn came to take the piece of cloth, and the guard went back to his post outside the door.

"What is it?" Luks asked as Sheyn took the fabric by two corners and held it up. Luks gasped. "That's a Muergathi battle standard!"

"What am I going to do with such a thing?"

"I told you they'd go raiding," Luks said. "It's your fault if they get in trouble with their commanding officers."

"All right, but what do I do with this?"

"Send it back. Here." Luks thrust a quill pen at Sheyn.

"What am I supposed to write on?"

"The flag. Say that you're flattered, but it isn't a suitable gift."

"What would be suitable?"

"Flowers or some such, but not this!"

Sheyn smiled at Luks's indignant expression, but he wrote the note and gave the battle standard back to the guard.

THE SURGEONS were amazed at Kashyan's recovery but insisted that he remain in bed for at least one day. He wasn't pleased and asked them to send a message to his brother. Kholya responded to Kashyan's request by sending two men to escort Sheyn to his brother's bedside.

Sheyn was not happy to be woken up, and he walked between the troopers in sullen silence. The soldiers didn't intrude on what they saw as grave concern for Prince Kashyan and waited outside the door as Sheyn went in.

"You look well," Kashyan said, his gaze traveling from the top of Sheyn's head to his feet and back again.

"My injuries healed almost instantly."

"Good." Kashyan hesitated before he spoke again. He wanted to talk about how his wounds had healed so quickly, but he wasn't sure how to approach it. So he asked about something else that was weighing on his thoughts. "How is Djenya?"

"Did no one tell you?"

"What?"

"The demon killed Djenya."

Kashyan was silent for a moment. "He shouldn't have tried fighting it alone."

"If you'd let me carry a sword, Djenya wouldn't have been fighting alone."

"Go away."

Sheyn stood up.

"You saved my life," Kashyan said. "But your words cut me deeper than the demon's talons."

"I was wrong to say it. I'll leave you alone."

Sheyn walked out of the room, leaving Kashyan staring after him.

LUKS PICKED up the remains of the midday meal and crossed the room. After setting the dishes on the side table, he filled the khai pot with water and hung it over the hearth fire. He added a handful of khai leaves and came back to sit with Sheyn.

"Your visitor will be here soon," Luks said.

"What visitor?" Sheyn looked up from picking at the embroidery on his robe.

"Prince Kashyan. The physicians have released him."

"You knew of this and didn't tell me?"

"I was afraid you'd find a way to avoid him if you knew beforehand."

"Sneaky," Sheyn said, not without admiration.

"I'll be leaving soon. Prince Kholya has requested my presence."

"Leaving me alone with the savage. How convenient."

"It isn't convenience. We planned it this way." Luks smiled. "And you can save those glares. They don't affect me."

Luks spent a little time primping and then left. It seemed like moments later to Sheyn when someone knocked. The door swung open before Sheyn got to it, and Kashyan came in.

"I came to thank you," Kashyan said. "You saved my life."

"I was just keeping my end of the bargain."

"Should I take back my thanks?"

"I don't—" Sheyn clenched his hands into fists as he fought back a wave of intense emotion.

"Are you all right? If you need more rest, I can—"

"No!" Again Sheyn battled the surge of emotion. "You can stay, if you want."

"You look ill."

"Well, I'm not. I'm as fit as… as you are."

"Actually, I feel a bit weak."

"Sit," Sheyn said. "Luks made khai, if you'd like some."

Kashyan grimaced. "I hate the taste."

Sheyn found himself thinking how adorable the expression was on the big man's face and coughed again. "Is there anything you'd like?"

Kashyan met Sheyn's eyes and held his gaze for several moments before looking away.

"What?" Sheyn asked sharply.

"I don't know how to talk to you." Kashyan pushed the wild hair back from his face. "I know how to talk to a daaksi, but that doesn't work with you."

"Just say what you want to say."

"I need ale."

"Now there's a taste I can't abide," Sheyn said. "Would you like me to send for some?"

"No. If I start drinking this early in the day, Djenya will…." Kashyan's voice trailed off as he remembered that Djenya would never tease him again.

"I'm sorry," Sheyn said sincerely.

"It's just so hard to believe that he's gone. He's been at my side for ten years, since I was fifteen and put in charge of my first troop. The best lieutenant I could've hoped for and the best friend. It feels so strange without him."

Sheyn reined in hard on the impulse to put a hand on Kashyan's head and murmur something soothing. "I'm sorry," he said again and then words tumbled from his mouth faster and faster. "It's my fault he's dead. I know that. If I hadn't wanted to go outside, he'd still be alive."

Kashyan looked up with tears standing in his eyes. "Djenya couldn't have wished for a better death. He fell in battle while protecting you. And he had a foe worthy of legend."

"He was so kind to me, even if it was only because he wanted to top me."

Kashyan's lips curved up in a small smile. "He did, at that, you and the Sumadi boy both." He paused. "At the same time."

"Did he have a reputation as a lover?"

"He was a legend among the troops for his stamina and appetite. Hearts will break the length and breadth of Savaan when his death becomes known." Kashyan paused. "I should ask Kholya if he's sent a message to Djenya's family. His wife will—"

"Wife?" Sheyn sat on the cushion that Luks usually occupied. "He had a wife?"

"You're surprised?"

"Yes, but I shouldn't be. Even if he preferred boys, your culture would demand that he take a wife and do his best to get sons on her."

"Djenya loved women as much as he loved men. You look surprised again."

"Well, that is a little unusual."

Kashyan frowned. "No, it isn't."

"It is in my land."

"In your land, a man must choose between women or men?"

"Not so much choose as…." Sheyn pursed his lips. "How did we get on the subject of sex?"

"I mentioned Djenya's wife."

Sheyn shifted in his seat. His *reyl* had been growing harder since he'd sat down near the barbarian, and he was terrified Kashyan would notice. "That's right," he said. "But are you telling me that everyone in Kandaar loves men and women equally?"

"I don't know how women feel about it, or the rest of the nation, but Savaani men don't limit themselves in that way."

"That's… I'm… I'm a little surprised," Sheyn said.

"I suppose your way is better."

"I didn't say that." Sheyn shifted positions again.

"I like men," Kashyan said candidly. "Women don't stir me."

"Nor I." Sheyn picked up a pillow from the floor and held it on his lap.

"I seem to have found a way to talk to you without a fight."

"I only fight when I'm provoked," Sheyn said defensively.

"Easy," Kashyan said. "I came here because I wanted to ask you about what you did. Kholya swears you put your hands on me and healed my wounds."

"I don't know how it happened. I remember being furious that you were going to die because of me and wishing so hard that you would live. Luks tells me it was his Goddess working through me. I think that's nonsense, but I don't have another answer."

"I don't know how to say this, but since you came to see me in the surgery, I feel that I want—" Kashyan swallowed and started again. "I want to be as close to you as I can."

Sheyn looked away from Kashyan. He had a clear choice here, but which was the wiser one? In the end, he told the truth. "I feel the same."

Kashyan held out his hand. Sheyn looked at it for a moment, noting the scars and calluses and the small hawk tattoo on the web of his thumb.

"I won't hurt you," Kashyan said.

"I know." Sheyn swallowed nervously and fell back on the thing he was good at: negotiating. "I think we should redefine our bargain."

Kashyan smiled in spite of himself. "I'm listening," he said.

"Apparently, you and I are caught up in some mystical nonsense that would have me obeying your every command and being available for sex whenever you're in the mood."

Kashyan's smile broadened. "The way you talk used to annoy me so much. Now…." He chuckled. "Djenya was right. It's charming."

Sheyn narrowed his eyes. "I don't think you're taking me seriously."

Kashyan chuckled again. "You're adorable."

"Are you trying to make me angry?"

"No. Does that word offend you? Djenya used to say it to pretty girls and boys."

"So you're trying to… seduce me?"

"Why would I need to seduce you? You belong to me."

Sheyn quelled his first reaction to Kashyan's words when he saw the gleam in Kashyan's eye. "You're joking with me," he said accusingly.

"Believe me, I'm as surprised as you are."

There was silence for a few minutes, and then Sheyn spoke. "Tell me what you expect from me."

"Do as you said you would. Treat me with respect when others are around." Kashyan cleared his throat. "And I will care for you as best I can."

"Will you help me get home?"

"If it was possible—"

"Why isn't it?"

"Get the Sumadi boy to explain it."

Once again, Sheyn quashed his exasperation and tried a new tack. "All right," he said. "Until I can find a way home, I'll stay with you."

Kashyan tried suppressing his grin and failed.

"Why are you smiling? Did I say something amusing?" Sheyn asked.

"Everything you say is amusing."

Sheyn stood up. "This isn't going to work," he said.

This time, Kashyan managed not to smile. "Tell me what you expect from me," he said.

"You want my respect? Then respect me in return."

"I'll do my best." Kashyan got to his feet. "I'm going now to let my men see that I'm well, but I'd like to visit you again later."

Sheyn bit his lip, but he couldn't stop the words from coming out. "I'd like to see you too."

Kashyan smiled, and Sheyn found nothing to object to. In fact, he found Kashyan's smile incredibly attractive. There was something in the way that the barbarian's pointed canines dented his lower lip that made Sheyn's legs go weak. Sheyn couldn't recall feeling quite like this before, and it made him uneasy.

"I'll return this evening and eat with you," Kashyan said.

Sheyn nodded, not trusting his voice, and watched Kashyan walk to the door.

"You look very fetching in black," Kashyan said from the doorway, and then he was gone.

Chapter 16

SHEYN PACED a circuit around the room as he tried to sort out his thoughts and feelings about his conversation with Kashyan. It appeared that he could manipulate Kashyan to some extent, but the barbarian's attitude was so maddening. Kashyan treated him like a bright child who had little understanding of the adult world. And then there was the distressing fondness for Kashyan that grew stronger every day no matter how hard Sheyn fought it. It was even more upsetting than the undeniable physical attraction.

"Are you well?" Luks asked as he entered.

"Why wouldn't I be?" Sheyn snapped.

"Softly," Luks said. "Here, I brought you some sweets."

Sheyn eyed the bowl of honeyed fruit. "Thank you," he said at last.

Luks sat, and Sheyn came to sit beside him. When Luks offered him a piece of fruit, Sheyn took it, chewed, and swallowed.

"Very good," he said. "What kind of fruit is it?"

"They're called sun apples, but they aren't really apples. Prince Kholya has a taste for them."

"You're getting along well, then?"

"Better than I could have hoped. He's a good man and an honorable one."

"What about…?"

"The sex?"

A tint of rose warmed Sheyn's pale skin. "I don't mean to be vulgar, but I'm curious."

"What do you want to know?"

"What does he expect of you… in bed?"

"Like most men, he enjoys any attention given to his jaavi, but he's very generous with his caresses as well."

"And you like that?"

"Of course. Don't you?"

Sheyn took another piece of fruit and put it in his mouth.

Luks studied Sheyn's face for several moments. "Have you never bedded anyone?"

Sheyn almost lied, but what would be the point? "Never."

"I'm sorry. It never occurred to me that you were… green. Though it does explain many things about your behavior."

"Does it really?"

Luks reacted to the chilly tone of Sheyn's voice. "I'm not saying there's anything wrong with you."

"Aren't you?"

"No." Luks paused before he spoke again. "I'm your friend, whether you believe it or not. I'd help you, if you'd let me."

"How?"

"If there were any questions—?"

"No!"

Luks sighed. "Someday the bond between you and your master will be too strong for him to resist. When that time comes, he will have you or go mad."

"You're wrong if you think he'd force me."

"The Savaani princes are not like most Kandaari men when it comes to sex, but your master won't be able to stop himself from taking you when—"

"How can you condone this?" Sheyn interrupted. When Luks looked blank, Sheyn spoke again. "What you're describing is rape."

"No!" Luks was horrified. "I'm not saying you should be raped. The bond grows stronger with time. You won't be able to resist it, either. I see by your smile that you think me a fool, but when the time comes…."

"What?"

"You don't want to listen, so I won't waste my words."

Sheyn made an exasperated noise. "The barbarian is coming back here to take the evening meal with me. If you have any advice, I'd like to hear it."

Luks didn't look convinced, but he obliged. "As I've said before, use a gentle tone and smile at him. Wear soft clothing and don't scold him if he touches you. My best advice is to let him do as he wishes."

"What if I don't care for what he wants to do?"

"How do you know if you've never done it?"

Sheyn thought about Luks's words. "I can't argue with your logic, but still, aren't there foods you know you won't like just by looking at them?"

"Your trouble is you only want to do what *you* want to do. Sometimes, we have to do things we don't want to do."

"Within reason," Sheyn said. "I didn't want to study anatomy, but I had to when I took a course in sculpting. But it did me no harm. Submitting to a savage is a different matter."

"Is it that you don't like men in that way?"

Sheyn laughed, making Luks give him an odd look. "No, it's not that. I'm attracted to men, but Kashyan—" He paused. "He's a savage."

"So this isn't a matter of taste. You fear bedding him."

"Yes. I fear it. Are you content now?"

Luks smiled. "Your fear is normal. Don't let it hold you back, and when your master touches you, you'll catch fire just as you should."

"I've asked before, but tell me again. Do you truly enjoy it?"

"What?" Luks asked coyly.

"You know very well what I mean. When the commander takes his pleasure of you, do you enjoy it as well?"

Luks nodded. "As I told you, Prince Kholya sees to my pleasure as well as his. We may hope that Prince Kashyan is the same. If not, there are things I can teach you to gently guide him in that direction. But I think, once he sees you unclothed and willing, he'll want to please you."

Sheyn changed the subject. "I'm hungry."

Luks smiled again as he got to his feet. "It will be time for the evening meal soon. I'm going to eat with the commander. Why don't you come with me, and we'll find you a new tunic?"

SHEYN OPENED another trunk and looked inside. "Does Kholya travel with all of these?"

"No, these were stored here," Luks said. "Look at this." He held up a diaphanous gown in a color somewhere between orange and red. "This would look well on you."

"The cloth is very… thin."

"It's warm enough in our room now that you don't need heavy clothing."

"I can see through it."

"Are you ashamed of your body?"

"No, but that isn't my style." Sheyn held a black tunic to his chest. "I like this."

Luks gave the knee-length garment a critical look. "The silver embroidery is very fine," he said. "It's not what I would choose, but it suits you."

Sheyn rummaged in the trunk again and came up with a pair of black leggings. "Finally!"

"Those aren't proper for a daaksi," Luks said, knowing his words were wasted.

"I don't care. I don't like my reyl and gaerys waving about in the breeze, and I can't wear that swaddle you manage so easily."

Luks didn't argue. He helped Sheyn into the tunic, which had dozens of tiny, knotted silk buttons. Sheyn pulled on the snug leggings and a pair of soft suede boots.

"Whose clothes were these?" Sheyn wondered aloud. "They're too small for Kholya, unless he wore them as a lad."

"They're fine enough for a prince," Luks said. He glanced at the filmy gown he'd suggested. "But not exactly suitable. If I were guessing, I'd wager they belonged to a daaksi."

"That's interesting," Sheyn said as the door opened and Kholya entered. He saw the tender expression on the commander's face when Kholya caught sight of Luks, and then Kashyan came in, and Sheyn's thoughts shattered. It took all his willpower to keep from running across the room to Kashyan's side.

"Will you stay and eat?" Kholya asked Kashyan.

Kashyan shook his head. "I have other plans," he said with his gaze on Sheyn.

Kholya grinned as he put an arm around Luks's lithe waist. "Then I'll see you at muster."

"Come," Kashyan said, gesturing to Sheyn.

Sheyn bit back a smoking retort and went to Kashyan. It was almost worth it to see the look of utter surprise on Kashyan's face. "Yes, my lord?" he said softly.

"I—I've arranged for food to be sent to your quarters," Kashyan said.

"Then we should go there," Sheyn replied.

"Yes, go now," Kholya said, "while this mood lasts."

Kashyan and Sheyn left Kholya's quarters and walked the hall in silence for several minutes before Sheyn spoke.

"I wonder if we could go somewhere before we eat."

Kashyan frowned. "Where?"

Sheyn cleared his throat. "I'd like to pay my respects to Lieutenant Djenya, if that's possible."

Kashyan broke the long silence that followed Sheyn's request. "All right."

KASHYAN LED Sheyn to the fortress bailey between the outer and inner walls. Here the paving stones gave way to packed dirt, except for one area where the earth was disturbed. At one end of a mound of dirt and rock, a sword stood upright, its point thrust into the ground. Sheyn recognized the blade and knew this was Djenya's grave. Kashyan hung back as Sheyn went to rest a hand on the curved hilt while he gazed on the barrow.

Sheyn remembered the kindness Djenya had shown him. He remembered how Djenya had protected him. And he remembered his disdain for a man he'd called savage, as well as the time he'd broken Djenya's nose. He was unaware that tears were streaming down his face until a drop fell on the back of his hand. A terrible rending pain in his chest put him on his knees, and he knelt at the graveside weeping like a child.

Kashyan's heart lurched at the sight of the chilly, wasp-tempered daaksi mourning for Djenya. Feelings he had shoved aside since childhood assailed him and drew him to kneel beside Sheyn. When Sheyn looked up with tear-blind eyes, Kashyan pulled him into his arms.

For the first time Sheyn could remember, he didn't feel suffocated by an embrace. He felt warm and consoled cradled in Kashyan's strong arms. Fresh tears flowed down his cheeks as his last vestige of control melted and he sagged against Kashyan's chest.

Tentatively, Kashyan stroked Sheyn's hair. He wasn't rebuffed, so he continued the soothing gesture until Sheyn stopped shaking and leaned against him, exhausted. Kashyan rested his cheek on the top of Sheyn's head and breathed in the daaksi's alluring scent.

"I don't want to be here anymore," Sheyn said in a voice with all its bones broken.

"I'm sorry," Kashyan murmured.

"I don't want anyone else to die because of me."

Kashyan held Sheyn tighter and kissed the part in his hair. "Spare yourself this guilt," he said. "Djenya would have attacked the demon whether you were there or not."

"I want to go home," Sheyn whispered, his words muffled by Kashyan's tunic.

Kashyan rose to his feet, drawing Sheyn with him. "Come. I'll take you to your quarters."

Sheyn didn't resist but let Kashyan lead him by the hand through the halls of the fortress. When they reached the room Sheyn shared with Luks, Kashyan led him to a seat and urged him to sit. Sheyn sank down onto the soft cushion, and Kashyan hesitated a few moments before he spoke.

"Would you—?" Kashyan cleared his throat. "Do you want to be alone?"

Sheyn looked up, and his gaze sharpened as he focused on Kashyan. "No."

"Tell me what you want."

"This isn't how it's supposed to be, is it?" Sheyn gave Kashyan a faint smile. "I'm almost certain, as Velvet explained it, that I'm supposed to ask what *you* want."

Kashyan made an exasperated noise. "Speak plainly, if you can."

"I'm sorry," Sheyn said contritely. "I'm not used to feeling badly when something happens to someone else, and I was trying to make us both feel better with a jest."

"I'm sorry too. I took much worse teasing from Djenya, but you...." Kashyan shook his head. "Your teasing gets under my skin."

"Are you accusing me of being a tease?"

"Only because you are one."

"Amazing. For a few moments, you forgot to be a barbarian."

"I'm a barbarian because I tell you the truth?"

"You're right. I shouldn't call you a barbarian when what you really are is primitive."

"If I'm primitive, what are you?"

"Civilized, educated, and well-bred."

"And what use are those things to you now?"

Sheyn took a breath before he replied. "Not much, I suppose."

"I don't know what life is like where you're from, but I think it must be very different from Kandaar."

"The people of Dey Larone revere learning above all, and our nation has been at peace for over a hundred years."

"So it's hard for you here."

"Hard? Have I not mentioned that I was abducted, not once, but twice? I was made a slave, and I was tortured by a madman." Sheyn paused. "And there are demons."

"I want to alter our bargain."

Startled by Kashyan's change of tack, Sheyn remained silent as Kashyan spoke again.

"I have a heart," Kashyan said. "And it's as soft as you guessed. It isn't in me to hurt anyone smaller or weaker."

"*Everyone* is smaller and weaker than you."

"Well, some of them attack me with weapons... and there are demons."

Sheyn tried to hold on to his outrage, but like his sorrow, it had faded in the glow of Kashyan's presence. "So there are," he said. "I suppose you could be forgiven for killing them." He paused. "Would it be insensitive of me to suggest we eat?"

"If you're hungry, you should eat."

Kashyan and Sheyn moved to sit on either side of the low table, and Sheyn removed the cloth that covered their dinner. For several moments, they were silent as they ate the roasted venison and yellowroot. As Kashyan set down his empty ale mug, Sheyn spoke.

"Aside from your table manners and your habit of killing things with your sword, you're not all that barbaric, are you? I'll have to find something else to call you."

Kashyan smiled. "As you wish, Pearl."

"No, as *you* wish, Bastard."

Kashyan froze at the sound of the mocking name on the daaksi's lips. After a moment, he relaxed and smiled again. "You can't help yourself," he said. "This is why we need to talk about our bargain."

"I'm listening."

"I'm not sure you *can* behave like a proper daaksi in public."

"That sounds like a challenge."

"It *is* a challenge." Kashyan leaned forward. "You're mine now and there's nothing I can do about it, but I can't have you making me a laughingstock in front of my men."

"I understand."

"I will give you the protection of my sword and my name… such as it is."

"This doesn't sound like a different bargain."

"There is one more thing I want."

"Name it."

"You can't guess?" Kashyan leaned closer. "Don't you feel the same thing when we're close like this?"

Sheyn shivered. Another difficult decision. Did he keep Kashyan at arm's length, holding out the possibility of sex as a reward, as he'd done with Aeriq? Or should he give the man what he wanted and count on him wanting it more than once? If it came to it, could he submit to Kashyan and retain his sanity? And could he really resist the attraction much longer?

Kashyan moved around the table and put his hand over Sheyn's. "I'd like an answer."

Another shiver ran the length of Sheyn's spine, and his body made the decision for him. The warm pressure of Kashyan's callused hand on his skin made him feel as though his insides were melting. The near-constant tension in his groin was winding tighter with each passing moment. Sheyn didn't know exactly what he wanted, but he knew he wanted something. No, he *needed* something, and he needed it *now*. Raising his head, he met Kashyan's eyes.

Kashyan looked into Sheyn's depthless gaze, and a wave of emotion swept through him that was frightening in its intensity. He stopped trying to hold himself back and gave his instincts free rein. He wrapped his fingers around Sheyn's slender wrist and pulled him into his arms, crushing him against his chest.

"I… can't breathe," Sheyn managed to say.

Kashyan eased his embrace. "Forgive me."

Sheyn's soft laugh rubbed against Kashyan's ears like a fur collar. "It still amuses me that you feel the need apologize to someone you consider your property." He tilted his chin up and widened his eyes. "Are you blushing? Is that even possible?"

"I feel… very warm."

"Luks is always telling me I put too much fuel on the fire, but it's so cold here in all this stone."

"You've started a fire inside me," Kashyan said, his voice dropping half an octave.

Sheyn's laugh came out as a giggle. "Is that what passes for courting talk in Kandaar?"

A crease appeared between Kashyan's dark brows. "Forgive me again for trying to please you."

"I'm sorry," Sheyn said swiftly. "Please don't be hurt. I didn't mean to—"

Sheyn's next words were muffled against Kashyan's lips as Kashyan brought their mouths together in a kiss. At first, Sheyn was so shocked that he didn't move a muscle, but after a few moments with Kashyan's warm, surprisingly soft lips pressed to his, he became aware of an amazing feeling. It flowed outward from his core, filling him from crown to soles with a delicious rush of tingling warmth. Each following wave of pleasure was stronger than the last, and he found the anticipation between them almost as exciting as the feeling itself. Seeking more of the exquisite sweetness, he nipped hungrily at Kashyan's full lower lip.

Kashyan responded with a swipe of his tongue along the curves of Sheyn's lips before he drew back. He looked down into Sheyn's eyes for several moments before he spoke. "I want you."

Sheyn took a few breaths and decided he could trust his voice not to shake if he spoke. He wanted Kashyan too. Not for any power it would give him over the barbarian, but because at this moment, he desired Kashyan more than anything he'd ever wanted in his life. He didn't care if it was Luks's silly magical bond or if he was finally feeling what Aeriq had called "growing his horns." He didn't care why. He wanted more of this bliss.

"Tell me you want me," Kashyan said. "Or I'll feel guilty for what I'm about to do."

"Kiss me again," Sheyn answered.

Kashyan cradled the back of Sheyn's head on his palm and took Sheyn's mouth with a passion too long deferred. After opening the front of Sheyn's tunic, Kashyan pulled it off Sheyn's shoulders and down his arms. He tasted everything he'd bared as he made his way down Sheyn's long neck to his collarbone. He turned Sheyn around and embraced him from behind to kiss a route along each bare shoulder, and back to the tender nape.

Sheyn trembled in the blasts of heat that billowed outward from his center each time Kashyan's lips brushed his flesh. Bolts of pleasure shot through him at every nip of Kashyan's teeth, and when Kashyan sucked at his skin, his insides turned to quaking jelly. If not for Kashyan's arm around his waist, Sheyn was sure he would fall to the floor. His reyl was hard and aching as Kashyan's rigid length pressed to his backside.

With a hand on the back of Sheyn's neck, Kashyan bent him over the pile of cushions, putting both of them on their knees. Kashyan pulled up the hem of Sheyn's tunic and ran a hand over Sheyn's ass cheeks before he tucked his kilt up into his belt. He worked up some saliva and spat into his hand. After adding the moisture to the leaking tip of his jaavi, Kashyan gripped his rod and brought it to Sheyn's dusky-rose opening. His heart pounded like Karkaran's hooves in a battle charge, and he felt an emotion impossible to describe as he watched the head of his jaavi enter Sheyn. It was so overwhelming that for several moments he couldn't move or even draw breath.

The sensual warmth that enveloped Sheyn was pierced by a chill that shocked him back to his senses. Tensing at the sensation of terrible pressure, he fought to draw air into his lungs. Vast, dark wings beat the air, and he felt the brush of phantom feathers against his skin, the prick of sharp talons. And then he felt Kashyan's soothing caresses that gentled the pain and tamed it. These were Kashyan's hands that touched him with such eagerness, not those of a stranger. And Sheyn was no longer a child. He accepted that he wanted this, that it wasn't being forced on him, and the claws of panic released him. He sailed free, as light as a mote in a sunbeam.

Kashyan stopped with less than half his length in the reluctantly yielding channel. Drawing back, he reached for the dinner tray and dragged his fingers through a puddle of uvardin oil, smeared it on his shaft, and eased back in. The tight heat that hugged his jaavi urged him to thrust. And thrust again. And again and again as the delicious friction burned hotter and hotter, stoking his release.

Sheyn tried to brace himself against the soft cushions as the feeling of intense fullness waxed and waned with each thrust. It was no longer painful, and the rhythmic rocking grew more pleasing with each stroke. A sound somewhat like a purr rose in his throat as he instinctively pushed back against the next thrust.

Kashyan swallowed at the intense pang of pleasure that gripped him when Sheyn responded. He hadn't been this aroused since the first time he'd had sex. And for the first time since then, he loosed his grip on a pleasure slave's flank and reached under him.

Sheyn shuddered as Kashyan squeezed his reyl, and a bone-deep pulse of pleasure shot through him. He mewled in a primal request for more, and Kashyan moved his hand in a pumping gesture. Sheyn cried out at the waves of bliss that tightened his groin.

Kashyan's world had shrunk to the feeling of silken skin under his fingertips, the clutching heat that massaged his jaavi, and his mate's sounds of approval. He thrust faster and moved his hand up and down Sheyn's hard length to the same tempo.

Just when Sheyn thought he couldn't take any more of the exquisite tension without flying into pieces, the biggest feeling he'd ever felt lifted him up and suffused his body and soul with pure ecstasy. It was so big that he couldn't contain it all, and he sent it into the bond he shared with Kashyan.

Kashyan came between one thrust and the next, holding tight to Sheyn as the strongest climax of his life hit him like a lightning strike. Pleasure rolled through him like a storm on the plains, leaving serenity in its wake. It was a long time before he realized he was still leaning on Sheyn's back. "Pearl?"

A soft snore answered Kashyan. He took hold of his spent jaavi and eased it out of Sheyn. As he moved away, Sheyn shifted, groaned, and opened his eyes.

"Am I still in Kandaar?" he asked drowsily.

Kashyan nodded.

"Is the tornado gone?"

Kashyan smiled. "I won't lie," he said. "I've never felt anything like that."

"Nor I." Sheyn yawned and closed his eyes and was asleep again in moments. His body still vibrated with pleasure, and he dreamed vague dreams of being topped on the grass under the sun, on a bed of swan feathers, on a boat on a slow-moving river, completely relaxed, warm, and aroused, savoring each thrust that filled him with feverish bliss. He moaned in his sleep and moved restlessly.

Kashyan grew hard again as he watched Sheyn writhe among the cushions. He scooped the remainder of the oil from the dinner plates and coated his jaavi. Pinning Sheyn to floor on his back, Kashyan hooked Sheyn's knees in the crooks of his arms and spread his legs wide. His lust blunted by the first bout, Kashyan took his time, thrusting in short, shallow strokes until Sheyn responded. Kashyan took hold of Sheyn's stiffening rod and caressed it.

The languid rocking merged with Sheyn's half-awake dreams. He felt like he did in those times when he stroked himself to release before he fell asleep. Before long, he came in a glorious unfurling that left glistening traces on Kashyan's scarred knuckles. His interior muscles clamped down on Kashyan's hardness, and Kashyan buried his length in the tight heat. Snapping his hips, he thrust hard a handful of times and spurted in several powerful streams.

With his seed unspooling deep inside Sheyn, Kashyan gathered him into his arms and held him tightly. "Pearl," he whispered, making a vow of the name.

Sheyn made a small sound as Kashyan's cock shifted in his passage. Kashyan pulled out, and Sheyn hissed at the burning feeling as he twisted away from it. Kashyan put a hand on Sheyn's thigh and murmured soothingly, and Sheyn settled down. After a moment, Sheyn let Kashyan pull him into a loose embrace.

"Did I hurt you?" Kashyan asked.

"Yes."

"I hope you took *some* pleasure in it."

"I did. There was more pleasure than pain." Sheyn pushed his hair back from his face. "I enjoyed it even more the second time, but... I wish I'd been awake for it."

"It was sweet watching you slowly rouse to my touch."

"Still, I'd rather be consulted about when the lovemaking starts."

Kashyan gazed into Sheyn's eyes in the dim light. "I'm sorry I didn't believe you when you said you had no training." He paused. "Was that your first time?"

"Yes," he said, refusing to count the nightmare of his rape. It had nothing to do with his new life. In this world, he was someone called Pearl, who could do things Sheyn could not. "You are my first."

Kashyan wanted to be amused by the irony, but the feeling that welled up in his chest had nothing humorous in it. He felt a heart-bursting love and a fierce determination to protect this precious life bonded to his. The Bastard of Savaan snared by a daaksi. How Djenya would laugh if he were here.

"Are you displeased?" Sheyn asked when Kashyan's eyes darkened.

"No." Kashyan pulled Sheyn closer and buried his face in the pale, sweet-smelling hair. "I'm very pleased. If it was physically possible, I'd be riding you again right now."

Boldly, Sheyn reached down and cupped Kashyan's crotch. "What will you give me if I make you rise again?"

"Why don't you tell me what you want?"

Sheyn ran a fingernail the length of Kashyan's shaft. Kashyan shivered with pleasure and closed his eyes for moment just as Luks had said he would. "I want a weapon," Sheyn said.

"You don't give up, do you?"

"No, I don't." Sheyn squeezed Kashyan's sac, and Kashyan's breath caught in his throat. Growing more confident, Sheyn did as Luks advised and handled Kashyan's reyl the same way he handled his own.

"Ayeesh! There's witchcraft in your touch," Kashyan said.

Sheyn was delighted to feel Kashyan growing harder. "And you could stand in for the town bull." He paused. "What about the sword?"

"What sword?" Kashyan said in a strained voice.

Sheyn stopped moving his hand.

"This isn't honorable," Kashyan said, but he was smiling. "We'll talk about your sword in the morning. Will that be enough to please you?"

Sheyn pumped his hand a few times, and Kashyan groaned in pleasure. Surging up from the pile of pillows, Kashyan bore Sheyn to the floor and rolled him onto his stomach. He pushed Sheyn's thighs apart with his knees and then pushed into the stretched passage in one long glide. Sheyn moaned and whimpered as Kashyan thrust and withdrew. The blunt head of Kashyan's shaft dragged over delicate tissues rendered sensitive by recent use and made Sheyn react each time it rubbed the front of his channel. Sheyn squirmed, thrashed, and bucked, and Kashyan leaned forward to hold him in place. Rolling and snapping his hips, Kashyan drove Sheyn to another peak before he spent himself in Sheyn's sweet cleft. He fell asleep spooned against Sheyn's back as he nuzzled his damp nape.

Chapter
17

KASHYAN WOKE at the sound of a knock. He picked up his sword, walked naked to the door, and opened it.

"Sorry to wake you," said the guard. "A message came for you." He handed Kashyan a rolled up strip of heavy paper.

Kashyan took the message and went back to sit on the mattress next to Sheyn. He unrolled the message and read the report from his new lieutenant. When he got to the end, he crumpled it in his fist and threw it across the room.

Sheyn made a soft noise in his sleep, and Kashyan looked down at him. The faint light of the shielded lantern gilded the smooth contours of Sheyn's face and body, half-covered, half-revealed by the fur blanket. Such profligate beauty, strewn before Kashyan's gaze like a treasure of ivory and gold. It made his heart soar to know Pearl was his, but it sickened him to be in thrall to a daaksi's charms. No matter how attractive, daaksim were formed around a core of spite, and their greatest delight was making others as miserable as they were. How could it be otherwise? If Kashyan hadn't such cause to hate daaksim, he would feel sorry for the wretched creatures in their unnatural bondage.

Sheyn stirred again, and Kashyan pulled his hand back, unsure when he'd begun stroking Sheyn's silken hair. "Are you laughing at me, Djenya?" he murmured. "I wouldn't blame you. I'd laugh too if this was mere lust, but he's under my skin now, as dear to me as my own life. He may be a viper in the form of a swan, but he's mine. I'm more sure of that than I've ever been of anything, and if this is my doom, I'll have to bear it bravely."

Sheyn opened his eyes and saw Kashyan staring down at him. "Is it morning already?"

"It's early," Kashyan said. "But if you're the sort to linger over clothing yourself, you should get up."

"Where am I going?"

"Kholya's morning briefing. Several interesting things happened last night."

Sheyn smiled as he sat up. "I know." In truth, it hadn't been such an ordeal. There had been some pain, but it had faded quickly, and the pleasure far outweighed it. He felt inordinately pleased with himself, as though he'd faced some great challenge and proven equal to it.

"I wasn't talking about our coupling."

"I'll get dressed, then," Sheyn said, his contentment withering in the coolness of Kashyan's tone. He went into the next room and returned with his face freshly scrubbed. He took the black velvet robe from its peg and belted it around his waist. "I wish Luks was here."

Kashyan looked startled. "Why?"

"I like the way he braids my hair." Sheyn pulled his waist-length locks into a tail and looked about for a bit of ribbon.

Kashyan unfastened his hair clasp from his belt and handed it to Sheyn, who took the hinged ring and clamped it around his hair. The silver was cool and heavy on his nape, an oddly sensuous feeling, and abruptly, he remembered the ring Aeriq had given him in another life. For a moment, the feeling of being hopelessly lost was so intense that tears sprang to Sheyn's eyes. All the confidence he'd felt upon waking vanished like mist in the sun. What was the point of trying if he was doomed to live as some sort of bewitched slave?

"What's wrong?" Kashyan asked, his blood surging with the need to destroy whatever had put those tears in Pearl's eyes.

"I mourn for all those who pick a quarrel with you." Sheyn threw his fur cape around his shoulders. For a moment, he'd despaired, but that mood had passed. He was Rosheyn Lir of House Merisolle, but he was also Pearl, and Pearl was a fighter. "I'm ready to leave when you are."

KASHYAN PAUSED outside the council room to caution Sheyn one more time. "You'll hold your tongue, yes?"

Sheyn nodded. "Yes, my lord."

Kashyan sighed. He didn't believe Sheyn was capable of curbing his tongue, but what could he do? He knew he was being nine kinds of fool, but he had no more control over his fate than Sheyn did. Whatever he might think of daaksim, the central truth of his universe was that Pearl was his and no one was going to take him away. The corollary was that Sheyn be always in his sight. If he couldn't see Sheyn, how could he protect him? With another sigh, he opened the door and committed a breach of protocol when he led Sheyn inside. Kashyan went to his seat on Kholya's right and sat down. Sheyn stood behind him, partially hidden by the high back of the chair, but close enough for Kashyan's comfort. Kashyan ignored the stares of the council.

Kholya leaned toward Kashyan and whispered behind his hand. "You brought your daaksi to this meeting?"

"You see him at my side, don't you?"

Kholya recognized that tone in Kashyan's voice. "You'll set a new fashion, or bring back an old one," he said before he faced the room again. "As you all know by now, a man sought sanctuary at our gate last night." He called out to a guard. "Bring in the prisoner."

Kholya's officers turned their eyes to the door as a pair of soldiers escorted a man into the chamber. Halfway across the floor, the stranger froze and stared at Sheyn.

Sheyn had never seen this man before, but he felt a dark connection to him. Without knowing how he knew, he was certain this man had done him a grave wrong. "Who are you?" he demanded to know. At his outburst, Kholya's officers broke into cries of disapproval.

"Silence!" Kholya said loudly, and the racket ceased.

"Thank you," Kholya said before he turned to Sheyn. "Pearl, do you recognize him?" he asked, pointing at the man under guard.

"I don't," Sheyn said reluctantly. "But he—"

"Quiet," Kholya said. "Yozif of Djenaes. How do you know this daaksi?"

"I performed the ritual that changed him," Yozif said.

"You doomed me to life as a slave!" Sheyn shouted. "I want this man punished."

"Where is the crime in performing such a ritual?" Yozif asked.

"I didn't want to be part of your ritual!"

Kashyan reached for Sheyn's hand and touched nothing but air as Sheyn dodged aside.

"Stop!" Kholya ordered with a glare in Sheyn's direction.

"Honor the bargain," Kashyan said softly for Sheyn's ears alone.

Seething, Sheyn moved back behind Kashyan's chair, out of sight of most of the officers.

Kholya nodded permission to speak when his commander of foot soldiers cleared his throat.

"A few senior officers have been discussing this problem, sir."

"What problem?"

"The Bastard's daaksi."

"Continue," Kholya said, putting a hand on Kashyan's forearm.

"This foreigner's behavior is unacceptable, and he's inspired an unhealthy cult among some of the men. They're conducting unsanctioned raids to avenge his abduction by the priests." The commander took a breath. "And he draws the demons to us."

Kholya's grip tightened on Kashyan's arm. "That certainly deserves a discussion, but just now, we're questioning a man who came seeking sanctuary from the Red Temple. Can we continue with that business before dealing with something new?"

The officer sat back down in his seat. "I beg your pardon. I'll raise the subject again at a better time."

"Yozif," Kholya said. "Tell me why you begged sanctuary at my gate."

"Gladly. I came to Muergath to perform a service for the king in exchange for gold. I was taken to the Red Temple and brought before Taankh's high priest. He explained what was wanted and I did as he told me."

"What did he want of you?"

"He needs daaksim for one of their rites."

"And you produced them for him?"

Yozif nodded.

"Idiot!" Kashyan said. "Don't you realize you're the one responsible for the demons? Those madmen use suffering as bait to summon those—"

"No," Yozif said "That would be a horrible perversion of Her gift. Sacrilege."

"So you really are that stupid," Kashyan said.

Kholya slapped a hand on the table. "I share my brother's sentiments if not his bluntness. Surely you must have known Taankh's servants would use the daaksim for an evil purpose."

"That—that is not my concern," Yozif said.

Kholya heard Sheyn's swift intake of breath and he spoke quickly. "None of your concern? What sort of priest are you?"

"That is between me and the Goddess."

Kholya's lips thinned to a grim line. "Finish your tale. Your presence is beginning to irritate me."

Yozif swallowed. "High Priest Chanesh made more and more demands on me. I explained to him that I had no control over the magic, but he chose not to believe me. He had those heartless Red Monks bring in boys by the cartload and ordered me to perform the ritual on each of them. When the change didn't happen often enough to please him, Chanesh grew so angry that I feared him more than any demon. When I saw a chance, I ran."

"And you came straight here?" Kashyan glanced at Kholya as he spoke.

"I wasn't followed, Bastard," Yozif said. "The commander has already made sure of that."

"My brother is a prince of Savaan," Kholya said. "If you address him as anything other, you'll wish you were back in the Red Temple."

"Please accept my apology," Yozif said to Kashyan. "Whenever I've heard talk of you, you were called by that name."

"An honest mistake," Kashyan said softly. "But you and I will have words at some point for what you did to an innocent boy."

Yozif nodded as though he'd expected Kashyan's speech. "I was very surprised when Chanesh mentioned him." He nodded again, this time in Sheyn's direction. "He was meant to be a gift from the king of Sumadin to Sumadin's champion. However, when Chanesh described him, I had no doubt of who he was. There could not be two such in this world."

Sheyn returned Yozif's stare like a bird watching a snake.

"I felt Her Presence when I woke the seed of magic in you. I knew you were exceptional, and that's when the last piece of my heart died. If She could let me raise the divine spark in you, and then allow you to be sold as a slave, my faith made no sense anymore. Why would She bestow Her greatest gifts on one who had never heard Her name?"

"She can have them back if She likes," Sheyn couldn't resist saying.

"I think you'll be glad of them before the end," Yozif said.

Kashyan put a hand on the hilt of his sword. "Are you threatening Pearl?"

"Not I. I appreciate him for the miracle that he is. It's Chanesh who means him harm. If he had Pearl at his disposal, he believes he could summon Taankh himself. He plans to establish the God of Death's dominion here in this realm. The High Priest lusts after your daaksi with a fire that could burn the world." Yozif paused. "That is why I came here to warn you."

"Thank you, but we already knew that," Kholya said.

"Listen to me. Very soon, Chanesh will attack, and he'll send every imp, goblin, and demon he can conjure at you."

"We've fought them before," Kashyan replied. "They die like any other creature when you put steel to them."

Yozif smiled. "You're a good match for Pearl."

Kholya cleared his throat. "If that's all you have to say, priest, I have other matters to attend to." He gestured to the door guards. "Take him back to his room. And make sure he doesn't leave it until I give word."

"Please put me in your deepest dungeon," Yozif said. "So there's at least a possibility I'll survive the night."

"If I were you, I'd be more worried about Kashyan than the demons," Kholya said. He looked up when Sheyn touched his shoulder. "Yes?"

"Lord Commander," Sheyn said. "I'd like very much to ask this man some questions… in private."

"No," Kashyan said before Kholya could speak.

"I can't grant that request just now," Kholya told Sheyn. He signaled the guards to take Yozif away and then beckoned Kashyan closer. "I sent a bird to the high king at dawn," he said. "I've requested his permission to go into Taar Muergan and wipe out the evil at its heart."

"Good," Kashyan said, clasping Kholya's forearm as he stood.

Sheyn turned his gaze to the wall to avoid giving Kashyan a glance of pure venom. He was so angry his body felt like a clenched fist. He needed to talk to the priest. If there was any chance Yozif could reverse what he'd done, Sheyn had to know. It took all of his willpower to stand in silence as Kholya ended the meeting and his officers left the room.

"Why?" Sheyn asked without turning around.

"I can't let you be alone with that scum," Kashyan said. "Kholya agrees, don't you, Kholya?"

Kholya was conspicuously silent.

Kashyan looked at his brother. "Tell him."

"You won't like what I'm going to say." Kholya stood up. "But this is how I see it." He took his sword belt from the back of his chair and spoke as he buckled it on. "Pearl was never meant to be a daaksi. If there's some way to return him to his former life, I think it would be the best thing for everyone." He met Kashyan's eyes. "The complaints about soldiers sneaking off to raid Muergathi and Sumadi camps are real." Trusting that Kashyan got the message in his words, Kholya left to direct the installation of some new defense measures.

"I'd like to go to my room now," Sheyn said.

"I'll take you."

"I'd rather have a different escort. Can you call for Leksi?"

Kashyan swallowed the rush of jealous words that rose in his throat. "No, I can't."

"You mean you *won't*."

"I said what I meant. Leksi is dead."

"What?"

"He was missing from evening roll call. This morning, his horse returned. He was tied to the saddle. There were so many arrows in him you could see he'd been used for target practice. The monsters that captured him likely tied him to a tree and made wagers on how long they could keep him alive. On how many arrows they could put in him without killing him. On whether he'd scream or—"

"No more!"

"Why? Does it hurt?"

Sheyn turned to face Kashyan. "Yes, it hurts. What do you think I am?"

"A member of a particularly heartless breed."

"How can you say that after—?"

"You're different from any other daaksi I've known, but you're still one of them. Though I ache for you and feel as though I'd die without you, I can't trust you."

"Tell me what I've done to make you distrust me."

"You are what you are. Daaksim are deceitful by nature."

"You're a fool."

"And you lure men to destruction."

"I didn't tell Leksi to go raiding. If I had as much influence as you seem to think, I'd talk some soldier into giving me an escort to the border."

"Leksi told his friends he was going to get a Red Monk's badge for you."

"That was a stupid thing to do, but I'm sorry he lost his life for it. He was kind to me."

"This can't go on."

"Tell me what to do and I'll do it."

"I need to talk to Kholya about this. Come with me."

"Are you really going to keep me at your side, day and night?"

"Yes. Aside from personal reasons, I can't let the Temple take you again. According to some, it would mean the end of the world."

"You believe what that madman said?" Sheyn asked as they walked down the hall.

"He sounded as though he believed what he was saying."

"He's probably a spy for the Temple."

"That's why Kholya has him under guard," Kashyan said as they walked into the courtyard.

As they crossed the cobbled expanse, Kashyan and Sheyn were aware of the murmurs that sprang up around them like leaves in a whirlwind. Kashyan was on the verge of ordering everyone in the courtyard to mind his business, when Sheyn preempted him.

"I'm stopping so you can get a good look," Sheyn said in a carrying voice. "And while you look your fill at the foreigner, you can listen as well."

Kashyan looked around and saw more and more soldiers gathering to hear Sheyn's words. He was glad to see most of his Black Hawk troop waiting for him by the gate.

"I had sad news today," Sheyn said. "A warrior who touched my life lost his last night. I can't speak of his death, but I would ask you to show more care for your safety. Obey your officers' commands, and don't go raiding without orders. To hear of another death would break my heart, and I am weary of weeping."

Sheyn took Kashyan's arm as they walked out of the gate. Kashyan's troop fell in behind them as Sheyn's audience watched in silence.

"Well done," Kashyan said softly. "I'll wager the raids stop after this."

"I hope so," Sheyn said as they reached the meadow where the cavalry horses were kept. He glanced around and saw the soldiers set to guard the horses watching him. A short time ago, he would have considered their interest ill-bred, but now he knew how he appeared to them. No wonder they stared as though seeing a ghost. Meeting the eyes of the nearest man, he smiled.

The soldier smiled back, and Kashyan turned to look at Sheyn. "What are you doing?"

"Showing them I'm as human as they are."

"But you're not."

"Why are you so contrary?"

Kashyan laughed. "You're asking *me* that question?" He took Karkaran's reins from the man who held them. "Get on the horse."

"Why make him carry double? Is there a shortage of mounts?"

"Always," Kashyan said. "Don't worry about Karkaran. He's strong and we're only going a short distance."

"It's an undignified position for me and it makes me feel like a child."

"You're behaving like a child right now. Lower your voice. Everyone can hear you."

"Surely not *every*one."

"Could you once do as I ask without an argument?"

"I've done everything you've asked that made sense to me."

"Then get on the horse so we can go talk to Kholya."

"If you want me on a horse—" Sheyn's words ended in a yelp of outrage as Kashyan swept him up and set him on Karkaran's back.

Kashyan got into the saddle and took up the reins.

"Your men look suitably impressed by your barbaric behavior," Sheyn murmured.

"Should we give them a show, then? You're good at that."

"Why won't you trust me? We could be a good team if you weren't so stubborn."

"Me?" Kashyan laughed again, and the men of his troop smiled as they assembled. "You're as stubborn as the most stubborn bull I've ever met."

"Don't compare me to livestock," Sheyn said as Kashyan gave a hand signal and the Black Hawks moved out.

Kashyan led his troop down from the peak and through the line of defense closest to the castle. When they reached the tree line, they found Kholya supervising the setting of improvised catapults in a ring around the fortress. Teams of men and horses used rope to bend the tops of the limber evergreens to the ground. Slings full of rocks were attached to the treetops and fixed to the ground with stakes and ropes. Each would be manned by four warriors ready to cut the ropes at the first sign of a flying demon.

"Kasha!" Kholya called out as Kashyan rode up.

Kashyan and Sheyn dismounted, but the Black Hawks rode on to patrol the outer perimeter of sentries.

"This will make the flying beasties take notice," Kashyan said as he inspected one of the simple catapults.

"You can't really aim them," Kholya said. "But we can turn the sky to stone."

"Why don't you use black powder?" Sheyn asked.

Kashyan and Kholya turned to look at him.

"Black powder?" Sheyn repeated. "Surely you know what I'm talking about."

Kholya exchanged a glance with Kashyan.

"Ask him," Kashyan suggested.

Kholya cleared his throat and addressed Sheyn. "What's black powder?"

Some of Sheyn's scholarly demeanor returned when he answered. "It's a mixture of three minerals that burn when you put fire to them. If the powder is contained in a tube, it explodes. It's used as a weapon to hurl stones for great distances."

"That's interesting," Kholya said. "If we had such a weapon on the parapet—"

"But we don't have this black powder," Kashyan said.

"It's not difficult to make. You could probably find the minerals near to hand. Are there caves close by?"

"Are you suggesting we go mining?" Kashyan asked.

"No, we'll find what we need lying around. There's plenty of daylight left."

"Are we doing this?" Kashyan asked his brother. "Are we taking military advice from a daaksi?"

"According to legend—and Luks—giving military advice was one of the duties of the first daaksim."

"I can't imagine what it was like back then." Kashyan shook his head. "Gods walking the earth. Mountains being born. Daaksim warriors."

"I have all the excitement I need right here," Kholya said. "Why did you seek me out?"

Kashyan glanced at Sheyn. "I'd like to talk about the morale problem General Pashan brought up at the last officers' meeting."

"If we must. Ride with me back to the cavalry encampment and we'll talk on the way."

Kholya's horse was brought, and he, Kashyan, and Sheyn mounted up. They took a route that led past several sentry posts, Kholya greeting each man as they rode past. In between, Kashyan and Kholya discussed the issue of Pearl's popularity while Sheyn bit his tongue.

"I know we have a problem," Kholya said. "I'm just not sure what can be done about it."

"You can give orders forbidding the men to—"

"Forbidding them to fall in love with your daaksi?"

"That's not what I was going to say."

"I know, but it's the root of the problem."

The trail widened, and Kashyan rode up beside Kholya. "You can say it," he said. "I should have more control over Pearl. That's what you're thinking."

"No, brother. That's what *you're* thinking."

"I don't enjoy being spoken of as though I were a poorly trained pet," Sheyn said.

"Then stop acting like one," Kholya said flatly as they reached the rise that overlooked the tree-bounded meadow where the cavalry was camped. Kholya drew rein and watched the troops moving to the staging area for the morrow's march.

"I don't know what you expect from me," Sheyn said. "I don't belong here."

"But you *are* here," Kholya said. "And you may never leave. How long are you going to pretend that you can stand apart?" He turned to look at Sheyn. "The things you do here have consequences. You won't be walking away from them even if by some miracle you're restored to your former life."

Several retorts sprang to Sheyn's lips. He wanted to tell these people that they were not his equals and had no right to judge him. He wanted to remind them that he hadn't chosen this fate; it had been forced on him. He wanted to scream that it wasn't fair. In a burst of insight, it came to him that everyone must feel this way at some time in their lives.

Kashyan felt the shiver that ran the length of Sheyn's body. "What's wrong?" he asked.

"Everything," Sheyn answered. He took a deep breath. "But I can't fix it all at once, so I'll have to solve one problem at a time. It'll take a good long while, but I don't see another way."

Kashyan and Kholya exchanged another glance, communicating their bewilderment at Sheyn's words. There were a few moments of silence, broken when Sheyn spoke again.

"If you're wise, Commander Kholya, you'll do nothing about my popularity with your men. If you're shrewd, you'll encourage it and use it to your advantage."

"I'm listening," Kholya said.

"I'm sure your army is a very good one," Sheyn said. "But an army that's inspired is unbeatable. According to the philosophers, soldiers with a cause will fight to the last breath."

"I won't encourage it," Kholya said. "But neither will I forbid it. If it happens as you say, I won't complain about it." He smiled at Sheyn. "I thought myself a cynical man until I met you, Pearl." He reached across and slapped Kashyan's shoulder. "You have a rare armful there, brother. Now go and make me some of this black powder."

Kashyan nodded and turned his charger's head toward the fortress.

Chapter 18

KASHYAN RODE Karkaran into the courtyard and dismounted. As a squire ran to take the charger's reins, Kashyan turned to Sheyn. "Return to your room and try not to cause any trouble while I'm gone."

"I'm going with you," Sheyn said as he slid down from the saddle into Kashyan's arms. "I'm the only one who knows what we're looking for."

Kashyan squeezed his eyes shut for a second and then opened them again. "That's true." He looked around the square and spotted a Black Hawk. After giving the man orders, Kashyan took Sheyn to a storage chamber. A few minutes of searching through trunks yielded a thick wool tunic, leather leggings, and a pair of gloves for Sheyn. Once he'd changed clothes and found a pair of boots, they went back to the central bailey where a group of men was waiting. The soldiers listened with bemused smiles as the Bastard's daaksi explained the mission.

"Bat shit?" Kashyan said after the teams had dispersed to locate two of the ingredients on Sheyn's list.

"It's called guano. Are you ready to go mining?"

Kashyan called for his horse.

"Surely you have one spare horse I can ride," Sheyn said. "I really do feel ridiculous riding in front of you like a stolen bride."

"That's too bad, because I enjoy having your backside pressed against my crotch. Now get on the horse."

"You're really quite tiresome," Sheyn said as he put a foot in the stirrup.

Kashyan got on behind Sheyn and put an arm around his waist. "I like the way your hair smells."

"Don't start being nice," Sheyn said. "You'll confuse me."

Kashyan laughed. He still believed this daaksi would eventually betray him and break his heart, but since he had no choice in the matter, he was going to enjoy as much of it as he could.

They rode through ever-sparser trees until they reached the bare rock of the next peak in the chain. Kashyan and Sheyn got down and led the horse around the scattered boulders on the slopes of the shattered mountain.

"This looks promising," Sheyn said as they neared the truncated summit. "It's just this sort of mountain where dragon tears are found."

"Dragon tears are a real thing?"

"It's the name of a kind of rock."

"Right." Kashyan kicked a stone out of the path. "In children's tales, dragon tears look like rocks, but they can start fires. Heroes were always using them to escape from caves."

"They weren't far wrong." Sheyn walked around a boulder and saw a crack in the mountainside. "And if we're lucky, we'll find what we need in this cave."

Kashyan looked at the tall, narrow entrance. "We'll have to leave Karkaran here."

Something in Kashyan's voice caught Sheyn's attention. There was an odd note that grated on Sheyn's ear, and then he realized what it was. Kashyan was afraid to go into the cave. Sheyn could feel the waves of anxiety Kashyan exuded. Knowing the big man was scared of the dark made Sheyn see him in a new light. Instead of taunting him, he looked for an excuse to leave him outside.

"I think you should stay here and stand guard," Sheyn said. "You don't know what to look for anyway."

"Do you think I'd let you go in there alone?"

"It's nothing I haven't done before. My geology instructor was very fond of going into the fields to look at rocks."

"You are so odd," Kashyan said. He draped the reins over Karkaran's back and gave the horse a pat on the withers. "I'm ready."

They walked for what seemed a very long way, sometimes stooping over, sometimes crawling. The whole way, Sheyn could feel

Kashyan's visceral fear, and it made him edgy. He found himself imagining what would happen if they were to become trapped, and he reached for Kashyan's hand. Kashyan wrapped his fingers around Sheyn's, taking as much comfort from the touch as Sheyn did.

Sheyn was beginning to think they wouldn't find what they sought, and then, through a crack to his left, he saw something glitter in the faint light. Using the pommel of Kashyan's sword, they broke off several large pieces of the crust of yellow crystals. They put as many as they could carry into leather sacks and made their way back out. Before they reached the cave mouth, they heard a horrible noise.

"What is that?" Sheyn asked.

"The horses!" Kashyan exclaimed.

Sheyn set his sack down just inside the cave and ran toward Kashyan's charger. Kashyan was already in the saddle and reached down to pull Sheyn up. At a reckless speed, they headed back to the meadow.

The cavalry camp was a scene of chaos. The soldiers struggled to get their horses to safety while fighting the pack of goblins that swooped down on them. Kashyan put Sheyn on the ground, drew his sword, and rode into the battle.

Sheyn cursed as he tumbled to a stop. Getting to his feet, he ran toward the fighting. When he came upon a wounded warrior leaning against a horse, he stopped. Driven by a sudden compulsion, Sheyn put a hand over the man's heart and left it there for a few moments. A nimbus of light appeared around his hand, and he felt an odd sensation, like the prickling that follows numbness. The warrior opened his eyes and gazed at Sheyn with a look of wonder. For a long moment, they looked into each other's eyes, locked together by the kindling miracle.

A shout of pain startled Sheyn, and he spun around to see a man knocked off his feet by a goblin. The soldier's sword flew from his hand and landed near Sheyn's feet. Sheyn didn't hesitate to pick it up and use it. Running forward, Sheyn leaped into the air and cut at the goblin's tail as it flew up. The hideous creature wailed in pain and flapped its leathery wings harder as the tip of its hairless tail fell to the ground. With a gobbling growl, the dog-sized demon dove on the downed trooper, and Sheyn lunged at it. The tip of the saber pierced a wing membrane, and Sheyn drew it downward in a long slice. The goblin retreated upward again, and Sheyn kept his gaze fixed on it.

When the monster swooped down to attack, Sheyn whirled away from the snatching claws and brought the sword around in an arc that nearly severed the thing's neck. It flapped slowly away with its head hanging gruesomely upside down. A moment later, it crashed to the ground and lay still.

"Are you all right?" Sheyn asked the soldier as the demon began to liquefy.

The young man stared at Sheyn in utter astonished silence.

"I have to go. Help that man get to safety." Sheyn pointed at the man he'd healed and sprinted toward Kashyan.

Karkaran was the only horse unaffected by the presence of the demons. While the other animals squealed and ran about in fright, the blue roan charger kept his head and obeyed his rider's commands. Kashyan was holding off three goblins while several troopers fought to get their mounts under control.

As Sheyn arrived, the trio of demons finally hit upon the idea of working together instead of diving on Kashyan one at a time. Sheyn launched himself from a flat-topped boulder and pulled Kashyan from the saddle. They struck the ground hard and flew apart. The three goblins collided in midair and fell to earth. One landed in front of Karkaran and was promptly trampled. The other two stunned monsters were cut down by warriors on foot. As Kashyan and Sheyn got to their feet, the remaining goblins rose up in a swarm, filling the air with shrill cries that spooked the last of the horses into bolting.

"What are they doing?" one of the soldiers shouted.

The question was answered as the small demons swooped down in a mass of slashing claws and gnashing fangs. For a few hectic moments, the humans on the ground swung their weapons while the goblins poured down on them. The overhead onslaught ended, but there was no respite as the grounded demons leaped at the soldiers. It was wet, grim work with little hope of victory, and then Kholya arrived with archers.

Kashyan lowered his sword as the last goblin was spitted by three arrows in quick succession. At his back, Sheyn relaxed and took a long, shaky breath. He didn't protest when Kashyan turned and put a steadying arm around his waist.

"So it wasn't a fluke, brother," Kholya said as he dismounted next to Kashyan and Sheyn. "Your daaksi can handle a blade."

"I should be able to," Sheyn said. "I've been taking lessons since I was eight."

"No one's going to tease you for getting a late start," Kholya said, and Kashyan laughed.

Before Sheyn could reply, the owner of the borrowed saber arrived.

"I wanted to say thank you," the soldier said. "Pearl saved my life."

"Thanks for the loan of your sword," Sheyn said as he offered the saber on his palms. "What's your name?"

"Dasha," the young man said as he took the sword with a mixture of awe and reverence.

"I'm glad you're not dead, Dasha," Sheyn said. "The Horde of the Hawk needs all its brave warriors."

"Go find the rest of your company, trooper," Kholya said.

Dasha saluted the commander with his saber. Stealing a last glance at the glowing daaksi, Dasha left to spread the tale of his rescue, embellishing it with details such as Pearl's eyes flashing like lightning, and the way he moved too quickly for the eye to follow. By evening meal, Pearl had grown wings and dispatched demons with bolts of fire from his hands. The soldier Sheyn had healed came forward with his story, and the legend grew by leaps and bounds. When Sheyn rode through the fortress gate with Kashyan, everyone stopped to watch them and a spontaneous cheer went up.

Sheyn and Kashyan began working on the black powder after the demon attack, and they'd just finished the first batch. Sheyn's face was smudged with charcoal, and he longed for a bath, but he smiled and waved as he walked slowly into the fortress.

"It's been a hard day," Kashyan said. "If you want to rest, I understand."

"Give me a little time to bathe and then come to me."

Kashyan grinned. "I hoped you'd say something like that."

"Go wash off the dragon tear smell." Sheyn wrinkled his nose. "And bring food."

"I will." Kashyan watched Sheyn enter his quarters and left him there.

"Luks," Sheyn called out. "I know you're here. I can smell that incense you like so much."

"Why are you shouting?"

Sheyn went into the next room and found Luks in a nest of cushions. "I need a bath."

"I can see that." Luks took a sip from his cup. "Would you like anything to eat first?"

"No. I need to be clean."

Luks got to his feet. "Come with me."

"Where are we going?"

"The engineers repaired the bathhouse."

"I'm shocked you'd suggest such a thing as bathing in public."

"There's a private bath for us."

"Of course. I should have guessed."

"You're in a pleasant mood."

"Am I?"

"I told you you'd be happier once you accepted the bond."

"Yes, yes, you're very wise," Sheyn said as he and Luks walked under an arched entry. He could smell the water and itched to be in it. "Which way?"

Luks took Sheyn's hand and led him to a room with a small pool in the center. Wisps of steam curled up from the surface of the water, and the air was lightly scented with a flowery perfume. Sheyn lost no time in dropping his robe and stepping into the pool. Luks watched for a moment before he joined him, enjoying Sheyn's childlike delight in immersing himself in water.

"Tell me," Luks invited as he and Sheyn leaned back against the edge of the pool to soak.

"First tell *me* how anyone heated this much water in this benighted castle."

"There are tubes that bring hot water in from the pools in the mountain."

"Ah, I see."

"You don't seem surprised at all."

"Because it isn't surprising. These are young mountains as the earth counts such things."

Luks stared at Sheyn. "One moment you sound perfectly reasonable, and the next, you start talking about young mountains."

"It's your ignorance that makes me sound strange."

"And it's your careless manner that keeps me from weeping at your cruel remarks."

"What?" Sheyn turned to look into Luks's eyes.

"When you insult me, it's with such lack of emotion that I feel foolish taking offense. Yet, it still hurts."

"I don't understand. When have I insulted you… recently?"

"A few moments ago, you called me ignorant."

"You *are* ignorant. That's not an insult. It's an observation."

"Well, it isn't very pleasant to be observed by you."

"Should I stop speaking the truth, then?"

"You could be kinder about it." Luks reached behind him for a cake of soap. "No one likes to be told he's ignorant, or backward, or a savage."

Sheyn's immediate impulse was to tell Luks to educate himself and behave in a civilized manner, but he held his tongue.

"Sit on the step and I'll wash your hair for you," Luks said to make up for what he said next. "Suppose I constantly reminded you that your nose is long? Or that your voice can be as harsh as a snarling dog? Or that you're never satisfied?"

Sheyn did as Luks instructed. "Is that how you think of me?" he asked as Luks worked the lather into his scalp.

"Sometimes."

Sheyn drew his knees up and rested his crossed arms on them. "I've never thought much about it, but all my life I've been surrounded by people who did nothing but praise me." He smiled. "I've always been the brightest, most sought-after person in whatever group I was in. My parents, my teachers, my friends all treated me like…." Sheyn paused. "No one has ever told me I was wrong, or that there was a thing I could not have. The one time my parents withheld their permission, I defied them, and that is what brought me here."

"Relax and lie back," Luks said softly. He supported Sheyn's shoulders as Sheyn let his feet float up. Letting Sheyn's head sink a bit, Luks rinsed the suds from his hair. "I don't think you're a bad person. And I don't think you're being punished."

"Why don't you think that?" Sheyn righted himself in the waist-deep water. "Doesn't it fit neatly into your religious views?"

Luks splashed Sheyn in the face.

"What did I say now?" Sheyn asked as water dripped from his chin.

"You were looking down on my faith again." Luks chuckled at the expression on Sheyn's face. "But it's all right. I truly believe you can't help it. You're just naturally arrogant."

"Never mind that. Do I still have charcoal on my face?" Sheyn said.

"A little smudge here and there." Luks took up the soap again and washed Sheyn's face. "There. Your skin is as fair as snow again." He tilted his head. "Actually, it's more like cream. You've been spending a lot more time outdoors."

"Don't tell me daaksim aren't allowed to tan their skin."

Luks laughed again. "No, that's not one of the rules. Are you hungry?"

"I could eat half a horse on toasted bread."

"I'm not surprised. Rumor has it that you defeated an army of demons single-handed."

"That's not true," Sheyn said as he got out of pool and offered Luks his hand. "The Bastard helped out where he could."

Luks pulled Sheyn back into the pool and climbed out while Sheyn was getting his feet under him.

"That wasn't very nice," Sheyn said as he pulled wet hair away from his face.

"No it wasn't," Luks replied. "But it was oddly satisfying." He held out a hand to Sheyn, only to pull it back when Sheyn reached for it. Laughing at the expression on Sheyn's face, he walked away from the pool to wrap himself in a large square of cloth.

Sheyn dove beneath the surface before emerging from the pool near where Luks was brushing his wet hair. He wrapped himself in his robe, made a rope of his hair, and squeezed out as much water as he could.

"I'll comb it for you in front of the fire when we get back to our quarters," Luks said.

"I'd like that," Sheyn said as he followed him out of the bathhouse. "Kashyan is coming to visit me later."

"You needn't worry that I'll hang about. I'll be staying in Prince Kholya's quarters."

"That's become a habit."

"I can tell when you're teasing me now." Luks gave Sheyn a sideways glance. "What are you planning to wear?"

"Plan?"

"You really are hopeless. Luckily, you have me to keep you from looking so ignorant." Luks took Sheyn's hand again and led him away. "Just do as I instruct, and you and Prince Kashyan will both be well-pleased."

KASHYAN OPENED the door to the daaksim's room and gestured for the guards to bring the trays inside. When the guards returned to their posts, Kashyan looked around for Sheyn. "Pearl?" he called in a voice very much unlike the one he used on the battlefield.

"I'm in here," Sheyn called from the next room. "And I'm too warm to move."

Kashyan grabbed one of the trays and a pitcher and carried them through the curtained entrance to the next chamber. His heart leaped and he nearly dropped the tray when he saw Sheyn sprawled across a large cushion in front of the brazier. The flames licked Sheyn's pale skin with tongues of red as he rolled onto his side.

"I hope it's all right," Sheyn said. "Luks tried to help me choose a robe, but after my bath, I didn't want to wear anything." He met Kashyan's gaze and smiled at the hunger he saw there. "No playing about until after I eat. I had an entire loaf that was left from Luks's midday meal and I'm still starving."

Kashyan set the tray down beside Sheyn and pulled off the cloth. "Start eating," he said. "I'll go get the rest of it."

When Kashyan returned, Sheyn looked up from the roast fowl he was tearing right off the bone with his teeth. "Wonderful," Kashyan said with genuine admiration. He had no use for dainty manners, and he preferred Sheyn's lean, hard angles to Luks's softer curves. Making himself comfortable among the cushions, he poured a cup of ale.

"I have a quarrel with you," Sheyn said after he wiped grease from his mouth.

"What have I done?"

"You've not kept your promise."

"What promise?" Kashyan bit into a sun apple and squeezed some of its juice into his cup.

"When I gave myself to you the first time, you promised me a sword."

"No, I didn't."

Sheyn sat up and sheaves of pale hair shifted, half veiling his body. "You deny it?"

"I said we'd speak of the possibility of a sword for you."

"Then speak." Sheyn paused. "My lord."

Kashyan grinned. "Giving orders comes so naturally to you," he marveled.

"Don't change the subject. I want a sword."

"This instant?"

"I wouldn't mind."

Kashyan chuckled. "I suppose you'll threaten to deny me your body if I refuse."

"I'd never make such a vulgar bargain… again."

Kashyan laughed heartily. "It's no secret that I desire you, but damn me if I haven't grown fond of you as well. Kholya was right."

"I see." Sheyn picked out a honey cake and reclined against a bank of pillows to nibble at it. "Would you say you're as fond of me as… your horse?"

Something in Sheyn's voice warned Kashyan that quicksand lay somewhere along this path. "Yes," he said cautiously.

"If something was causing him pain, such as a sharp bit or a shoe nail, you'd remedy it."

"Yes."

"Then why do you deny me the thing that will give me the greatest comfort?"

"A sword?" Kashyan guessed.

"Surely you can imagine how vulnerable I feel without a weapon."

"I've heard some daaksim carry jeweled daggers. Would you like one of those?"

"How can I make you understand?" Sheyn said in frustration. "How do I make you see me as a person? You'd never deny a man the means to defend himself, but you do it easily enough to me. Why?"

"You don't need a weapon. I'm here to protect you."

"I'm not a chest filled with gold and jewels. I can defend myself if you'll let me." Sheyn clenched his fists. "It maddens me that I'm forced to ask permission."

"I can see that." Kashyan took a drink and set his cup down. "By law, you belong to me, which makes you a slave. Slaves cannot carry weapons."

"*Your* law," Sheyn retorted. "Not mine. I refuse to—" His words broke off as he remembered what Kholya had said to him earlier that day. The full reality of his situation hit him again. He couldn't send for his parents, or Aeriq, or an agent of Eastern Coach to come and fetch him. And worse, he had no one but himself to blame for his plight.

Sheyn felt a pang of despair, but instead of fighting it, he let it bloom and fade. When it had passed, he replaced it with renewed resolve. If this was to be his home, he would have to shape it to his liking or let it shape him.

"Pearl?" Kashyan said softly so as not to startle Sheyn. The look in Sheyn's dark eyes was enough to spook the battle-hardened warrior.

"I'm sorry," Sheyn said as he focused on Kashyan. "Did you ask me something?"

"Do you know what maddens *me*? It maddens me that you affect me. I can't put you out of my mind, no matter how hard I try. You confuse my head, and my body aches for you. If you're out of my sight, I can barely stand it."

"I don't think that's my fault."

"Why couldn't you be an ordinary daaksi like Luks? If you were biddable and waited on my pleasure, I could dismiss you, but you put yourself forward at every turn, and you're smart, so smart you frighten me sometimes. You're brave as well and unlike anyone I've known."

"That's...." Sheyn swallowed. "That's the most wonderful thing anyone has ever told me."

Kashyan widened his eyes at this unexpected response. "I'll never understand you."

"Even so, will you take pleasure with me?"

Kashyan grinned and lunged over the tray to pounce on Sheyn. "To your heart's content," he growled as he crouched over Sheyn.

Sheyn looked up into Kashyan's eyes. "You've been very good to me, by your lights," he said.

"I thought we were done with words."

"Then you don't know me well enough yet." Sheyn smiled. "Now listen, because I'm trying to thank you."

Kashyan let some of his weight rest on Sheyn. "I can think of a way you can thank me."

"Easy," Sheyn said softly. "This isn't a race." He reached up to stroke Kashyan's shaggy hair. "Thank you for being patient with me. I know by your law you can do whatever you like with me, but you endured my insults and outrageous behavior. Never mind that I think your laws and customs are backward and barbaric. You could have had me in chains, or even chopped my head off, but you chose to bear it… for the most part. Do you understand what I'm saying?"

"Probably better than you think." Kashyan rolled his hips, rubbing his hardness against Sheyn's crotch. "If it makes a difference to you, I don't think of you as a slave."

Sheyn blinked back the tears that filled his eyes. He wanted to be annoyed that the barbarian's opinion meant so much to him, but his heart didn't have room for petty emotions right now. He put a hand around the back of Kashyan's neck and pulled him down into a kiss. He molded his lips to Kashyan's and did his best to convey the passion he was feeling.

"No one has ever stirred me the way you do," Sheyn said breathlessly when the kiss ended.

Kashyan knelt between Sheyn's thighs and pushed Sheyn's legs apart. He was surprised when Sheyn sat up and knocked him over. He was even more surprised when Sheyn removed his belt and his leather kilt. Kashyan collapsed onto his elbows with a long groan of pleasure when Sheyn grasped his jaavi.

Sheyn gazed on Kashyan's face, noting the changes of expression as he moved his hand on Kashyan's reyl and gaerys. Gathering his nerve, he did as Luks had shown him and lowered his head to kiss the tip of the shaft. Encouraged by Kashyan's response, he enveloped the head in his mouth and tongued it thoroughly, before taking it deeper. Luks had warned Sheyn, so Sheyn wasn't surprised when hot liquid splashed the back of his throat. He swallowed quickly, as Luks had advised, and was gratified by Kashyan's unreserved reaction.

Kashyan wrapped a strand of Sheyn's hair around his finger and drew Sheyn up to crouch over him. He pulled Sheyn's head down for a kiss that went on for several heartbeats.

"Witch," Kashyan said, his lips moving against Sheyn's.

Sheyn smiled. "That's Luks's delusion, not mine."

"If you aren't casting a spell on me, how is it I'm still hard?"

Sheyn flexed his thigh muscles and dragged his hard length over Kashyan's. Kashyan clamped an arm around Sheyn's lower back and took hold of his jaavi with the other hand.

"Wait," Sheyn said as Kashyan tried blindly to enter him.

"For what?" Kashyan frowned in puzzlement. "Don't you want to?"

"In time." Sheyn smiled. "First let's talk about my horse."

Kashyan laughed and rolled Sheyn over. "A sword. A horse. What else do you want, Pearl?"

"I want to be loved."

Such sweet yearning was in Sheyn's gaze that Kashyan nearly confessed his love. But the bitterness in him whispered that deception was part of a daaksi's nature and pretending to be in love was what they did best.

"You're mine." Kashyan contented himself with these words as he claimed Sheyn's mouth again. Rolling onto his side, he pinned Sheyn's thigh with his knee and rested a hand on Sheyn's chest. As he thrust his tongue into Sheyn's mouth, he ran his hand slowly down Sheyn's body, wrapped his fingers around Sheyn's arousal, and stroked it firmly.

Sheyn wanted to ask Kashyan to stop, to slow down, to make this wonderful feeling last just a little longer, but it felt so good that he didn't really want it to stop. And then the escalating feelings of pleasure peaked, and he exploded, thrusting into Kashyan's fist as he came in several strong spurts.

"So beautiful," Kashyan said as he reached up to trace the line of Sheyn's cheek.

Sheyn was filled with a sweet languor that made him disinclined to move or speak. He sank into the pillows, his eyelids drooping and his limbs sprawled wide. Supremely relaxed, he looked up at Kashyan from under his lashes and gave him a drowsy smile.

"You shall have your sword," Kashyan murmured as he seated the tip of his rod against Sheyn's dimpled port. "And a horse, even if I have to go raiding for it." He leaned forward and breached the ring of muscle that guarded Sheyn's passage. "For good or ill, you also have my love, if a fool's love is what you want."

Sheyn moaned as Kashyan forged ahead, finding the act much more pleasurable since Luks had shown him how to prepare himself. Being oiled and stretched beforehand spared Sheyn the uncomfortable part of being topped and allowed him to enjoy the action from the beginning. He found he enjoyed being *taken*, as Luks termed it, and his reyl got hard again as Kashyan inched forward.

"That's all of me," Kashyan said. "I'll give you a moment to catch your—"

"Move, Bastard!" Sheyn commanded, smacking his palm against the floor. "Let me feel you moving in me."

Kashyan obliged, thrusting in long, firm strokes, pulling back to the brink before plunging back in. Cradling Sheyn's hard shaft in one hand, Kashyan cupped his other hand under Sheyn's ass and lifted it off the cushion. Rolling his hips and flexing his thighs like a long-distance rider, Kashyan advanced and withdrew to a sweet and steady rhythm.

Sheyn moaned with pleasure each time the head of Kashyan's cock rubbed against the front of his passage while Kashyan pumped his arousal. Getting the soles of his feet against the floor, Sheyn gave Kashyan something solid to push against as he tilted his pelvis to a better angle. It seemed impossible that the feelings of pleasure could increase, but they became more intense each time he found joy with the barbarian prince. The more he learned about Kashyan, the more he liked him, and the feelings grew ever stronger.

"G-great Leynys," Sheyn stammered. "I didn't know I could feel this good."

Kashyan's eyes glowed with pride. "I'm going to make you feel even better," he said. Doubling his speed, he shuttled his hand up and down Sheyn's hard length while slowing his hips until just the tip of his jaavi was moving in and out.

Sheyn's breath came short and fast as he yearned for release. He thrust in an attempt to take in more of Kashyan's cock, but Kashyan pulled back and shifted positions. Lifting Sheyn's calves to his shoulders, Kashyan took hold of Sheyn's rod again.

"Come ride with me," Kashyan said as he stroked Sheyn. A needy little whimper escaped Sheyn's lips, and Kashyan resumed thrusting.

"Thank you!" Sheyn said breathlessly and then lost himself in the waves of pleasure that crashed through him each time Kashyan thrust. Caught up in all-consuming bliss, he could almost believe Luks's babble about mystical power. He couldn't deny the connection he felt with Kashyan as they moved together toward the same goal. He could feel Kashyan's excitement climbing higher and higher, matching his own eagerness to reach the summit. Giving his instincts free rein, Sheyn reached another level in which he felt joined to Kashyan in body and spirit, sharing his feelings, his thoughts, and his memories. The communion grew almost too intense to bear, and then Sheyn crested in an explosion of pleasure that overwhelmed him and spilled over into the link. Sheyn felt Kashyan climax a moment later, and Kashyan's joy crashed into him like a wave on the shore. He felt drained and yet full of fire. He couldn't move, but if Kashyan asked, he'd stretch out his hand and pluck a star for him. He could do anything, but all he wanted to do was float in this timeless limbo of contentment.

Kashyan shifted, and Sheyn made a wordless sound of displeasure. "I'm sorry," Kashyan said. "I don't want to crush you."

Sheyn wrapped his arms and legs around Kashyan and burrowed his face into the crook of Kashyan's neck. As slowly as ice melting, Kashyan disengaged by tiny increments, placating Sheyn with little pats and strokes when he fidgeted. At last, Kashyan was able to roll onto his back and relax. He gathered Sheyn into his arms and held him close until morning came and a loud bang woke them.

"What *is* that noise?" Sheyn mumbled.

"There's someone at the door," Kashyan said.

"Kill them for me." Sheyn nestled into the cushions and went back to sleep.

Kashyan stepped naked into the hall to speak with Kholya's messenger. After a few words, he sent the man away and went in to get dressed. As he threw his cloak over his shoulders, he felt the unfamiliar weight in the left-hand pouch, and he glanced at Sheyn. The gift would have to wait until later. The Savaanim had visitors.

Chapter
19

"WHAT TOOK him so long?" Kashyan said as he and Kholya gazed down on the camp of the Sumadinim just beyond the tree belt.

"Ognyan must have been delayed trying to get his queen with child," Kholya answered.

Kashyan spared a thought for the woman who'd been passed to the man who'd claimed her husband's throne before it grew cold. He supposed, if she became pregnant, she would fear for the life of her son with the former king. A short time ago, her plight wouldn't have entered his mind. It would have been simply the natural consequence, but now Kashyan felt pity for the bereaved Sumadi queen. And he felt guilty for killing her husband.

"Save that scowl for Ognyan," Kholya said. "What is in your thoughts?"

"I had to kill Yevdjen."

"I know. I'm still not happy you killed him, but I know your honor demanded it."

"I did it for our mother." Kashyan shook his head. "Now I'm not sure it's what she would have wanted."

"It's done, little brother. Don't get into a brood." Kholya slapped Kashyan on the shoulder. "Go back to your daaksi. He always manages to get your blood up."

"It's only one of his many virtues."

"Can this be the same man who swore he'd never succumb to daaksim charms?"

Kashyan grinned. "I'm still a little upset that I'm no stronger than any other man when it comes to resisting a daaksi's wiles, but I'll not struggle against it. Because you're right. Pearl suits me." He reached under his cloak. "What do you think of this?" he asked as he held out his hand.

Kholya picked up the old-fashioned hair clasp and held it to the torchlight. It was a simple design of a silver crescent that wrapped around the hair and was secured with a separate wooden pin thrust through it. The pin was ornamented with silver filigree, and a large pearl hung from the knobbed head. "It's beautiful," Kholya said. "Pearl will like it."

"What a relief." Kashyan put the clasp away. "Now let's talk about the lesser problem. What do you want to do about Ognyan?"

"Frankly, I never thought he'd bother seeking vengeance since you gave him what he wanted when you killed Yevdjen."

"Or maybe he just took advantage of the situation to claim the crown."

Kholya shook his head. "Ognyan's seizing of power was quick and smooth, as though it had been planned for years, which I believe it was."

"Then why do you think Ognyan came all this way with an army?"

"I'm sure he'll tell us when he's ready."

"Did you really call me up here just to look at some Sumadinim scurrying around like ants?"

"I have a decision to make and I'd like to hear what you think."

"I'm not known for my wisdom."

"I wanted you to see how far away the Sumadinim are before I asked my question." Kholya crossed his arms over his chest as he gazed out over the evergreen forest. "Do we go, or do we stand and fight?"

"I assume you're talking about organizing the men to slip away in groups over the back of the mountain to meet up with the wagons on the border of Savaan. That would be very risky and the last few might be trapped here. On the other hand, I hate a siege." Kashyan paused. "I could join the Black Hawks at the cavalry camp, and we could raid the Sumadi army in surprise strikes. We know this ground. It'll be child's play to attack them and get away."

"I like the idea. It'll keep you from being penned up here where you'll be a bigger danger than the army outside."

"Make fun of me. I'm used to it."

"That reminds me… what will you do with Pearl while you're off raiding?"

"Raas blast it!" Kashyan smacked his palm against the parapet wall. "I have no choice. He goes with me."

"If you're taking Pearl with you, promise me one thing." Kholya smiled. "Save a few Sumadinim for the rest of us."

"I'll see that he spares a few."

"Do I have your answer?"

Kashyan nodded.

"Then we're in agreement. I'd rather fight in the open, but there's a chance this won't turn into a siege. I think with enough men outside the gates, we can hammer Ognyan like iron on an anvil." Kholya smiled again. "And besides, I just got comfortable here."

"I'm going to get Pearl and leave as soon as I can."

Kholya gave Kashyan a hug and let him go. Kashyan left, giving orders to a sergeant to have his gear packed and his horse saddled. After a moment's thought, he requested a second mount and went to find Sheyn.

"My lord!" Luks exclaimed when Kashyan strode into the antechamber.

"Where's Pearl?"

"We just returned from the bath." Luks nodded toward the next room.

"Who are you talking to?" Sheyn asked as he appeared in the doorway. His gaze went to Kashyan, and he smiled. "Back so soon? People will gossip."

"You're coming with me for a few days," Kashyan said. "Wear clothing suitable for riding." He glanced at Luks. "Don't let Pearl dawdle. I'll be back in a few minutes."

Luks stared at the door that closed behind Kashyan. "Great Goddess!"

"Was he serious?" Sheyn asked as he drew a comb through his hair.

"Let's act like he was." Luks gave Sheyn a shove back into the other room. "Find your outdoor boots. You can wear those leather leggings, and I'll see if I can find…." He began sorting through the chest of clothing Sheyn had collected.

When Kashyan returned, Sheyn was dressed in a singlet of knitted silk under a thigh-length tunic of thick wool over leather leggings and knee boots. Kashyan approved but took the fur cloak away from him.

"Wear this," Kashyan said, handing Sheyn a weatherproof cavalry cloak. "And this." He held out a sword belt with a slender, curved scabbard.

Sheyn closed his fingers around the wire-wrapped pommel as though shaking hands with an old friend. He drew the blade smoothly from the sheath and held it at arm's length as he ran his gaze down the gleaming length of metal. The saber was light, well-balanced, and without blemish. Sheyn flexed his wrist, and the sword did his bidding almost effortlessly. "I like it," he said.

"It was made for Kholya when he was sixteen, but he grew so much that year that he switched to the broadsword. It's a tradition in my family." Kashyan took the hair clasp from his pocket. "I'm spoiling you, but I see no reason you shouldn't have this now."

"It's beautiful!" Sheyn took the clasp and went to admire it in the mirror.

Kashyan turned to Luks. "You did a good job."

"Thank you, my lord."

"My brother tells me you treat him well."

"I do my best."

"My thanks." Kashyan raised his voice. "Pearl! No time for primping."

Luks handed Sheyn a leather pouch with a few items Luks deemed essential, among them a hair comb and a bottle of oil. "Take care," Luks said.

"You can be sure of it," Sheyn said. "Don't cause trouble while I'm gone."

Luks pretended to be offended and turned to Kashyan. "Take care of him, my lord."

"I intend to. That's why he's going with me." Kashyan chucked Luks under the chin. "Just take care of Kholya, and Pearl will be back soon."

Luks kissed Sheyn's cheek. "Remember what I said about—"

"I remember everything you say." Sheyn smiled at Luks and then followed Kashyan.

"Don't dawdle," Kashyan said as he walked swiftly down the hall.

Sheyn matched Kashyan stride for stride until they reached the courtyard again. Kashyan's charger was waiting, laden with a pair of saddlebags, a quiver of javelins, and a large bedroll. Next to the warhorse was a tall gray courser with a bridle and saddle of black leather. Sheyn glanced at Kashyan, and Kashyan nodded. Smiling delightedly, Sheyn went to the gray horse and made his acquaintance. The gelding seemed to approve of Sheyn, accepting half a honey cake and standing docilely as Sheyn got into the saddle. Sheyn put his saber in the sheath sewn to the saddle skirt and noted the pair of long knives, one on each side of the pommel.

"Thank you," Sheyn said to Kashyan.

"He's yours until the couriers need him again. There should be a pair of gloves tucked away somewhere."

Sheyn found the gloves under the sheepskin saddle pad and put them on, snugging them down between his fingers and pulling the cuffs up. The leather was supple but thick enough to protect his hands from rein burn and long enough to save him the sting of a bowstring. He looked up when Kashyan spoke to him.

"I'm not taking you with me on a whim," Kashyan said. "This will be hard on you, but I can't bear to leave you here. We'll be living in the saddle except for a few hours' sleep in the middle of the day. It'll be rough, but I won't let anything happen to you."

"I know you won't."

"Are you ready, then?"

Sheyn nodded.

"We're going out the postern gate and making our way along the back of the ridge. We don't want Ognyan's scouts knowing we're leaving the fortress."

"Ognyan!"

"I assumed you'd heard already. The Sumadinim are camped just below our outer ring of sentries. They haven't declared their intentions yet, but it seems plain what they want."

"Your head?" Sheyn guessed.

Kashyan didn't answer. He was looking up at the wall where a sentry was raising a horn to his lips. The signal for approaching enemy riders rang out against the stone, and Kashyan leaped down from the saddle. As Kashyan ran for the stairs, Kholya charged out of the fortress with his sword in his hand. Kashyan waved to Kholya and they climbed to the parapet together. After a few moments, Sheyn followed them.

"Kholya of Savaan!" called out the herald at the head of the small party of Sumadi nobles. "King Ognyan requires speech with you."

"That's Sumadi manners for you," Kholya said to Kashyan. "I suppose I should see what they want."

"Stay out of arrow range," Kashyan said. "Sumadi honor is a lot like Sumadi manners. They have none."

"We really should talk about your cynicism, little brother." Kholya stepped forward and raised his voice. "I'm Prince Kholya and leader of the Horde of the Hawk. What says Ognyan of Sumadin to me?"

"*King* Ognyan!" roared the big man in the center of the Sumadi delegation.

"Come and say it to my face," Kholya invited.

Ignoring the protests of his officers, Ognyan spurred his horse forward until he was beside the herald. "I'll shout your shame to the Gods," he told Kholya.

"Be so kind as to tell me first."

"You know your offense. You're hiding the man who killed King Yevdjen."

"Hiding?" Kashyan came to stand next to Kholya. "All the world knows where the Bastard of Savaan is. What took you so long to find me?"

Kholya somehow managed to keep the smirk from his lips, but he thoroughly enjoyed Ognyan's reaction to Kashyan's implied insult. "We're not here to exchange pleasantries," Kholya said. "What is it you want, Ognyan?"

"The Bastard's head on a pole."

"That is not mine to give, I'm sorry to say."

"Then you leave me no choice but to come and take it for myself."

"That didn't work so well the last time we met," Kashyan said.

"So you admit you were in Sumadin when the king was murdered," shouted the herald.

"I was in Sumadin to kill the man who dishonored my mother, if that's what you mean."

Sheyn stifled a snort behind Kashyan's broad back. He was certain his amusement would not be well received, and for once, he didn't want to attract attention. He'd only met Ognyan briefly, but he remembered him well and didn't care to meet him again. As though he'd cursed himself, his blood went cold when Ognyan spoke again.

"You have something else that belongs to me," Ognyan said. "A white-haired daaksi."

"You claim Pearl as yours?" Kholya asked before Kashyan could answer.

"He was a gift to me from King Yevdjen, and I'll have him back."

"No, you won't," Kashyan said.

"You're wrong, Bastard," Ognyan shouted. "I'll have your head and your brother's too, if he stands in my way. I'll take my pleasure of the white witch before your blood cools. And mark me, witch, if you're listening… you'll pay a price for your disloyalty."

"You won't put a hand on him," Kashyan said. "You'll never be that close."

"You sound very sure of that."

"I am sure, because I'll always be standing between you and him."

"You think I can't best you?"

Kashyan smiled. "You already know the answer to that."

"Before you start swearing oaths at one another, I'd like to speak," Kholya said. "King Ognyan, I've heard your demands and I can satisfy neither. I'll leave you now to consider your reply. I'd suggest you break camp and go home, but it's up to you. You can stay and be slaughtered if that's your pleasure." He gestured for Kashyan to go down the stairs. "By the way, Your Majesty," he said to Ognyan. "Has anyone warned you about the demons that come in the night?"

Kashyan turned, saw Sheyn, and gestured curtly for Sheyn to follow him.

"Disloyalty!" Sheyn said indignantly as soon as they were out of earshot. "I was kidnapped. How can that be called disloyalty?"

Kashyan didn't answer as he reached the bottom of the steps and stood aside to wait for Kholya. He put Sheyn behind him as Kholya descended.

"Ognyan's on his way back to his camp," Kholya said. "We can expect his men to start moving forward in the next few hours."

"We'll do what we can to hinder them," Kashyan replied. "We should leave now while everyone's eyes are on Ognyan."

Kholya gave Kashyan a hug. "Come back," he said.

Kashyan and Sheyn mounted their horses and rode to the northern side of the fortress. Set in the thick wall was a door just large enough to accommodate one rider at a time. The guards recognized Kashyan and let him through, looking curiously at Sheyn as he rode by.

Kashyan led the way down the steep, narrow path that followed the western flank of the ridge. Sheyn found the gray gelding to be sure-footed, so he relaxed in the saddle and trusted the horse to make the important decisions. Sensing the rider's confidence, the courser ignored the drop-off on the left and followed Kashyan's stallion down to the tree line. Footing was less precarious here, and Sheyn took the opportunity to braid his hair and fasten it with the new clasp. He let the braid hang down his chest and pulled a soft cap of gray wool over his head.

"My ears are freezing," Sheyn muttered to his horse.

Kashyan glanced back but said nothing until they reached the Black Hawks' camp. "Don't embarrass me," he said as Sheyn dismounted.

Sheyn gave Kashyan a cheeky look but held his tongue as a trooper came to take care of their horses. He looked around curiously while Kashyan spoke with his lieutenant and issued orders.

"They'll be ready to ride in a moment," Kashyan said to Sheyn as the officer strode away. "We should get back in the saddle." He watched in amusement as Sheyn stretched out in a lunge before going to his horse.

Four companies of six men left the camp, taking different directions. Each was under orders to cause as much mischief as possible for the Sumadinim without getting caught. Sheyn considered it more of a dare than a mission and hoped the eager raiders would respect the danger they were in as they harried the enemy. After the first curious stares, the Savaani cavalry seemed to make an unspoken pact to pretend that Sheyn didn't exist as he rode on Kashyan's left.

"Is it all right to talk?" Sheyn asked.

"If you keep your voice down, you'll make no more noise than the horses."

"I'm surprised none of your men have said anything about my presence. Aren't they worried about having a civilian along on a mission like this?"

"A civilian?" Kashyan glanced at Sheyn and smiled. "You know so many words and you learned our tongue so quickly."

"You're changing the subject."

"My men trust me not to put them in danger on a whim."

"Admirable," Sheyn said. "I was afraid they'd think you brought me along to warm your lap."

"Are you certain I didn't?"

"It's too late to play the brute. I know you now."

"And I know almost nothing of you."

"I told you my sad history when you brought me to your brother's tent the first time."

"Did you? I must not have been listening. Everything you said sounded like a complaint anyway."

"Have I improved, then?"

"I love you as you are," Kashyan said wisely.

"Why don't you tell me what you expect me to do on this outing?"

"If you were Luks, I'd hide you and come back for you after the mission was over. But you're not Luks. Why don't you tell me what you think you should do?"

"I think you should use me as you think best. You're the military man. I have some skill with a sword, but strategy is not a talent of mine."

"I could argue that." Kashyan held up a hand, and his little troop halted. He led them into the cover of a stand of long-skirted pines, and they gathered in a circle. "We're nearing the Sumadi sentry line," Kashyan said. "They have whistles made of boar tusk that they'll blow as soon as they see anyone unfamiliar to them. I favor shooting the sentries in the throat with arrows, but there's always a chance of missing."

"Creep up, hand over the mouth, knife across the throat," said one of the troopers.

"Risky, Lanzha," said another. "And we can't always be sure we'll have cover."

"You could lure them from their posts and ambush them," Sheyn said.

"They're Sumadi soldiers," Kashyan said. "An old hunter's trick isn't going to work on them. What do you think we could lure them with?"

"I thought it would be obvious."

"Well it isn't."

"They're warriors, yes?" Sheyn waited for Kashyan to nod. "And which of us here is supposed to be irresistible to warriors?"

"No," Kashyan said. "I'm not putting you in danger."

"I'm in danger simply by being in this barbaric country."

"It would work, Captain," one of the men said. "And Pearl wouldn't have to be in danger. All he'd have to do is show himself and duck back under cover where we'll be waiting."

"I could be a fair distance away from the sentry," Sheyn said.

"Why do you want to do this?" Kashyan asked.

"Too many reasons to explain right now. Ask me after we make camp."

"I'd like to hear them now, if you don't mind," Kashyan said sharply

Sheyn sighed in exasperation and glanced aside as he spoke. "I owe you this much."

"That wasn't so hard to explain after all." Kashyan looked around at the five other men. "We'll walk the horses from here. Be as quiet as possible. Whisper if you need to speak."

Kashyan had studied the Sumadi army's movements through Kholya's telescope, and the placement of troops was fixed in his head. He brought his men within sight of the first sentry post, and they stopped well back in the trees. The sentry was on the far side of a meadow, leaning on his spear, turning his head from time to time to scan the area.

"What are you planning to do?" Kashyan asked Sheyn.

"I'm going to walk to the edge of the trees, wave, and run back here as fast as I can."

"That's a good plan." Kashyan looked around at his men. "Who wants this one?"

"Me, Captain!" a young trooper said quickly.

"Very well, Dasha," Kashyan said. "Make sure he doesn't blow that whistle."

"Wait. How do we know he won't raise the alarm when he sees Pearl?"

"Would you?" Lanzha asked.

"I guess I wouldn't," Dasha said. "I'd want to see if the vision was real, and if it was, I probably wouldn't want to share."

"That's what I'm counting on," Sheyn said as he loosed his hair from the braid. After tucking his gloves into his belt, he finger-combed the rippled, waist-length tresses as he moved away.

"Pearl," Kashyan said in a loud whisper.

Sheyn turned with an inquiring look on his face.

"Don't dawdle."

Sheyn smiled as he resumed walking toward the forest's edge. He stepped out into the sunlight and waited until he was sure the sentry saw him. With a little beckoning gesture, he stepped backward into the shadows, turned, and ran. He reached the area where he thought he'd left the Black Hawks, but he didn't see anyone. As he ran past a lightning-blasted trunk, someone reached out and grabbed him by the waist. Sheyn stilled the cry in his throat as Kashyan pulled him close. He peered around the tree and saw Dasha step from hiding into the sentry's path.

The Sumadi raised his whistle, but it flew from his hand as Dasha plowed into him. The fight was over quickly, as Dasha gained the upper hand with a crushing grip on the sentry's throat. Dasha suffered a cut from the Sumadi's knife, but it wasn't deep, and he earned Kashyan's praise as well as Pearl's.

Until dark, Kashyan's troop rode down the Sumadi line taking out sentries. When night fell, they changed tactics, sneaking up on the Sumadinim under cover of darkness. Not until dawn did Kashyan call a halt. They made camp in a holly thicket, under cover of the dense canopy of leaves, and the horses were tethered among some nearby pines that enclosed a grassy clearing. The men fashioned lean-tos from their cloaks and spread their bedrolls beneath. They made no fire but sat in a circle anyway as they ate jerky and cracked grain washed down with water from their canteens.

"You all did well today," Kashyan said. "Get a few hours' sleep and dream up new devilry."

The men wrapped up in their bedrolls while one stood watch. Kashyan took Sheyn by the wrist and led him to a spot a significant distance away from the others where a makeshift tent covered their bedrolls.

"When did you find time to do this?" Sheyn asked as he looked at the shelter. "You haven't left my side."

"I didn't. It was like this when we came back from feeding the horses."

"Sly savages." Sheyn chuckled. "I think you're meant to *enjoy* me, as you Savaanim say."

"Bad idea. I lose my wits when I top you."

"You're right." Sheyn yawned. "I'm going to sleep."

Kashyan spoke to the sentry for a few minutes and then went to lie down. He wasn't sure he could sleep with his daaksi lying so close, but he would try to rest. Fully clothed, he stretched out behind Sheyn and put an arm around his waist. Burying his face in Sheyn's hair, Kashyan closed his eyes. The sweet scent of Sheyn's nape reminded him of something. He'd smelled that perfume before when he was much younger. It had come to him on the breeze from the river where he liked to play. Down among the marsh reeds, he had beaten down pathways and chambers of an elaborate fortress where he could play without anyone teasing him. Closer to the water's edge were banks of frostflowers. He was holding a bouquet of them when he got his first kiss. He'd never forgotten the delicate sweetness of their scent.

Half-asleep, Kashyan spread his hand over Sheyn's lower belly and pressed Sheyn's ass firmly against his crotch. Sheyn snuggled back into the pleasant warmth with a happy little moan, and Kashyan moved his hand lower. Sheyn sighed when Kashyan took hold of his reyl, but he didn't wake. Kashyan yanked his kilt out of the way and pulled Sheyn's tunic up. It took a bit of maneuvering to get Sheyn's leggings down over the curve of his ass, but finally Kashyan was able to press his hard shaft into Sheyn's cleft.

Sheyn woke and his breath caught in his throat. Kashyan was fondling his reyl in the most pleasing manner, and he could feel the heat of Kashyan's arousal rubbing against his backside. It was an entirely agreeable situation as far as Sheyn was concerned, and he bit his lip to keep from crying out and drawing attention. The shadowy panic that had once paralyzed him had no power over him any longer. He didn't feel as though he was being split open and suffocated at the same time. He felt warm and secure and wrapped in bliss like a cloak made of sunlight.

"Didn't we speak about this?" Sheyn purred.

"Aye, but you liked it so much before, and I love waking you up like this. Should I stop what I'm doing?"

Sheyn smiled drowsily. "No. You can keep doing that for as long as you like, my lord."

Kashyan replied by holding Sheyn tighter and stroking him faster. Sheyn's jaavi jerked against his palm, and hot liquid filled his hand. He continued to pump the spurting shaft, coating it with the slick fluid, as he spilled his seed against the small of Sheyn's back. Shuddering in release, Kashyan pressed his cock into the damp groove as he hugged Sheyn tightly.

"Are you well-satisfied?" Sheyn asked.

Kashyan let out a breath that stirred the silky hair at Sheyn's nape. "Ayeesh! You have truly conquered me."

Sheyn smiled into the darkness. Putting a hand over Kashyan's where it rested on his lower abdomen, Sheyn snuggled back against him. "We should try to sleep, then."

"I love you," Kashyan whispered a few moments later, but Sheyn was already asleep. He settled himself a little more comfortably and dozed off but woke an hour later. Sheyn was restless in his arms but quieted down when Kashyan murmured soothingly in his ear. This happened twice more before Sheyn fell into a deep sleep. Kashyan lay awake until the watch changed, and then Sheyn's calm breathing lulled him into drowsiness. He slept well and didn't wake until first light.

"AYEESH! GET on the horse," Kashyan said impatiently as Sheyn fiddled with a stirrup.

Sheyn looked at Kashyan over his shoulder. "If I'm reluctant to ride, whose fault is that, Bastard? Who's the cause of my soreness?"

Kashyan glanced around to see if anyone had heard, and of course everyone had. His glare discouraged the smirks, but he found he wasn't all that angry with Pearl. What harm was there in letting his men know he was enjoying Pearl's charms? It would only enhance their respect for him. If only it didn't make him feel weak.

"Did you hear me?" Kashyan asked. "We need to be in the wind. The longer we stay in one place, the more likely it is that a Sumadi scout will find us."

"As you command," Sheyn said as he got into the saddle. "But next time, be a bit less enthusiastic when you take me."

Kashyan heard the muffled snickers, but he didn't acknowledge them. "I'll take you in whatever way pleases me."

"To be sure," Sheyn answered, eyes twinkling. "But don't complain if I can't ride the next day."

"I should have brought a silk pillow for your precious behind," Kashyan said as he mounted Karkaran. He looked around at the five troopers. "Who's ready for a little sport before the sun gets much higher?"

The Black Hawks slapped the hilts of their swords to signal their readiness, and Kashyan led them away from camp. Once they were gone, there was little sign they'd ever been there.

After riding for some time, Kashyan called a halt. "The Sumadi have moved their lines back," he said. "We'll have to go farther away from the fortress to find them." He paused, but no one had anything to say. "All right. We'll water the horses and ride until we find some Sumadinim to discourage."

Keeping to the trees, Kashyan led his band to a rock-strewn brook that cut through the thick moss of the forest floor. While the horses drank, Sheyn walked a short distance away along the bank of the stream. He could feel Kashyan's presence behind him, coming nearer, but it was no longer an odd feeling to know where Kashyan was or what he was feeling. It had become as natural as breathing.

"Don't stray too far," Kashyan called softly.

"I won't." Sheyn paused. "I can't."

"I feel it too," Kashyan said as he came closer. "It's as though there's an invisible rope tying us together. The farther I am from you, the tighter it grows."

"I keep forgetting that you're a victim as well."

"I don't mind so much now."

Sheyn leaned his back against a tree and watched the water slide by. "I've heard how you despise daaksim. You even told me so yourself. Isn't it odd that bedding me could change you so completely?"

"You think it's your divine ass that converted me?"

"What else am I to think? Bedding you certainly had a profound effect on me."

"Haven't I told you that I love your fire and your courage? I love how you stand by your beliefs. I love that you never once showed any real fear of me. You fascinate me, and I'm willing to look like a fool for loving you. What more can I say?"

"Isn't this a fine turn of events?" Sheyn swallowed, and his voice was a trifle unsteady when he spoke again. "Of all the suitors I imagined for myself, not one resembled you."

"I know I'm not what you'd have chosen."

"Hush! It doesn't matter what I would have chosen. I'm not known for my wise decisions."

"Pearl?"

Sheyn took a deep breath and let it out again. "Yes, my lord?"

"Can you love me?" Kashyan looked away as if fearing what he'd see in Sheyn's face. "Or will the manner of our meeting always stand between us?"

"You really have no idea how I feel about you? That's interesting. I guess that connection doesn't work both ways."

"I don't understand."

"Haven't I said that I love you?"

"No," Kashyan said without a shade of doubt in his tone. "Never."

"Well… perhaps not in words, but I gave myself to you."

"Of course you submitted. You're my daaksi."

Sheyn snuffed a spark of annoyance with a sticky-sweet smile. "You're so witty, my lord."

"You're making fun of me again, aren't you?"

"I assumed we were both joking."

Kashyan snorted. "Will I ever get the better of you?"

"You shall always have my best," Sheyn said softly.

Kashyan swept Sheyn into his arms and held him with fierce tenderness. "It's all worth it," he said. "To feel like this for even one moment."

Sheyn hoped for a bit more than just moments, but he kept silent and enjoyed the sublime feeling of being held in loving arms.

"The horses have probably had enough to drink by now," Kashyan said.

"Then we should go." Sheyn paused. "You'll have to let go of me."

Kashyan loosed his hold, and Sheyn stepped away. They walked back to the others and got back on their horses. Kashyan noticed the smirking and winking among the troops, and abruptly he missed Djenya so intensely his chest hurt.

"Are you well?" Sheyn asked, leaning in the saddle toward Kashyan. "You look as though you took an arrow in the back. I've recently seen someone take an arrow in the back, so I know what it looks like."

"I wish Djenya was here," Kashyan said. "He'd have enjoyed this."

"He'd be teasing you unmercifully."

"I miss his teasing. He was so clever. And no matter how ill things were going, nothing dimmed his high spirits." Kashyan tightened his grip on Karkaran's reins. "I still owe the Red Temple a blood debt."

"One enemy at a time," Sheyn said. "Get rid of the Sumadinim, and you'll have a clear path back to Taar Muergan."

"You're right." Kashyan squared his shoulders. "Let's send the Sumadinim home so Djenya's spirit can rest easy."

At midday they found a Sumadi camp. Leaving the horses in a thicket, they crept close and watched the Sumadinim for a few minutes. The soldiers walked about picking body parts from the ground and trees and pitching them into a bonfire. Kashyan gave a signal, and the Black Hawks met where the horses were tethered.

"They were attacked by demons," Kashyan said.

"It certainly looked that way," Lanzha said. "That must be why they pulled their men back."

Kashyan nodded. "It's easier for the monsters to pick off a small number of men." He looked around the circle. "I'm changing our orders. Dasha, you'll go to the rendezvous point and wait for the other squads. The rest of us are going back to the fortress. I need to talk with Kholya." He looked in the direction of the Sumadi camp. "And I think they're demoralized enough for the moment."

Chapter

20

KASHYAN WENT directly to Kholya and found him in his chambers. Luks was there and offered khai before Sheyn declared he'd kill all of them for a bath. With a two-man escort, Sheyn and Luks left for the bathhouse while Kashyan spoke with Kholya.

"It looks as though the Sumadinim had a visit from the Red Temple's pets last night," Kashyan said.

"We heard nothing of it here." Kholya sipped from his cup. "Why would the high priest send demons to attack the Sumadinim?"

"I doubt he even knows they're here. The demons probably attacked the first men they happened upon."

Kholya nodded his agreement with that theory. "They don't seem to be very bright."

"The demons or the Sumadinim?"

Kholya chuckled. "I should include that in my next dispatch to the high king. Djulyan will—" He broke off at a knock on the door and called out permission to enter.

"Commander," said the messenger. "A delegation from the enemy is at the gate."

"Ognyan has no sense of timing," Kholya said as he rose. "I was looking forward to seeing our daaksim when they returned from their bath."

"Is there a better smell in the world?"

Kholya chuckled again as he buckled on his sword. "I can't think of a single one. Unless it's the smell of their sweat after they—" He grinned at Kashyan. "But I don't have to describe it to you. Are you coming with me?"

"Of course." Kashyan followed his brother out of the room.

"YOU'LL REWRITE all the rules before you're finished," Luks said as Sheyn massaged lather into his scalp. "I still find it hard to believe that you went on a raid."

"Rinse," Sheyn said, pushing Luks's head down into the water.

Luks stayed under for a minute to get all the suds out before he surfaced facing Sheyn. "What did you do while you were in the wilderness with all those men?" he asked with a sly smile.

"Most of the time, I watched them kill Sumadi soldiers. Once in a while, I helped."

"That's—" Luks shook his head. "I'm sorry, but I just can't make myself believe it."

Sheyn sighed. "I know I'm not a proper daaksi, but you'll simply have to forgive me."

"Forgive you? No. You misunderstand me."

"But everything I do and say scandalizes you."

"Yes, you're scandalous, but I… I admire you. I wish I could be half as brave." Luks smiled shyly. "That probably surprises you, but you're my hope that daaksim will one day take their rightful place again."

"I'm speechless."

"Surely not." Luks smiled again. "Let's dry off and get dressed. I'd like to hear Prince Kholya's plans for the evening."

"You should see your face. Does it make you so happy to care for him?"

"Yes, it does. It's what I was trained to do, but I enjoy my duty. The prince is kind. He cares for me, so why shouldn't I care for him?"

"It's good to see you happy. With all that's happening around us, everyone is so grim."

Luks wrapped a large square of cloth around his torso and tucked the end in at the top. "That's why I'll do my best to make my lord comfortable when he's in his chambers."

In a rare affectionate gesture, Sheyn leaned to kiss Luks's cheek as they left the baths.

"What a pretty sight," said a man who was leaving the officers' bath.

Sheyn froze at the sound of Yozif's voice.

Luks glanced at Sheyn and then at Yozif. Confused, he fell back on etiquette. "Sir," he said, looking at the floor. "We're not acquainted, so please don't approach us with familiar words."

"I know you well enough," Yozif said. "Pearl and Velvet. You belong to the Savaani princes." He smiled. "Princes in exile, I should say."

"Please clear the way," Luks said.

Sheyn found his voice. "Why are you walking around free?"

"I have an escort here somewhere. There was a lot of steam and I lost sight of him." Yozif smiled as he let his gaze travel over Luks and Sheyn. "You really are two of the finest daaksim ever created."

"Do you know what you did to me?" Sheyn asked. "You changed my life completely without asking permission. What gives you the right to do something like that?"

"There's never just one reason," Yozif said as a Savaani soldier appeared in the doorway. "And I don't have time to explain. However, if you want to speak with me, I'm not terribly busy at any time of the day."

"Can you change me back?"

Yozif shook his head. "That's quite impossible. The divine spark is part of you. To remove it would mean death, and only the Goddess can take back what She has given."

"Then I have nothing to say to you."

"There are many things I could teach you about yourself."

"What could you tell me that Luks doesn't know?"

Yozif showed his teeth in another smile. "Luks was clearly awakened in stages by the monks at the Shrine. He has the best breeding and the finest training. He is the current ideal of a daaksi, and he can share much knowledge with you, but he can't tell you anything about how you were made."

"What are you talking about?" Luks said. "There's only one way to make a daaksi."

"So they teach at the Shrine, but it isn't true. You're the pinnacle of what Anaali's faithful are creating these days, but it's possible to make a lesser form."

"That's sacrilege."

"So I was taught, yet I've performed the ritual many times since I left Her service and She hasn't seen fit to blast me." Yozif's eyes glittered as he fixed his gaze on Sheyn. "I wonder if you have any idea what kind of miracle you are."

"It's time to return to your room," said the Savaani soldier at Yozif's back.

Yozif bowed to Sheyn and Luks. "I hope I'll see you again."

"I'd sooner have a conversation with a demon," Sheyn said.

"You should be careful what you say," Yozif said as he turned away. "Words have power, and the Gods have a cruel sense of humor."

"My apologies if the prisoner upset you," the guard said to Sheyn and Luks without looking directly at them.

"Take him away," Sheyn said as Luks murmured something polite. "That man makes my skin crawl." Sheyn shuddered dramatically.

"I don't like what he was saying about the ritual." Luks glanced at Yozif's back as the sentry led him down the hall.

"It wasn't news to you, was it? With all of these demon attacks, you must have figured out the Temple was getting daaksim from somewhere for their filthy ceremonies."

"I suppose I didn't want to think about it."

"If you'll pardon me saying it, you should think a bit more." Sheyn put his arm around Luks's shoulders as they walked. "You're not stupid, but you're used to pushing aside the things you consider unpleasant. You'll never solve your problems like that. You have to… take your troubles by the horns, as Aeriq used to say."

"It seems to work for you," Luks said. "But I'm not you."

"I understand that you have a lifetime of training to overcome, so start with small steps." Sheyn nodded his thanks as the guard at the daaksim quarters opened the door for them. "First, you should decide what you'd like to change."

"I'd like to change this drying cloth for a soft robe that will tempt my lord to stroke it."

"Is seduction all you think about?" Sheyn asked as he threw his drying cloth over a rack. Naked, he walked to the collection of trunks he and Luks had amassed. There wasn't a lot to choose from in the stores of clothing left at the fortress over the ages, but the items were all of good quality and kept the wearer warm.

"I wish there was one pretty thing here." Luks sighed as he put aside another dull gray garment. "Why do we have all these colorless wool tunics?"

"They fit me," Sheyn said as he slid his arms into the sleeves of a jacket of leather and woven wool. "Which is a true miracle. Are all Kandaari men formed like the God of War?"

"They were formed *by* the God of War," Luks answered. "Most Kandaari nobles and warriors are descendants of the tribe created by Raas at the dawn of this world."

"It makes sense, then." Sheyn smoothed his leggings and sat to pull on a pair of boots.

"There are also Kandaari descended from the children of the God of Harvests and the Lady of the Forests and the King of Winds. The Ocean God's people haven't been seen for ages, but maybe they exist somewhere deep in the Sunred Sea."

"Your head is so full of fanciful thoughts that I'm astounded you're so practical." Sheyn buckled his sword belt around his waist and turned to look at Luks. "You're beautiful."

Luks adjusted the circlet of tiny golden leaves on his auburn curls and shrugged the shoulders of the thigh-length white tunic back into place. "Do you think anyone will notice that I'm not wearing an undergarment?"

"No one will notice anything except how beautiful you are." Sheyn paused. "Aren't your legs cold?"

"Foreigner," Luks said as he twirled a cloak around his shoulders. "If you're too cold, your blood is too thin."

"The cold certainly doesn't seem to bother anyone else. Half the army walks around bare-chested most of the time."

"Is that right? I hadn't noticed." Luks led the way to the door and out into the hall. "I see you've taken to wearing that sword all the time."

"It comforts me."

When they reached Kholya's quarters, the guards told them that the commander had gone up to the parapet. Since no orders had been given concerning the daaksim, Sheyn and Luks weren't hindered when they walked away.

"This is not a good idea," Luks said as they approached the main entrance to the fortress.

"Aren't you curious?"

Luks looked out at the bustling courtyard. "If it's important, someone will tell me about it."

"You're not serious, surely." Sheyn stepped outside. "Come on. I've been up there before. Just follow me." For a moment, it occurred to him that Luks was probably right, but his curiosity spurred him on. "Take my hand."

Sheyn and Luks climbed the stair to the parapet, and none barred their way. At the top, Sheyn saw Kashyan and Kholya standing near the sentry tower over the gate. He edged closer with Luks's hand in his until they could hear what was being said.

"You can't deny it," Ognyan shouted. "You used sorcery against me, sending monsters in the night to slay my men."

"If monsters slew your men, you should be having this talk with the high priest of the Red Temple," Kholya answered.

"You lie like the coward you are. Yesterday you threatened me with a plague of demons and they came in the night. You'll answer to the high king's court for your crimes."

"I would welcome a chance to face you before the high king's judgment, but isn't it a somewhat unmanly thing for a Sumadi warrior to suggest?"

"You'll not trick me into a trial by combat," Ognyan said.

"I don't think I'm the coward here," Kholya said. "If you fear demons, you should return to your camp before it gets much darker."

"Yes, run away," Kashyan told Ognyan. "You know how to do that."

"You'll pay for your taunts, Bastard," Ognyan shouted. He gave the sky a wary glance before he spoke again. "You killed my king and stole my daaksi and you will answer for those crimes."

"Ware away south!" the topmost lookout called out. "Ware the sky!"

Every man looked up at the southern quarter of the cloudless sky. Five black blotches against the serene violet dusk grew larger until they resolved into the shapes of winged demons. The pack soon reached the fortress and wheeled overhead like vultures.

"Why aren't they attacking?" Kashyan asked Kholya.

"They're looking for something," Kholya said.

One of the demons opened its beak and gave a loud, croaking cry. All five monsters dove on the Sumadinim. Kholya shouted an order, and the Savaani archers on the wall loosed their arrows. The demons roared in pain as the bolts pierced their flesh, but they were not deterred. Kholya shouted again, and clay balls filled with black powder were flung into the air with fuses alight. The balls exploded and rained fire on the demons as the Sumadinim desperately tried to control their maddened horses. Ognyan's champions did their best to protect their king as the demons swooped on them. Slashing and snapping, four of the demons hovered over the Sumadinim as the warriors thrust at them with swords and spears. The fifth monster used the speed of its dive to propel it up to the top of the fortress wall.

A sentry shouted an alarm as the beast opened it wings and stopped in midair. Clutching a merlon with its lower limbs, it snatched Luks up and prepared to launch itself back into the sky. Sheyn brought his saber around in a short arc and severed one of the demon's claws. The monster began to rise with Luks's tunic still clutched in its talons. Luks twisted wildly in an effort to shed the garment as Kashyan and Kholya ran toward him. Sheyn cut at the thing's tail as it lifted off, and then ducked as a knife flew past his head. The beast squealed as the blade sank into its back, but it kept flying.

"No!" Sheyn screamed. "You can't have him!" He reached up as though he could pluck Luks from the demon's grip as he willed his friend back to his side. It was unthinkable that the horrible old man in the Temple should get his hands on Luks. Sheyn utterly rejected the very notion of Luks suffering through the demon-summoning ritual. He would not let it happen.

Something stirred at Sheyn's core, and something ancient rolled over in its long sleep. Propelled by an unknown force, Sheyn leaped to the top of the wall and flung out his hand in a grab for Luks's ankle. As Kashyan wrapped his arms around Sheyn's knees, a beam of eye-searing light shot from Sheyn's hand and struck the demon. The beast vanished in a flash of purple-white light, and Luks plummeted toward the ground. Sheyn snagged Luks's burning tunic with his outstretched hand and swung him over the wall. Kholya caught Luks and smothered the flames as Kashyan lifted Sheyn down from the merlon. They were all stunned by what had just happened, but it was no time to be frozen by shock.

Kholya gave Luks over to Sheyn, ran back to the wall, and looked down with Kashyan at his side. "At least it was quick," he said.

Kashyan counted eight human corpses: some Sumadi, some Savaani who'd gone out on Kholya's orders. Four demons decomposed at the usual rapid rate, while one flapped slowly in the direction of Taar Muergan. "If Ognyan doesn't clear the road soon, I'm taking a few Black Hawks on a raid to the Red Temple."

"I forbid it."

Kashyan stared at his brother. "You forbid it?"

"Yes. This one thing I'll deny you. Don't go alone to Taankh's Temple. If you do, you'll no longer be my brother."

"Then I'd better start making new plans for tomorrow."

"For now, let's see to Pearl and Velvet. I'd like to hear what they were doing up here."

Luks's burns were mild and already healing as he and Sheyn accompanied Kholya and Kashyan to Kholya's quarters for the evening meal. After food was set out, Sheyn insisted on serving everyone and scolded Luks if Luks even looked as though he was going to move.

"Stay as you are," Sheyn said for the tenth time as Luks shifted on his cushions.

"I wish I healed as fast as you. I'm tired of lying on my stomach," Luks said.

"I never thought to hear those words from your mouth," Sheyn said drolly.

"Don't tease him," Kholya said. "I'd rather hear how you destroyed that demon."

"For which I'm grateful," Luks said.

"But how did you do it?" Kholya asked.

"I'm not sure," Sheyn replied. "When that creature grabbed Luks, it made me so angry. I couldn't bear the thought of Luks in that horrible temple and I just felt like… I felt like I could stop it from happening because I didn't *want* it to happen. I… wished him back, I suppose."

"What about that light?" Kashyan asked.

"I was as surprised as you were," Sheyn said. "I reached for Luks and I could see that I was going to miss, but I couldn't let that monster have him. I felt something sort of rise inside me, and then that light shot out and burned the demon."

"It rose in you?" Kashyan said. "Like a belch?"

Sheyn gave him a chilly glance. "I suppose a certain sort of person might describe it that way."

Kholya smiled. "I should spend more time around you, Pearl. You're always amusing."

"My lord," Luks said coyly. "I wonder that you would speak such words where I can hear them."

"Are you jealous?" Kholya asked with something akin to delight in his tone.

"Jealousy and envy are vulgar emotions," Luks said. He shifted again and grimaced in pain.

"Is your back hurting you?" Kholya asked. "Would you like me to put salve on your burns?"

"You should probably stay naked to the waist until you heal," Sheyn said. "Modesty be damned. Burns need air."

Luks sighed. "I'm doing my best to be a good daaksi, but fate conspires against me."

"Then thank your stars," Sheyn said. "Now eat this pudding." He set a bowl and spoon in front of Luks.

"Bossy," Luks said, making Kholya smile again.

"This is my thanks for tending you?" Sheyn sat down next to Kashyan. "That's how it is with some people. All that sweetness goes the way of the wind when they fall ill."

Luks threw a pillow awkwardly at Sheyn and knocked Kashyan's ale from his hand. Luks's rapid change of expression made Sheyn and Kholya laugh heartily.

"I'm sorry, my lord," Luks said. "Let me fetch something to dry you off."

"Stay as you are," Sheyn said, flattening his palm against the small of Luks's back as he got to his feet. "I'll take care of it."

"I've already taken care of it." Kashyan finished blotting up the ale with his cloak and held out his cup for more. "Sit down and pour."

"Even though I know you order me around just to get a rise out of me, it still gets a rise out of me," Sheyn said as he sat. He picked up the pitcher of ale and poured for Kashyan.

"Does it make your blood stir?" Kashyan asked with an inept leer.

"If you want to enjoy my body, you know what you have to do," Sheyn said, smiling at the sound of Luks's gasp.

"Remind me," Kashyan said coolly.

"You have to ask, my lord."

Kholya drowned his chuckle in his ale cup.

"What is it about Pearl that captivates you so?" Luks asked. "He's forward and headstrong."

"You've answered your question, my own," Kholya said.

"Then why are daaksim trained to speak softly and always agree with their lords?"

"I don't know. You'd have to inquire at the Shrine." Kholya plucked at the lacing that ran up the back of Luks's tunic. "Let me take this off. I'm sure it would be a relief."

"I promise not to pounce on you in crazed lust at the sight of bare flesh," Kashyan said.

"And if he *is* driven mad by your charms, I won't let him force himself on you," Sheyn said. He took over unfastening the laces as Kholya brought out the pot of salve.

Sheyn sat next to Kashyan again and nibbled on a few cakes while he watched the scarred warrior prince tenderly apply ointment to Luks's burns. Kholya was nearly finished when one of his officers requested entry. After a few moments speech at the door, Kholya returned.

"Ognyan has decamped and marches toward Taar Muergan," Kholya said.

"Ognyan and Kezlath will make interesting bedfellows," Kashyan said.

"If the bed isn't already too crowded with Chanesh and the Red Priesthood in it."

"You have a point," Kashyan said.

"I often do. You should try it."

Sheyn snickered, and Kashyan gave him the wounded look he used to save for Djenya. "Shouldn't you be doing something to soothe my pride?" he asked.

"I would," Sheyn said. "But I happen to agree with Kholya."

Even Luks laughed at Kashyan's expression.

"You don't seem troubled at all by the thought of Ognyan allying Sumadin with Muergath." Kashyan returned to the subject.

"I'm not worried," Kholya said. "I'm curious, because I can't see the future, but I'm confident in my allies."

"What aren't you telling me?"

"Almost everything," Kholya said as he put the salve away. One hand lingered on the smooth, cinnamon-brown skin of Luks's back as he spoke again. "You've refused every attempt of mine to elevate you to a rank above captain, so you can't be surprised when I don't share every detail with you. If you were a general—"

"Ayeesh!" Kashyan cursed. "I'm your brother."

"You're a hothead."

"That's true," Sheyn said.

Kashyan glared at Sheyn. "While you are the soul of restraint," he said.

"I haven't killed *you* yet," Sheyn drawled.

Kholya laughed so hard he started coughing. Luks tried to get up to fetch some water, and Sheyn lost his balance while trying to prevent Luks from rising. Kashyan stared at his red-faced brother and the daaksim entangled in a mound of pillows.

"And you all think *I'm* the simple one," Kashyan said.

"Stop," Kholya begged with tears in his eyes. "If I laugh any harder I'll have hysterics."

"Well, I would hate to strap you to your bed and pour snow melt over you until you returned to your senses," Kashyan gestured to Sheyn to attend him. "We'll go to your quarters now."

Luks waited for Sheyn's blistering retort to the command, but it never came. "Go on," Luks said to his oddly quiet friend. "Prince Kholya will see that I survive until morning. By then, my burns will have healed."

"Are you sure?" Sheyn said as he rose to his knees among the scattered cushions. "I feel awful about burning you."

"You saved me." Luks kissed Sheyn's hand. "Now go and find joy with your master." He smiled. "After what you did tonight, you'll need to recover some energy."

"Are you telling me to get a good night's sleep?"

"No. I'm telling you to let Kashyan fulfill his half of the bond. Each time you find release with him, it adds to your power."

"You're choosing to tell me this now?"

"Well, I didn't know before that you could shoot lightning from your fingers."

Sheyn smiled, kissed Luks's forehead, and took the hand Kashyan offered him. He fancied he felt a small jolt when his flesh touched Kashyan's. The tingle became a spreading warmth that raced up his arm into his chest. "Sleep well," Sheyn said to Luks as he went to the door, suddenly eager to be gone.

"I wish you a good night," Kholya told Kashyan.

"I wish you the same." Kashyan opened the door, and Sheyn followed him into the hall.

"Take me to the baths," Sheyn said.

"You want another bath?"

"Yes, and so do you."

After a brisk walk through the fortress, Kashyan and Sheyn reached the bathhouse, and the guard let them enter the daaksim's room. Sheyn quickly shed his clothing and left it in a pile as he waded into the waist-deep pool. Kashyan unlaced his leather vest and kilt and joined Sheyn in the water.

"Have you *ever* washed your hair?" Sheyn asked, eyeing Kashyan's spiky mane.

"Not often. When it's clean it just lies there and isn't very intimidating."

"I can show you how to do the same thing with beeswax. Here's the soap. Wash your hair."

Kashyan washed and rinsed his hair and looked around for Sheyn. In the next moment, Sheyn had grabbed one of Kashyan's feet, yanked his leg from under him, and lifted it high. Kashyan floundered for a moment, unable to raise his head until Sheyn let go. Spinning agilely, Kashyan grabbed a handful of Sheyn's hair and reeled him in.

Sheyn laughed as he fetched up against Kashyan's broad chest and bobbed up to kiss his lips. He put his palms against Kashyan's shoulders and shoved Kashyan back against the wall. Sheyn rested his arms on the side of the pool and looked down into Kashyan's eyes. "How like you this?" he murmured.

Kashyan took hold of Sheyn's hips. "How can I judge on a mere taste?"

Sheyn wrapped his legs around Kashyan's waist. "Judging by what I feel, you approve." Leaning back, he grasped Kashyan's arousal and seated the tip at his entrance. Sheyn braced one hand on Kashyan's shoulder and sank slowly down on the hard shaft. When he'd taken the full length, he put his other hand on Kashyan's opposite shoulder and levered himself up. Using the buoyancy of the water, he rose and sank, rhythmically clenching his interior muscles on the rod that stretched them.

"You can keep doing that for as long as you like," Kashyan said in a strained voice.

"Stroke me," Sheyn said throatily.

Kashyan reached under the water between them and took hold of Sheyn's shaft. Sheyn wasn't hard yet, but it took only a few pumps of Kashyan's hand to rouse him. With his calves gripping Kashyan's flanks, Sheyn bobbed up and down, taking Kashyan to the root before pulling off. His cock pushed into Kashyan's fist, and Kashyan licked at his nipples on each upstroke.

"I'll not last long." Kashyan panted in Sheyn's ear.

"Don't hold back," Sheyn answered. "We have all night to play."

"You'll be the death of me, Pearl." Kashyan groaned as Sheyn squeezed his jaavi. "I still expect to wake from this dream, but I don't want to anymore."

Completely in control of the depth and speed of the stroke, Sheyn rode Kashyan's reyl, glorying in being in charge for a change. Kashyan had no objections at all to this position. He kept an arm wrapped around Sheyn's back to steady him, but otherwise, he had nothing to do but caress Sheyn, lean against the wall, and enjoy it. Not until his pleasure peaked did he take active part. Planting his feet on the bottom of the pool, he thrust into Sheyn's tight heat and sank his fingers into the resilient muscles of Sheyn's ass.

Sheyn bent backward at the waist, his hair fanning out in the water. He raised his legs to rest his feet on the edge of the pool and spread his arms wide, floating on the surface as Kashyan rocked him.

"I can't—" Kashyan gasped before his hips stuttered and his seed unspooled in Sheyn's passage. He gazed down at Sheyn, his chest heaving as he panted for breath. "My love," he mouthed.

Sheyn braced his feet against the wall and pushed. Kashyan's sated cock slid free, and Sheyn flipped over in the water to grab it with one hand. Using Kashyan's shaft to anchor himself, Sheyn floated in front of him. "You look almost sad after you come," he said.

"I'm not," Kashyan assured him. "My knees are a little weak, but I don't feel sad at all."

"I feel glorious."

"I haven't given you pleasure yet."

"Anticipation is half the fun."

Kashyan shook his head. "That's foolishness." He snaked an arm around Sheyn's waist and pulled him close. "Let me show you what fun is."

Sheyn giggled as Kashyan spun him around and put him belly down on the edge of the pool. Kashyan reached under Sheyn and cradled his jaavi and naaks. As he gently massaged them, he eased a spit-slickened finger into Sheyn's passage. Thrusting gently, he rubbed his fingertip around until Sheyn shivered and moaned.

"Is that what you like, Pearl?" Kashyan asked in a low voice. "Tell me you like it."

"It feels good."

Kashyan applied a bit more pressure, circling his finger around the small swelling at the front of Sheyn's passage. He shuttled his hand slowly up and down Sheyn's hard shaft as he moved his finger in Sheyn's narrow channel. It wasn't long before Sheyn's moans of pleasure inspired Kashyan's rod to rise again. Taking himself in hand, he nuzzled the head of his jaavi against Sheyn's spit-shiny opening.

"Yes," Sheyn said breathlessly. "Give it to me."

Kashyan resisted the strong urge to plunge his shaft into Sheyn and thrust until he exploded. He wanted Sheyn to take as much pleasure in the action as he did. Holding his instincts in check, he rubbed the leaking tip of his cock up and down Sheyn's cleft and around his crinkled entrance. He was gratified when Sheyn moaned loudly and tried to push backward.

"You want me to give you more of this?" Kashyan asked as he pressed harder against Sheyn's port. "Or do you want me to play with you for a while longer?"

Sheyn made a frustrated, demanding noise and gave Kashyan a smoking glare over his shoulder. Kashyan smiled as he resumed teasing Sheyn, growing even harder as Sheyn made it plain how much he wanted to continue. Kashyan took a firm grip on his shaft and eased the head through the flexing ring of muscle that squeezed it so rousingly. Reining in his excitement, Kashyan moved his hips in subtle arcs, shunting the tip in and out. The short, shallow strokes tagged the spot inside Sheyn that made him shudder and cry out in bliss. Patiently, Kashyan thrust and stroked Sheyn's arousal as Sheyn's cries of pleasure grew louder.

Sheyn pressed his fingertips against the cool stone and tried to hold himself together, but it was no use. His consciousness blew away like milkweed fluff on the hot winds that gusted through his body each time Kashyan thrust. The fire at his core had consumed him and expanded to engulf the world. And he was the heart of the flame whose name was joy.

Kashyan felt the tremor that ran the length of Sheyn's body. Leaning forward, he sheathed his jaavi to the root as he stroked Sheyn to a faster rhythm. He kissed and nipped at the smooth skin of Sheyn's back and churned his hips, driving Sheyn over the edge. Kashyan wrapped an arm around Sheyn's waist, holding him fast as Sheyn shook with the force of his release. Without faltering in his cadence, Kashyan reached his climax while Sheyn was still trembling in the aftermath of a soul-shaking experience.

It was several moments before Sheyn remembered he needed to breathe. His gasp was loud in the empty room and echoed oddly. Kashyan's arms tightened around him, and he smiled contentedly. "I feel as though I died and was reborn," he said softly.

"Is that a good thing?"

"It was for me." Sheyn groaned as Kashyan disengaged and then turned in his embrace. "You're quite a handsome fellow. Did you know that?"

"Djenya used to tell me I was handsome. I never believed him."

"Surely you believe me."

Kashyan smiled. "Daaksim are trained to flatter their masters."

"Bastard." Sheyn returned the smile. "You know I've had no training in pleasing a man."

"That's obvious to anyone who knows you." Kashyan held Sheyn tighter as Sheyn tried to splash him. "Hush, I didn't mean it." He kissed Sheyn's eyelids. "You've just given me the greatest pleasure I've ever known. Don't be cross. I want to kiss and pet you until I'm hard enough to top you again."

"I suppose I could allow it. Lift me out of the pool."

Kashyan set Sheyn on the edge of the pool and then climbed out. The sight of Sheyn's long, smooth muscles gleaming in the lamplight made Kashyan want to lay him down on the bench and get his fill of touching. He caught the drying cloth Sheyn tossed to him and wrapped it around his middle. "Let's go," he said impatiently as Sheyn wound his hair into a loose braid.

"You can't be hard again already."

Kashyan looked down. "This is one effect of your witchcraft that I can't complain about."

"And to think you found me so repellent when we met," Sheyn said as they left the baths.

"You despised me."

"I had every reason to. When we met, you were a savage brute who abducted me and made me your slave."

"I guess you could see it that way." Kashyan leaned close to sniff at Sheyn's hair. "Why are your quarters so far away?"

Sheyn chuckled. "You could take me against this wall and no one would gainsay you."

"I won't share you, not even with other men's eyes."

"Sometimes I fear I'll never be able to civilize you."

"I don't think you want me *too* civilized." Kashyan took Sheyn's elbow and steered him into the right-hand hall. "Finally," he said as he saw the door to Sheyn's rooms. He saluted the guards and pulled Sheyn into his arms as soon as the door closed behind them. "I'll have my pleasure of you now," he growled.

Sheyn grinned, bent his knees, and slipped down out of Kashyan's hold. He spun on his heel and lunged to his right, leaving Kashyan grasping at air.

"You really are fast," Kashyan said as he faced Sheyn from across the room. "But so am I." On the last word, he charged toward Sheyn in great strides. Feinting to his left, he reached to his right and just missed getting a hand on Sheyn's arm.

Sheyn leaped over the mattress and turned back to laugh at Kashyan.

"Stop dancing around and get on the bed."

Sheyn laughed again, a bit giddily. "After you."

"On the bed, or I *will* take you against the wall."

"Oh, my lord!" Sheyn said with an exaggerated quaver in his voice and then paused. "Sorry, I'm not sure what I should say next. Should I compliment the size of your… jaavi, or should I praise your might in battle?"

Kashyan shook his head. "Sometimes I fear I'll never turn you into a proper daaksi."

Sheyn jumped on the bed and sprang at Kashyan. He wrapped his arms around Kashyan's neck and his legs around Kashyan's waist. "Keep trying," he said.

Kashyan lowered Sheyn to his back on the bed. "You may rely on that."

Chapter
21

"CAPTAIN!" DASHA shouted as he knocked at the door of the daaksim quarters.

"Let him in," Kashyan called out to the guard as he laced his kilt.

"A message from the commander," Dasha said as soon as the door opened. "You're to attend him as soon as may be in your finest garments. And bring Pearl with you."

"Where do I meet him?"

"He'll be in the saddle. Your mount is waiting."

"Go join the Hawks. I'll be there presently." Kashyan went to wake Sheyn as Dasha returned to his duties. "Something's stirring," Kashyan said when Sheyn sat up. "Kholya wants us to attend him in our finest. Pack enough for a few days."

Sheyn got to his feet. "I'll meet you at your quarters."

Kashyan pulled Sheyn into a kiss and let him go. "Don't dawdle," he said as he left.

As SHEYN and Kashyan walked into the courtyard, Sheyn was surprised to see Luks in a light two-horse carriage with trunks strapped to its back. When Luks waved Sheyn over, Kashyan told Sheyn to go.

"For some reason, we're being very formal," Kashyan said. "Ride with Luks for now."

Sheyn walked to the carriage as Kashyan mounted Karkaran. A soldier climbed into the driver's seat and took up the reins as Sheyn sat down next to Luks. Sheyn settled his fur cloak over his lap, thankful for the thick layer of cushioning on the bench seat. He turned to speak to Luks and was jostled as the carriage began moving.

"Where are we going?" Sheyn asked as they passed under the gate.

"Prince Kholya and Prince Kashyan have been called to court."

"What court?"

"The high king arrived at Taar Muergan last night."

Sheyn glanced up at Kashyan and Kholya riding at the head of the small column. "Don't make me ask. Tell me what you know."

"I did. King Djulyan arrived in the night with four other kings and established a court outside the gates of Taar Muergan. He sent immediately for my master and yours."

"This is serious, isn't it?"

"I can think of only one reason the high king would come here now. He's been asked to render a judgment. Ognyan must have sent him a message after King Yevdjen was killed."

"Why is Kholya going to this court? Why not—?"

"Prince Kholya is a man of honor, and High King Djulyan is his liege. He can't refuse a summons."

"No, of course not." Sheyn leaned back against the seat and pulled his fur collar up around his ears. "My nose will probably fall off before we get there."

"You slept outdoors just the other day."

"I had my lord to warm me."

Luks took Sheyn's hand. "Don't worry too much," he said. "Prince Kholya is clever. And it will be warmer when we reach the plains."

"I remember when it was me telling you not to worry too much."

"A lot has changed in the short time since we met."

"Really? I hadn't noticed." Sheyn smiled at Luks.

"Can I give you one more piece of advice? While we're in the high king's presence, do as I do."

"I'll try."

Luks squeezed Sheyn's hand. "I've been to a high court before. Mostly, a lot of men who don't like one another stand around arguing. We'll be there as ornaments, unless the high king doesn't approve of our presence. Then we'll be a pair of daaksim cooling our heels in some boring antechamber with guards on the door."

"If I just had one book," Sheyn muttered.

"What?"

"Never mind. How shall we pass the time until we reach Taar Muergan?"

"We could play some sort of game, I suppose."

"Or you could tell me why the Bastard doesn't trust daaksim."

"What makes you think I'd know something like that?"

"You know every piece of gossip that relates to daaksim."

"I'd feel uncomfortable telling you this story."

"I love Prince Kashyan," Sheyn said, lowering his voice. "And he tells me he loves me, but I know he doesn't trust me… because of what I am."

Luks looked into Sheyn's eyes and then started talking. "This is only a story pieced together from rumors, you understand. You know that Prince Kholya is some six years older than his brother. When Prince Kholya was eighteen and went to swear his fealty as knight to the high king, his father gifted him with a daaksi. King Nakhol of Savaan would not have it said that his son lacked for any royal trappings."

"Are you going to tell me that this daaksi seduced young Prince Kashyan?"

"Indeed he did!" Luks frowned at Sheyn. "If you already know the story, why did you ask?"

"I was guessing. I tried to imagine what could possibly happen to turn Kasha against daaksim so thoroughly. Being caught having a romp with his beloved elder brother's toy would have been horrible for him."

"What an awful thing to have so much shame bound up with his first taste of sex."

"Yes, a terrible thing." Sheyn cleared his throat. "But I flatter myself I've made it enjoyable for him again. What happened to the daaksi?"

"As it turned out, Honey wasn't very discriminating. He'd somehow managed to bed most of the royal guards as well as Prince Kashyan and any number of visiting noblemen. He was very wicked indeed."

"Or perhaps he'd been so well-trained to please men that he couldn't stop pleasing them."

Luks pursed his lips. "Perhaps. It was Prince Kholya's right to have Honey executed, but since there was no bond between them, he sent him back to the Shrine. Honey ran away so many times that they stopped bringing him back. He walked into the first brothel he found and began making his fortune."

"That last part isn't true, is it?"

"I don't know. I wish it was." Luks sighed. "What's sure is that it left a deep scar on Prince Kashyan. He feels such a deep debt of honor to his brother."

"He was just a child." Sheyn was quiet for a moment. "That wasn't gossip," he said. "The commander told you about it, didn't he?"

"He mustn't find out."

"He won't hear it from me. Now tell me how things are with you and the commander."

Sheyn and Luks spent the day talking and eating from the basket at their feet and slept on the carriage seats that night. They struck the Muergathi royal highway at noon the next day, and the smoothness of the road allowed them to go at a much greater speed. The sun hadn't begun to set when they saw the walls and towers of Taar Muergan across the plain. To the left, a city of pavilions and tents occupied the parkland where the Horde of the Hawk had once camped. From poles on the tops of the pavilions, the high king's bear banner rode the breeze slightly higher than Sumadin's boar, the Lake King's stag, the horse of the Sea of Grass, and Long Isle's leaping dolphin.

Four mounted royal guards met the Savaani party on the road with instructions from the high king. One man took the company of Black Hawks to the area where they would tether their mounts. The mules carrying the presents for the high king were taken by another guard to the royal tent. The two remaining guards escorted the Savaani princes and the daaksim to the high king.

No one noticed when one of the mule drivers slipped away behind one of the tents. Removing the dust wrap from his head, he struck out for the city gates. Halfway there, he was met by a party of Red Monks.

"Welcome back, Brother Yozif," said their leader.

DJULYAN AND his fellow monarchs sat at a large table under a sunshade of dark blue silk when Kholya's group approached. The high king rose to greet the newcomers, and the others at the table followed suit.

"Prince Kholya," the high king said. As he stepped out of the shade, his thinning hair glinted with copper lights. "I hope you will stand for your father, King Nakhol, at this council."

"Sire," Ognyan said as he moved to Djulyan's side. "I remind you of the matter we spoke of."

"I remind you of my orders not to raise this issue until I give leave."

Ognyan subsided with ill grace to stand beside Kezlath.

Djulyan gestured to the line of men standing just under the sunshade. "Kholya, let me present King Ognyan of Sumadin, King Kezlath of Muergath, Lukha, King of the Sea of Grass, King Preth of Long Isle, and the Lake King, Agneth-Khol."

Kholya and Kashyan bowed to the gathered sovereigns.

"Come and sit," Djulyan said. "I've declared a ban on any talk of tomorrow's business." He leaned close and spoke in Kholya's ear. "You'll have to stand in court and hear charges, but I don't want to speak of it this evening."

"I understand, sire," Kholya said.

"I haven't taken a journey for a long time," Djulyan said. "I'd forgotten how much I enjoy being in the saddle. In an attempt to keep this mood, I've decreed that tonight is for feasting."

"Before we sit," Kholya said, "we have a duty to attend." He gestured toward the carriage.

"Good, you brought the daaksim." The high king smiled.

"Where shall they wait for us?"

"My daaksi will see to their comfort," Djulyan said as he looked around vaguely.

"Your daaksi, sire?" Kezlath said.

"Yes, my daaksi. Djeyd. The most enchanting creature you ever saw."

"Well, I've not seen him," Kezlath replied.

"Is he not here? What an odd thing." Djulyan paused. "He does tend to drift, though."

"I didn't know you'd acquired a daaksi, sire," Kholya said.

"Oh yes. Shortly after I saw you last, he came to me."

"Congratulations."

Djulyan nodded. "I never felt I needed a daaksi until my queen died. I wasn't sure it would agree with me, but he's a great comfort."

"Then I hope you won't mind if we keep Pearl and Velvet close to hand."

"Not at all. Djeyd sleeps in my tent, and I assume your daaksim will share yours."

"Sire!" Ognyan burst out, pointing at the carriage. "That daaksi belongs to me!"

"Did I not bid everyone be silent on this matter until tomorrow?" Djulyan said mildly.

"But sire! By letting him keep the boy, you're winking at his crime."

Djulyan looked over at Sheyn. "It doesn't look like he's being held against his will."

"He is bonded to my brother," Kholya said.

"Your brother is a thief!" Ognyan burst out.

Kezlath put a hand on Ognyan's arm. "Forgive my guest," he said. "He's wroth at the injustices done to him, but he will wait until it's time to make formal accusations."

Ognyan glared at Kashyan. "This is all your fault, Bastard."

"I beg your pardon?" Djulyan said.

Ognyan contained himself with an effort. "May I have your leave to go?" he growled. "I must prepare for court tomorrow."

"Will I not see you until then?" Djulyan asked. "Or will you be at the feast tonight?"

"Excuse me, sire, but there will be those at your table I don't care to break bread with."

"Until tomorrow, then."

Ognyan bowed and turned away. Sheyn was the only one who saw the sneering glance Ognyan exchanged with Kezlath as the Sumadi left the high king's presence.

As Kholya and Kashyan joined the table of kings, Djulyan's seneschal showed Sheyn and Luks to a nearby tent where they could wait in ease. The silk pavilion had been made comfortable with carpets and cushions, and a low table held a pot of khai and several small cups. As Luks poured, Sheyn helped himself to a selection of small, flat cakes soaked in honey.

"After we've refreshed ourselves, we should begin dressing for the feast," Luks said.

"Did you bring a full wardrobe?"

"Weren't you listening when the high king's seneschal was talking? Garments have been set aside for us to choose from."

"How very hospitable. Where are the clothes?"

Luks took another sip of his khai. "I imagine they're being brought here right now, since that's what I requested."

"How clever of you! Now tell me what I can expect from this feast."

"I'm sure it will be quite as usual. Boars roasted whole. Naked dancing. Duels with daggers."

"What? Oh… I see." Sheyn smiled. "You're teasing me."

"I've learned to enjoy it." Luks returned Sheyn's smile. "Now, what are we going to do with all that hair?"

"I'll wear my clasp as I always do."

"I don't think so. Not tonight. Tonight, I think you should wear it loose."

"Why?"

"Because we want to make a favorable impression on the high king. It might help Kholya and Kashyan's cause."

"And we'll do this by dazzling the eyes of the high king?"

"A daaksi can be very persuasive without saying a word."

"I find this somewhat distasteful, but if you think it will help, I'll wear whatever you like."

"Someday I'll tell you the tale of Fawn Fairskin."

"Tell me now."

"It's a very affecting story. I don't want to tell it now and have red, puffy eyes at the feast."

"You're very softhearted." Sheyn poured more khai for both of them.

"The tale concerns a daaksi who went before the king who'd conquered his master and begged so prettily for his master's life that—"

"The conqueror was charmed and granted the daaksi's request."

"Not exactly. The conqueror *was* charmed, but he couldn't spare the defeated king's life. He claimed Fairskin for himself and ordered him sent to the royal harem. Fairskin asked for some of his personal belongings to give him the comfort of familiarity. The new king gave his permission but with a condition. Fairskin could only take what he could carry. So he—"

"The daaksi picked up his master and carried him away," Sheyn said.

"It's very annoying when you finish my sentences."

"Did Fairskin and his master escape?"

"No. The invader was amused, but he executed Fairskin's master and took the daaksi into his harem." Luks swallowed. "I can't finish it. It makes me sad just thinking about it."

"I don't wonder! That's an awful story. I like tales with lost princes meeting their true loves by a well in the forest. I like them even better if the true love is a witch with the power to change into an animal. And if the prince becomes enchanted and stays in the forest forever with his love, that's the best ending I can imagine."

"Why would the prince fall in love with a black-hearted witch?"

"Not all witches do evil."

"How many witches do you know?"

"None. Witches are characters in books."

Luks rapped on Sheyn's skull with his knuckles. "How can a person so smart be so dense?" He chuckled. "After seeing demons, it's too much for you to believe in evil witches?"

"Yes, it is. Demons are beasts of some sort. But you want me to believe a human could acquire magical powers and dedicate his or her life to doing evil. It doesn't make sense. Why would magical abilities turn someone into a monster?"

"I don't know why," Luks said. "But in Kandaar, witches are known to be evil."

"I think we should talk about something else. You're starting to get upset."

"I'm not upset!" Luks said loudly and immediately clapped a hand over his mouth.

"At least you aren't sad anymore," Sheyn said.

Luks's reply was preempted by a royal guard requesting permission to enter the tent. The guard was accompanied by four servants carrying two litters piled with trunks. The litters were unloaded, and the guard led the servants away. Luks opened one of the chests, and his eyes widened when he looked inside.

"It looks as though the high king's daaksi has lent us his personal wardrobe," Luks said.

"I hope he's not short."

Luks held up a diaphanous gown of deep blue-green with white gems sewn around the neck.

"It suits you well," Sheyn said.

"I agree." Luks laid the garment aside and beckoned to Sheyn. "Let's hope it's that easy to please you."

"I told you I'll wear whatever you choose."

"What a temptation this is! I could tell you to appear naked except for a dragon's hoard of jewels." Luks paused. "But that would be vulgar."

"The entire situation is vulgar. Why must I sway the high king's crotch? Why can't I simply explain what happened?"

"It won't harm your case if you have his attention."

Sheyn sighed. All this fuss over clothing was tiring. He missed the scholar's gowns that he'd worn almost every day since he'd entered the university at twelve.

"This," Luks said triumphantly as he drew a length of flame-red silk from the trunk. "Put it on."

Sheyn removed his clothing and pulled the crimson gown over his head. It flowed down his body in a sensuous whisper to brush the floor. The slightest movement molded the fabric to the contours of Sheyn's torso. "It's beautiful," he said as he looked down. "But I should probably wear something underneath it."

Luks tilted his head to the side and regarded the bulge at the junction of Sheyn's thighs. "I'll find a pair of leggings," he said. "A loin wrap would look ridiculous, but some knitted leggings will hold everything in place and give a *tasteful* indication of your charms." He tossed Sheyn something soft and black.

Sheyn pulled on the clinging garment and arranged his reyl and gaerys before letting the gown fall to cover his crotch. "I've never been any good at this. It's not the kind of attention I've ever wanted to attract."

"You attract attention whether you want it or not. You may as well turn it to your benefit rather than letting it make you unhappy."

"I'm not sure I agree, but I don't want to argue." Sheyn pulled on a pair of suede boots and admired the silver stitching over the toes. "I like the look of these." He glanced up. "And you look exquisite."

Luks bowed, and his blue-green gown gathered in graceful folds around his slender figure. "Now let's see what sort of jewelry the high king's daaksi travels with," he said.

Sheyn picked out a belt of silver discs on black velvet and fastened it around his hips. Luks clasped a choker of green gems around his neck and decorated his bare arms with several bracelets. He looked up from adjusting his anklet and let his gaze linger on Sheyn.

"I'm not sure why I'm bothering to primp," Luks said. "Everyone will be looking at you."

"They'll be staring because they've never seen such a freak."

"They'll be staring because you're Pearl."

"How will they have heard of me?"

"Soldiers talk, and the Black Hawks have been in the high king's camp for hours now."

"Your head is full of moonbeams. What did they teach you in that Shrine of yours?"

"First tell me why you're so set against any romantic notion."

Sheyn abruptly remembered speaking similar words to Aeriq during one of the many arguments Sheyn had engineered to discourage intimacy. "Poor Aeriq," he murmured.

"What?"

"Nothing. I'm sorry if I belittled your sense of romance. I assume it's part of your training."

"Sit," Luks said a bit more sharply than he'd intended. "I'll brush your hair."

"I really am sorry." Sheyn sat on a cushion in front of Luks. "I didn't mean to insult you."

"I know you didn't, but you hurt my feelings all the same," Luks said as he drew a brush through Sheyn's hair. "I believe you're truly sorry."

"Good. I want to keep your friendship."

"Then be still and let me finish with the brush."

Luks arranged Sheyn's shining, waist-length hair to spill down his back and over his shoulders onto his chest. Pronouncing Sheyn ready to dine with royalty, Luks fluffed his mahogany ringlets and tweaked them to nestle in front of his ears and on his forehead.

"Do you ever wear scent?" Sheyn asked.

Luks laughed softly. "Here's another thing I've forgotten to tell you. Each daaksi has a unique natural perfume that doesn't smell the same to any two people. Whoever smells it is reminded of a scent from one of their happiest memories."

"Is there some sort of daaksi reference book I could read?" Sheyn asked. "It would be quite useful to me."

"There's a library at the Shrine," Luks said, ignoring Sheyn's sarcasm.

"I'll have to go there soon."

"I should laugh at your silliness and reprimand you for your boldness, but I'm beginning to believe that you can do whatever you set your mind to."

"I can't return to the moment before I left on my journey."

"No, you can't, and Prince Kashyan can't return to the moment before he was seduced by his brother's daaksi."

"It's very annoying when you point out that I'm not the only victim of fate."

"You told me you love Prince Kashyan. Did you mean it?"

"You know I do. You can feel what I'm feeling."

"That's true, but it's still courteous to ask." Luks took Sheyn's hand. "Finding love isn't such a bad fate, is it?"

"Are you asking me or yourself?" Sheyn cupped Luks's cheek. "Does finding love with Kholya wipe away all you suffered before him?"

"I choose to begin a new life with him."

Sheyn looked into Luks's doe eyes for a long moment. "Is it that easy?" he murmured.

Luks pulled Sheyn into a hug. "We'll see," he said.

TWO RED Monks escorted Yozif to the high priest's quarters and were admitted right away. An acolyte showed Yozif into Chanesh's private sitting room and left them alone. The high priest gestured Yozif to a seat across from his and offered wine. Yozif accepted a cup of the restorative before giving his report on the Savaanim and Pearl.

"You saw the Gate?" Chanesh asked eagerly as he set down his cup.

"I saw him and spoke with him." Yozif held out his cup for another dram.

"Tell me all you remember." The high priest turned his chair so he was facing the fire and took up his cup again.

"I was able to get quite close to him," Yozif said. "It was a very profound experience being so near to something so near to perfection."

"He's just another sack of rotting meat," Chanesh said.

"According to the teachings of the Shrine, a daaksi is the closest thing to a deity that still walks the earth."

"I might say the same of a demon."

"I can't argue that point. All I know is that Pearl is like the first daaksim. He's smarter, swifter, and stronger than any pure human. He's set custom at naught, doing just as he pleases, and no one lifts a hand to him." Yozif leaned toward Chanesh. "If you'll take my advice, don't try bringing Pearl back to the Red Temple. He might bring it down on top of you."

"So you not only failed to find a way to bring the daaksi to me, you advise me to leave him alone?"

"I think it would be wise. You weren't there. You didn't feel the power radiating from him. He has the Savaanim in his palm. By this time, he's probably enthralled the high king."

"I saw none of this power in him when he was in my hands. To be sure, he's the most powerful daaksi I've encountered, but hardly a demigod."

"That was before he'd completed the bond with his master."

Chanesh grimaced. "You mean he let the Bastard prong him, the filthy little piece."

"My faith doesn't look upon sex in the same way yours does."

"Fornication is an untidy and futile act. Lust makes animals of men and desire drives them mad. And what is it all for? For pleasure? To bring another slug of flesh into the world?"

"It's the union of two souls using crude flesh to become one with the only means available in this world. It's a joyful, transforming—" Yozif stopped in the middle of his sentence. "Or so I used to believe."

"We are born alone. We live our lives alone and we die alone," Chanesh said. "That is the central truth of existence. We and everything around us are dying from the moment we're born and we do it alone. When you recognize the truth of this, it gives you freedom."

"To do what?"

"Whatever you like. I choose to serve Taankh, Lord of the Shadoworld. After my inevitable death, He will give me a kingdom in His realm." Chanesh took a drink of his wine. "Now tell me more about Pearl."

Chapter
22

LUKS AND Sheyn turned as Kholya entered the guest tent.

"It's time to join the high king," Kholya said.

"Remember," Luks said quickly to Sheyn. "Do as I do."

Sheyn nodded and then followed Luks out of the pavilion. Though Sheyn professed not to care about such things, he was pleased by the admiring glances Kashyan gave him.

"You look quite presentable with your hair braided," Sheyn said to Kashyan.

"You look…." Kashyan looked to Kholya in appeal.

Kholya didn't notice. He only had eyes for Luks.

"How do *I* look?" Sheyn prompted.

"I've never seen anything so beautiful," Kashyan said truthfully. "You're too beautiful to be made of the same flesh and bone as everyone else. You look like you were conjured out of stardust and wishes."

Kholya glanced at his brother. "Pearl has made a poet of you."

"Attend to your own concerns," Sheyn told Kholya without taking his gaze off Kashyan's face.

Kholya cleared his throat. "We should go now."

When Kholya's party left the tent, they were met by an escort of four royal guards and shown to the center of the camp. On a flat stretch of turf, tables and torches had been set up in a horseshoe shape, and chairs waited for the high king's guests. Djulyan and a few others were already present, drinking from horns of wine and speaking cordially.

"Come and sit at my table," Djulyan called out. "I want a closer look at your daaksim. You're the only ones who brought companions to this court."

"Perhaps the others were afraid I'd steal them," Kashyan said.

Djulyan laughed heartily and then gave Kashyan a stern look. "I'll have no more of that sort of talk tonight," he said. "Now let me have a look at these beauties." Djulyan turned his gaze on Sheyn and Luks. "I've never been one for pretty boys. I loved my wife and I love my mistresses, but there is something about my daaksi that I can't resist." Djulyan drew breath to comment on Sheyn's exotic beauty when his eye strayed to Luks. He froze, staring at Luks like a man seeing a vision. "Who are you?" he whispered.

"You may answer," Kholya said formally to Luks.

"I'm called Velvet, Your Glory."

"Tell me how you came to be here. Begin at the beginning and don't worry that you'll bore me."

"I was raised and trained in the Shrine at Djenaes. When I was sixteen, I became a daaksi and was given to Yevdjen of Sumadin. I was with him for twenty-five years, and when he died, I was claimed by Prince Kholya."

"How did you come to the Shrine?"

"I was left there as a baby, Your Glory."

"And how old are you now?"

"I'm forty-two, Your Glory."

"You look no more than—" Djulyan called out. "Ardjul, where are you?"

A richly dressed young man broke off his conversation with the captain of the guard and hurried to the high king's side. "Yes, sire?"

"Ardjul, my son. Stand next to that boy."

"By Raas's Thunder, they could be brothers," Kholya said.

Djulyan stood. "My brother kings," he said to the assembled monarchs. "I must attend to an urgent personal matter. Please enjoy the food and drink and I will return to feast with you." He gestured to the people who stood closest to follow him and led them to his tent.

"What's this about?" Prince Ardjul asked.

Djulyan looked around at Kholya, Kashyan, Sheyn, and lastly, Luks. "I can scarcely dare to hope what I suspect."

"That doesn't make it any clearer, father."

"I have eleven sons as alike as pups from the same litter, saving the difference in height." Djulyan sighed. "But I should have twelve."

"Ah, this is the Little Lost Prince story," Ardjul said. "I grew up hearing it." He drew himself up in a majestic pose and affected a grand manner. "It's a family legend."

"Don't make light of it," Djulyan said. "After we lost our firstborn, it took your mother and I a long time to have another. She said she was too full of sorrow to carry a child. But then we had Daryan, and Ardjul, and they kept coming. Her sons made her happy, but I know she never forgot the child that was taken from her." His gaze rested on Luks as he spoke. "He was only three months old when he and his nursemaid disappeared from the royal gardens. She returned twelve years later and confessed she'd taken my child at her lover's bidding. However, she knew nothing of the people he'd sold the baby to. My agents spoke to every slaver that could be found, but no one remembered buying a babe with red hair. By then, the trail was too cold."

"What became of the nursemaid?" Sheyn asked.

"I ordered her execution, but I could not go through with it. I hoped that if she lived, she might someday remember a clue. She works in the palace laundry."

"Is there a way—?" Kholya began.

"Yes," Djulyan said. "There's a way to confirm whether Luks is the lost prince. I told you that all the children of my getting look alike. And they have one more thing in common: a birthmark shaped like the paw print of a bear."

Kholya and Luks exchanged a glance full of conflicting emotions.

"You have a mark like that," Sheyn said to Luks. "Those big freckles on your left hip."

"Is this true?" Djulyan asked.

Luks nodded.

"You're the right age, you look as much like me as any of my sons, and you have the birthmark." Djulyan cleared his throat. "I can only believe that you're my eldest son come back to me after so many years."

"But what does this mean?" Ardjul asked. "Is Daryan still crown prince?"

"Yes," Luks said, surprising everyone. "There's no reason for anything to change."

"But some things must change," Djulyan said gently. "My son can't be a daaksi."

"If you know a way to change it, Your Glory, please tell me," Luks said. "I know Pearl would be grateful."

Djulyan looked troubled as he ran his hand over his thinning ginger hair. "We should return to the feast, though it's not my wish. It's dangerous to leave a pack of kings alone for too long." He glanced at Luks and couldn't look away. "Djulz," he said. "That's what we named you. I only wish your mother was alive to see you."

"I wish that too," Luks said. "Your Glory, if I am your son, I think you should keep it a secret. The other kings will never accept me as a prince of the Misty Vales."

"I don't care what they think about you," Djulyan said. "If you don't wish to be acknowledged, I'll respect your decision. However, I must insist that you consider yourself part of my family. I want you to come to the Misty Vales and meet all your brothers."

Luks glanced at Kholya before he spoke. "My lord high king, I wish I could tell you of the joy in my heart right now. To know that I have a family—" He swallowed and went on in a steadier voice. "I want to speak more of this, but I can wait until the fate of the Savaani princes is decided, if it pleases you."

"I wish I could tell you how it feels for me to see my firstborn as a grown man." Djulyan stepped forward and pulled Luks into a hug. "If you have the strength to get through tonight and tomorrow, then I will find the strength inside myself to endure it as well." He let Luks go and stepped back.

Tears streamed down Luks's cheeks as he met Djulyan's eyes. "I will not call you father yet, but I hope to soon."

Djulyan ran a hand over Luks's hair and turned to leave the tent. Ardjul moved to his father's side as they set out and the rest followed him.

"I have to say." Sheyn leaned toward Luks as they walked side by side. "That was much more affecting than Fawn Fairskin's story. I came close to shedding tears myself."

"My face will be red and blotchy after all."

"Would you rather not attend the feast?"

"It's not my choice. I go where my master goes."

Sheyn put a hand on Kashyan's shoulder, and Kashyan turned his head. "Do we have to attend this feast?" Sheyn asked.

Djulyan overheard and stopped. "There is a tent set aside if your daaksim want to rest away from curious eyes," he said. "It's well-guarded."

Kholya met Luks's gaze for a long moment before he spoke. "Thank you, my lord. We'll take Pearl and Velvet there and then join you at the table."

The tent was a very short distance away, and Luks and Sheyn were soon made comfortable. However, despite the presence of a squadron of royal guards, Kashyan was reluctant to leave.

"We've an army around us and we're under the high king's protection," Kholya said. "But if it troubles you that much, Kasha, you can stay here too."

Kashyan shot his brother a black look before turning his gaze to Sheyn again. "We're too close to the Red Temple for my comfort."

"King Kezlath is at the banquet," Kholya said. "Do you think the Temple would attack and risk a demon gutting their king?"

"Yes, I do." Kashyan stroked a strand of hair away from Sheyn's face. "I think they'd do anything to get Pearl back."

"If they try, they won't find me as helpless as the last time," Sheyn said.

"You hear that, brother?" Kholya said. "Don't forget that your daaksi has the heart of a hero."

"That's what frightens me," Kashyan said. "Pearl, I forbid you to put yourself in danger. Do you hear me?"

"I hear you," Sheyn said. "You're adorable."

"Your mocking isn't amusing at this moment."

"Are you certain? *I* found it quite amusing."

"Not now," Kashyan said in a strained voice. "Please."

Sheyn framed Kashyan's face between his hands. "I promise," he said. "At the slightest sign of demonic activity, I will call for the guards."

Kashyan wrapped his arms around Sheyn and hugged him tightly. "My love," he whispered in Sheyn's ear. "Thank you for not wearing your sword to the feast." He kissed Sheyn and followed Kholya out of the tent.

"One thing's for certain," Sheyn said as he sat next to Luks. "You've made an impression on the high king."

THE NIGHT passed in peace, and Kashyan, Sheyn, Kholya, and Luks woke early in the tent the high king had provided for them. A servant arrived just after they'd dressed, leaving a tray of khai and cakes that Sheyn immediately pounced on. They'd just finished eating when they received a summons from Djulyan.

"I want to go with you," Sheyn told Kashyan, setting himself for an argument.

"Are you ready as you stand?"

"Am I—?" Sheyn narrowed his eyes. "Yes," he said as he picked up his cloak.

"Then come with me."

Kholya grinned at Sheyn's reaction to Kashyan's easy capitulation. "The high king invited you in his summons," Kholya told Sheyn.

Sheyn turned to Luks. "Aren't you coming?"

"No. I couldn't bear to be so near Ognyan. He has always frightened me."

"He makes my skin crawl," Sheyn said. "But I want to hear what's said in the court."

"You can tell me about it later. I'll wait here and perhaps the high king's daaksi will make an appearance. I'd like to meet him."

"I suppose it would be nice for you to have someone who wants to discuss the many methods of brewing khai or the most provocative way to recline on a pile of pillows."

Luks laughed. "You can't fool me any longer. I know you're teasing."

"Not this time." Sheyn dodged the pillow Luks threw at him.

"This may take some time," Kholya told Luks. "Are you certain you'll be all right alone?"

"If I suddenly long for company, I'll send word to Pearl," Luks said.

Kholya, Kashyan, and Sheyn walked to the pavilion where the high king was holding court. As at the feast, three tables were set up.

Djulyan sat at the center table, and the other kings sat at his left and right. Kholya took a seat on the right-hand side while Kashyan was instructed to stand in the area between the tables. Sheyn was given a seat on a couch behind Djulyan. When all were settled, the high king began to speak.

"I, Djulyan of the Misty Vales, High King of Kandaar, will now hear Ognyan of Sumadin on a matter of grave concern. Yevdjen of Sumadin is dead, and the new king sues for justice over the manner of Yevdjen's death. Step forth, King Ognyan, and speak your piece before your fellow rulers."

Ognyan rose from his seat and came to stand in the center of the room a few feet away from Kashyan. "Before I lay my charges at the feet of the villain, I raise another issue."

"You have leave," Djulyan said.

"I object to the presence of Kholya of Savaan on this Council of Kings. He is brother to the accused, and he took part in the crime. You cannot let him stand here for Savaan."

"Can't I?" Djulyan raised an eyebrow. "I was under the impression that I could appoint anyone I liked." He glanced at the other kings. "Am I wrong?"

Ognyan saw he had no support and let the matter drop. Kholya was only one vote, and Ognyan was certain the other kings would side with Sumadin. After all, if the Bastard could murder the king of Sumadin with impunity, which of them was safe? At the least, Kezlath's vote would cancel Kholya's.

"Your Glory," Ognyan said, bowing to the high king. "I am here to charge the Bastard of Savaan with the murder of King Yevdjen. I also charge him with the theft of my property. I would sooner meet him outside with a sword in my hand, but the new laws require me to bring my grievance to this council." He met the gaze of each man in turn. "With my own eyes, I saw the Bastard cut Yevdjen down. After killing the king, he stole my daaksi, the one who sits yonder looking like a cat in cream." Ognyan pointed at Sheyn. "When you're back where you belong, I'll slap that smirk from your face, slut."

"King Ognyan," Djulyan said loudly. "I have heard your grievance. If you've no more to add, you may sit or stand as it pleases you, but be silent until called upon."

Ognyan acknowledged the high king with a slight bow in Djulyan's direction and then went back to stand near his chair.

Djulyan looked to Kashyan. "And what is your answer?"

"I went into Sumadin for revenge on the man who dishonored my mother, the Queen of Savaan. I challenged him. He accepted and lost."

"And what of Pearl?"

Kashyan shifted his weight, bringing his hip forward and placing his sword in easy reach. "Pearl is mine."

Djulyan held up a hand to forestall Ognyan's protest. "When I received the request for a judgment, I sent my agents out to gather what information they could on this matter. I've formed what I believe is a clear picture of the events, and this is my judgment.

"Prince Kashyan acted within the bounds of honor in killing King Yevdjen. My agents, having spoken with Yevdjen's widow, find her description of the king's wounds quite telling, and their report leads me to believe Kashyan's account of the duel." Djulyan paused when Ognyan made a sound of strangled rage. "Hold your peace until I've finished," he said sternly.

"On the matter of the daaksi, Pearl." The high king glanced at Sheyn. "I have met with Kashyan and Pearl together, and I judge them to have a true bond. Therefore, it's not within my right to separate them. If you require a daaksi, Ognyan, I will require Kashyan to procure one for you. Now I will hear your thoughts on this judgment."

"Is this the will of the council?" Ognyan asked.

"The council advised me, and I considered their advice when I made my decision. You may address the council, if you wish."

"Is it truly your will, my lords, that Yevdjen of Sumadin go unavenged?" Ognyan asked. "Are you such cowards that you dare not go against the word of the high king? You all know the Bastard murdered my liege. He abducted my daaksi and Yevdjen's and ran to his brother who hides him still. Against my instincts, I brought this matter before you, trusting in you to judge fairly, but you're naught more than sheep led by a bellwether."

Djulyan held up a hand to still the outraged cries of the council. "You accuse me of having no naaks. Where were yours when your king was fighting for his life?"

"He was fleeing as fast as his horse could carry him," Kashyan said before Ognyan shouted him down.

"Prince Kashyan has the right to speak," Djulyan said.

"All of his words are lies," Ognyan said loudly.

"You're the liar," Kashyan said. "You were there when I fought Yevdjen, but you weren't at his side. You were in a bedchamber forcing yourself on an unwilling boy like the swine you are."

"No insults or threats will be tolerated here," Djulyan warned.

"I beg your pardon, sire," Kashyan said. "It irks me to see Ognyan of Sumadin standing there pretending to be a man."

"I will meet you whenever you like," Ognyan said. "Be sure you bring your sword."

"No more threats," Djulyan roared, and for a few moments, there was dead silence until he spoke again. "King Ognyan, have we heard your last word on this judgment?"

"I do not accept this judgment," Ognyan said.

"Ognyan!" Kezlath burst out, before he got himself under control.

"That's treason, Ognyan," said King Agneth-Khol.

"Defy me, and you will find the combined armies of the nations of Kandaar at your gates," Djulyan said.

"Then may I have your leave to go? I wish to return to Sumadin where the old ways are still honored."

"You may go," Djulyan said and waited until Ognyan had marched away before he resumed speaking. "Now *I* would like to raise a matter. Kezlath, I've had reports of banned rites being performed in the Red Temple."

"Sire, I—" Kezlath got to his feet.

"I could forgive you if this were a case of a king being unduly influenced by one of Taankh's Servants, but I understand that you conspired with the high priest. It's said you gave him leave to use such of your subjects as he found suitable for sacrifice. If you betrayed the sacred trust between a ruler and his people, you are no fit king."

"Who told you those filthy lies?" Kezlath asked, his voice rising on each word.

"The rite of summoning was witnessed by men whose word I trust. It's forbidden to call Taankh's Children into this world. You know this."

"I've called no demons," Kezlath said. "I gave you permission to enter the Temple and take back your daaksi. This is the doing of the white witch at your back. Ognyan told me how that unnatural daaksi called monsters down upon him."

"Yes, it's clear that Ognyan wishes harm to the Savaani, but you can't tell me you believe this daaksi wields sorcerous powers."

"My high priest believes it," Kezlath said.

"Thank you for reminding me." Djulyan cleared his throat. "High Priest Chanesh is charged with kidnapping Pearl and attempting to summon a demon."

"If you are punishing me for standing with Ognyan—"

"I'm thinking of charging you with treason. Do you wish to lose your crown?"

"You can't do that!"

"In fact, he can," said the Lake King. "But I for one would be disturbed if he did without showing evidence."

"Aye," agreed King Preth of Long Isle. "I'd want to see proof of Kezlath's perfidy before I consented to dethroning him."

"Then we shall have a tour of the Temple and give the high priest a chance to explain," Djulyan said. "And no one is to leave this assembly without my permission."

Kezlath broke off whispering to his aide and gave the high king a sickly smile. "I would be honored if you would all be my guests in Taar Muergan."

Djulyan called for the captain of the royal guard. "Keep watch over King Kezlath," he said. "Make sure he sends no messages ahead of us to the city."

"It will be done," the captain said.

"Then we should all go and prepare." Djulyan got to his feet and so did everyone else. "We'll meet before the gates of the city."

OGNYAN WENT from court into Taar Muergan. After stopping at the palace, he went to the Red Temple. He and his companion were admitted to the high priest's presence.

"Your Majesty." Chanesh greeted the king of Sumadin with a respectful bow. "I fear from the set of your face that the ruling did not go as we hoped."

"It was as you foretold," Ognyan said. "Djulyan brought his weight down on the side of the Savaanim. The sooner Kezlath takes the crown of high king, the happier I'll be."

Chanesh glanced at Ognyan's companion. "This must be the lad you told me about. Welcome to the Temple of Taankh, Prince Djenosh. Such a handsome young man. How old are you?"

"I'm to be sixteen in two months," the crown prince of Sumadin answered.

"Your uncle—" Chanesh glanced at Ognyan. "King Ognyan tells me you're very special."

"He shouldn't listen to my mother so much, sir," Djenosh said with one of his winning smiles.

"What a fetching lad," Chanesh said as he came from behind his writing desk. "I promised you a tour of the Temple, I believe."

Djenosh's eyes glowed at the thought of the morbid marvels that lay ahead in the fabled Red Temple. He couldn't believe his luck in being allowed to ride with his stepfather's honor guard, and now he was inside the ancient building whose stones were said to be steeped in blood. He was excited and a little bit scared, but he knew Ognyan would not allow him to come to harm.

"This way," Chanesh said as he led the way into the hall. "The building we're entering is the oldest structure in Muergath. It was constructed rather like a beehive. You probably noticed from the outside that the walls slope inward as they rise."

Ognyan grunted his lack of interest. Djenosh nodded politely, but he didn't care about the construction, either. Secretly, he hoped to see a demon, or at least an imp. He'd been fast asleep the night the creatures had attacked the camp at Karkaran Fortress, and he was keenly disappointed that there wasn't so much as a scale or a talon left in the morning.

"Before we continue to the Gate Chamber, I'd like you to meet someone." Chanesh paused before a door and the Red Monk on guard opened it.

"What happens in here?" Djenosh asked as he looked around the curved walls of the room. The only piece of furniture was a long table with candles burning at each corner.

"I'll show you," Yozif said as he moved into view.

Chapter
23

DJULYAN DISMISSED the council, and Kholya, Kashyan, and Sheyn went to their tent. Luks was very happy to hear of the high king's judgment but not overjoyed at the news that they were going to Taar Muergan.

"No good will come of this," he said.

"We're King Kezlath's guests," Kholya said. "He won't break guest-law. Djulyan's already threatened to take his crown away."

"I don't understand, my lord."

"The high king has the power to dethrone a monarch if that monarch proves himself rankly unworthy of his crown. Of course, enforcing such an order would require a war."

"I didn't know that," Luks said. "My lord?"

"Yes?"

"I've been afraid to ask, but do you believe I'm the high king's child?"

"How can I doubt it? Even if you aren't his lost firstborn, you are at the least one of his bastards. You and Prince Ardjul could be twins."

"I agree," Sheyn said as he handed around cups of snow-chilled water. "It's like a grand tale, isn't it? A stolen baby is revealed to be a prince." He paused. "Except the part about the prince being made into some sort of mystical pleasure slave." His eyes widened as he saw Luks's change of expression. "I'm sorry," he said quickly. "That was a thoughtless thing to say."

"But it's true," Luks said. "I'm glad to know I have a family, but I can't simply take my place with them. How could any of them see me without thinking about my past?"

"You surprise me," Sheyn said. "I thought you were proud to be a daaksi."

"I was." Luks looked down into his cup. "But the things I was proud of belong to the past. To be a daaksi in this age…. You're right. I'm merely a pleasure slave."

"Not to me," Kholya said. "I should have spoken before now, but I feel a true bond with you."

"I'm happy to hear you say it." Luks smiled, though tears trembled in his eyes.

Sheyn exchanged a glance with Kashyan and then spoke. "I can't bear to hear more of this. You'll have me weeping like a jilted bride, and we have to meet the high king at the city gates."

"You're going into Taar Muergan?" Luks said in surprise as he wiped his eyes.

"I want to see the high king pass judgment on the high priest. I know I'm a petty person, but I'll take pleasure in watching Chanesh humbled."

"Djulyan is skilled at humbling," Kholya said. He held out a hand to Luks. "Will you come with me?"

"You are my lord. I go where you go," Luks said, the words taking on a formal cadence. He took Kholya's hand and rose to his feet.

Kashyan watched Sheyn buckle on his sword belt. "Are you ready?" he asked.

Sheyn put his cloak around his shoulders, hiding his saber. "Yes, my lord. Now go, so I can go with you."

"What's it like kissing someone with a tongue that sharp?" Kholya asked his brother as they left the tent.

"I like the taste of blood," Kashyan said.

Kholya smiled as he greeted the royal guards who were waiting to escort them. They mounted their horses and rode to the gates of Taar Muergan. Djulyan was waiting with Kezlath and a troop of royal guards, but the other kings were not present.

"The council voted to abide by my judgment in this matter," Djulyan said when Kholya asked about the others. "I think they're unwilling to go any closer to the Red Temple."

"It has a fearsome reputation," Kezlath said. "But so do some of us."

"If you're speaking of me, my bloodthirsty reputation is true," Kashyan said.

"You follow the old ways in Savaan," Kezlath said easily. "It was all right in my father's day to ride out to war, but I'm content to let my officers lead my army."

"You sound very civilized," Sheyn said, and everyone turned to look at him. "My lord," he added.

Kezlath regarded Sheyn steadily for several moments. "So you're Pearl," he said. "You live up to the stories about you."

"I don't know if that's a compliment or an insult, my lord," Sheyn said. "I never listen to gossip."

"Very amusing," Kezlath said. "Are you looking forward to seeing Taar Muergan?"

"I can't in honesty say yes. I've been inside your Red Temple, and I didn't find it agreeable."

"He's absolutely unique," Kezlath told Kashyan. "What's it like to top him, though?"

"You'll never know," Kashyan said as he stepped in front of Sheyn.

Kezlath chuckled as though Kashyan had made a jest, but Djulyan's frown was like a thundercloud.

"Pearl," the high king said. "I've read the reports of your ordeal in the Red Temple, but soon I'll ask to hear an account from your own lips. Are you prepared to speak of what occurred there?"

Sheyn called on the manners learned while attending his mother's council meetings. "If Your Glory commands it of me, I will accomplish it," he said with a graceful bow.

Djulyan smiled warmly. "Are you a swan or a falcon? I'm damned if I can tell."

"Somewhat of both, sire," Kashyan said.

Djulyan chuckled and then turned to Kezlath. "I'd be pleased to see your city now."

Kezlath gestured to the high king to precede him, and they went through the gates down a street cleared of people. The citizens of Taar Muergan lined both sides of the road and stared curiously at the nobles who rode by. A few cheers were raised for King Kezlath, but the people were for the most part silent.

At the center of the city, the party rode into the vast square that surrounded the Red Temple. They drew rein before the clusters of stepped pyramids around the lumpy cone of the central building. The yellow bricks of the original temple were rounded with age, and some were missing, but no birds built nests in the handy niches.

"Gods of my fathers, what a sad pile of rocks," Djulyan said under his breath.

"Shall I send a runner to the high priest and let him know of your visit, sire?" Kezlath asked.

"No. If he hasn't already been warned, I'd like to take him by surprise."

"Are you sure that's wise, sire?" Kezlath raised an eyebrow. "If what you suspect is true, surprising him might have disastrous results."

"If what I suspect is true, the results will be disastrous for Chanesh whatever befalls," Djulyan said. "Any person who deliberately summons a demon forfeits his life."

With an escort of eight royal guards, the high king entered the Red Temple. In front of him were four guards. To his left was Kezlath. On his right was Kholya. Behind Kholya walked Kashyan, Sheyn, and Luks, and behind them, four more guards. A Red Monk approached to guide them, and Luks took Sheyn's hand.

"It was foolish to come here," Luks said softly as they followed the monk. "I can feel this place wanting to swallow me whole."

"You're not making it better," Sheyn whispered. "Think about how easily demons die when you cut them with steel."

"Aren't you frightened?"

"I'm so scared I can barely speak." Sheyn took a shaky breath. "But I'm not going to let my fear rule me. This is an evil place and I'll do what I can to see it destroyed." As he said the words, he felt the truth of them, and he knew this was his purpose. He was here in Kandaar to rid this realm of Taankh's pollution. He'd never had a cause before, other than satisfying his own wants and needs, and it was a marvel to him how much he'd changed in such a short time. With a sense of renewed purpose, he lengthened his stride until Luks's tug on his hand reminded him of his place. Once he would have chafed at the reminder, but now he merely slowed his steps and twined his fingers with Luks's.

Luks squeezed Sheyn's hand in gratitude for the comforting touch. The sense of something huge looming overhead waiting to crush them grew stronger with each step until Luks could barely hold his head up.

"Wait," Kashyan said when the Red Monk turned left at a junction in the arched passageway. "We want to go right."

"That is First Temple. Only Taankh's Servants may enter there," the monk said.

"I give my leave as King of Muergath," Kezlath said when Djulyan looked at him.

"As you will, sire." The monk bowed before leading them down the right-hand corridor. He saw no point in arguing with the king. If the visitors saw anything they shouldn't, this part of the Temple had ways of protecting itself. It was here long before Muergath had a king, and it would be here when this city was dust. The monk didn't fear a human king whose life was just a firefly flash in the great night of the world.

"STOP! PLEASE!" Prince Djenosh wailed as the high priest made another precise cut on the young man's abdomen.

"Shut up!" Ognyan ordered. "A Sumadi warrior doesn't howl like an infant who misses his mother's teat."

"Please, make it stop," Djenosh begged, as he had begged many times since he woke shackled to this altar. He couldn't understand why Ognyan stood by while the high priest hurt him. No matter how Djenosh pleaded, his stepfather answered with a growled command to be quiet. Nor did he understand what had happened to him, but he knew he was somehow different. The first cuts Chanesh had made were already healed, and he'd swear he could hear the high priest's thoughts. Abruptly, he received a very clear vision of what Chanesh hoped to achieve, and he began to scream and pull at his manacles again.

SHEYN LET go of Luks's hand and began walking faster. He passed Kashyan, Kholya, and Djulyan as he broke into a trot.

"Pearl!" Kashyan shouted.

"This way," Sheyn called back as he passed the Red Monk. Following the emanations of extreme distress, he found the repaired door of the Gate Chamber. "In here!"

Kashyan reacted to the urgency in his daaksi's voice. Drawing his sword, he pushed past the royal guards and grabbed the door handle. "Kholya!" he shouted when the door didn't budge.

Kholya put his shoulder against the door, and two royal guards jumped to help. The four men crashed into the door.

"Merciful Mother!" Djulyan exclaimed when he could see into the chamber. "Guards! Stop this evil."

Ognyan stood before the altar with his sword in his hand as Chanesh continued chanting. Djenosh's scream cut through the turmoil, and everyone looked up when the demon materialized near the ceiling.

"Kill that thing," Djulyan roared.

Kholya and the eight guardsmen rushed across the room, and Chanesh saw his dearly held plans crashing around him. Pulling an amulet from under his robes, he incanted a spell. The demon swept the high priest up in one of its six limbs and disappeared with a sound like a cork being pulled from a bottle.

"Ognyan, put down your sword," Djulyan called out as Sheyn brushed past him.

"I've waited too long for this, Bastard," Ognyan said. "Now we fight man to man as it was meant to be."

"You are no true man." Kashyan made the first move, leaping high and angling to the right as he slashed downward at Ognyan.

The king of Sumadin dodged aside and parried Kashyan's strike. As Kashyan landed behind Ognyan, Ognyan whirled with a speed that belied his bulk. Kashyan bent his knees and threw himself sideways to avoid the blow that would've decapitated him. As momentum pulled Ognyan around in a half circle, Kashyan rose from his crouch. Ognyan flung himself forward, and Kashyan's potentially crippling blow at Ognyan's legs was foiled. Kashyan's blade slid across the back of Ognyan's left knee, slicing into one hamstring but leaving him upright and mobile. Furious that Kashyan had drawn first blood, Ognyan released a bellow of pure rage and swung his blade harder and faster, raining blows on Kashyan. Kashyan gave ground under the barrage until he was at the altar. As he parried another hammering strike, his heel came down in a pool of Djenosh's blood. Kashyan's foot went out from under him, and Ognyan's next swing passed harmlessly over his head.

Sheyn saw Kashyan slip, and he saw Ognyan prepare to take advantage of his downed foe. He ceased trying to free the boy on the altar and drew his saber. Leaping down to the floor, he deflected Ognyan's whistling strike at Kashyan's neck.

"Poisonous witch!" Ognyan said from between clenched teeth. "I'll gut you like a sackfish!"

Djulyan had kept his men from the fight out of respect for a duel of honor, but now that Sheyn had joined the fray, it was a different matter. "Arrest Ognyan of Sumadin," Djulyan ordered the captain of his honor guard.

Kashyan scrambled to his feet as the royal guards gathered in a circle around the combatants. For a moment, Kashyan watched in fascination as Sheyn slid fluidly away from Ognyan's thrusts. And then one of the Sumadinim's blows grazed Sheyn's forearm, and a line of red appeared on Sheyn's pale skin. A rush of intense emotions blasted through Kashyan like a furnace wind and propelled him forward.

"Stay back," Kashyan ordered the royal guards as he pulled Sheyn behind him.

Kashyan said not a word as he engaged Ognyan again. He fought without hesitation, as a man certain of the outcome. He felt stronger than he ever had in his life, and each move he made felt preordained, as though he'd practiced this dance many times. Methodically, he broke through each of Ognyan attempts to counter his strikes or go on the offensive. He saw Ognyan's eyes change as the possibility of defeat entered his thoughts, and he pressed the attack, driving Ognyan backward, step-by-step, until his back was against the altar. Kashyan raised his sword high and swung with all his might at Ognyan's neck. Ognyan brought his blade up to block the slashing strike and watched in horror as his broadsword was cut in two. The blow struck Ognyan with diminished strength, and he kept his head but suffered a terrible cut to the side of his face. Dazed, Ognyan dropped to his knees.

"Take him!" Djulyan shouted at the guards. "Kashyan of Savaan! Put down your sword!"

Kashyan stood over Ognyan, breathing hard, trembling with the effort of standing still. The one who had hurt his love was a breath away from the point of his sword. A single thrust between the ribs, hardly any effort at all, and a stain would be scrubbed from the world.

"Bastard." Sheyn's voice pierced the red mist that surrounded Kashyan.

Kashyan looked up at the touch of a hand on his arm.

Sheyn smiled at his lover. "If anyone's going to kill this beast, it will be me. Let the high king have him."

The royal guards swarmed over Ognyan and bound his hands behind him. Through a mask of blood, Ognyan glared balefully at anyone who glanced at him.

The high king ignored Ognyan and gave another order. "Free him," he commanded, pointing at the altar.

"You'll need the key," Kashyan said after inspecting the shackles.

"The key probably disappeared with Chanesh," Kholya said. "Call for a stonemason with his mallet and chisel."

"I don't believe it!" Djulyan said as he came closer. "I met this boy yesterday. This is Djenosh, the crown prince of Sumadin." He gave Ognyan a disbelieving look. "When your fellow kings hear of this, they'll demand I take your crown."

"None of you are fit to judge me," Ognyan answered. "Look at you, you bunch of women."

"Take him out of here and send for a mason," Djulyan told the guards. "Kezlath, go with them to your palace and prepare a chamber for a court of judgment. Send for the council of kings. I want to pass sentence swiftly."

"What of me, sire?" Kezlath asked.

"I have no proof you condoned your high priest's actions. Until I have such evidence, you retain your rights as a sovereign lord. However, keep in mind that a good king would have known what was happening here."

"Yes, sire." Kezlath bowed and accompanied the guards and their prisoner out of the temple.

Sheyn bent over the unconscious young man on the altar, and the sight of the marred flesh reignited his fury at Taankh's Servants. "Help me," he said as he reached for Kashyan's hand.

Kashyan took Sheyn's hand in his. "Tell me what to do."

Sheyn made a frustrated noise. "I need your strength."

Kashyan squeezed Sheyn's hand. "What I have is yours."

Grasping one of the chains in his fist, Sheyn channeled his rage into a pure beam of energy. The metal flew apart, sending shards flying and freeing one of the sacrifice's hands. Sheyn concentrated, and the shackles around Djenosh's ankles and his other wrist disintegrated into powder. "Someone take him out of here," he said wearily.

Kashyan lifted Djenosh down and put him in Djulyan's arms. When Sheyn swayed on his feet, Kashyan swept him up with an arm around his back and one under his knees. With the high king in the lead, they let the royal guard clear a path to the palace. Along the way, the people stared at Djenosh's injuries and muttered among themselves.

Chapter
24

OGNYAN STOOD in the center of the chamber, unrepentant in his chains. He sneered openly at the monarchs gathered to pass judgment on him.

"Majesties all," Djulyan said as he entered the chamber. "I regret that I had to call you together again so soon, but this is matter so grave, I am not willing to take it on myself."

"We are here to aid you in way we can," said Lukha, King of the Sea of Grass.

Preth of Long Isle and Agneth-Khol nodded their agreement.

"Ognyan of Sumadin," Djulyan said sternly. "I charge you with conspiring to raise demons. I charge you with the attempted murder of the crown prince of Sumadin. I charge you—" He broke off as the other kings began speaking at once.

"What's this about the crown prince?" Preth asked. "Djenosh is my queen's nephew."

"Ognyan turned him over to the Red Temple for use in the ritual of summoning," Djulyan said. "I saw this with my own eyes."

Preth focused his gaze on Ognyan. "You filthy—" he shouted before outrage choked his voice.

"Can this be true?" Lukha asked.

"I can bring the lad in and let him tell it in his own words," the high king said.

"Sire," Preth called out. "Allow me the honor of cutting Ognyan's head off."

"None of you dare touch me," Ognyan shouted. "I don't recognize your authority over me."

"Yet you will answer for these crimes," Djulyan told him. "I strip you of your crown, your title, and all rights that go with them. As soon as a suitable spot is found, your head will come off. Does anyone have anything to add?"

"I volunteer for the job of headsman," Preth said immediately.

"Granted." Djulyan looked around the room. "I find I cannot condemn Kezlath of Muergath without more evidence. Are you content with this?"

"Aye," the council answered in unison.

"If I may, sire," Kezlath said. "It would please me greatly if you would all be my guests at a banquet tonight."

After everyone accepted the invitation, Kezlath hurried away to arrange a sumptuous feast to begin buying his way back into favor. Djulyan dismissed all but the Savaani princes and their daaksim. Together, the five retired to a bedchamber where Djenosh was being cared for.

"Poor lad," Djulyan said. "He'll have nightmares all his life."

"And what sort of life will it be now that he's a daaksi?" Sheyn asked.

Djulyan cursed as the reality of Djenosh's situation came home to him. "Beheading is too good for Ognyan."

"This raises interesting questions," Kholya said. "Djenosh is the crown prince of Sumadin, Yevdjen's only male child. But the other kings won't accept a daaksi on the throne."

"Then let there be an end to the worship of Taankh and the practice of creating daaksim!" Djulyan's voice filled the chamber, and silence reigned for several moments after he finished speaking.

"Are you banning them completely?" Kholya asked. "If so, you have my wholehearted support. Though I pity the kings who won't know what it is to be owned by a daaksi."

"If this incident does not convince my fellow rulers that worship of the Demon God and the custom of daaksim should be done away with, then I do not know what will. This could have happened to any one of their sons."

"If you put it that way, they'll demand you ban Taankh's Servants," Kholya predicted.

"The first thing we need to do is find the high priest," Sheyn said. "As long as he's free, this dark faith will never die."

As though it were the most natural thing in the world to take advice from a daaksi, Djulyan gave his captain orders to perform a search for the high priest. "Though I hold out little hope of finding him. Who knows where the demon may have taken him? He might be in the next room or he might be in the Shadoworld."

"I still don't understand this religion," Sheyn said. "Why would anyone choose to worship a God whose greatest desire is their destruction? I could feel the minds of the demons. All their thoughts are of rending flesh and basking in misery."

"They do it to gain power," Djulyan said. "If a man can coerce a demon to do his bidding, he can easily do away with his enemies."

"I don't understand the kind of person that would court such an ally," Sheyn said. "And I hope I never do."

"Well said, Pearl." Djulyan smiled for the first time since entering the temple. "And now that's settled, when will we have your trial for using witchcraft?"

"Trial, Your Glory?" Sheyn said, looking up Djulyan with wide eyes.

"I'm joking with you," the high king said. "But that was a very winning look." He chuckled. "Don't be concerned. Though I saw you use magic, it wasn't in service of evil."

"On my honor, sire," Sheyn said. "I'm not a witch." He looked up at Kashyan.

"A witch he may be," Kashyan said to Djulyan. "But there's no evil in him. Spite he has in plenty and enough pride for a God, but no evil."

"Spite?" Sheyn repeated.

"You do tend to hold a grudge."

"Still, I think you might have chosen another word."

"Sire," Kholya spoke up. "When you have leisure, I'd like to speak with you about...." His gaze went to Luks.

"You love him," Djulyan said.

"With all my heart, sire."

"I see." Djulyan paused in thought, his eyes on Luks's face. "I think my son will find happiness with you. And I know you'll care for him as though he was porcelain from Weijan. But you must promise me one thing."

"Yes, sire?"

"You must let me host a bond fire for you."

"I'd be honored." Kholya bowed. "And if you did not already know it, you have my loyalty to my last breath." He glanced at the prince who moved restlessly in his sleep. "I should go and let Prince Djenosh have peace and quiet."

Djenosh woke then and cried out. After a few minutes, he realized he was safe, and he calmed down. When he saw Sheyn in the crowd around his bed, he spoke. "I know you. You freed me."

"I helped," Sheyn said, coming forward. He put a gentle hand on Djenosh's forehead, and a frown creased his brow. "Kashyan," he said softly, and Kashyan came to put a hand on his shoulder, lending his energy to Sheyn's healing of Djenosh. Sheyn looked into Djenosh's eyes for a long moment and then stepped back.

Djenosh relaxed against the pillows and the haunted look left his eyes. "Thank you all for saving me," he said. "Could someone send to Sumadin and tell the queen what has happened?"

"I'll send a scribe to you to take down your words," Djulyan said. "And one of my couriers will carry your message."

"Where is Ognyan?" Djenosh asked. "What has become of him?"

"Ognyan of Sumadin is under arrest and will be executed as soon as you give the word," Djulyan said. "You are the heir to Sumadin's throne, and as Ognyan is now your subject, it is your right to name the manner of execution and to conduct it if you wish."

"I wish he could be cast into Taankh's realm to suffer endless torment," Djenosh said fiercely, and then his eyes filled with tears. "Why did he do this to me?" he asked in a choked voice. "All my life I called him uncle, and he gave me to the priests as if he cared no more for me than a buzzing fly."

"I don't know, but you're safe now," Djulyan said. "Rest if you can. Someone will be with you to tend your needs."

"Don't leave me here," Djenosh said. "Please take me out of this place."

"As you wish," Djulyan said. "My royal guards will escort you to my camp. You'll stay in my tent until you're fully recovered." He gestured to Kholya and Kashyan to accompany him and left the chamber.

"I know it's soon to think about it," Kholya said. "But perhaps you could set one of your older sons to rule Sumadin for a time."

"There would be many among the Sumadi nobility who would oppose an outsider, but it would go a long way toward preventing a civil war."

"Especially since the Sumadinim would know that your regent would have the backing of your armies, sire," Kashyan said.

"I don't like putting a nation under martial law," Djulyan said.

"Think of it as setting an example," Sheyn said. "And as a deterrent to treachery."

Djulyan swiveled his head to look at Sheyn.

Sheyn cleared his throat. "And of course, when you lift martial law, the people will hail you as a liberator, Your Glory."

"I hope Prince Kashyan takes no notion to rule Kandaar. With you at his side, I think he'd accomplish it."

"Prince Kashyan is loyal to you," Sheyn said. "And he'd rather be flayed alive than rule a kingdom."

Djulyan chuckled. "You remind me a bit of my daaksi. Not that Djeyd has your sharpness of wit, but he's very amusing when he wishes to be."

"When will we meet him?" Sheyn asked.

"Djeyd comes and goes with the wind. Locking him in a room does no good, so I've stopped trying to keep him. He always returns and is never gone longer than two sunsets." He paused. "And what did I say to earn that sweet smile?"

"You're not what I expected in a Kandaari high king. Since you know my reputation for a forward tongue, I'll tell you that I expected you'd be the biggest brute of all. Yet you're kind, and wise, and not at all barbaric."

"You cannot judge all of us by Ognyan," Djulyan said.

"Sadly, he was the first Kandaarim I met, unless you count Brother Yozif."

"Ognyan is worse than an animal," Djulyan said. "No animal would behave so badly." He paused as they reached the front of the palace. "I should send to King Preth. There's no reason to delay Ognyan's execution." He looked at Kholya and Kashyan in turn. "I'd like you to attend, along with the council of kings. I want as many witnesses as possible, and I want the sight of Ognyan's severed head to be a warning in case another ruler considers conspiring with Taankh's Servants."

AT THE hour named by the high king, he and a number of nobles gathered in a small courtyard of the royal palace in Taar Muergan. True night had not yet fallen, and a soft twilight exalted the plain gray stone of the paving, the walls, and the block set in the center of the grass. Beside the block stood Preth of Long Isle with a broadsword in his hand. Prince Djenosh, having recovered with a daaksi's swiftness, was at the side of the high king to see justice done.

Servants came to light torches, and then the prisoner was brought forth. A wooden door opened in the west wall, and four royal guards marched in with Ognyan in chains between them. Ognyan was brought to the block and by the strength of all four guards was made to kneel. His head was forced down until it rested against the stone, and he was tied there to await the killing stroke. Preth looked to Djulyan, and the high king stepped forward.

"Ognyan, late of Sumadin, you've been judged guilty of terrible crimes. Your life is forfeit and the sentence will be carried out now. If you wish to name others who took part in this crime, this will be your last chance to speak."

"So the sheep will kill the wolf," Ognyan said. "That is how it is in Kandaar now. Everything is upside down and backward. I only wish I could live to see Chanesh take the crown from you. I'd like to see you grovel when—"

Ognyan's words were cut short when Preth brought his sword down. The sharp, heavy blade sliced cleanly through Ognyan's neck and clanged on the stone. A blood-chilling shriek followed the decapitation, and a huge demon dropped from the sky onto Ognyan's body.

"Kill it," Djulyan shouted, and the royal guards ran toward the monster.

Before the soldiers reached the demon, the creature beheaded Preth with a swipe of a claw and sent the broadsword flying. Sinking its talons into Ognyan's flesh, it bent to snuffle at the limp, headless body. With a scream of rage, it flung the corpse at the oncoming guards and extended its wings.

"Stay," Kashyan told Sheyn and followed Kholya across the courtyard.

"Why doesn't it fly away?" Sheyn muttered. He tightened his fingers around the hilt of his saber as he watched the battle. The demon was nearly twice the height of a man, with six long arms that ended in talons like daggers. Each sweep of its limbs dealt horrible wounds while the Kandaarim could not come within sword's reach. Several throwing knives were embedded in the monster's flesh, but it took no notice of them. Sheyn watched Kashyan duck under a black claw to slash at the demon's legs. He cursed when one of the creature's heel spurs caught Kashyan in the lower back and toppled him.

"Sheyn!" Luks cried out as Sheyn left his side. "No!"

Sheyn paid no attention to anyone's orders for him to stop. He bounded past the guards, weaving through them as he dodged the demon's claws with a daaksi's phenomenal speed. Seeing Kashyan on his feet, Sheyn moved toward him.

"Get back," Kashyan shouted when he saw Sheyn. In the next instant, he parried a swooping claw and sheared the tip off. He reeled back from the force of the blow but kept his footing as the demon attacked again. In his peripheral vision, he saw Sheyn coming closer and his heart froze. "Get away," he yelled.

"I can help," Sheyn said, wondering again why the beleaguered beast didn't simply fly away. He assumed the high priest had sent the demon to rescue Ognyan but too late. With its mission failed, it only made sense that it return to its master. Or was the demon's lust for blood and suffering stronger than Chanesh's command of it?

Abruptly, the demon's head swung down, and the four gleaming eyes between its ram horns fastened on Sheyn. Its leathery nostril slits whistled as it leaned over him, sniffing loudly. The creature's maw opened, exposing row after row of needle teeth, and it let out a great bellow of triumph. The basso roar ended in a shriek of agony as Kashyan's sword severed one of its legs at the ankle joint.

Sheyn closed his eyes and reached for the power that had come to him when he needed to save Luks's life. He waited for the force to rise in him so he could blast the demon, but he felt nothing. Opening his eyes, he gripped his saber tightly and stabbed up at the monster.

The demon flapped its wings to stay upright as viscous fluid poured from the stump of its right leg. It kept up a constant keening of pain as it hovered, avoiding the blades of Kashyan and the royal guards, as it grabbed at Sheyn. The creature suffered several stab wounds from Sheyn's saber, but at last it snagged its claws in Sheyn's long hair and bore him aloft.

Sheyn cut at the demon's limb, but it grasped the sword in its mouth and flung it away. Hauling Sheyn higher, it took hold of him with two more claws. The freezing cold of the demon's knobbed hide quickly penetrated Sheyn's clothing, chilling him to the bone. Staving off panic, he once again tried to summon the power to blast the demon. He didn't care that he might fall to his death. Anything was preferable to being in the clutches of Taankh's Servants.

"Pearl!" Kashyan shouted.

Sheyn looked down and saw Kashyan clutching the beast's maimed lower limb.

"Hold on. I'm coming for you."

Kashyan sheathed his sword and reached up. At the same moment, the demon kicked backward with its uninjured leg. A cloven hoof the size of an anvil struck Kashyan in the chest and sent him flying. Sheyn looked down and saw Kashyan land on a tower not too far below. He watched Kashyan get to his feet and saw his mouth moving. Though he was too high to hear Kashyan's voice, he knew what his man was saying. Kashyan would come for him.

KHOLYA MET Kashyan halfway up the tower stairs. "It's all right, Kasha. We're going to get Pearl back. And the council of kings has approved my proposal to burn down that filthy temple."

As they descended to ground level, Kashyan reached out to clasp Kholya's forearm and give it a squeeze. "Good. I'm going to the Red Temple to fetch Pearl. If anyone tries to hinder me, he forfeits his life."

"I've sent a runner for the Black Hawks," Kholya said as they left the tower.

"Then they can meet me there." Kashyan took off at a dead run.

Kholya paused long enough to bow to Djulyan and give Luks a reassuring look before he followed Kashyan. It wasn't far from the palace to the temple square, but the demon could get there a lot faster than a man running through the streets. And the high priest could cause a lot of grief in a few minutes.

They heard the footsteps of a large group behind them and turned to see a company of Djulyan's royal guards. The captain saluted and stayed on the Savaani princes' heels as they raced to the square. When they poured into the plaza, they saw several ranks of Red Monks assembled to block entry to the temple.

Chapter 25

"NO!" SHEYN gasped as he regained awareness and felt the rough, cold stone under him. He hadn't forgotten the gritty, greasy feel of the altar in the Gate Chamber. Fear flooded in, and he reached out with all his senses as he tried to gauge the immediate threat. The air was heavy with the smoke of the human lard candles, and overlaying that was the rotted-meat smell of a demon's breath. He raised his head as the door opened, but the shackles made it impossible to move his arms or legs.

"Quickly!" Chanesh said as he entered the chamber. "We haven't much time."

Sheyn glanced behind the high priest and saw no one, though he could feel the presence of a demon. He followed Chanesh with his gaze as Taankh's Chief Servant went around the room lighting more of the thick candles. Pushing aside the weight of dread that threatened to suffocate him, Sheyn spoke to the high priest.

"You're all alone now, aren't you? Ognyan is dead. King Kezlath has renounced you, and the high king's men are hunting you. But those are the least of your worries. The Bastard of Savaan is coming for me, and he won't be gentle with you, if you're still here when he arrives." He took a shuddering breath. "You should leave here now. Run as fast as you can and go as far away as possible."

Chanesh gave no sign he'd heard Sheyn. His head was bent over an array of objects on a stone shelf. After choosing one, he went over to the altar.

Sheyn's eyes were irresistibly drawn to the gleaming metal of the small knife in the high priest's hand. "Get away from me, monster," he said.

"You call me monster?" For the first time, Chanesh looked directly at Sheyn.

"Because you *are* a monster. Who else but a monster would take up a knife and calmly cut another person over and over in the hope of raising a demon?"

"Why do you fear the knife so? I've always wondered, but the ritual doesn't allow for personal communication, so I've never asked."

"You are truly mad. I fear it because it hurts."

"But you heal right away. I've never seen a daaksi heal as quickly as you."

"It still hurts." Sheyn steadied himself as the knife neared his thigh. "And besides the pain, the stench of evil in this chamber makes me ill."

"If you're going to be sick, turn your head so you don't choke on your spew. If you die, you're of no use to me."

Sheyn shivered as the cold blade touched his skin. "Why are you doing this?" he asked. "Your evil has been exposed. What can you hope to gain by torturing me?"

"Yozif tells me you're much stronger now. I'm going to use you to bring Taankh across the Threshold into this world. When Taankh has come, He will destroy all who oppose me. Kezlath shall be high king and do my bidding."

"Isn't it more likely that your God will pull your head off and drink your blood?"

Chanesh raised a hand to stroke an amulet around his neck. "Taankh knows who his Servants are. He might devour you, though."

"Kasha will be here before then."

"The demon at the door will keep him busy for a while." Chanesh pressed down with the blade and made the first cut. He chanted as he circled the altar, and the emanations of Sheyn's pain and horror carried his message to the Shadoworld and the ears of the God of Death.

Taankh raised his massive head, crowned with the horns of a bull, and savored the intoxicating draughts of distress. He stirred from his throne-nest of burning coals and followed the alluring scent. The coils of his tentacles carried him over the bone-strewn floor to a roofless section of the chamber. Taankh snatched up a scuttling imp with a whiplash of his tongue and ate the scavenging creature in two bites. His hunger assuaged, he prepared to endure the burning cold of the space between the worlds.

THOUGH OUTNUMBERED, Kholya, Kashyan, and the royal guards kept the temple's militia at bay until the Black Hawks arrived. The Savaani cavalry turned the tide, their battle-wise chargers bowling over the enemy as they rode through them. Kashyan grabbed on to a stirrup strap and ran beside the horse, slashing at the monks until they reached the steps of the temple. Kashyan patted the rider's calf and dashed up the stairs and through the entrance, outstripping his allies. He could feel Sheyn's agony, and it drew him unerringly to the Gate Chamber.

The demon that guarded the door to the chamber roared when it saw Kashyan. The grating bellow echoed off the stone walls as the creature raised its forelegs and scissored its pincers.

Kashyan didn't slow down. He charged directly at the monster with his sword in front of him. As he came within reach of the thing's barbed pincers, he reversed his grip on the hilt and sprang high. As he passed to the left of the clacking claws, he slashed downward, severing the insectile forelimbs at the middle joint. He collided with the demon, and the beast staggered back but stayed on its hooves. Kashyan shouted in pain as needle teeth sank into his shoulder. Bringing his sword around, he sliced the creature's snout and it let go. With a turn of his wrist, he shortened the return arc of the heavy blade and sheared through the demon's skull from jaw to gnarled scalp. The monster dropped like a puppet with its strings cut, and Kashyan left it where it fell.

KHOLYA, ALONG with the surviving guards and Black Hawks, entered the temple over the bodies of the Red Monks. Behind him came the high king and the members of the council as well as Kezlath. As they crossed the slate-paved antechamber to the temple, the ground shook and tilted under their feet with a menacing rumble.

A PUFF of smoky darkness appeared between the altar and the ceiling of the Gate Chamber. It spread rapidly, becoming denser until it was a depthless hole boring straight to the Shadoworld. Sheyn clenched his fists and his teeth, determined not to scream when the monster appeared. Ruthlessly, he clamped down on his panic, calmed his breathing, and slowed the racing beat of his heart.

"What are you doing?" Chanesh barked. He gazed up at the lightless tunnel, troubled when he saw no sign of his God. "Stop or I'll cut off your fingers. Then we'll see if you're able to grow new ones."

Sheyn ignored the threat and concentrated on mastering his emotions the way his fencing master had taught him in another life.

With a snarl, Chanesh went through the door in the opposite wall and returned with a young man bound in chains. The high priest brought the lad up to the altar and put the knife to his throat. "This is—" Chanesh paused. "Which one are you?" he asked the captive.

"Moksha," the young man said dully.

"Pearl, this is Moksha, and if you don't stop blocking the Threshold, I'll use him to finish the ritual." Chanesh drew the blade against Moksha's skin, and blood trickled down Moksha's neck.

On the other side of the Threshold, Taankh bellowed and thrust a tentacle through the small gap that had opened. Chanesh cut Moksha again, and Sheyn cried out. In a few more moments, the ceiling was a writhing nest of purple-black tentacles with phosphorescent greenish-white suckers. The chamber was fetid with the choking reek of a stagnant swamp full of putrid corpses. Taankh bellowed in triumph, and the Red Temple shook to its foundations.

"Master!" Chanesh cried out, pushing Moksha away and lifting his arms in worship as more of Taankh's bulk squeezed through the gap.

Kashyan burst through the ruined doorway of the chamber and ran at the high priest. Before Chanesh could react, Kashyan ran him through. Pushing the high priest's body off his blade, Kashyan leaped aside from the whiplash of a tentacle. He swung at the thick limb and lopped off the tip. Dodging the thrashing tentacle, he moved toward the altar, but several more barred his way. Determined to get to Sheyn, he began hacking his way through the ropy limbs.

Sheyn lost his calm when he sensed Kashyan near, and he yanked desperately at his shackles. Blood ran from gouges in his wrists and ankles, but still he tried to pull free. When he felt a touch on his arm, he froze.

"I can help you," Moksha said. Turning his back to the altar, Moksha leaned against it, feeling under the lip for the bolts that fastened the chains to the stone. It was difficult with his hands bound, but he found the metal tongue that released the king bolt. With all his strength, he leaned against the latch, and it flipped over.

The next time Sheyn pulled on his chains, they slithered through their brackets. The manacles were still attached to him, but he was able to get down from the altar. "How do I free you?" he asked Moksha with his gaze on Kashyan.

"High Priest Chanesh has the key."

Sheyn crawled to the high priest's body and searched it. He found a key on a chain around Chanesh's neck and took it along with the amulet before he unlocked the chains that bound Moksha.

"Thank you," Moksha said as he sank wearily to the floor and leaned against the altar.

Sheyn turned away to do what he could to help Kashyan. "Bastard!" he called out. "It looks as though you've found a challenge at last."

A tentacle rippled across the floor in front of Sheyn, too big to jump over. He wrapped his fingers around the chain dangling from his wrist and lashed at the tentacle.

"Again!"

Sheyn flinched at the sound of an unfamiliar voice, but he couldn't take his eyes off the tentacle. In another moment, a slim young man with vivid red hair was at his side, cutting at the tentacle with a dagger. Sheyn caught a flash of aquamarine eyes as the stranger slashed at a feeler that reared up between them.

"I'm Djeyd," he shouted. "How do you feel? Are you weak?"

"Aside from these chains, I'm well."

"Good. We need to keep Taankh from emerging completely. The only reason we're still alive is that he can't see into this realm yet."

"Kashyan," Sheyn gasped.

"Stay here! Kashyan will be fine for a few minutes." Djeyd stomped on a small tentacle, and it went wriggling off. "They don't seem to be attacking you anymore," he observed.

Sheyn pointed to the necklace wrapped around his hand. "I took this from the high priest. I think it's some sort of—"

"It's an amulet that identifies you as a Servant," Djeyd said. "Clever of you. Now, come with me."

Leaping over and dodging around flailing tentacles, the daaksim reached the stone table against the wall. Djeyd searched the objects atop the table and took up a scroll. After unwinding it, he read the words written there.

"Memorize this," Djeyd said as he handed the scroll to Sheyn. "While the Savaani prince distracts Taankh, you will chant the spell of closing."

"And that will get rid of… that thing?"

"We may hope." Djeyd's pale gaze fixed on Sheyn's. "If Taankh succeeds in fully entering this world, he will lay waste to it. Demons will roam freely, butchering any living thing they find. And when they run out of prey here, they'll look to other lands. We must stop this."

Sheyn looked at the scroll and frowned. He was familiar with the script and could sound out the words, but he had no idea what they meant. "I'll try my best," he said at last.

"Go back to the altar," Djeyd said. "And be ready when I give the signal."

"Wait! What signal?" Sheyn called as Djeyd moved toward Kashyan.

"I'll shout at you to start the chant."

Sheyn bit his lip as he watched Kashyan sever a tentacle as thick as a tree trunk and leap back from the spray of black blood. Every instinct screamed at him to go to his beloved, but he believed Djeyd's words. He could save Kashyan, or he could save the world. It wasn't an easy choice, but he knew what he had to do.

Abruptly, Sheyn pulled the amulet over his head and shouted to Kashyan. "Bastard! Catch!"

Kashyan ducked under a tentacle, saw Sheyn toss the necklace, and caught it in his left hand. Immediately, the tentacles ceased attacking him and thrashed about aimlessly. With a fierce grin, he began chopping the waving limbs into pieces as he waded toward their source.

Taankh emitted a whistling wail of pain and lashed his tentacles wildly as he redoubled his efforts to cross the Threshold. After losing three more limbs, he drew his tentacles up and tried to gain some purchase against the domed ceiling of the chamber.

"Now!" Djeyd shouted. "Begin the chant!"

Standing on the altar, Sheyn spoke the first line of the incantation.

"Louder!" Djeyd called out.

Sheyn took a deep breath and spoke the next line. He raised his voice and fixed his eyes on the hideous bulk of the God of Death as though aiming his words like stones. As he intoned the third line, his voice took on a measured cadence dictated by the syllables themselves. The fourth line flowed from his lips, and he fancied he could feel the words stacking up like bricks to bar Taankh's access.

Wisps of steam rose from Taankh's hide, and the ear-piercing wail cut off to be replaced by a burbling gobble. Smaller tentacles began to melt and drop off. Taankh stopped halfway through the Gate and let out a roar of frustrated rage and defiance. Lashing blindly, one of his arms brushed against Sheyn. Recognizing the aura of a daaksi, the tentacle threw a loop around Sheyn's ankle and pulled. Sheyn's words broke off on a yelp of alarm as he was dragged off the altar.

"Keep chanting!" Djeyd shouted.

Sheyn began the chant again as he kicked at the tentacle. He saw Kashyan leaping toward him and heard Djeyd yell at Kashyan to keep Taankh at bay. And then Sheyn read the last line.

The temple shifted with the deep rumble of stone grinding against stone and then settled. Grains of sand sifted down from the ceiling, but they never touched the floor. They were sucked away as all the air in the chamber began to pour out through the widening rip in the Threshold.

Taankh released Sheyn, and his tentacles stretched as he maintained his foothold in the temple. With a mighty heave, he pushed back against the force that attempted to repel him.

"Prince Kashyan!" Djeyd shouted, and Kashyan turned from Sheyn to attack Taankh once more. "Pearl! Repeat the chant!"

Sheyn got to his knees and held up the scroll. In a voice of steel, he chanted the words that flew from his mouth to strike Taankh like spears of molten metal. He was vaguely aware that others had entered the chamber and were moving to help Kashyan, but all his will was set on expelling the writhing horror.

"It's working!" Djeyd cried out as Sheyn began the spell again.

Taankh hung on with all his strength as he was sucked back through the Gate. Kashyan leaped at one of the tentacles braced against the temple wall and slashed it deeply with his sword. The force of the suction doubled suddenly, and Kashyan was dragged across the Threshold with the God of Death.

"Close it!" Djeyd shouted as he ran to Sheyn. "Say the final words one more time."

"As soon as Kashyan is back, I will."

"You can't save him. He's past the barrier."

"I can see him."

"Close it now, or risk Taankh's return."

"I won't. There has to be a way to—"

"There isn't." Djeyd touched Sheyn's hand. "I'm sorry."

Where Djeyd's flesh touched his, Sheyn felt a peculiar but pleasant warmth. It spread throughout his body, calming him and taking away his sense of urgency. He looked upon the chaos around him with a serene gaze. He had a task to perform, and that was his only concern.

A voice that rang like a silver bell echoed in Sheyn's head. "Close the Gate, child."

Sheyn fixed his gaze on Kashyan, his heart yearning toward the man he'd come to love. As he watched Kashyan swing his sword at the God of Death, he chanted the words for the last time. Kashyan and Taankh grew smaller and smaller, and the blackness dwindled until it was a smudge against the ceiling. And then it was gone and the chamber was still. Sheyn bowed his head and wept.

"DJEYD!" HIGH King Djulyan called out. "What happened here?"

The red-haired daaksi came to stand before his master. "The high priest summoned the God of Death, but fortunately, we managed to send him back. And also, King Kezlath was part of a plot to depose you and take the crown of high king for himself."

"Fortunately?" Djulyan repeated. "You want me to believe it was luck that brought you here?"

"My Goddess brought me here," Djeyd said. "Call it what you will." He looked over his shoulder to where Kholya was staring up at the ceiling. "You should say something comforting to him."

"Yes, I should."

"I'll see to Pearl."

Djulyan nodded and went over to Kholya. He put a hand on Kholya's shoulder and spoke in a low voice. "It was a very brave thing your brother did."

"Is he really gone?" Kholya continued to look up at the spot where Kashyan had disappeared.

"We may have to question Taankh's Servants about that, but I feel his absence in my heart."

Kholya bowed his head at last. "So do I," he said hoarsely.

"He died a hero."

"Yes." Kholya swallowed. "He would like that. I—" He turned toward the sound of Sheyn's angry voice.

"No!" Sheyn shouted again as he batted Djeyd's hand away. He rose to his feet and fixed his dark gaze on the other daaksi. The wetness on his cheeks glimmered in the torchlight as he spoke. "Don't touch me."

"I only meant to offer you comfort."

"You can't—" Sheyn took a shaky breath. "You can't comfort me. No one can."

"You did what was necessary."

"I did what you told me to," Sheyn shouted. "I chanted those words and now Kasha is gone."

"He sacrificed himself to save all of us. I know he doesn't regret it."

"No, he doesn't feel regret. Or sorrow. Or love. Or anything else. He's gone." Sheyn clenched his teeth. "And you—you made me kill him."

"Prince Kashyan was a warrior," Djeyd said as Kholya came to stand beside Sheyn. "He knew he could die at any time in battle. He accepted that."

"That's true," Kholya said.

"I don't care." Sheyn looked up as Djulyan put a robe around his shoulders. He looked puzzled and then remembered that he was naked. Pulling the robe around him, he addressed Djeyd again. "Stay away from me."

"I can't do that, Pearl. I must do as my Goddess commands and serve you."

"I don't care about your Goddess unless She can bring Kashyan back to me."

"Let me take you out of here," Kholya said. "Velvet will be glad to see you're unharmed."

"Unharmed?"

Kholya tensed, cursing his choice of words. "I'm sorry," he said sincerely. "Come with me, please. I want to be out of this ill-fated place."

"You shouldn't be alone," Djeyd called after Sheyn.

"And yet I will," Sheyn said under his breath as he let Kholya lead him away.

"LIE DOWN," Luks said as he pressed a damp cloth to Sheyn's forehead.

"I don't have a fever," Sheyn said. "I lost the one I love."

"You do have a fever," Luks contradicted gently. He sat on the mattress beside Sheyn and stroked his hair. "I'm sorry about Prince Kashyan."

"I want him back," Sheyn sobbed.

"Of course you do." Luks kissed Sheyn's forehead. "Sleep and forget for a while."

"I can't sleep," Sheyn said, but in a few minutes, he fell into exhausted slumber.

Luks lay down next to Sheyn and fell asleep holding his hand.

Chapter 26

Sheyn woke and knew immediately that something was wrong. He raised his head and looked about but saw no imminent danger. All the sounds that came to his ears were the usual ones. He settled back, closed his eyes, and reached for Kashyan. And then he remembered.

Kashyan was gone.

Sheyn felt as though his ribs were caving in and crushing his heart in a shrinking cage of jagged bones. Tears welled up and overflowed, and he clenched his jaw to keep from sobbing. He'd never felt grief like this, and he wasn't sure he'd survive it. It was not fair that Kashyan had been taken from him just when he'd fallen in love. Sheyn clenched his hands into fists and willed his anguish to become anger. He let his rage at the temple have free rein, and it filled him until he thought he would burst.

Getting quietly to his feet, he left Luks sleeping and dressed in his most practical clothing. He buckled his sword belt around his waist and walked out of the tent, aware that he was glowing like the full moon. Telling the nervous door guard he needed time alone to mourn, he promised to stay in camp and then headed for the field where the cavalry mounts were pastured.

One of the men guarding the horses saw Sheyn approaching and hailed him. "Pearl! What are you doing here alone?"

"Dasha, where are the Black Hawks?"

Dasha vacillated between his desire to do Pearl a favor and his absolute certainty that a daaksi had no business visiting a barracks. "Why do you ask?" he said finally.

"Because my lord is dead."

Dasha had no answer for this statement. He called over a lower-ranking trooper and turned over his sentry post. "I'll take you to the Hawks," he told Sheyn.

"You have my thanks." Sheyn gave the young soldier a sideways glance and saw the effect of his words. He would have to remember how susceptible these men were to his unique charm. True, he intended to use any influence he might have to sway the Hawks to his side, but he didn't want things to get out of hand. He felt confident he could defend his honor with his sword, but the odds changed when an entire cavalry troop was involved. Brusquely, he swept aside these unhelpful thoughts. They had no place in his mission.

Dasha cleared his throat. "Are you certain you should be out alone?"

"I'm not alone. I'm with you." Sheyn felt Dasha's frustrated anxiety and spoke again. "My lord is dead and from now on, I'll be alone. However, I'm not going sit in a dark room weeping for the rest of my life. I'm going to honor my lord and make his name known to the world when I avenge him."

Dasha was so overcome with admiration for this brave, beautiful boy that he couldn't speak for several moments. "There is no other like you," he said when he found his voice.

"For that, the world may be thankful."

"What do you mean? I wish there were more like you. Maybe then I'd—" Dasha stopped speaking abruptly.

"Maybe what?"

"You must know it's every warrior's dream to earn enough glory to deserve a daaksi."

"I've heard anyone with enough wealth can buy one."

"Those aren't true daaksim."

"You sound like a man with a strong opinion. May I hear it?"

Dasha's cheeks flushed red. "It's foolishness. I shouldn't even be talking to you."

"Please tell me."

"How can I say no to you?" Dasha ducked his head. "Even though you'll think me foolish." He sighed. "I always loved hearing stories of the dawn time about the daaksim and their lords. I think it would be a fine thing to have a companion at my side in battle and in bed."

"Couldn't you choose one of your comrades?"

"I could if any of them roused me, but none do. Some of the other men share blankets, but I don't want a warrior like myself. I want...." Dasha smiled sheepishly.

"What do you want?"

"I want someone like you. I'm just the fifth son of a minor king, but I have royal blood. If I win honor enough, someday a daaksi might come to me. He'll be beautiful as a new sword, brave, wise, and sweet. And I will love him and protect him for all my life."

"You remind me of the Bastard," Sheyn said, and a tear rolled down his cheek.

"Ah, Pearl! Don't cry." Dasha stopped in his tracks, left helpless by the look of utter sorrow on Sheyn's face.

Sheyn wiped the wetness away with his gloved hand. Sternly, he tamped down his grief and focused on his goal. "Why are you stopping?" he said. "We have work to do."

"Yes, Pearl," Dasha said as though the daaksi was an officer.

On the far side of the horse pasture, small tents were arranged in neat rows under the shade of a grove of nut trees. Black Hawks in various versions of the cavalry uniform sat or stood about in small groups. There was no laughter, no raised voices, and none seemed inclined to do anything but mourn their lost leader.

Until Sheyn entered their midst.

It didn't take long for a crowd to gather, and after word went around, all the Black Hawks assembled. Under the weight of so many stares, Sheyn lifted his chin and reminded himself of who he was. He was Rosheyn Lir, a prince of House Merisolle, and he was Pearl, beloved of Kashyan, the Bastard of Savaan. He needn't lower his head before anyone. As for the physical danger he might be in, he counted on respect for his lost lord to keep him safe.

"What's this about, Dasha lad?" asked a soldier with wolf-brindled hair.

"Pearl wanted a word with you," Dasha said. "Will you hear him?"

A few older men muttered about the unseemliness of a daaksi addressing warriors, but the majority were prepared to listen. They stood silently watching Sheyn and waiting for him to speak. Sheyn took his time, letting the silence draw out, letting them look their fill before he spoke.

"You all know me," Sheyn said and waited for a round of comments to die down. "I did not come to Kandaar intending to stay. I'm kept here by a force I don't understand, a force you call magic. I found little to like here until fate brought the Bastard to me. I didn't want to love him, but in spite of all our differences, I loved him more than my freedom."

Sheyn waited again while the Hawks cheered their captain. "I know you loved him well, and he often told me that he commanded the best men in Kandaar." He paused. "Are you as angry as I am that he was taken away?"

Such a roar went up that several of the warhorses answered with ringing neighs.

Sheyn unsheathed his saber. "I have such a rage in me as will only be quenched by the blood of Taankh's Servants. I'm going to the Red Temple to get vengeance for my lord. Any who wish to come with me are welcome."

Another roar filled the air, and the Black Hawks strode away to arm themselves. Not one man brought up the question of mutiny.

"Dasha."

"Yes, Pearl?"

"I need a horse. Saddle Karkaran for me."

Dasha bowed and left to do Sheyn's bidding.

KHOLYA HEARD the guard's challenge and looked up from the pile of dispatches he was trying to read. He needed distraction from his grief, but he couldn't concentrate. An interruption was welcome just now. "What is it?" he called out.

A messenger hesitated in the doorway of the guest tent. "I'm sorry, Commander, but your daaksi—"

"What?" Kholya got to his feet. "What's wrong?"

"He asks you to come to him, my lord. He says it's urgent and he couldn't entrust the news to anyone but you."

Kholya cursed under his breath. "Return to your duty," he said as he left the tent.

"Thank the Lady you came," Luks said when Kholya arrived. "Pearl is gone."

Kholya looked around as though he might spot Sheyn behind a mound of pillows. "How long has he been missing?"

"I woke a few minutes ago and he wasn't here."

"What did he take with him?"

Luks looked around wildly, noting what items were missing. "He's probably wearing a green tunic."

"I don't need a description. That hair of his stands out a bit."

"I found this." Luks held up several strands of long, moon-colored hair. "He cut his hair. Why would he do that?"

"Perhaps it's a sign of mourning in his land. Did he take a pack?"

"No." Luks paused. "His saber is gone, though."

"If he didn't take a pack, he probably hasn't gone far. Taking the sword—"

They heard the sound of running feet, and someone shouted for the commander.

"In here!" Kholya called out, and a courier ran into the room.

"Commander." The man bowed briefly. "The Black Hawks have left camp and are riding to Taar Muergan."

"Is that all?" Kholya asked.

"My lord?" The man gave Kholya a puzzled look.

"Fire isn't raining from the sky?"

"No, my lord."

"You're certain you don't have any other disasters to report?"

"No, my lord. I mean yes, my lord."

"Go back to your post and tell your superior officer that I'm on my way."

The courier saluted and left at a trot.

"Well," Kholya said. "Do I look for Pearl or go after the Black Hawks?"

"I don't think you need to choose," Luks said.

"I fear you're right, and I should go." Kholya put a hand on Luks's cheek. "So soft," he said. "I wish I could lie down in your arms and let you ease my sore heart, but I have to go see why the Hawks have gone off without orders."

"Come back as soon as you can," Luks said. He took Kholya's hand, turned it over, and left a kiss on his palm.

Kholya closed his hand around the kiss. "As soon as I can," he said.

KHOLYA RODE into Taar Muergan and found Djulyan at the palace. He borrowed a troop of Djulyan's royal guards and led them to the Red Temple. Several streets away from the square, they knew something was wrong. People were fleeing the area like birds before a storm.

"What's happening?" Kholya called out.

"They're burning the Temple," someone in the crowd yelled.

"Make way!" Kholya shouted as he urged his horse through the mass of people.

Wailing of Taankh's wrath, the Muergathim parted for Kholya and the guards and closed in again behind them. It was like swimming in quicksand, but at last they reached the great square. The statue of Taankh lay on its side with the body of a Red Monk crushed beneath it. Smoke and the smell of black powder hung in the air. From the red-lit doorway of the Temple poured priests, acolytes, and novices, some with their clothing on fire.

"Get down," Kholya shouted at the fleeing Servants. "All of you. Get down on the ground." He ordered the guards to herd the priests together and put out the flames. It took several minutes, but the Servants recovered from their panic and helped tend their burned brethren. Kholya left them and entered the temple.

With his sword in his hand, Kholya hurried down the curved corridors, hoping he remembered the route to the Gate Chamber. In every room he passed, the furniture had been piled in the center and set alight. At every step his boots crunched on the clay shards of smashed votive statues of the God of Death. Now and then, he came upon the body of a Servant bearing multiple wounds. When he reached the Gate Chamber, he found a Black Hawk guarding the door. "Out of the way," Kholya ordered.

"I'm sorry, Commander. I can't let you in."

"What's your name?"

"Dasha, my lord."

"You know me, don't you?"

"Yes, Commander."

"Then stand aside."

"I have orders not to let anyone in."

"Orders from who?"

"From Pearl, my lord."

"You'd better be joking, lad, and if you aren't, I'll beat you myself." Kholya took a step, and Dasha raised his sword.

"Please don't, Commander," Dasha said. "We're doing this to honor the Bastard." He paused. "The captain, that is. Prince Kashyan."

"What exactly are you doing?"

"We're destroying this place."

"Then I have no quarrel with you. Let me speak to Pearl."

"Let him come," Sheyn called out. "It's useless, after all."

Dasha stood aside, and Kholya brushed past him into the ruined chamber. Sheyn stood before what remained of the altar. The great slab of stone had been reduced to gravel and dust.

"Did you do that?" Kholya asked.

Sheyn nodded. "Yes, and I've been standing here ever since asking myself why this power wouldn't come to me when I needed it to save Kashyan."

"I don't know. I'm just a soldier," Kholya said, and silence fell for several long moments. Twice he started to speak, and then he reached out and put a hand on the raggedly cut hair that framed Sheyn's face.

Through the contact of flesh on flesh, Sheyn felt Kholya's grief. "I'm sorry," he said.

"I know you loved him too."

"I'll always love him."

Kholya stroked Sheyn's hair. "Are you done here?"

"I hoped to find a way to him, a way to bring him back, but…. I'm not strong enough or smart enough."

Kholya had never seen anything sadder than the droop of Pearl's proud head. "Come with me," he said, as he'd said earlier. "Let me take you out of here. Velvet is worried sick."

Sheyn squeezed his eyes shut and then opened them again. "I don't want to cause him pain. Now that I know what true pain is, I don't want to hurt anyone."

"Except the Servants of Taankh."

"Yes. I intend to rid Kandaar of every trace of their slime."

"By yourself?" Kholya asked as they left the chamber.

Sheyn glanced at Dasha, who fell in behind him. "No. Not alone."

"I can't have you inciting my soldiers to mutiny."

"That doesn't concern me. The only thing in my mind is the destruction of the Red Temple."

Kholya brooded on his thoughts as they traveled to the camp outside the city walls. He brought Sheyn to his tent and watched as Luks greeted him like a lost child returned. Dasha stood just outside the entrance until Kholya called him in.

"We have to talk about this," Kholya said to Sheyn. "I know, though you're a daaksi, you feel a need to avenge Kashyan. But what happened today cannot be allowed to happen again."

"It *will* happen again," Sheyn said. "It will happen as many times as there are temples dedicated to the worship of Taankh. I will fill them with black powder and blast them to dust."

"I can't let you defy my authority by stealing my soldiers."

"What are you talking about?" Luks asked as he set cups of khai in front of Sheyn and Kholya. "Dasha, would you like a cup?"

The corporal shook his head and went back to watching the entrance.

"Pearl and the Black Hawks went into Taar Muergan and attacked the Red Temple," Kholya said.

"No!" Luks sat and took Sheyn's hand. "This isn't true, is it?"

"Why do you say it as though it's beyond belief?" Sheyn asked.

"Daaksim don't…. But you're not an ordinary daaksi, are you?"

"An ordinary daaksi," Sheyn repeated. "I think I'll do away with those as well."

Luks gasped.

"Would it be so wrong?" Sheyn asked. "Why should one more boy be enslaved like this?"

"You're right," Luks said. "If daaksim were the beings the Goddess intended, it would be a glorious thing, but as it is…."

"I should make finding Yozif a priority," Sheyn said. "If he has his freedom, he'll keep making daaksim for whoever can pay him."

"I think your cause is a noble one," Kholya said. "I agree with your goals, but I really can't let you destroy discipline in my army."

Dasha cleared his throat.

"You have something to say?" Kholya asked.

"You could solve the problem easily, my lord," Dasha said. "All you need do is make Pearl an officer." He looked around at the shocked faces. "I know it's never been done, and it will take time for some to get used to it, but if Pearl was an officer—"

"A daaksi warrior?" Kholya interrupted. "Who will accept this?"

"The Black Hawks already do, Commander," Dasha said. "You should have seen him when he came to us and told us he was going to avenge the captain. Flames burned in his eyes and a light surrounded him. I fell to my knees and pledged myself to his service."

"You've already taken an oath," Kholya reminded Dasha. "To me."

"I know, my lord, but I couldn't help it. When Pearl took my hand, his light went into me and my heart was his. My comrades all say the same."

Kholya shook his head. "Well, I can't execute my finest cavalry troop for treason." He sighed. "I can't believe I'm going to say this, but I see no other way unless I put Pearl in chains. Dasha, see if a uniform can be found to fit Master Long Legs. And don't forget to salute him. He's a captain now."

As Dasha left, Sheyn looked at Kholya with suspicion. "What sort of trick is this?"

"I wish it were." Kholya took a drink of his khai. "But I think giving you a rank will cause less trouble than you enthralling my men."

Luks looked a bit shaken as he offered more refreshments.

Sheyn squeezed his friend's hand. "It's a giddy feeling when things change quickly."

"I feel a bit queasy." Luks took several deep breaths. "A daaksi warrior. Are all the old legends going to come to life?"

"Great Raas, I hope not," Kholya said. "I'll go now to arrange a ceremony of passage for Kashyan. It won't be the first time we've had a pyre without a body, and the men will want to pay their respects. I'll send an escort for you at sunset."

"I need sleep," Sheyn said as soon as Kholya left.

"I'm surprised you have the energy to speak." Luks put a pillow under Sheyn's head. "I'll wake you when it's time for the fire."

"Thank you." Sheyn reached out to stroke Luks's arm. A tear trickled down his cheek and made a dark spot on the pillow.

Luks lay down with Sheyn and held him until a messenger arrived to call them to the ceremony.

THE SUN had set and torches had been placed around the empty platform draped with the Savaani royal flag. The vagrant wind pulled the flames into streamers of yellow silk, illuminating the wood piled at the foot of the bier. The Black Hawks stood in a single line as an honor guard, each man holding his sword aloft in tribute to their fallen leader. When Sheyn appeared, the troop dipped their weapons once in a somber salute to their captain's bereaved daaksi.

Kholya nodded to Sheyn and Luks as they took places behind him. Now that their eyes were no longer blinded by the torches, they could see the vast crowd surrounding them. It looked as though the entire Horde and all of the high king's guests had come to say farewell to a hero.

Taking a step forward, Kholya unsheathed his sword and began to speak. "I am not here tonight as a prince, or as your commander. I'm here as a brother. You all knew Kashyan, some better than others, but even if you never met him, you knew of him. He was already a legend while he lived. Now he's taken his place among the great heroes. Tonight he drinks with Lahar, first king of Kandaar, and with General Uerman, who repelled the invading armies of Teijal Warmaster. And he can hold his head proudly, for his glory is equal to theirs. How many heroes can boast that they fought a God?"

Kholya paused for a few moments, and there was not a sound other than the wind in the trees and the popping of the flames. Unable to find words, he pulled one of the torches from the ground and approached the pyre. Kholya threw the torch, and the Black Hawks raised their voices in a dirge as old as legend, singing to their captain's memory as the oil-soaked kindling caught fire. They sang until the flames reached the empty bier and then stood their posts in silence to guard the fire until it went out. Kholya turned away and found High King Djulyan watching him.

"May we speak?" Djulyan asked.

"Of course, sire." Kholya wrenched himself up from the pit of his grief. "How can I serve you?"

"I'd wait if I could, but—"

"Please speak your mind."

"Kezlath will be executed in the morning. As he has no heir, it falls to me to make the same decision I made for Sumadin."

"What did you decide for Sumadin?"

"Sumadin's queen will stand regent for Djenosh until he's ready to rule. When that time comes, I'll stand with him against any who oppose his rule."

"Yevdjen had an heir, Kezlath does not."

"Indeed." Djulyan put a hand on Kholya's shoulder. "I know this is a hard time for you, but I need you, so bear up."

"Yes, sire."

"I've decided to put you on Muergath's throne."

"Sire?"

"You may well look surprised, but once Djeyd suggested it, I could see it was the ideal solution."

"You leave Savaan without an heir."

"Until your father names another, you are still his heir."

"Will you have me rule two kingdoms, then?"

"We'll speak of that when Nakhol of Savaan dies."

Kholya nodded. "If this is your will, I accept."

"Good. We'll speak more of it later, but I want you to cleanse Taar Muergan and all Muergath of the Red Temple's stain. Make this place a worthy home for Djulz… or Velvet, if you prefer."

"It will be as he prefers, sire. The rest of his life will be one of ease without fear. I'll make sure of it."

Djulyan gave Kholya's shoulder a squeeze. "See that you do." He smiled. "And let him visit the Misty Vales from time to time."

"Whenever he wishes, and I hope you won't be a stranger to my court."

"You make me hopeful for Kandaar's future. Perhaps it's unmanly of me, but I'm weary of war."

"I wish Kashyan might have lived to see such days." Kholya's lips curved in a slight smile. "I'm not sure where he'd fit in a world without battles, but I wish he had lived."

"Walk with me to my tent. There is one more thing I'd like to discuss." Djulyan cleared his throat as they started off with the royal guards around them. "What will become of Pearl?"

"I don't know, but I've just made him a captain in my army."

"I didn't think the day had any surprises left in it." Djulyan cleared his throat again. "Your men are willing to follow a daaksi?"

"The Black Hawks are. They already have."

"I've seen Pearl fight, and he's skilled with that pretty blade of his, but I can't quite make myself believe it. He's a daaksi."

"I've learned a lot from Velvet," Kholya said. "Daaksim are not inhuman creatures designed for one purpose. They're flesh and bone like you and I, and they have all the same feelings, the same fears and desires as anyone else. For hundreds of years, they've been forced into a rigid and narrow nature that perverts their original purpose." He took a breath. "I believe Pearl is the embodiment of that original purpose."

"You're an educated man, so I suppose I should accept your opinion. Djeyd agrees with you."

"Whether you do or not, Pearl will make you change your mind before he's done."

"What is it he's doing with your cavalry?" Djulyan asked as they came in sight of his pavilion.

"To honor Kashyan's spirit, Pearl has dedicated himself to destroying every trace of Taankh's worship." Kholya stopped as the royal guards hailed the sentries outside Djulyan's tent. "I think this campaign will ease his grief. At the least, it will keep him busy."

"Then he has my blessing." Djulyan turned to acknowledge the guard captain and then addressed Kholya again. "I'll say good night. Take my best wishes to your companion."

"I will, sire." Kholya bowed and left for his tent.

Kholya found Luks and Sheyn entwined in sleep and quietly removed his clothing. He blew out the oil lamps and candles and lay down beside the daaksim. Carefully, he pressed himself to Luks's back and put an arm around him. He thought he wouldn't be able to sleep, but before he knew it, morning had come.

Chapter
27

LUKS STIRRED and instinctively nestled into the warmth at his back.

"Are you awake?" Kholya asked.

"Yes, my lord."

Kholya pulled Luks into an embrace, turning the young man to face him. "How would you feel about living in the palace of Taar Muergan?"

"My lord?"

"The high king has offered me Muergath's throne."

Luks was quiet for a few moments, and then he asked, "Could Pearl live with us?"

"If you wish it."

"I do wish it. He's all alone now." Luks looked over his shoulder at the empty space where Sheyn had slept. "I heard him get up before first light."

"He's probably with the Hawks."

"I worry about him so much."

Kholya kissed Luks's forehead. "I know. You're as beautiful as a daydream, but it's your kind heart that made me love you."

Luks smiled shyly. "Does my lord wish to…?"

"Of course I do, but I don't think this is a good time for bedplay." Kholya sighed. "Kandaar is changing, and I think soon the days will be gone when a man ate, fought, slept, rutted, and shat whenever and wherever he felt like it."

"Are you sorry?"

"I think we'll be a better people when we stop seeing others as property."

"You haven't answered my question," Luks said boldly.

"Haven't I?"

"Maybe you have. I'll think about it. Now, my lord, if you have no pressing business, will you go and see that Pearl is safe? The thought of him alone with twenty-four young warriors...."

"What do you fear will happen to him?"

Luks sat up. "Are you joking?"

"Do you really think a man of Kashyan's troop would harm Pearl or allow Pearl to be hurt?"

"They're men—warriors—and he's a daaksi."

"I'll go and find him to ease your mind, but I truly believe Pearl can look after himself now."

Luks rose and donned a robe of white silk. "I remember when I first saw him," he said as he went to put the khai kettle on the brazier. "I could see that he was confused and terrified, but no one would have known it by his face. He looked as fierce as a hawk defending a nest. I knew as soon as I saw him he was trouble. I could hardly stand to be in the room with his defiance and Lord Ognyan's desire to dominate him."

Kholya finished putting on his uniform of kilt and tunic. "Ognyan won't be bothering anyone like that again," he said as buckled on his sword belt.

"Ognyan was never Pearl's master," Luks said softly.

Kholya swallowed. "Only one man could have been that," he said in a voice squeezed small by sorrow.

Luks came across the floor, and Kholya opened his arms to him. For several minutes they stood in silence with Luks wrapped securely in Kholya's strong arms, his head resting on Kholya's chest. "I can't believe how lucky I am," Luks said. "I feel guilty being so happy when you're so sad."

Kholya kissed Luks's auburn curls before he let him go. "I'm truly glad you feel lucky to be with me. I'll go now and see about Pearl. There's also the rest of my army to be called from Karkaran Fortress, and your father has asked me to attend him today."

At the words "your father," tears flooded Luks's eyes, but this time, they were tears of joy. "I'll begin packing such belongings as we brought with us," he said. "I'll be ready to move to the palace when you give the word."

"I'll send the quartermaster a message to loan you some men."

"Thank you, but I'd rather do it myself, my lord."

"As you prefer." Kholya ran a hand over Luks's hair and walked from the tent.

It didn't take the commander long to find Pearl. As he'd expected, Sheyn was with the Black Hawks. When Kholya reached the meadow where the cavalry mounts were kept, he found a ring of men, jostling and shouting, and for a moment his heart froze. And then he heard the sounds of metal on metal, and a wave of relief swept through him. Kholya pushed his way into the circle and saw Pearl fighting a Black Hawk called Kaastas. As he watched, Pearl swayed fluidly to one side to avoid a thrust and brought the hilt of his saber down on Kaastas's wrist. Kaastas's sword fell from his numb fingers, and he went to one knee in surrender.

"Pearl!" Kholya called out. "I would speak with you."

Sheyn sheathed his sword and followed Kholya away from the troop.

"You've gotten even better with that blade," Kholya said. "But I'm a little surprised Kaastas gave in so quickly. Losing your sword is no reason to stop fighting."

"This is how we practice. When a man is disarmed, the bout is over."

"I see." Kholya stopped beneath a large tree. "Velvet is worried about you."

"I'm honored that someone like Velvet cares enough about me to worry, but I have a mission."

Kholya started to speak and then changed his mind about what he would say. "High King Djulyan had given his blessing to your mission."

"That's very kind of him."

"Yes, it is." Kholya glanced at the young man's face and saw no trace of emotion. "You've been riding Karkaran. Would you like to keep him?"

"Do you think you could take him from me?"

"Pearl, I know you're grieving, so I make allowances but—"

"If it's too much effort for you, then don't bother. I don't need your leave or your tolerance." Sheyn's voice grew in pitch. "If I wished it, I would ride from here now with *all* your men at my back. You speak to me as though I'm still that lost boy Kashyan rescued. You have no idea what I've become."

Kholya met Sheyn's eyes for a long moment before he looked away, shaken by the fathomless, frozen dark. "You're right. I've no idea what you are. Do as you please, then. For Velvet's sake, you'll have the protection of my name, whether you want it or not." He took a deep breath. "We move today to the palace. Velvet will set aside rooms for you."

"Thank you." Sheyn turned on his heel and walked purposefully back to the troop.

Later that day, the Black Hawks conducted their second raid under Pearl's command. In the town of Gathmaar, they attacked the local temple of Taankh, killing those who resisted and gathering the rest in the town square. The Servants who renounced the God of Death were spared, and those who didn't were executed. The farmers and merchants who'd lived under the rule of Taankh's Servants cheered as the men who'd stolen so many of their children were put to death. When the swift beheadings were over, Sheyn called upon the power that came more and more easily to his hand. He no longer had need of the black powder. With a gesture and his will, he blasted the temple with the force of his fiery hate and left it to burn to the ground. And thus the pattern was set for the days to come.

EACH NIGHT after raiding, Sheyn fell into an exhausted sleep and dreamed vivid dreams of Kashyan. The dreams were always of Kashyan alone in the dark he'd feared so much in life. And sometimes Sheyn woke convinced that the battle with the God of Death had been nothing but a nightmare and Kashyan was still alive. But the illusion never lasted for long, and he rose to plunge into the day's battle to distract himself from his grief. He vowed he would not rest until all of Taankh's temples were ashes.

News of Pearl's campaign spread, and people spoke with wonder of a daaksi who commanded warriors. After a time, others took up the banner, and Red Temples were burned in every nation. Songs began to be sung about the moon-haired daaksi on the big blue horse who came from the west to destroy the evil cult of Taankh.

None of this eased Sheyn's grief as he had supposed it would. After three seasons, the feeling of loss was as keen as the moment the Gate had closed. And when at last he turned Karkaran's head back toward Taar Muergan, he did so with no sense of joy.

Luks, however, was delighted to receive the news that Pearl had returned and was in the palace. Throwing a light robe over his loincloth, he hurried to the guest quarters.

"Pearl!" Luks called out as he entered the chamber set aside for his friend's use. He got no answer and passed through the antechamber into the sitting room. "Pearl?"

Sheyn turned from the window with its view of the life-sized statue of Kashyan astride Karkaran with his sword raised in challenge. "I miss him," he said brokenly.

"Of course you do," Luks said as he stroked Sheyn's hair. "He was your lord and your love."

"I miss the way he teased me and ordered me around. I miss the way it felt to be in his presence. I even miss his stubbornness… and more."

"Tell me," Luks said gently.

"I can't. It's too embarrassing."

"You miss his body?"

Fresh tears flowed down Sheyn's face. He nodded. "I never thought I would miss his touch so fiercely. At times, I remember how he made me catch fire like dry grass and I can scarcely breathe. I burn for him and there is nothing now that can quench the flames."

"That's normal."

"Did you miss Yevdjen like this? If you did, I'm sorry I wasn't more understanding."

"No." Luks wiped Sheyn's tears away. "I didn't have a true bond with him, though we each pretended it was so."

"But you love Kholya."

"With all my heart. He is everything I could wish for."

"He's a good man. The Muergathim are lucky to have such a king."

"I'm glad they accepted him so quickly."

"They see him as their savior. He delivered them from the nightmare of being ruled from the Red Temple. They don't have to worry anymore about their children being taken away and used as sacrifices in nasty rituals."

"It's you… and Prince Kashyan they should thank."

"I don't need their gratitude but I rather like the statue. I think Kasha would've liked it too."

"It's beautiful," Luks said. "And looks so much like him."

"The sculptor did well enough with the face, but I think Kasha would've liked the big sword, and the way Karkaran is rearing with his mane and tail flying."

"It's a grand statue." Luks watched Sheyn's face as he talked, alert for signs of fatigue, distress, or madness. He didn't approve of Sheyn riding with the Hawks and killing Taankh's priests with his own hands. He didn't understand why Sheyn couldn't give his orders and let the soldiers do the bloody work.

"Because it's my work to do," Sheyn said, meeting Luks's gaze.

"Don't!" Luks gave Sheyn a reproachful look. "You promised you wouldn't listen to my thoughts."

"Sometimes I can't help it."

"Why won't you let Djeyd teach you how to block it out?"

"Has he been here again?"

"He's here now with the high king."

"Djulyan's here?" Sheyn finally smiled. "Did he bring any of your brothers? I truly believe that someday you'll meet all of them."

"He doesn't have that many sons."

"I thought there were thirty, thirty-one counting you."

"Twelve." Luks tweaked Sheyn's nose. "Are you coming to dinner?"

"I suppose I have to eat sometime." Sheyn rose. "Can I assume you've provided suitable clothing?"

"You can." Luks pointed to a small door in the east wall. "Would you like to see?"

"How long before we eat and who will be there?"

"Kholya will be there and Djulyan and Djeyd, of course. I think you should dress now and come keep me company."

"I could as soon resist a kitten as that look on your face. Very well. Show me the clothes I'll be wearing."

Sometime later, Luks led Sheyn from Sheyn's quarters to the royal apartment. Sheyn wore a clinging silk robe of bright Savaani red belted with gold. The small golden discs that hung from the belt chimed together as he walked, creating a musical ringing. His hair had grown long enough for Luks to plait into swirling, bejeweled patterns on the sides. Along the top and back, the loose hair had been coaxed into a mane by Luks's skill and a jar of beeswax. More jewels gleamed in his recently pierced ears and the wide bracelets on his forearms. It was a look of barbaric splendor, but he found it suited him now.

"I feel a bit plain beside you," Luks said. "But wait until you see the gown I'm going to wear."

"I look forward to seeing you in it," Sheyn said as they emerged into the large courtyard in front of the royal quarters. He stopped abruptly. "What is this?" he asked.

"Surely you recognize your own men," Djulyan said as he came forward.

Sheyn stared at the twenty-four mounted Black Hawks assembled in the courtyard. Each man wore a new uniform of black leather with a black-and-red hawk crest on the breast. Every horse had new tack of silver-studded black leather. As one, the troopers drew their new swords and raised them in a salute to their leader.

"Do you like your present?" Djulyan asked.

"Your Glory," Sheyn said with a bow. "It's a magnificent gift."

"Consider it a reward for ridding my land of a great evil."

"Thank you." Sheyn bowed again. After telling his men how fine they looked, he dismissed them with orders to enjoy themselves. He turned to find Djulyan with an arm around Luks's shoulders. Luks's smile warmed Sheyn's heart for a few moments. "Thank you," he said again.

"You're most welcome," Djulyan said. "And now, I'll leave you to prepare for the feast."

The high king left, and Luks and Sheyn continued to the royal apartment. Everywhere Sheyn saw the influence of Luks's quietly elegant style, and he remarked on it.

Luks's blushed with pleasure at the compliments. "I took great enjoyment in having a free hand with the furnishings," he said as they entered his private sitting room.

Djeyd got up from a comfortable chair, swallowed the bite of cake in his mouth, and greeted Luks and Sheyn. "I hope you don't mind. A servant let me in to wait for you."

"Of course not," Luks said. "You can talk with Pearl while I dress."

Sheyn shot Luks a glare that said his friend would pay for this later. Ignoring Djeyd, he sat at the other end of the table and heaped a plate with cold meat, cheese, and honey cakes.

"Would you like some wine or water?" Djeyd asked.

"Is your blood on offer?"

"Still so full of anger."

"It makes me strong."

"It will burn you hollow."

"Until then, it will keep me warm."

Djeyd yanked the plate away from Sheyn. Sheyn leaped to his feet, reaching for the saber he'd left in his room. They faced each other across the table, eyes locked, each determined not to break the stare first.

"Now that I have your attention, will you walk outside with me?"

"Why?"

"You wouldn't believe me if I told you. I must show you."

Intrigued despite himself, Sheyn followed the red-haired daaksi into Luks's private garden. He stopped when Djeyd stopped beside a pattering fountain. After trailing a hand in the cool water, Djeyd flicked droplets from his fingers into Sheyn's face. Sheyn blinked, and the world wavered, wobbled on its axis, and started spinning again at a new tilt.

"What did you do to me?" Sheyn asked slowly. His voice sounded muffled and distorted to his ears as though he were underwater. He sensed a vast presence hovering on the edge of becoming, unimaginably ancient and powerful. And then it arrived, not like Taankh trailing terror, but like a bird alighting.

Djeyd closed his eyes. When he opened them again, they were liquid silver, and someone else was looking out of them. "My dearest child." It was the sweetest voice Sheyn had ever heard.

Sheyn's skin puckered into gooseflesh. "Who are you?"

"I am the avatar of Anaali."

Sheyn refused to give the avatar any sign of homage. "What do you want?"

"Thank you for defeating my old enemy and bringing surcease of pain to the people of Kandaar. You have suffered much, but you have also accomplished much, and I thank you."

"I didn't do it for you."

The avatar reached out, and Sheyn shied away. "It's not my purpose to hurt you, child."

"Should it make me feel better to know that all the pain you've caused was an accident?"

"I know it's hard for you to understand, however—"

"Hard!" Sheyn said loudly. "Hard? Don't speak to me of hardness, Lady. I am the hardest thing you will ever know, and you made me this way."

"Then change."

"Why should I? Doesn't my hardness suit your purposes?"

"When you do things with hate in your heart, you blight the good you mean to do." Anaali's avatar put a hand on Sheyn's head, and he didn't rebuff it this time. "Let go of your hate and your rage. I know it has sustained you, but trust yourself to be strong without it."

"Sometimes you have to use your enemy's methods against him."

"No. Never. For then you become your enemy."

Sheyn was silent for a moment before he spoke again. "Answer me one thing. Why did you take Kasha away from me? Why did it have to be him?"

"He was the strongest, strong enough to fight a God." Anaali's avatar stroked Sheyn's hair. "You made him strong."

"I made him strong so he could fulfill your plans?"

"He saved your world from a future of darkness and pain."

Sheyn looked up, narrowing his eyes against the brightness of the Goddess's aura. "Do you know how cruel it is to maneuver two people into love so you can sacrifice one of them?"

"You wonder if I care what happens to my children?" Anaali's avatar lifted Sheyn's chin until their eyes met. "I own a sorrow deeper than any ocean. My despair encompasses the world." The avatar smiled gently. "But I also have hope now, and it is more boundless than the sky."

"Hope."

"Yes, hope. Hope that the light will be a little brighter tomorrow. Can you feel that flutter in your heart? That is hope. Let it in, and oh, the miracles you'll perform. You think yourself powerful now? Act out of love and know true power."

"My love died with Kasha."

"No, it did not. You still love him, or your anger at his loss would not be so huge. But this is not the way to honor his spirit."

"Why should I listen to you? You ruined my life."

"I showed you what it is to love and be loved in return."

"And then you took it away from me."

"No. Love never dies."

"But Kashyan is dead."

"Then mourn him and love again." Anaali's avatar smiled. "You will touch many lives with happiness, my Pearl."

"All but mine." Sheyn turned his face from the Goddess's avatar. "Please leave me alone," he said as he hurried away.

The spirit of the Goddess departed as well. Sad but still hopeful, Djeyd shivered in the aftermath of possession as he watched Sheyn walk away. The foreigner's spirit still resisted, but it was that very stubbornness that had allowed him to survive and made him perfect for the Goddess's purpose. Djeyd would be patient, though it pained him to watch Pearl suffer. Pearl was clever and would soon admit he needed Djeyd's help to control the forces he wielded.

THE MORNING after Sheyn returned to Taar Muergan, he sought High King Djulyan's daaksi. Djeyd greeted him joyfully and bade him be at ease. Sheyn sat on a well-cushioned divan and accepted a goblet of wine. Before he spoke, he devoured a cake from the plate set thoughtfully in front of him.

"How can I serve you?" Djeyd asked.

"I'd like to talk about you. You're more than you seem."

"Aren't we all?"

Sheyn ignored the arch remark. "You said you had things to teach me. What sorts of things?"

"If you're willing to submit to my instruction, I'll teach you to control the power inside you."

"I believe that would be wise. Sometimes I feel as though the power will get free and burn everything in creation." Sheyn paused. "Luks told me that my power increased each time—" He paused again. "When Kashyan and I—"

"Your power increased each time you found joy with your master," Djeyd said.

"Yes, but even though Kasha is gone, my power increases every day."

"You're like the first daaksim. Your spirit is connected to the boundless energy that flows all around us. You alone in all of this world can channel that power. You can continue to be a force for good, or you can allow your dark emotions to overwhelm you and lead you to do great evil."

"Then I suppose you'd better teach me."

"There is naught I'd rather do," Djeyd said with a warm smile. "Shall we begin?"

Sheyn nodded.

Djeyd set an empty cup on the table. "Can you move the cup without touching it?"

"Of course." Sheyn focused his will, and the cup flew across the room to strike the wall.

Djeyd picked up the cup and set it on the table again. "Try to move it a short distance."

"Tell me how."

"I cannot." Djeyd gave Sheyn another smile. "But I can show you."

"How?"

"You know how. Let it happen."

"I've always detested teachers like you," Sheyn said, but he didn't sound annoyed at all. He reached for the serenity that stole over him when Luks brushed his hair. In this stillness, he could hear Djeyd's thoughts as though Djeyd was speaking to him. "Is it really so easy?"

Djeyd nodded.

Sheyn pictured the cup sliding smoothly over the polished wood. The cup moved slowly across the table until it was in front of Sheyn. It didn't stop there but rose into the air where Sheyn caught it in his hand.

"Remarkable." Djeyd sat back. "You've just mastered something that should take an entire day of practice."

"You said it was easy, and it was."

"I must remember to repeat it, then. Do you feel tired?"

"Not at all."

"Very well, lesson two."

While the Black Hawks enjoyed a time of ease in Taar Muergan, their leader spent his days and nights under the tutelage of Djeyd Flamehair. Djeyd taught Sheyn to call up the power as easily as whistling for a hound. Djeyd taught him how to control the power until Sheyn could use it to bring a cake to his hand or blast a wall of solid granite into dust. In a handful of days, Sheyn acquired a mastery that had once taken years to learn.

"Honestly, it's as though you know what to do by instinct," Djeyd said after observing Sheyn light a candle from across the room.

"And what of you?" Sheyn asked. "How long did it take you to learn?"

"Do you still not know me?" A tear ran down Djeyd's smooth cheek. "But how could you?" Another tear fell. "It breaks my heart that all I may do is offer advice."

Djeyd's sorrow and regret was a cold wave that chilled Sheyn to the bone and threatened to drag him under. "I didn't think you cared," Sheyn whispered. He took Djeyd's hand between his and pressed it warmly.

"You wanted to hate me."

Sheyn nodded. "I blinded myself. I keep hoping I'll outgrow the habit."

Djeyd kissed Sheyn's hands. "You will. Promise me you'll never give up hope again."

"That's not an easy thing to do. Kasha—"

"Promise me."

"I can't."

"Then I've nothing more to teach you. Go and do as you will."

"How do you know you haven't trained me to go out and wreak more destruction?"

"I can't know that for sure," Djeyd said. "But in my heart, I feel you want to do good." He leaned close to kiss Sheyn's cheek. "I'll just have to trust you."

"You really are a master manipulator, even better than my mother." Sheyn stopped speaking abruptly.

"You miss your mother," Djeyd said. "There's nothing wrong with that. Go ahead and weep if you need to."

"No, I'm fine." Sheyn willed his tears back with an effort. He couldn't remember the last time he'd thought of his home or his family.

"You *are* fine, Pearl, but you have flaws. I don't want those flaws to crack you wide open. The things that would escape might eat you alive."

"Charming," Sheyn said. "If we're done here, I should see how lazy my troop has become."

"I'll go with you if you like."

"To see the Hawks or to finish the mission with me?"

"Either or both."

Sheyn gave Djeyd one of the few genuine smiles Djeyd had seen since Kashyan was lost. "No," he said. "I don't want to compete with you for the men's attention."

Djeyd smiled back. "Then I'll wish you good fortune."

"Thank you… for everything. There are only a few temples left now that people have risen against them. This shouldn't take long."

"And when all Taankh's Servants are gone, what will you do?"

"You've asked me that a dozen times. I still have no answer for you."

"But you'll return to Taar Muergan."

"Yes, that much I know. I'll come back because Velvet is here and because this is the last place I saw Kashyan alive."

Djeyd drew breath to speak but thought better of it. Why add to Pearl's sorrow? "You must come to the Misty Vales with Velvet. It's beautiful country and soothing to the spirit."

"Is that where you're from?"

Djeyd smiled. "I never satisfied your curiosity about me, did I?"

"Who are you really?"

"I'm a daaksi called Djeyd Flamehair. I was sent by My Lady to teach you."

"But you're also the avatar. The perfect creature Velvet told me about."

Djeyd laughed. "The truth is that all daaksim are avatars of the Lady, but I was one of the First Ten. For centuries I have dwelled in the Unseen Realm until She called me to serve again."

"Why didn't She use you to get rid of the Red Temple?"

"Because I am not you."

Sheyn waited for Djeyd to say more, but he was left with that cryptic answer. He sighed and then bowed to Djeyd. "Until I see you again."

Djeyd pulled Sheyn into an awkward hug. Sheyn let his hands hover over Djeyd's back and then relaxed into the embrace, wrapping his arms around Djeyd.

"If I haven't said it, I'm sorry for what this has cost you," Djeyd whispered.

"If I haven't said it, I don't hate you anymore," Sheyn said. "You had no more choice than I did. It isn't pleasant to be a chess piece of the Gods."

"Chess?"

"A game of mock battles."

"Ah, I see. No, it's not always pleasant, but we have the solace of knowing we saved the world."

"There are times I'd trade this world for one of Kasha's kisses."

"Go," Djeyd said, giving Sheyn a shove. "I'm not in the mood to weep."

Sheyn went to bid farewell to Luks and left the palace for the royal stables. He collected Karkaran and rode to the building where the Hawks were billeted. The troopers were happy to hear they'd soon be in the saddle again. They'd enjoyed the pleasures the city had to offer, but they were becoming restless. After a feast provided by King Kholya, the Hawks went to bed in anticipation of an early-morning ride.

Chapter
28

NEAR THE isolated village of Gaaz on the western border of Sumadin was the last known temple of the God of Death. It was not much more than a shrine in a cave, but the priests held the villagers in sway, collecting tithes of food, coin, and sacrifices. With the lives of their children at stake, the people of Gaaz obeyed the Servants of Taankh when they were called to worship.

At sunset, a large fire had been built in front of the sacred cave and tended through the night. At dawn, it was hot enough for the ceremony, and the people of Gaaz gathered around it. The bound sacrifice was led from the cave where he'd spent the night. Two priests supported the man as he tottered between them to the fire. A priest struck him behind the knees, and the prisoner dropped to the ground. The Servants picked him up and crammed him into the waist-high metal cage. A rope was attached to the ring at the top of the cage and thrown over a thick bough of the shrine's blood tree. With threats, the priests coerced six of the cowed villagers to haul the rope and raise the cage from the ground. The sacrifice writhed frantically as a priest used a pole to push the cage over the fire. A priest chanted, and the village men waited for the signal to let go of the rope.

The people who'd been forced to gather at the edge of the forest looked around uneasily at the sound of running horses coming closer. The priests called out for order as the first horseman appeared between the trees. The Servants of Taankh had heard no rumors of the campaign against the Red Temple, and the attack on them came as a total shock. The first rider charged in, sweeping a priest's head from his shoulders with a swing of his sword. The villagers screamed and shouted as they fled the approach of the white-haired creature on the giant horse. Sheyn reined in as he recognized one of the priests.

"Yozif!"

Yozif dropped the pole he was using to hold the cage over the fire. The men holding the rope ran, and the cage fell free, slamming into Yozif. The priest toppled into the fire, and the cage landed atop him. Sheyn shouted an order, and a Black Hawk lassoed the cage and pulled it from the flames. Yozif was dragged out of the fire, but he was dead. Sheyn had wished to kill Yozif himself, but he was not unhappy with the means of death.

"Free any prisoners," he called out as the chaos subsided. He noticed the men trying to open the cage's lock and bent his will on it. The metal bolt popped out of the hasp, and the door fell open, allowing the Hawks to pull the victim free. Sheyn walked Karkaran over to address the villagers. "You are free," he told them. "Never again will the Servants of the God of Death steal your children for their rituals. You may keep the fruits of your fields and orchards to feed your families. You need not fear revenge, for the evil of the Red Temple has been scoured from Kandaar and the high king's men will once again patrol the borders."

As he turned from the grateful thanks of the people, a great weariness came over Sheyn. Leaving the Hawks to clean up, he rode back to camp. Sheyn unsaddled Karkaran and let the charger wander to crop grass. After drinking as much water as he could hold and pouring the rest over his head, Sheyn sat with his back against a tree and finger-combed the hair away from his face. He was falling into a doze when he heard the troop returning and was surprised to see they'd brought the prisoner with them.

"Pearl!" Dasha called out as he leaped from the saddle. "Are you well?"

"Well enough." Sheyn stood. "I'm wondering what I'll do with myself now that all the Red Priests are gone."

"You could come home with me." Dasha grinned.

Pearl gave him a tired smile.

"I can see you need to rest, but this—" Dasha's words were cut off by a shout from the former prisoner.

"Sheyn!"

Sheyn tensed. He knew that voice. When the troopers tried to restrain the stranger, Sheyn gestured to them to let him go.

"Sheyn!" the tall man said joyfully as he stopped in front of Sheyn. "They took everything except this. This one thing they couldn't take from me." He held out a delicate ring on the palm of his hand.

Sheyn stared at the piece of jewelry and then looked up at the man's face. "Aeriq?"

"Yes!" Aeriq paused. "I'll look more like myself when I've shaved."

"How?"

"With a razor, of course."

"I meant how did you come to be here?"

"It's quite a tale. Is it possible I could recount it somewhere more comfortable?"

Sheyn stared at Aeriq for another long moment and then threw his arms around him as the Hawks muttered in confusion. "I can't believe it. It's so odd to hear Laronese." He let go when Aeriq winced. "Are you wounded?"

"I have a few bumps and bruises, and I think my left arm is broken."

"Come with me and let a healer look at it."

Sheyn refused to answer any of his men's questions about the foreigner who behaved so familiarly with him. He took Aeriq up behind him on Karkaran and headed for Taar Muergan. The city was a day and a half away, and the Hawks made camp that night at the foot of the mountains on the Muergath border. As the men built fires and cooked dinner, Sheyn sat and talked with Aeriq.

"I can hardly believe you're here though I see you sitting in front of me," Sheyn said.

"I'm having a little trouble believing it myself." Aeriq flexed his arm in the tightly wrapped bandage. "You make a fair healer."

Sheyn's eyes opened wide as a thought occurred to him. Taking Aeriq's arm gently in his hands, he focused his will. "How does it feel now?" he asked.

"It doesn't hurt at all," Aeriq said in tones of wonder. He touched the point of the break. "It's… it feels as though it isn't injured at all. How?" he asked as he unwrapped the strip of linen.

"It's something I learned to do while I was here. I'll tell you about it later, but now I want to hear your story."

"Very well. When I realized you were gone, I searched for you with every resource I could muster. I had to stop and rebuild my fortune, but then I began searching again. And after all that effort and money, the clue came to me by chance.

"I was attending an auction of precious metals, and a jeweler of Moon Trine house approached me. He was surprised that the ring he'd made for me was up for sale as he remembered it being a very special present for someone I held dear. I knew instantly what ring he meant, and I think I frightened him with my loud demand that he show me where it was. After that, it was simply a matter of backtracking each time the ring had changed hands."

"But surely that trail went cold at the Greiwoll."

"As your parents always suspected, I have friends in the smuggling trade. It's true that the trail seemed to end with the caravan, but I held out hope you hadn't been killed and tossed in a river. Being a merchant at heart, my next thought was that you'd been sold as well as your belongings. I appealed to my more disreputable friends and eventually I was given the name of a man known to traffic in slaves who was said to do business on the other side of the Greiwoll. I didn't believe it, of course, but I was wrong. This merchant actually bragged to me about selling you to some savage king."

"And you followed that clue to Kandaar. You're braver than I ever gave you credit for."

"I was obsessed." Aeriq smiled. "Tell me your tale."

Sheyn offered more khai, and Aeriq finished two cups before Sheyn finished speaking.

"I'm astounded," Aeriq said. "When I reached Kandaar, I began to hear tales of Pearl, an ice warrior who rid Kandaar of demons, but though the stories described a beautiful youth with hair like moonlight, I never dreamed it was you."

"I'm not the Sheyn you knew in Dey Larone. What I loved most was taken from me and it changed me forever." Sheyn sighed. "I'd like to sleep now. You should too. Morning comes early for us Hawks."

Still marveling at the changes in Sheyn, Aeriq accepted a blanket and lay down on the ground with the troopers. At first light, they rose and rode to Taar Muergan.

LUKS LOOKED away from the sleeping man in Sheyn's bed. "He came all the way from the Farthest West to find you," he said.

Sheyn nodded. "Poor man. I was never kind to him, and he loved me nonetheless."

"What will you do with him?"

"Let him recover and send him home, if that's what he wants." Sheyn glanced at Luks. "What's in the pretty head of yours?"

"He's very handsome." Luks brushed a finger over Aeriq's freshly shaven cheek.

"Yes, he is. He's handsome and brave and loyal. What of it?"

"Nothing. I just wish you weren't so alone."

"I'm not alone. I have you and Kholya and the Hawks."

"Don't you want someone to—?"

"If you know a way to bring Kashyan back, please tell me. If not, please don't speak of such things to me."

Luks folded his lips and let the subject drop for the time being. However, it had been a year since Taankh was repelled and banished, and it broke Luks's heart to see Sheyn still grieving. If there was no man of Kandaar who would do for Pearl, perhaps this foreigner could coax him into a happier mood.

"I'm sorry," Sheyn said softly. "I didn't mean to hurt your feelings."

Luks took Sheyn's hand. "I know you didn't. There's so much pain in you that sometimes it leaks out and spills onto those close to you."

"I'll try to be more careful."

"Good, and try to be happier as well." Luks squeezed Sheyn's hand and let it go. "And get some rest. We can wait until tomorrow to feast with your friend."

Sheyn embraced Luks and went to lie down on the divan. He slept for a few hours and woke to find Aeriq looking down at him.

"I didn't mean to startle you," Aeriq said. "I was watching you sleep. You're as beautiful as you ever were." He reached out to touch one of Sheyn's daaksi scars but drew his hand back. "It's difficult to credit your talk of magic and Gods, but there *is* something otherworldly about you."

At the sound of a knock, Sheyn called out permission to enter. A palace servant came in with a tray and set it on a table. Sheyn thanked the man, dismissed him, and hurried to the food. Aeriq followed a bit more slowly, smiling at the amount Sheyn piled on his plate.

"Sit and eat," Sheyn said. "It's quite good."

"Thank you." Aeriq helped himself to a plate and a cup of ale. "Now that I've recovered from the treatment those lunatics gave me, I'd like to talk about why I'm here."

"You said you came to find me."

"I came here to find you and take you home."

"Kandaar is my home now."

"Surely not. I can see you've made a place for yourself, but you're not happy here."

"Happy?" Sheyn set down an unbitten sun apple. "No, I'm not, but I'm tied to this land now, and there's a possibility that I won't be this miserable forever. My closest friend assures me that the worst grief fades in time."

"Did you love him that much? Whoever the man was who left you."

Sheyn heard the raw pain in Aeriq's voice, but he had no balm for him. "I love him more than my life. If my death would bring him back, I'd kill myself."

"But you still wouldn't be together."

"I know."

"Could you love me?" Aeriq asked. "Is there even the possibility that one day you might?"

"How can I answer that?"

"You just did." Aeriq studied Sheyn's face for several moments. "You're definitely not the boy who left Dey Larone almost three years ago."

"Only three?" Sheyn thought briefly of all that had happened to him, and it didn't seem possible that so little time had passed.

"It seems like a decade at least, doesn't it?"

"At least." Sheyn met Aeriq's eyes. "And the honest answer is no. I'll never love you the way you want me to." He paused. "I guess you've had a long trip for nothing."

"No, not for nothing. I know you're alive. Not knowing your fate would have haunted me to my grave. And I can tell your parents that you survived."

"My parents." Sheyn fell silent.

"They're well," Aeriq said. "Heartbroken but healthy. Your mother is chief councilor now."

"Yes, her work would be a distraction for her. And for my father. It's what they love."

Aeriq sighed. "Do you truly intend to stay here?"

"Since that rogue priest changed me, I don't think I *can* leave. My destiny is bound up with Kandaar's and it will not release me." Sheyn looked down at his hands. "Perhaps you'd carry a message to Mother and Father."

"I will do whatever you ask."

Sheyn put his hand over Aeriq's. "You're a good man. I'm sorry I was so horrid to you."

"I didn't mind. I loved everything about you."

"I understand that now. When you love someone, the things that annoy you become endearing."

"Just so." Aeriq smiled. "It's odd. For years I've pursued this vision of you, and now that I've found you, you aren't you."

"I'm sorry."

"So am I, but I also feel like a great weight has lifted. I no longer have a purpose, but I'm free."

Sheyn gazed on Aeriq's face for several moments. "I know how that feels," he said at last. "So much has happened. I'm twenty-one, but I feel as though I'm one hundred." He smiled at Aeriq. "Would you mind terribly if I went back to sleep?"

"Would you mind if I watched you?"

Sheyn's smile was a shade brighter this time. "Always the flatterer," he said fondly and rose to go to the divan.

"Take your bed back," Aeriq said. "I'll be quite comfortable here in the sitting room."

Sheyn changed directions and went to lie down on the soft mattress Luks had chosen for him. "Call me if anyone knocks," he said before he closed his eyes. He heard Aeriq respond, but the sound was faint as though it came from a great distance. The sea of dreams had already pulled him in and swept him away.

In his dreams, Sheyn drifted from one life to the next in an unfolding of Kandaar's history from the dawn of time. In each era, he was a daaksi, close to a great king, as companion, lover, guide. He wielded enormous power in the service of his lord, destroying enemies, providing healing, bringing comfort and victory in equal measure. In each life, his power diminished and the gold-edged dreams became tarnished. Deeper and deeper he sank until he came to a place where the light couldn't penetrate.

For an age, Sheyn fell through the freezing, lightless void, paralyzed and helpless to slow his descent. Incapable of resisting, he hurtled downward faster and faster until he lost all sense of motion. He and the dark were moving at the same speed. And he remembered where and when he'd last experienced this sense of being enveloped by darkness.

"Kasha," Sheyn gasped, and Kashyan was there in front of him.

The Bastard's great muscles bulged and gleamed with sweat as he grappled with Taankh on the Threshold. It was as though Kashyan and the God of Death were frozen in the moment Taankh had been pushed back through the Gate. Sheyn's heart broke at the thought of Kashyan locked forever in this inimical embrace. And then Kashyan looked back over his shoulder and met Sheyn's eyes.

Help me, he said.

Sheyn tried to go to Kashyan, but something held him back.

Wake up!

Sheyn struck out at the tentacles that bound his arms.

"Sheyn, wake up! You're having a nightmare!"

Sheyn opened his eyes and saw Aeriq bending over him.

"You were screaming," Aeriq said. "Are you all right?"

Sheyn took a deep breath and willed his galloping heart to slow down. "No," he said breathlessly. "I'm not all right."

"It was just a nightmare. You're safe."

"No, it wasn't." Sheyn sat up. "There's something I need to do."

Aeriq stood aside so Sheyn could get out of bed. "I'm not sure I like how you look. Is there a physician I could call for?"

"I'm not sick." Sheyn swiftly shed the clothes he'd fallen asleep in, oblivious to Aeriq's astonished stare. He pulled on the royal blue court robe Luks had sent over and pushed his feet into a pair of low boots.

"Where are you going?" Aeriq asked as Sheyn strode to the door.

Sheyn paused in the doorway. "All this time I assumed Kasha was dead. But what if he isn't? What if he's doomed to bar Taankh's way for eternity? What if I *can* bring him back?"

Chapter
29

"ARE YOU certain this is a good idea?" Aeriq asked when he and Sheyn reached the great square where the Red Temple had once stood.

"You don't have to be here, but if you're going to stay, please stay quiet."

Aeriq moved out of Sheyn's line of sight. Sheyn blocked out all extraneous sounds and smells and concentrated. In moments, he found the spot where the altar of the Gate had been located. There was nothing now to mark where so many had suffered at the hands of madmen bent on domination. All traces of the Red Temple had been scoured away, and new paving stones had been put down. However, Sheyn could sense the maw of the Threshold when he stood beneath it.

Gathering himself, Sheyn loosed the flood of his memories of Kashyan. The first time he'd seen the warrior prince, the sheer height and breadth of him, the shaggy black hair, bronzed skin, and pale green eyes, the bloody sword. He remembered his exasperation with the ignorant, overbearing savage, and he remembered the moment he'd seen him as a person with fears of his own. The memory of their first joining swept through him like a warm wave, and he clenched his hands into fists as though he could hold on to it. He let the memories fill him like points of light, and then he let them shine forth in a beacon of pure love.

Child, what are you doing?

The Goddess's voice rang in Sheyn's skull, and his teeth and bones vibrated with its timbre. He tried to ignore it, but it was impossible. "I'm going to bring Kashyan back," he said.

Aeriq looked around to see who Sheyn might be talking to and saw no one but himself. "Are you speaking to me?" he asked.

You must not do this.

"I must!"

You risk allowing the God of Death to return.

"I can't leave Kashyan there. He suffers horribly."

He suffers willingly to keep you safe.

"I don't want to buy my safety with that coin. The price is too steep."

And what of the rest of your world? Would they count the price too steep?

"I don't care."

You don't mean that.

Sheyn calmed himself. "If someone must block the Threshold, let it be me."

No, my most beloved child. You will serve better in this world.

"It's my life to trade."

You are right.

Sheyn almost went to his knees as the weight of Anaali's sorrow fell on him. "Will you help me?" he asked.

I cannot refuse you now. The bond of service runs both directions.

"Sheyn?" Aeriq touched Sheyn's forearm. "Who are you talking to?"

Sheyn didn't answer, but the warmth of Aeriq's touch penetrated his trance. Taking heart again, he asked the Goddess a question. "Why must someone guard the Threshold? Why can't we close it?"

If the Threshold is closed, there can be no crossing from one realm to another. The demons but also the Gods and Goddesses would be barred.

"Maybe it's time we learned to live without them."

As you will, my own.

Sheyn felt the phantom caress of cool fingers on his cheek, and his hair lifted in the breeze that blew only on him.

Well done. You are worthy to take your place as my incarnation in this realm. Now prepare for the hardest battle of your life.

"I'm ready."

"Sheyn?" Aeriq stared as Sheyn rose a few inches off the paving stones. After a few moments, he realized he could see the other side of the square through Sheyn's translucent form. When he grabbed for Sheyn's hand, his fingers passed through with no resistance.

Be strong.

"I am strong," Sheyn answered.

There is a crack in the heart of the universe.

"I feel it."

It will require an enormous amount of energy to fill it, maybe more than you possess. Do you still wish to do this?

"I do." Sheyn felt Anaali's approval and pride like the sun shining on his bare skin. He absorbed the heat and light and let it radiate outward from his core. He was the moon. He was a sword made of light. And he shone so very brightly.

"Sheyn?" Aeriq whispered as Sheyn rose to shoulder height.

Though it was a moonless midnight, the square was lit as though it were noon. People gathered in ones and twos until a large crowd formed a ring around Pearl's floating, glowing figure. There were a few reverent murmurs, but for the most part, the people were silent with awe. Aeriq jumped when someone touched his elbow.

"What's happening here?" Kholya asked.

"I swear by Leynys, I don't know," Aeriq said.

"How long has Pearl been like this?" Luks asked.

Aeriq glanced up. "Not too long, I think. A quarter hour, perhaps." He fixed his eyes on Sheyn again. "He keeps talking to someone."

Luks left Kholya's side and went to Sheyn. Bowing his head, he cleared his mind and let his life force flow out like the breath from his lungs. He felt the Goddess's presence, and he felt it when his energy was drawn to Sheyn, strengthening his friend. As he grew weak, he stretched out a hand to Kholya, and Kholya took it between both of his. More strength flowed into Sheyn, and the light in the square grew brighter.

Child.

"Yes, Lady?"

Our wills are not enough. We need more energy.

Sheyn gritted his teeth and extended the sphere of his influence until he was drawing on the crowd in the square. His every cell screamed in pain as he pushed his way into the Unseen Realm. The cold was so intense he felt as though he was being burned alive, and a terrible pressure squeezed him like a giant fist. He was afraid a breath would freeze his lungs, and he kept his eyes closed for fear they'd turn to ice. And then he sensed Kashyan's presence.

Sheyn opened his eyes on darkness and saw Kashyan braced against Taankh's bulk, both outlined in cold, blue light. "Bastard! Let go!" he called.

Kashyan wavered.

"It's all right," Sheyn told him. "You can come home now." The cold sank deeper, and he knew in a few more moments, he wouldn't be able to speak or do anything else. He would be a frozen cinder sucked dry. "Take my hand."

Taankh focused his malevolent will on Sheyn, and the crushing pressure increased. *Tasty one.* The Demon God's words grated on the inside of Sheyn's skull. *Come closer that I may swallow you and the spark of the Bitch that shines in you.*

"Go back," Kashyan said in a strained voice.

Sheyn moved closer, forcing his way through the numbing nothingness of the Threshold to the only warm spot in creation. Fending off the enormous pressure of Taankh's will, he reached Kashyan and put a hand on his shoulder. Kashyan's love for Sheyn and determination to protect him filled Sheyn like spring water poured into a crystal goblet. Sheyn called for power, and it came to his hand. "I love you," he managed to say before he ripped Kashyan from Taankh's hold and flung him away. As Kashyan hurtled through the Gate to the Waking World, Sheyn took his place blocking Taankh. Instantly, knives of ice pierced every particle of his being, and he screamed at the searing agony. He didn't see how he could withstand this for long, but he knew that he had to.

No, child. I will not let you make this sacrifice.

Anaali's voice was a cool balm that gave Sheyn the strength to answer. "You said I could trade my life for his."

And so you have. But I need you in the mortal realm.

Sheyn felt the ephemeral touch of the Goddess as invisible lips brushed his forehead in a kiss of blessing and farewell.

I will stand guard at the Threshold until the rift is mended.

Tears froze in Sheyn's eyes. "Thank you. I'll honor you as best I can."

The group in the center of the square gasped in surprise as Sheyn dropped from the air. Aeriq caught him and steadied him on his feet. Sheyn looked around and saw he was back in Taar Muergan surrounded by a crowd of curious onlookers.

"Pearl!" Luks said weakly.

Sheyn reached out, and Luks took his hand. "The way is barred," Sheyn said. "Kandaar need never fear an attack by demons again." He looked around once more. "Where is Kashyan?"

"Pearl," Kholya said gently. "Have you forgotten—?"

"Quiet." Sheyn closed his eyes and concentrated. Every fiber of his being strained to find some trace of Kashyan as he prayed the Bastard hadn't been lost in between this world and the next. Blindly, he turned his face to the moon, questing like a hound for an elusive scent. A red glow appeared against the darkness like a burning coal in the night. Abruptly he dropped to his knees and stretched out his hands, reaching for something only he could see. After a few moments, Kashyan materialized on the stones in front of Sheyn.

"Great Raas!" Kholya exclaimed as he knelt beside Sheyn. "Can it be true?"

Kashyan stirred and opened his eyes. His gaze met Sheyn's, and a slow smile formed on his lips. "Why did you dawdle for so long?" he asked hoarsely.

Sheyn threw his arms around Kashyan and held him tightly. "I'll never let you go again," he said in Kashyan's ear.

Kholya put his arms around Sheyn and Kashyan, and Luks knelt to be part of the glad embrace. The four stayed that way for some time, giving thanks for the return of their lost loved one. The crowd drifted away, but the people did not forget what they'd seen, and Pearl's fame grew a hundredfold by morning.

KASHYAN SLEPT soundly in Sheyn's arms until midday. At noon, Kholya and Luks couldn't bear to wait any longer and invaded Sheyn's quarters with a platoon of servants. Food was set out, and the servants left the royal brothers alone with their daaksim.

"I still can't believe it," Kholya said as he hugged Kashyan.

Kashyan hugged back until Kholya's ribs creaked. "I'm sorry I caused everyone so much worry."

"I'm glad you're back, my lord," Luks said with a shy smile.

Kashyan swept Luks up and soundly kissed his cheek before setting him on his feet again. "Are you really happy I'm back? I seem to remember being harsh with you."

"Your harshness is much easier to bear than Pearl's grief."

Kashyan turned to the young man at his side. "You grieved for me?"

Sheyn slapped Kashyan's arm hard enough to make him wince. "I cried like a lost child, but now I wonder why."

Kashyan put his arms around Sheyn, holding him close. "Tell me to stop teasing you and I will."

"Barbarian," Sheyn said in mock irritation. "You've returned to me. You can do whatever you like."

"If that's so, I'll ask Kholya and Velvet to leave us alone."

"Not until I've eaten," Sheyn answered instantly.

Luks laughed as he went to the table. "Come and eat, all of you. I'm so happy I could float about the room like a fish in a pond."

Sheyn came over to hug Luks. He picked up a cluster of red fruits and put one in his mouth before feeding one to Luks. He smiled when Kashyan opened his mouth and begged for a treat.

"It's as though you were never gone," Kholya said, slapping his brother on the back.

"No, it isn't," Sheyn contradicted.

"Well, at least you haven't changed," Kashyan said, squeezing Sheyn. "Are you laughing at me?" he asked when Sheyn reacted to his statement.

"I think he's laughing because he's changed so much," Aeriq said, and everyone turned to stare at him. "May I come in?" he asked from the doorway.

"Come here and meet Kashyan," Sheyn said. He could feel Kashyan's sharp curiosity edged with tension, and he hurried to speak again. "Aeriq Toureyn is a very good friend of mine from my homeland."

Kashyan insisted on hearing the tale of Aeriq's journey as they ate. When Aeriq ended with his rescue by Sheyn, Kashyan reached across to clasp Aeriq's forearm. "You're a brave man," he said sincerely.

Aeriq smiled. "No braver than you. I admire any man who can survive Sheyn's love."

Kashyan looked perplexed for a moment before he broke into hearty laughter. "There were more than a few moments when I feared for my life, my sanity, or my naaks."

"You're both very amusing," Sheyn said.

Kashyan winked at Aeriq. "When you knew Pearl, did he often say one thing when he meant the opposite?"

Aeriq laughed. "Often."

"Before you goad Pearl into violence," Kholya said, "I'd like to know what Aeriq's plans are."

"Now that I know Sheyn is alive and well, I shall return to Dey Larone to give the news to his parents. And I have a business to run."

"I hope you won't leave right away," Kashyan said. "I think coming back from the dead deserves a celebration of some sort, and I think Pearl would like you to stay for that."

"Don't start thinking you know what I like or don't like," Sheyn said.

"I know one or two things you like." Kashyan smiled at Sheyn.

"You see this?" Sheyn asked Aeriq as he gestured to Kashyan's comical leer. "This is what I've been contending with in this primitive country."

"I'd say you've coped rather well," Aeriq answered. "I hope your friends know you're joking."

"We learned to accept Pearl's odd sense of humor," Luks said.

Sheyn shot Luks a betrayed look, but then he smiled. "It took me some time to learn the local ways. Thank the Lady I had Velvet to teach me better manners."

Luks kissed Sheyn's cheek. "If you don't mind," he said, "I'd prefer to be called Djulz now."

"I'm so proud of you," Sheyn said. "You actually asked for something you wanted."

Aeriq stood. "I'll leave you now. I only came to see if Sheyn was well, and I can see that he is very well indeed."

"We should go too, my lord." Luks looked to Kholya.

"Yes, Djulz is right," Kholya said. "I'm sure I have some business or other to attend to. Ruling a kingdom is not as easy as commanding an army."

"If you have time, Your Majesty, I'd like to have a word with you about opening trade routes into Kandaar," Aeriq said.

"We have always stood apart," Kholya said. "Kandaar has never wanted anything from the world beyond the Kurais." He paused. "But so many things are changing. Perhaps that will change too."

"I hope so. I've seen quite a few things in Kandaar that the west would find worth trading for. I'd like to start importing khai as soon as possible."

"Come, then, and we'll discuss it." Kholya turned to Kashyan. "I'll see you this evening. In the meanwhile, don't tire yourself out."

"I came back from death. The last thing I want is sleep," Kashyan said.

"I'll make sure the Bastard spends a fair amount of time on his back," Sheyn said. "Close the door as you leave."

Kholya took Luks's hand and gestured to Aeriq to follow. Kashyan lounged back on the divan and gave Sheyn an inquiring look. Sheyn let his robe drop to the floor and welcomed his lord home in every way known to him.

Chapter
30

AERIQ TUCKED his gloves into his belt and walked briskly toward the main courtyard of the palace. It had taken him longer than expected to pack the personal belongings he'd collected while he was a guest of King Kholya. In the past three months, he'd received so many presents that he needed six trunks to carry them.

As he entered the breezeway between the palace and the guardhouse, someone called out to him. Aeriq stopped and turned to see Kashyan hurrying after him. "Yes, Your Highness?"

"I wanted a word with you alone."

"I see." Aeriq felt a twinge of apprehension, but he smiled politely.

"You and Pearl…. You were more than friends, weren't you?"

Aeriq answered honestly. "I wanted to marry him." He smiled. "He didn't feel the same way."

"I'm not here as a jealous lover. I'm simply curious. Is there anything you can tell me that will help me to please him better?"

"Nothing I did seemed to please him." Aeriq paused. "Although he did like receiving gifts."

"All daaksim like presents. I was hoping for something more personal."

"Prince Kashyan, simply wanting to please him will take you far in his regard, but you don't need advice from me. Sheyn—Pearl loves you."

"I thank you for being so honest."

"You look as if you have another question."

"How can you bear to let him go without a fight?"

"I don't find it easy to give him up. Since the first time I saw him, I was obsessed with having him for my own. I came to Kandaar to find him and take him home, but after I found him, I realized that he's already home."

"And you're content with that?"

"Are you asking if I plan to return with an army to try and take him back?"

Kashyan met Aeriq's eyes. "You would fail."

"I know. When I stood with him in that square and saw what he was willing to sacrifice for you, I knew he'd never be mine." Aeriq smiled. "You have a rare treasure. Guard it well."

"I will."

"Good. Now I believe people are waiting to see me off."

Kashyan put a brawny arm around Aeriq's shoulders and walked with him to the great courtyard in front of the palace. A train of a dozen pack mules accompanied by a troop of royal cavalry was drawn up before the gate. Under the grand arch of the main entrance stood Kholya, Luks, and Sheyn.

"Fare well on the road," Sheyn said after giving Aeriq a hug. "Tell Mother and Father I love them and miss them."

Aeriq patted the breast of his new tunic. "I have your letter right here," he said. "I hope someday you'll come back to Dey Larone, if only to visit."

Sheyn looked up at Kashyan and then back at Aeriq. "You understand that if I come, I'll be bringing a veritable army of savages with me?"

"You'd be a seven moons' wonder." Aeriq chuckled and then bowed to Kholya. "Your Majesty, accept my thanks once again for the sampling of goods. I'm certain that I or one of my agents will soon return with orders for more. I hope this will be the beginning of a mutually beneficial exchange between west and east."

Kholya gripped Aeriq's forearm for a moment before letting go. "I hope so too. There will be many who oppose the opening of trade routes, but I'm hoping to sway the high king to my side." He glanced at Luks with a fond smile. "And I have the perfect emissary."

Aeriq mounted the fine bay gelding Kholya had given him and rode through the gate with his small caravan behind him. He turned and waved and then passed out of sight.

"What shall we do with the rest of the day?" Kashyan asked.

"I have a kingdom to manage," Kholya said. "With the help of my able councillor." He gave Luks's hand a squeeze.

"I think the Hawks would like to greet you," Sheyn told Kashyan. "And then, no doubt, they'll lure you into a day of riding, feasting, and drinking."

"Is there anything wrong with that?" Kashyan asked.

"Not as long as you find time amid all that to top me."

"Then let's ride," Kashyan said. "If Karkaran will have me back."

Sheyn grinned. "I'll race you to the stables," he said. On the last word, he sprinted away.

"I'll never get the best of him," Kashyan said.

"Not unless you catch him," Kholya said.

With Luks's soft laugh in his ears, Kashyan ran after Sheyn.

IN THE fullness of time, Kholya, King of Muergath, was crowned high king when Djulyan stepped down. When his father died, he put his brother, the Bastard, on the throne of Savaan and never had a more loyal vassal. High King Kholya brought the warring nations of Kandaar together under one flag and one law, though it took the greater part of his lifetime. Trade routes were opened to the west and to the eastern shore. He did away with the practice of taking slaves from a defeated enemy and made it illegal to create daaksim. Existing daaksim were elevated to their former status, and the worship of Anaali came back into favor.

Sheyn remained dedicated to bettering life for the people of Kandaar, whatever their station might be. However, his greatest passion was for the Bastard of Savaan, and he was at Kashyan's side until the end. After Kashyan died, Sheyn spent his time in the saddle, dispensing justice with succeeding generations of Hawks. He passed into legend long before his years were up and retained the look of a youth of eighteen until the day he was taken into Anaali's embrace forever. But that was not for a long, long time.

Glossary

Aanki—a spoiled child, a brat

Ayeesh—an expression of disgust, annoyance, or exasperation

Daaksi, pl. daaksim—a pleasure slave imbued with irresistible appeal and mystic power

Gaerys—a slang word for testicles in the Deysian Protectorate

Jaavi—a Kandaari slang word for penis

Kataash—Kandaari naturally occurring herb. The dried leaves are smoked in a pipe to produce a euphoric state

Khai—Kandaari cultivated herb. The dried leaves are brewed with hot water to make a strong, black tea

Naaks—a Kandaari slang word for testicles

Reyl—a slang word for penis in the Deysian Protectorate

Uvardin—a small fruit pressed for its oil

THE EAST

NATIONS OF KANDAAR

Grus, The Sea of Grass is located roughly in the center of Kandaar, a vast, windy plain covered in grass. The nomadic tribes are known for the swift, greathearted horses they breed. Their God is Grusa, and their banner is a rearing horse in white on a green field.

Kesh, The Utmost East occupies the eastern seaboard of Kandaar. The coast has many friendly harbors and cities dedicated to trade. It is known that if an item cannot be found in the markets of the Utmost East, then it does not exist. The Moon Goddess's Sanctuary is located in the capital of Weijan. Their Goddess is Anaali, and their banner is a coiled sea dragon in gold on a field of white.

The Land of the Lake is one of the westernmost Kandaari nations, north of Sumadin, cradled between the highlands of Savaan in the east and the Kurais in the west. The largest geographical feature is Lake Khol, seventy leagues across at its widest part. The rest of the land is marsh and lush forests. Their Goddess is Laris, and their banner is a royal blue stag on a pale green field.

Long Isle is the southernmost nation of Kandaar, an island separated from the coasts of Sumadin and Muergath by the Small Sea. The people raise fine-coated goats, spin and dye the wool, and weave all manner of goods. By tradition, the royal palace is located on an islet called The Maiden. Their God is Wei, and their banner is a silver leaping dolphin on a field of bright blue.

Macsaar is located in the northeast of Kandaar, and the landscape varies from the grain fields of the south to the forested mountains of the north. It is the most self-sufficient of the nations and least likely to become involved in war or alliances. Their God is Macs, and their banner is a white wolf on a golden field.

The Misty Vales comprise an area of green mountains with gentle slopes and valleys threaded with silvery streams and cascades. The people raise sheep, cattle, and khai, an herb whose dried leaves are brewed with water to make a refreshing drink. Their Goddess is Besh, and their banner is a golden bear on a field of dark green.

Muergath covers much of southeastern Kandaar and is made up of fields and forests surrounding a broad central plain. The capital, Taar Muergan, is located near the center and is the home of the oldest Red Temple of Taankh, God of Death. Their God is Taankh, and their banner is a red bull on a black field.

Raadana is a long narrow nation with no remarkable geographical features between Muergath and the Utmost East. In ancient times, it bustled with caravans and prosperous way stations, but the principle industry now is raiding. Their Goddess is Raada, and their banner is a rampant lion in orange on a field of yellow.

Savaan is country of soaring peaks and evergreen forests populated by fierce clans uneasily united into a nation under one king. Their reputation as warriors and weaponsmiths is second to none, and the chargers they breed are coveted warhorses. Their God is Raas, and their banner is a black hawk on a red field.

Sumadin occupies the southwest corner of Kandaar. The land is best described as rolling with many hills, forests, and lakes. In the north is a region of marshes that borders Lake Khol. The people are fiercely competitive, and their history is one of invasion and conquest. Their God is Suma, and their banner is a red boar on white.

GODS AND GODDESSES OF KANDAAR

Anaali—Moon Maiden, Goddess of Love, Lady of Swords, Mother of Daaksim. Her symbol is a sword.

Besh—Sky Mother, Maker of Rain, Lady of Light. Her symbol is a star.

Grusa—King of the Winds, Father of Foals. Usually depicted as a centaur. His symbol is a running horse.

Laris—Lady of the Forests, Goddess of Spring, the Flower Queen. Usually depicted with a crown of antlers. Her symbol is a leaf.

Macs—God of the Harvest, Fire Bringer, Lord of Plenty. His symbol is a scythe.

Raada—(twin sister of Raas) Goddess of Victory, the Red Lady. Her symbol is an arrow.

Raas—(twin brother of Raada) God of War, Lord of Thunder, Storm King. His symbol is an anvil.

Suma—Lord of the Hunt, The Beast God. His symbol is a spear.

Taankh—God of Death, the Demon King, Shadow Lord. His symbol is
a serpent.

Wei—the Ocean God, Lord of the Deep, the Sun Father. His symbol is
a shell.

The West

The story of the Bastard's Pearl takes place mostly in Kandaar in the east, but I'd like to say a few words about the lands west of the Greiwoll. The Deysian Protectorate is comprised of six large, cultured, very civilized city-states, innumerable towns and villages, and seven Buffer States. Beyond the Buffer States is the soaring mountain range called the Greiwoll or Kurais that separates west from east. In the west, there is only one God, a man named Leynys who was elevated to divinity by his wisdom and kindess.

CONNIE BAILEY is a Luddite who can't live without her computer. She's an acrophobic who loves to fly, a faultfinding pessimist who, nonetheless, is always surprised when something bad happens, and an antisocialite who loves her friends like family. She's held a number of jobs in many disparate arenas to put food on the table, but writing is the occupation that feeds her soul.

Connie lives with her ultralight designer husband and Ickle the Wonder Whippet at a small grass-strip airfield halfway between Disney World and Busch Gardens. Logic and reality have had little to do with her life, and she likes it that way.

DSP PUBLICATIONS

visit us online.
WWW.DSPPUBLICATIONS.COM

9 781632 168788